The Hanged Man *and the* Fortune Teller

The Hanged Man and the Fortune Teller

LUCY BANKS

AMBERJACK
PUBLISHING

IDAHO

AMBERJACK
PUBLISHING

Amberjack Publishing
1472 E. Iron Eagle Drive
Eagle, ID 83616
http://amberjackpublishing.com

10 9 8 7 6 5 4 3 2 1

Book design by Aubrey Khan, Neuwirth & Associates.

Library of Congress Cataloging-in-Publication Data
Names: Banks, Lucy, 1982- author.
Title: The hanged man and the fortune teller / by Lucy Banks.
Description: Eagle, ID : Amberjack Publishing, 2019.
Identifiers: LCCN 2019010130 (print) | LCCN 2019013340 (ebook) | ISBN
9781948705554 (ebook) | ISBN 9781948705547 (hardcover : alk. paper)
Subjects: | GSAFD: Mystery fiction.
Classification: LCC PR6102.A64 (ebook) | LCC PR6102.A64 H36 2019 (print) |
DDC 823/.92--dc23
LC record available at https://lccn.loc.gov/2019010130

ISBN 978-1-948705-547
eBook ISBN 978-1-948705-554

To my husband, Al,
who kept saying I could, even when I felt I couldn't.

ONE

— 2017 —

HE REMEMBERS LOVE.

Her fingers, laced with his. The smoothness of skin. Eyes meeting, before they sank under the water.

He remembers it *here,* where his stomach once was. The force of feeling lies in the moments when she laughed, the warmth of her nearness, and those quiet times, just the two of them. It is *here,* in his memories, botched and scarred as they are.

I know love, the ghost tells himself, because it is important. It's the rope that ties him here, that keeps him anchored through the centuries. He holds the *knowing* close, and knows he will never, never let the memory of his wife go, no matter how many decades he moves away from her.

Though it has been a long time, and times have changed.

People are different, he finds. Larger, louder, more unkempt. They use peculiar words and rattle away on incomprehensible machinery. But this isn't the worst aspect of this sparkling, gritty modernity. The true agony is that he is diminishing, losing more of himself with every passing day. This has nothing to do with his lack of physical form. Death has made sure that he is never more than a stillness in the air, a patch of coldness that causes the occasional shiver. Rather, it's his mind that is alarming him, by slowly, surely unravelling at the edges. He is *drifting.*

This is the twenty-first century. He knows it, because it is written in their newspapers, stamped on their glowing screens. Every wall has a calendar, it seems; and there is the year, over and over again; 2017. Bragging how far the world has come, muddling his thoughts.

The modern world confuses him. It is a mechanical forest, a landscape of metal and glass. Of course, cities expand, he remembers that from his living days. But this? This growth is parasitical, out of control. It sprawls outwards until he can no longer find his way out to the countryside of his childhood. He doesn't even know if it exists anymore.

He is in one of those modern places now, though it is past midnight. An *internet café,* they call it, with rows of glaring screens and sombre silence, broken only by the noise of fingers tapping at buttons. He dares not come too close; machinery startles at his presence, like a skittish horse. It is safer to remain at a distance.

He is here because of the boy.

The boy in question sits at one of those screens, a lonely figure hunched in a chair that spews stuffing from its burst seams. The ghost cannot remember his name, though knows it's something clipped and efficient, as so many names seem to be these days.

He cannot leave the boy; he knows that too. For better or worse, he is tethered here, at least for now.

The glow makes the boy's face ghoulish, and this is emphasised by his frown, the ceaseless flit of his pupils. He is a creature in motion, fingers dancing across a board of printed letters. Each press of a letter produces a corresponding letter on the screen, and so poetry is written, page after page of words that tug at the rags of the ghost's memories. So much has changed, yet this remains the same, this all too human torrent of emotion. It heats him, if only for a moment or two.

He first found this boy by London Bridge, staring at the Thames. A week ago, a year ago, perhaps; it is difficult to keep track of the passing of time. The ghost was drawn, pulled by his fever-filled heart, his tumultuous mind. This was a boy in love, he realised; and watched while the boy rubbed his brow, much as he rubs it now, while hiding in this internet café, gazing at the white glow of his writing.

He is always staring at screens.

"You like him," the Fortune Teller whispers. A trace of a finger touches where his arm once was, startling him.

It has been a while since he's seen this other ghost. The contact makes him tighten, sputter, then fade briefly. He does not want to talk to her. It has been too long, and she's been too persistent. Her presence is *wrong*. This is *his* boy, not hers, and she should leave.

"Why do you follow me?" he asks. The words are soundless, yet she hears them. This is how all spirits converse, not that they've had much experience talking with any others. For some reason, they are two of only a few that remain, wandering aimlessly among the living. And so, they linger together, connected by a history that the ghost struggles to recollect.

"You know why I follow you." She glides past the rows of chairs, past the dull hum of the screens. The air shudders, then stills.

Love. The word chimes inside him. *It is always love. I must remember that.*

He looks to the boy, who is yawning, mouth a distended circle of exhaustion. His hair is a street-urchin mop, and he is from the Orient, perhaps, with deep brown eyes and a pale complexion, though it is hard to know exactly where people come from now. Skin tones are alchemically blended, a chaotic coalition of ethnicity, matching the ambience of the capital perfectly. Old with new. Strange with familiar. Kinship with isolation.

The Fortune Teller looks over the boy's shoulder. The shade of her shawl remains, beads glittering a trail of tiny orbs, all the way to the ground. He spies a glimpse of knowingness in her expression, a lock of unruly curl, before she fades completely. Ghosts are an unusual manner of creature, impermanent, restless, full of pain; and she is particularly complex; his coy, confusing stalker.

"He is writing to her again," her voice echoes, somewhere in the semi-darkness.

He doesn't reply. It is a given that the boy is writing again, pouring love onto the screen. That's all he ever does here, night after night, rather than return to his home. The ghost wishes he could tell the Fortune Teller to go away. It pains him to see her here, not least because he forgets the *details*. Once, he knew everything about her, he is certain of it. But he cannot recollect anything of her existence now, not even the moment they met. Time stretches his memory, and all he can do is cling to the thought of his wife; his anchor. This Fortune Teller is *not* her, and as such, she must leave him be.

His turmoil brings her into visibility for a moment, before she dwindles against the brick wall, melting back to nothing. For now.

Show me love, he thinks, and reads the strange, printed words on the boy's screen.

Zoe,

Work was terrible today. Every hour drags without you, but I'm glad your course is going great. Your happiness is what matters, that's the truth.

I loved that photo you sent. I love you, more each day. I meant what I said. Marriage, kids, all of that. It's going to happen.

Tell me more news. My phone is still cut off, email me. You are my world, babe.

Bo x

The ghost smiles. *Bo.* That is the boy's name, short as a hasty breath. He knows the photo; the boy had it on the screen last night. A girl, brightness pouring from her, standing by a tree. Her stomach showed, but he understands this is the way females dress now. It is acceptable to show flesh, to take photos, to share with others. The strength of her jawline, the warmth of defiance in her eyes, they remind him of someone, though he cannot remember who. *She is what connects us; myself and the boy,* he reminds himself, knowing he will forget soon enough.

Certain words in the letter make no sense to him, but everything else is soothing, blanketing him in clarity. For a second or two, his past becomes clearer; a series of disjointed, hazy images. A cosy cottage overlooking the river. A metal-framed bed, the rise of his wife's shoulder beside him, shining in the morning light. And laughter, endless laughter. The memories rise then fall, like the breath he once had, and he wishes he could clasp hold of them, but it is impossible. Sure enough, they retreat like the tide. He knows better than to try to chase them down, there is no point.

I cannot continue like this, he thinks. But what choice does he have but to carry on, day after day, year after year? *Perhaps there are other options,* he muses, and shivers at the thought. He knows the Fortune Teller does not like him to dwell on such things.

It is strange and silent, that place of screens; aside from a vague hum, like the distant throb of a beehive. This is another thing the ghost recollects from his youth. The bees in the back garden, the sheep, blank-eyed and chewing in the neighbouring field. The name comes to him, *Battersea;* as does the knowledge that it has changed, that it's a village no more. The world has turned and left him behind.

The boy shrugs his rucksack over his shoulder, then choruses a hoarse farewell to the old man behind the desk, who doesn't reply. The night outside is balmy, noisy. Men shout from pub doorways, black cars fly past, with bright signs printed 'taxi'. Even this late, the street is alive, energy seeping from the cracked pavements, buzzing off the surrounding buildings. The boy doesn't notice, only slips two acorn-shaped things in his ears, then drives his gaze to the ground. They pass late-night revellers, a drunken woman clutching her shoes in one hand. It is not a London he recognises.

The boy's tiny dwelling is a few minutes away, a pitiful bedsit within the attic of a terraced house. It pains the ghost each time he slides through the door; the broken furniture, the fraying rugs, the windows covered in black sheets. It is a place of despair and loneliness. He can feel the residue of previous residents; the echo of an unhappy wife, running from room to room to escape her husband, the memory of a child, cowering under a bed. Sadness stains every corner, which is why the ghost suspects it is cheap to live here. No one would choose to, unless there was nowhere else to go.

Sometimes, the ghost can access the boy's thoughts. Not the exact words, but rather the *feel* of them, the emotion that drives them through his head. Tonight, it is *anxiety*. Deep-rooted panic, unable to be voiced. Growing dread at the prospect of losing the one he loves. The ghost shifts further away. To be swathed in human emotions can be a painful, disorientating experience; especially if those emotions are raw and brutal.

The boy is too young to be burdened with such love. Yet the ghost has a memory of marrying at a similar age, before he turned his twentieth year. He doesn't know where, or what date, he only recalls the stiffness of his collar, and the shine of his hat when he threw it to the air. *Why did I do that?* he wonders. He cannot imagine being so frivolous now.

The night deepens, then departs, and the ghost waits, watching the slow rise of the sun through the crack in the curtain. The boy goes to work, as the ghost knew he would; to the loud, metallic kitchen, where colleagues squeeze around him like rats in a hole. He turns burnt meat on a slab of metal, then piles it in a corner to be collected. Others talk to him from time to time, but he does not listen. His ears are trained inward, to his thoughts. And his thoughts are of her, only of her.

During this time, the ghost wanders. There is no point remaining there, with the hiss of oil, the muggy air, and the scent of dead animal. Nothing unusual ever happens; the workers merely repeat the same actions throughout the day; meat-flipping, slicing open pieces of bread, squirting bright red sauce on to slithers of fried potato. Instead, he drifts outside to the busy streets and heads towards St Magnus the Martyr, which is only around the corner, its spire now dwarfed by the surrounding towers of glass and metal. The interior is familiar, soothingly white, lofty pillars flanking the aisle. He thinks he must have once walked down it before, when he had feet to walk with.

An old woman sits, head bowed, on the pew nearest the altar. There is something in her posture that stirs a memory within him, of another ancient lady, in another time. *She called me a cursed creature,* he thinks. *I remember nothing else about the event, but I do recall those words. But was I dead or alive, back then?* It disturbs him that he cannot recollect even that.

She shudders as he floats past, a sign that she senses him, on a subconscious level, at least. Sometimes this happens with those who are more sensitive, and it is often the elderly; perhaps because they are closer to death than the younger ones.

I remember churches, he tells himself. Every Sunday, a morning service. Another memory, this time of his mother, bonnet ribbons trailing over her chest, and his two brothers, his one sister. He doesn't know their names, they are lost to him, much like the face of his father. And later, the church for his wedding day, though he forgets which church it was. The lack of memory pains him, so he moves on, out to the streets, where the sun pours through him, hitting the steel-grey pavements below. A homeless man shifts under his lumpen blanket, then settles again.

All the while, he thinks of what might have passed before, on these streets; which are so familiar and yet so alien. He is confident he was here the previous day, and that he gazed out to the Thames only a few hours earlier. But what of the year before that? A decade previously? A hundred years ago? Where was he then? What had happened? And why is it becoming harder to seize these facts, which once he would have grabbed effortlessly, without thought or strain?

Of course, he knows the truth. A part of him is gradually departing, the part that made him human. The essence of the man he once was is slipping away like sand from a timer, leaving him a vacant vessel. What will he be left with, once all memory and feeling have gone? Will that be the end of it all?

It would be a relief, he thinks. *Finally, to come to an end.*

TWO

— 2017 —

THE GHOST FINDS the boy later, back in the internet café. It is cave-like in there, primitive and dark, though this time, a few other people are present, tapping away at their letter boards. There's a girl with blue hair, though how such a thing is possible, he does not know. Perhaps it is the breeding of the races again, producing shock-haired children. An older man too, clutching a bottle, which he taps at the desk like a nervous tic. Lonely people. Their sadness shimmers from their shoulders, soaking the air.

But the boy is happy, because she has replied; his love, *Zoe*. He smiles, and the ghost does too, or would if he had lips to smile with. These are the moments he yearns for. Communication. Hearing from a loved one. Kind words, written down. They warm him and provide a welcome contrast to all the unhappiness.

The ghost moves closer, though he is wary of the screen and the way it flickers if he drifts too close. He floats just near enough to read the words and feel the crash of the boy's pounding heart.

Hey Bo,
Sorry work sucks.
  I am doing good, though heard that Gran ain't so great, she's in hospital. Maybe you could go see her, give her love from me? You need to ask for Bernadette, not Bernie. That's her real name.

We still lovers, Bo. But you need to get lighter, yeah? This time
is about fun. I still love you, but you've got to stop putting pressure
on.

Peace out.

Zoe

The ghost watches the boy's smile, the way it freezes, falters, then
crumbles. It is like watching a wounded animal die. He retreats from
the pain before it seeps in too deeply, taking him to darker places that
he does not want to visit. *This boy's energy will finish me, if I let it,* he
realises. The name *Bernadette* clangs strongly as a bell, before being
lost in the turmoil. He closes his eyes, resisting the pressure of it all,
dimly aware that he *knew* her, this grandmother. But how? Now is not
the time to wrestle with long-forgotten memories.

Somehow, he finds himself out on the street, though the buildings
still spin around him. The ghost knows if he stops moving, things will
eventually return to calm, and he will be able to order his thoughts
again. Still, the passing scenery reminds him of the merry-go-rounds of
the travelling fair, and how they turned the surrounding fields to a blur.

A travelling fair. Another memory, a strong one this time. Not a fair
though, that isn't quite right; it's a circus he's thinking of. The name
flashes, *Captain Otto,* then disappears again. He remembers a Strong
Man, in gladiatorial boots and tight, shining undergarments. Sawdust
scent, the press of people, surging to see the spectacles, an elephant,
tethered to a post. *When was this?* he wonders. The Fortune Teller, she
was there too, in her tent, concealed by draped fabric and darkness.
Living then, not dead, and unhappy, desperately so.

The memory teeters, whirls, then vanishes. Perhaps it was never
there at all, only the false recollection. Now, all he feels is the dusty
remains of a *thing* that might or might not have happened. He heads
down the road, through throngs of suited young men, not knowing
where to go or what to do. Recovery is necessary. Such doses of emotion drain him.

The Fortune Teller is waiting for him by a metal pillar, one of many holding up yet another of the city's behemoth buildings. The setting sun passes through her, making her seem a creature of glitter, if only for a moment or two. He thinks he sees a reflection of her human face; high cheekbones, a crooked smile. Then it fades to grey.

"I was thinking of you," he says, by way of greeting. They both look out to the river.

"I know." She smiles, shimmering in and out of view. "I think I must have sensed it. Were you remembering something of the past again?"

Why does she have to ask? The Fortune Teller has pressed him on this before, he knows that. He shakes his head, and hopes that it will suffice.

A boat passes by, people clustered on its deck, taking photos of the skyline. They are happy, relaxed, immersed in their experience of the city, much as thousands of others have been before them, sailing on the sludge of the River Thames. *Joking. Laughter. The joys of a pleasure cruise, until there is no joy left.* The sight is a dagger, a merciless jab that sets the world spinning once more. He quickly looks away.

The Fortune Teller slips a spectral hand in his. It shudders the air, before returning to normal. "You cannot go on like this."

The words jolt him, then he realises her meaning; quite different to the secret feelings hidden within himself. "I don't understand," he replies.

"You do. You understand very well."

Perhaps, he thinks.

She wants him to change, he knows; to return to something more like what he once was; and to reclaim the memories of his past life. But she doesn't realise that he is in free fall, cascading along a path that he has no control over. It has been this way since he left his living body; a slow, crushing decline to forgetfulness. *Towards a total lack of being.* But isn't that what he yearns for, after all? To put a stop to all of this?

"Since when was memory such a desirable thing anyway?" he says wryly, watching her out of the corner of his eye.

A smile tugs at the mist of her lips. "I remember my life. Parts of it, anyway. And I take pleasure in those memories."

"I don't wish to remember. And don't tell me your memories either, I cannot endure it, not at present."

"You were there for part of it, some of my memories are your memories too." She waits patiently for him to meet her gaze before continuing. "It's because of you that I'm here now. Don't you want me to tell you, to help you remember it?"

He moves away, closer to the breeze of the river. It is a cooler night than yesterday. Sometimes, he lifts his head to the sky and imagines the air, tickling his skin; the kiss of a gust of wind, before it flies to a neighbouring tree. *The living don't know how lucky they are,* he thinks. Nature caresses them ceaselessly, and they don't even notice it.

"You spoke to me, when I was alive." The Fortune Teller is behind him, beside him, suddenly all around him. He cannot keep track of her movements. "You used to beg me to look for your wife. Then you talked to me about love . . . ."

"Stop it," he whispers.

"You said you'd keep looking for her, no matter how long it took. But instead of remembering, it's all becoming distant, isn't it? Do you even recall my name?"

He shakes his head, though it pains him to admit it. A cloud slips over the sun, and the water loses its shine, fading to gunmetal grey.

The Fortune Teller stops. Her form quivers, restless and anxious. *She is worried,* he realises. *She is just as frightened about what is happening to me as I am.*

"You don't remember me at all, do you." It is a statement, not a question.

"I'm sorry."

He feels a tingle at the crook of his elbow. It is her hand, squeezing him briefly, making the air glisten. Then she is gone, absorbed into the surroundings as though she'd never been there at all. Goodness knows where she vanishes to each time, though her disappearances have been less regular as of late. He knows he should feel guilty, driving her away with his taciturn comments, but as it is, he relishes the chance to be alone.

After all, he thinks, as he glides back to the boy, to his sorrowful messages of love, *it isn't personal that I can't remember who she is. I don't remember myself, either.*

Night sets in and the ghost returns, back to the hovel at the top of the terraced house. The boy does not go to work the following day, nor the day after that. Long hours pass, and the ghost settles by the empty fireplace, waiting and watching. It confuses him, how someone can spend so much time doing so little. He remembers, as a child, reciting a line about the devil, and his ability to make work for idle hands. Though, presumably, Satan has eased his grip on twenty-first-century dwellers, who seem to enjoy spending hour after hour doing nothing at all.

The boy reads a book, some scrappily bound tome with a skeleton on the front. He eats, discards empty bowls, then lies on the floor, staring at the dirty ceiling. The ghost wishes he could offer some comfort, but the boy's pain is too raw, and he fears getting too close. It may cause disruption to them both. Instead, he merely observes, seizing the chance to focus on someone else's emotions, rather than his own. Better to be the invisible observer, the bit part in someone else's life performance. It's far less agonising to endure.

Finally, the boy grabs his jacket and heads for the door. It's obvious where he's heading to. The ghost has sensed the boy's yearning for hours, gnawing at him, causing his mind to fray at the edges. He *needs* to see a message from his lover, like a drowning man needs a helpful rope to pull him from the waters. Without it, he will surely fade, every bit as much as the ghost himself.

It's a chillier night than usual, but the boy seems oblivious, thudding along the pavements, intent on his destination. He fails to greet the proprietor of the place of screens, only slams his bag on the desk and throws himself into the nearest chair. Music tinkles from a machine out back, from a room that's filled with boxes and old magazines. It is a cheery tune, something with a frenetic drumbeat, which the ghost understands is popular these days. The boy doesn't seem to notice. He only has eyes for the screen, the singular screen, which even now is glowing and whirring to life.

An image of a rolling field appears, triggering another half-remembered thought in the ghost's mind. He watches as the boy moves the mouse around, jerky motions that betray the truth of his heart. The truth of panic, fear, and desperate, overwhelming love.

The ghost senses this will not have a happy outcome. There is a darkness, a thick syrup of anticipation, which humans seem unaware of; and as it appears, the ghost gags, knowing if he follows the dark to its root, he will find the knot of it, the tangled heap of knowledge that leads to the future. He doesn't want to know this boy's future. The responsibility is too huge.

Let it be a kind message, he wishes instead, positioning himself behind the chair and waiting for the boy to start reading.

Bo,
I hate to say this, but I think it's better if we cool it for a while. I need to focus on stuff here. We can still talk, just not every night, okay? Please don't be sad.

Zoe x

The boy's agony envelops him like a cloud, sending the room into a storm of colour and speed. The ghost knows it is too late to move away, so braces himself, pressing into the floor, fighting to find a root of calm amongst it all. He isn't angry at the boy, he understands it only too well. *I have been here too,* he thinks, waiting for the madness to pass. *I know what this feels like.*

Finally, the ghost can open his eyes again. The boy's forehead is pressed against the desk, hands braced at the back of his neck, and dark lingers around him, a brooding cloud of misery. The ghost does not dare come too close, for fear that it will submerge him, that he'll be forced to *see* what lies ahead.

"It is a monstrous thing," he whispers, to no one in particular.

The boy lifts his head, turns, and his eyes narrow. For a brief moment, the ghost feels watched, or at least *sensed*. The invisible thread that ties them together tightens, like a tug-of-war rope, then slackens and drifts.

He isn't surprised to see the Fortune Teller beside him, waiting to be noticed.

"Can you see this boy's future?" he asks, refusing to meet her gaze, to peer through the misty remnants of a spectral face.

"No. Not unless I enter the black, which I have no intention of doing."

The ghost laughs. "I thought that telling the future was what you did."

"Not like this. Not without my cards."

He nods, hearing the truth in her words. Half-remembered visions of her deck spin into mind—bright images of people, coins, swords, cups—printed onto a grubby, well-handled pack. Others had been charlatans, but she'd had real talent.

That's how she spoke to me, he remembers. *While staring at her candle, in her tent. The only living creature to hear my voice.* Suddenly, he can see the blotchy mirror hanging on an Asian screen, the scratched table. An obligatory crystal ball, smaller than he'd originally imagined. It is there, in his mind, blisteringly clear, and he bathes in the certainty of it, knowing that it will pass before too long.

"I recall them," he mutters, remembering one card in particular; a man, suspended from a strange, T-shaped tree, one ankle strung to the branch, the other crossed neatly behind the knee. He'd had a halo circling his head, a grim interpretation of saintliness. *The Hanged Man.* That was what it had said, in rough capitals at the bottom. He shudders, remembering a hushed woman's voice. *You will make a sacrifice.* Strange, those words. Hastily, he puts them from his mind.

The boy cracks his knuckles, bringing him back to the moment.

"You remember my aunt's tarot pack?" The Fortune Teller smiles. "That is good. What else can you remember?"

This is what she fails to understand, every time they talk like this. Her continual questions stopper him up, corking the flow of his thoughts. Just like that, the memory slides away, leaving him disorientated. *What did I just see?* he wonders. Already, it seems like a half-remembered dream, floating into the distance.

A rattle of noise sends the memory even further adrift. It is the boy, pressing at the letter board, fingers flying from button to button. The ghost cannot follow at such a speed, so studies the screen instead, watching the words, stunted and baffling as they are, fill the whiteness.

Zoe,

You're breaking my heart. You're killing me. Why are you treating me like this? What about that night, before you left, when you said you would never get tired of me? Was that just lies? You let me hold you, all night, and you said going to college wouldn't change anything. But you lied. Are you hooking up with someone else? Is that it?

The ghost and the Fortune Teller glance at one another, and instinctively back away. He notices a tear on the boy's cheek, and watches it travel slowly towards the side of his mouth. It leaves a snail-trail of sadness, closely followed by another tear, which follows a different path.

It is like life itself, the ghost thinks. *We're all carried along by the forces that drive us, and where it will take us, no one knows.*

"If he carries on writing this, he will regret it," he says.

The Fortune Teller sighs, and he can almost imagine feeling the tickle of breath on his cheek. "Maybe it is for the best. Who knows?"

But the ghost remembers the darkness before, the low-hanging fug that almost submerged the boy's head, touching his scruffy, childlike hair. The meaning had been clear, even without stepping too close to it. *One path, leading to trouble. A single version of the future, hanging in the balance.*

Like a Hanged Man, he thinks, then wonders why.

"His heart will break," he says.

"Then it will mend soon after." The Fortune Teller may be right, but then, has she ever had her heart broken? Does she know the agony, palpable as a punch to the chest, or the inability to escape it? He doesn't think so. She's never known the perpetual pain of losing the one she loves. Heartbreak is only interrupted by the short bliss of falling asleep, simply to realise, on waking, that the torment is still there. It is a nagging, persistent weight that will not lift.

I knew it once, he realises. A glitter of pain bursts within him, like the aftershock of a distant earthquake, then settles and dies. He is more sensitive to these feelings when he's around the boy, which perhaps explains why he clings to him.

"He is still writing." The Fortune Teller points. More words of pain, black and ragged across the screen. The boy is falling, he can tell; plummeting into greater despair with every tap on the letter board.

The blackness thickens like sauce. The ghost would struggle to breathe, if he had lungs to inhale with. *I must stop him,* he thinks, unable to guess why, but only convinced that the dark will be worse if the message is sent, if Zoe reads the boy's open wound, dripping through the words.

He edges closer to the screen. It flickers in response.

"What are you doing?" The Fortune Teller stills, tensing.

"I'm not doing anything." *I don't have much time,* he realises, and steels himself.

The buzz of the machine is tracing through him now, disturbing the strange energy that makes up the ghost's form. Like a lifeline, it pulses, and as he draws nearer, the vibrations grow into a throb. It fascinates him, this proximity to self-damage. Both he and the boy, thinking the same dark thoughts, driven by the same unhappiness.

The Fortune Teller grasps at his shoulder, before pulling away.

I will do it, he thinks. *For the boy. And for myself. I will stop the darkness from falling.*

He hears the Fortune Teller's voice, a vague echo of a scream, as he dives towards the screen, breaking like a water drop against the bright, buzzing surface. For a moment, there is only noise; the sizzle of burning, the snap as something tightens and breaks deep within the machine itself. Another part bangs, breaking against the elements of himself that are spreading through the strange wires and metal components.

It is agony, though agony of a different kind to when he was living; a sense of unbearable pressure, noise, and *loosening*, as though the very essence of himself is bleeding outwards and diluting away. He closes his eyes and endures, with relief in his heart.

Then, silence.

It is done, he thinks. And finally, he rests.

THREE

— 1877 —

"GOODNESS, YOU LOOK the part." Arthur stood back to admire me, then resumed smoothing down his suit jacket. The buttonhole flower was already wilting in the heat, petals curling like peeling wallpaper.

I grinned. "I should jolly well think so. After all, if a man isn't dandied up to the nines on his wedding day, when can he be, eh?"

"Well, you look positively afternoonified." He straightened my waistcoat, then picked up the top hat, thumping it on my head before I had a chance to protest. "There. A fine gentleman and no mistake. I can scarcely believe you're my brother."

It was a splendid day for a wedding, as Mother had predicted yesterday, peering into her usual morning tea leaves. I told her it was all stuff and nonsense, which had made her chuckle. Dear old Mother, she still clung to her superstitions. It was part of living in a village, I presumed, where the local residents still crossed themselves at the sight of a black cat. We'd always laughed about it as children, and it still amused me as a full-grown man.

I wondered how Eleanor was getting on, and whether she was feeling as nervous as I was. No doubt her aunt was fussing over her right at this very moment; dabbing her eyes and muttering about her poor, dear parents, as she always seemed to do at every opportunity. Eleanor once confided in me that she wished she felt more grief over her parents' death, but then, she'd been a baby at the time; and the only lasting impact was her reduced circumstances in life, moving from a London townhouse to a diminutive terraced cottage in Battersea. Her misfortune had been my gain though, for if she hadn't come here, I'd never have known her.

How fate moves us in strange, unexpected directions, I thought, reviewing my appearance in the looking glass, and smoothing down my morning jacket. *We never know what the future has planned for us.*

"Here," Arthur said, smoothing down my collar. "You've got a bit of dust on you, and we can't have that."

"You're as bad as Mother, fussing over me."

"Well, enjoy it while it lasts. It will be your lady wife doing this tomorrow morning."

My lady wife. I took a moment to let the words sink in. As children, we'd all played together; running through the woods, fishing in the local pond, eating buns on the church wall. It seemed astounding to think that the pretty, curl-headed girl I'd adored as a child should now be my wife. *Thank heavens she chose the right brother,* I thought, with a rueful smile. *Things could have easily turned out differently.*

Our new house was ready and waiting, already filled with furniture; some new, other items generously donated by Mother from her cluttered collection. It overlooked the Thames, and I could scarcely wait to move in. *To be a husband, at last. To provide for my wife and keep her in a manner to which she can become accustomed.* Lord knows I felt ready enough for the task; I'd been working hard at the office.

"So," Arthur declared, interrupting my thoughts, settling into the armchair by the fireplace. "Is Fred coming?"

I darkened at the mention of my older brother's name. *Not today, of all days.* "You know as well as I do," I replied, trying not to sound testy. "In fact, probably better, given that you spoke to him only last week." Arthur may have been younger than me by a year and a half, but he was far better at keeping the family peace than I ever was.

"Fred is a damned nuisance sometimes. I do wish he'd considered your invitation."

"Fred only considers himself, I believe."

Arthur's eyebrow shot up. "That's hardly fair. Life hasn't been kind to him, has it?"

Fred's hardly been kind to life, either, I thought childishly, but kept my thoughts to myself. I knew, deep down, that I'd contributed to my older brother's unhappiness, which made my cruel thoughts even more unacceptable, I supposed.

"Well," I replied in a lighter tone, determined not to let anything spoil the day. "He declined to come, so let's discuss other matters, eh?"

Arthur nodded. "Quite right, we can't sit here debating ridiculous family squabbles. We've been over it far too many times in the past. He'll come around in the end."

Or not, I thought, musing on Fred's general surliness and bad manners. Still, it was pointless to dwell on it, particularly today.

Arthur caught my eye, then grinned. "I say, hadn't we better go? Time's getting on, we don't want to be late."

I nodded. "We should. And let's agree to not mention Fred again. It'll only upset Eleanor."

For a moment, Arthur looked as though he would say something else. Then he shook his head and stood aside, letting me depart the room. My jaw clenched involuntarily. Arthur had a way of making me aware of my own inadequacies, though of course, he never meant to do so. His good nature often made me look unfeeling by comparison; but then, I'd always been the rational, level-headed son, and it wasn't my nature to be otherwise.

We headed downstairs, which was strangely silent without my mother and sister, who were already at the church. I wished I could rid Fred from my mind, just for this one day. Eleanor had been his sweetheart first, though he'd treated her badly. That was typical of him; possessive, casually hard to others, not to mention perpetually jealous of both myself and Arthur. Hardly surprising really, given how far we'd both come in life. Poor Fred, he'd ended up down at the Docks, just like Uncle Harold. A filthy, noisy, thankless job, with not much in the way of reward for all the hard labour involved.

Arthur stood, then patted my arm. "You look troubled, Brother. Come on, no woeful feelings are permitted. This should be the happiest day of your life. Let's get you to the church."

The neighbours had turned out to watch the spectacle. Mr and Mrs Harding were hanging over their garden wall and waved enthusiastically as we passed. Even Mrs Jones from down the road had made the effort to hobble to the church gate. That was the thing with village communities, any event was an event for *everyone,* regardless of whether they were invited or not, a fact that warmed and irritated me in equal measures. *It'll be nice to move into London itself,* I thought, straightening my shirt collar, aware of eyes upon me. *In the city, anonymity isn't nearly so hard to achieve.*

Mother was waiting for us at the corner of the road, still fussing over Martha's ribbon sash, which had drifted down over her dress like a stream. At the sight of us, she pulled a face; the light dappling on her bonnet from the tree above.

"I'm so glad you're both here," she said, without preamble. "Will you tell this young lady to carry herself properly? She refuses to listen to me."

I laughed. My sister grimaced, then tugged at her skirt, looking every inch the reluctant flower girl. It wasn't surprising. She loathed dressing up and was never happier than when racing through the fields, climbing trees, or fishing in the local pond. No wonder Mother despaired so much, especially now that Martha was coming to an age where such behaviour was considered indecorous for a female.

"I feel ridiculous," Martha muttered, then folded her arms.

Mother promptly sighed, patting down her cheeks, which had grown ruddy in the heat. "She's been like this all morning. I honestly believe she's more like a boy than you two put together."

"Martha, behave," Arthur chastised. "It's a big day today, the first of your brothers to get married. Don't ruin things by being a silly little prig."

"I'm not being a silly little prig, don't be so mean."

"Well, don't kick up a tremendous fuss over nothing, then." Arthur's eyes twinkled with merriment. He never could resist teasing poor Martha.

"See how you like it, being dressed in a big, silly—"

"—That's enough, the pair of you!" Mother, normally so composed, looked set to collapse. She turned to me, then a slow smile broke out over her face, lighting her like a candle. "But enough of this nonsense. Look at you, looking so smart and handsome. Eleanor is a fortunate lady."

"I'm a fortunate man," I corrected. And it was true. While courting Eleanor, I'd constantly wondered what she'd seen in me, a man with an expression that I've been told looked continually harassed. Fred was far more handsome, inheriting the swarthy, sharp looks of our late father. But, as Eleanor often reminded me, it was the heart of the man that was the important thing, not the physical form that housed it. For all his good looks, Fred had lost her, and that was that.

I really must stop thinking about it, I thought. *For today, at least.*

Two local lads tittered as we passed through the church gates, threw their browning apple cores to the ground, then waved. Urchins from down the road, no doubt, their faces grimy with dirt. I winked at them, then delved into my pockets for a couple of pennies to give them. For luck, of course. It was always fortunate to be charitable on such a day as this.

"Come on," Arthur whispered, nudging my shoulder. "Stop delaying and get in there. We need to make an honest man of you."

Behind me, Mother sobbed, blowing her nose loudly on her handkerchief. Arthur and I caught one another's eye and grinned. *Still the same old Mother,* I thought. *Always so emotional about everything.* I dared not turn to comfort her, for I knew it would bring about a fresh wave of blubbing, which wasn't desirable for the ceremony. Thankfully, Martha took on the task herself, or rather hissed at Mother to calm down, before entering through the wide wooden doors.

The church was as refreshing as a cool bath, despite the number of people already congregated inside. I'd always loved the solemn, airy dimensions within; the simple wooden roof, the stained glass sending rainbows over the altar. A few friends smiled from the pews, some already with wives of their own, a few with babies, snuggled in linen and ribbon. I returned the smile, knowing that in the future, I would be sitting where they were now, with Eleanor by my side, and possibly a child or two, God willing. *A boy,* I thought, allowing my thoughts to drift. *It would be wonderful to have a boy. What we would call him?*

"What a turnout," Mother muttered behind me, still sniffing. She fussed a little more with Martha's dress, only to be batted away furiously.

"Let's just hope the bride arrives." Arthur laughed, ushering me down the aisle. "I wouldn't blame her if she changed her mind."

"Really, Arthur, do stop teasing your brother, it's most—"

I waved her protestation away. "Don't worry, Mother, I know he's only joking." To be honest, I'd hardly registered the comment. My nerves were rising, bubbling in my stomach like a whirlpool. Now, all I needed to do was compose myself while the crowds chattered and shuffled behind me. *What if she doesn't go through with it?* Even imagining the crushing anxiety, the humiliation of waiting and wondering, was deeply unpleasant.

But of course, in the unlikely event that did happen, I would wait. I would wait until the world ended, if necessary. Some creatures mate for life, and I sensed, from the day I first kissed Eleanor, that I was one of those fortunate beings. I remembered the day with astonishing clarity. The breeze had lifted her on that afternoon, rendering her almost airborne; flickering at her skirt, sending a stray curl bouncing on her forehead. Her composure had been demure, much as it always was, but her eyes had gleamed with energy. I'd felt myself lost inside them, like a drowning man.

Fred's loss is my gain. I wondered what he was doing today, at this moment. Brooding, no doubt, back in his hovel by the Docks. Angry? Vengeful? Possibly, I wouldn't put it past him. Although he wasn't a violent man, he'd been involved in fights in the past. Would he stoop so low as to hit his own brother? I wasn't sure.

No, he wouldn't, I reassured myself, nervously plucking at my cuffs. *I do him a disservice to even imagine him capable of such a thing.*

"Look lively, here she comes!" Arthur poked me in the ribs, just as the organ reached its crescendo, rippling through the air like rich butter.

This is it, I thought, my heart quickening. *What I've been waiting for.*

I turned, and there she was, framed by the arch of the doorway, flower girls and well-wishers trailing behind her, like small planets orbiting the sun. Time slowed, until each movement seemed a deliberate step in a dance that my heart already knew the rhythm to. She was radiant—seeing her took my breath away.

Martha raced up the aisle to join her, her grumpiness at her attire now forgotten in the excitement. The congregation stood, expectant.

I smoothed my suit and waited for the service to begin.

FOUR

— 2017 —

FOR A MOMENT, he is drowning.

The dark slashes at him. Had he a body to feel with, he knows he would have felt brutal, unrelenting pain. As it is, the machinery's energy soars and swoops through him with predatory power, until he feels himself breaking apart, coming loose at the seams.

The deed is done. That is his final thought, for better or for worse. *It is finally over.*

And yet, it is not.

Somewhere, from the deadened husk of all the darkness, a hand seeks him out. A lifeline, albeit a ghostly one, reaching for him, gathering his particles and pulling him back to safety. He resists, but the age-old instinct to survive overcomes him, and he allows himself to be yanked free.

Then comes the shock of light. The glare of seemingly endless screens, the wavering buzz of electrical energy, still sputtering and spitting in the aftermath.

He fights to compose himself, straining against the raging urge to *combust* and scatter himself once again. Energy crackles around and within him, sparking through the echoes of his limbs, motoring his heart. Again, the ghostly hand settles upon him, tender as a mother stroking a child, but he can feel its hesitancy and terror. He has *transgressed*, ventured to virgin territory, and upset the natural rule of things. He has frightened her.

The Fortune Teller's face swims into focus, a transparent moon of horror.

Why did you do that? her expression screams, and it is too much for him to bear. He drifts away.

The boy is clutching his head. The ghost watches as a shining red line slides past his eyelid and over his cheek, glittering in the dim light. *Blood.*

"Did I hurt him? What happened?"

"The machinery exploded when you entered it. Some of the screen must have hit him in the face."

I hadn't meant to, he insists to himself, horrified by the unexpected outcome of his actions. *I'd meant only to save him. And end myself.*

The Fortune Teller moves closer to the boy, drawn by the essence of life itself, as it dribbles over his face. *Perhaps she is mourning for the time she once had blood too, so long ago,* he thinks, waiting for her to turn to him.

"I didn't know that would happen," he says finally.

She glances at him, knowingly. "Perhaps. Perhaps not."

The room stills to a halt. The ghost steadies himself and assesses the situation with a more rational eye. He can see the smouldering wreck of the machine, screen gaping like a feral scream, black smoke seeping from the back. Something inside the mess still crackles, a hiss of threat lashes ceaselessly at the torn metal components. It is carnage, in modern-day form.

The proprietor of the internet café is now beside the boy, pressing a towel to his head, muttering the same words over and over: "I don't know how this could have happened, I don't understand it."

Of course he cannot understand it, the ghost thinks. *I fail to grasp it myself, and I'm the one who caused it.*

The boy is numb to it all. It's easy to tell from the absence of aura, the lack of friction in the air that surrounds him. *It is for the best,* the ghost thinks, knowing that the physical pain is easier to endure than the cacophony of emotions that came before. Still, he wishes that the boy had not been hurt. It is not in his nature to cause injury to any living creature. Even though he has forgotten himself, he is certain he was never a violent man when he was alive.

But my brother was, he thinks, then questions himself, wondering where the thought came from. He cannot even remember either of his brothers' names, let alone their character traits. Who is he to say what they were like? And what does it matter now? They are long dead and buried in their graves, and if their ghosts wander the earth as he does, he has yet to encounter them.

"Let's leave this place." The Fortune Teller flits anxiously by his side. The event has disturbed her, he can tell by the wideness of her eyes, her skittish posture. Every darting motion reveals her panic.

"We can't." He points at the boy. "I need to check that he's not badly hurt, and—"

"—you were far more badly hurt than he was. You nearly . . ."

The unsaid word hangs, unspoken, between them.

"I stopped him from sending his love that terrible message," he protests, objecting to the weight of her judgement. "I stopped the darkness from falling on him. Doesn't that make it worth it?"

She stares, then shakes her head, a tiny motion of defeat. "Come on. Let's go."

The Thames calls to them both, as it often does. The syrup-waters gleam under the street lamps, slurping at the muddy banks like a hungry animal. Why he is tied to this area, he doesn't know; all he understands is that it's *here* he feels most himself, yet also most afraid. The river is dark, and he wonders what is beneath the surface. What dead things hide below, undredged and forgotten? *There are bodies down there,* he thinks, and shivers.

Despite everything, there is a part of him that is glad to be back, looking out on the sparkling skyline of the city. London brings him peace, despite its continual motion, its never-ending pulse of people, pumping through the streets like arterial blood. *All of the living,* he thinks, with both fondness and a sense of loss, *getting on with their lives, without appreciating that one day, it will all be over. Then, they'll either cease to exist, or wander as we do, slowly losing their memories and their minds.*

The Fortune Teller waits, pressed against the fence, fingers tapping the railing, before passing through it. Her patience with him is formidable, yet oppressive. He feels battered by her stoic ability to forgive, suffocated by her continuous, unrelenting support. *Surely there is more for her than this,* he thinks. It demeans her to linger after him, as though her existence had no other meaning. But anger is not the answer here, nor pity for her. He owes her more than that.

"You want to know why I did it," he says finally, aware that he'll find it difficult to justify, because the memory is already fading. He recalls an explosion, the dull whine of exposed electrical wires. Blood on the boy's face. But all else is blurring, becoming fuzzy and forgotten. In a short while, he won't remember it at all.

"Yes," she says simply. "I want to know."

The broken part of him that is still human aches, like an old scar. "I wanted to stop all this."

"You wanted to come to an end?"

He nods. "I wanted to come to an end."

"But what else is there for us, if not this?"

Nothing, he answers silently. And that was the whole idea, after all. Oblivion. Snuffing out like a candle, stopping the confusion of disconnected memories, finally finding some peace. The Fortune Teller cannot understand, because she still has her thoughts, her recollections, her knowledge of what happened and when. She doesn't know what it feels like to lose yourself a little more every day.

He sighs, knowing he needs to give her something more. But what? No words adequately capture the despair that he feels. "It is torture to continue," he whispers.

She winces. He can feel the echo of her sadness, rippling through the spectral cloth of her shawl. "Can't you look to the future, rather than trying to grasp the past?"

Can't I be your future? It's the unspoken plea, always there between them. The neediness, the desire that he can't answer. He can't provide what he wants, because he cannot share this misery with anyone. It is his, and his alone.

"I had a wife," he says finally, shaking his head. "I know I did, because I can feel it in my core. And I have lost her, so I must find—"

"Forget your wife! Don't you remember what happened? Dear God, how can you have forgotten? We were both there! Don't you remember how you felt, when you saw her?"

Her rage is hot as a furnace. It is out of character, and he recoils instinctively, turning back to the water, unable to stand firm in the face of her fury.

"I remember nothing," he murmurs, knowing that is not quite true. There are feelings, leftover scraps of instinct; subtle dregs of *knowing*. Something happened to his wife. Something happened to him. And there is a darkness, much like the darkness surrounding the boy and his screen, which clings closely to him.

The Fortune Teller shakes her head, her features solidifying for a second, before fading into fine mist.

She is sad, he realises. *I make her unhappy.* That wasn't his intention. *Perhaps she should leave me for good,* he thinks, then imagines an existence without her, spanning for years, decades, centuries into the future. The thought of it chills him.

He waits. She waits. A lone rowboat passes, oars turfing the still surface of the river.

"I wish I could make you understand," she says quietly. "You *need* to understand, then you can move on."

"Understand what?"

Silence; a pause that could have lasted moments, or perhaps a cold, desolate lifetime.

Finally, she answers him. "You will *never* find your wife. *Never.*"

FIVE

— 1877 —

I ALWAYS TOOK great delight in watching her. It was never the grand moments that thrilled me, but rather the mundane, simple actions. A hair comb, slipped nimbly into her mass of curls. A sigh as the church bells disturbed her from her reading. Small, tender seconds that carried such weight in my heart. I knew I would never forget them.

Her bodice was causing her pain, I could tell. Yet despite this discomfort, I still revelled in that thrill of assisting her; of being at liberty to place my hands around her waist, to rest my chin upon her pale shoulder.

"You are the most beautiful woman alive," I whispered.

Eleanor laughed, eyes still fixed on the looking glass. "I don't feel it in this ridiculous garment. How I wish someone would invent a more comfortable thing to wear!"

I agreed with her, once again pitying females, with their elaborate dress codes and lengthy beauty regimes. Eleanor scarcely needed assistance in my opinion; her waist was already tiny, and her face quite splendid enough without powders or lotions.

"Mother will be impressed that you've gone to such an effort," I said, giving the ribbon of her bodice a final tug. "Though you needn't have worried so much, it's only a casual family gathering, after all. It's not as though we're dining at some exclusive establishment in the city."

Her expression darkened, and I knew immediately why. It wasn't Mother she was concerned about, but rather Fred's presence, and the discomfort that was likely to accompany it. Goodness knows why he'd decided to accept this particular invitation to luncheon, when he'd rejected so many in the past, but there was little point dwelling on it. He would be there, and there was nothing that could be done about it. Still, it was hardly surprising that Eleanor was apprehensive. I felt much the same way, which seemed rather ridiculous given that he was my brother.

"Arthur will be there too," I said, stroking her arm. "It won't just be *him*. And you know Arthur, he's more than capable of lightening the mood."

Eleanor climbed into her dress with the grace of a ballerina, toe pointed with discreet delicacy. "Yes, of course, I know dear Arthur will do his best. Fred will be bringing his fiancée, that's what your mother said, wasn't it?"

"Yes, though heaven knows what she'll be like. Mother's already met her, and she implied the woman was something of a strumpet."

"Goodness me!" Eleanor giggled, before covering her mouth with her hand. "Still, if he met her down the Pig and Whistle, she's bound to be, isn't she?"

Eleanor wasn't wrong. The Pig and Whistle was one of the most notorious spots down by the Docks, usually filled to the brim with whiskered workers, shifty-eyed pickpockets, and women of ill repute. I dreaded to think what Fred's wife-to-be was like, or what her previous profession in life might have been. Still, my brother had clearly recovered from his heartbreak over Eleanor, and that was the most important thing.

"Poor old Arthur." I buttoned her dress, then spun her around, kissing her gently on the nose.

She blinked in surprise. "Why?"

"Well, he's the only brother not to have a sweetheart, isn't he, now Fred is engaged? I do hope the lad isn't feeling too hard done by, I should think he's rather surprised by it, given how much fuss everyone used to make about his blonde curls and rosy cheeks."

"He'll be fine." She glanced a final time in the looking glass, before scooping up her bonnet and pressing it delicately on to her curls. "He's a charming man; I'm sure he has no problem attracting female attention. Now, shall we go? I don't want to be the last ones there."

I seized an umbrella on the way out. Although the sun was high in the sky, grey clouds loomed over the distant buildings, rolling uneasily, like sea-tossed boats. We were surely in for a bout of bad weather before too long; it was all too evident in the still, humid air.

Our house was diminutive, but perfect for the two of us. Every time I closed the front door, a swell of pride rose within me; pleasure at what I'd achieved in life, and how I'd managed to provide for my wife. Perhaps Eleanor would have liked a larger dwelling, with a few servants to assist with the running of the house, but if this was the case, she never once said it. Arthur's home was grander, but then, he had no one to share it with, which rendered it immediately less charming than my own. As for Fred's, well, it was better not to think of Fred's current situation, renting a grim room overlooking the Thames. I'd not visited, but Martha had avidly filled me in on the dirt, the damp, the broken windowpane. It sounded like a filthy, desperate little hole.

How far Arthur and I have come, I thought, musing on the house we'd grown up in, where Mother and Martha still resided. It was a dear little cottage with a beautifully overgrown flower garden, but was decidedly cramped. Still, it had been a happy childhood, for the most part. Even after Father had finished chastising us for one misdemeanour or another, the house had never lost its warming glow. *Though Fred may feel differently,* I acknowledged. He'd always come off worst with Father; there'd been something about their personalities that simply clashed, like two clanging cymbals. Poor Mother had often found herself in the role of mediator, along with Arthur, desperately trying to keep the peace. I'd often secretly agreed with Father; but then, everyone always said I was more like him than the others; even more so after he passed away.

It was a pleasure to see that Mother's door was wide open, as it always was when she was expecting guests. At the sound of our feet on the doorstep, Martha tore from the parlour, wide-eyed as a puppy, her apron streaked with flour and water. Eleanor squeaked in surprise, before letting herself be enveloped in her sister-in-law's chaotic embrace.

"Gosh, you've got a lot of energy today," I commented, placing my umbrella in the corner. "Kindly release my wife; you'll do her some damage with a grip like that."

Martha let go, then grinned. She had a smudge of coal by the side of her nose. "Mother's cooked rabbit, and it smells wonderful. I was making bread earlier, but then it was too wet, so I gave up and Mother took over. Won't you come in?"

"I would," I remarked dryly, "if I could get through the door. You're rather blocking the passageway, Martha."

"Are the others here yet?" Eleanor asked, glancing over Martha's shoulder.

"Arthur is, he's lazing around outside. Typical him, he expects us women to wait on him hand and foot. Won't you come through? I'll pour you both some lemon cordial. We're sitting out in the garden for lunch, don't you think that's a splendid idea? Though the wasps are dreadful today. I've already had to swat three with my book. Shall we sit outside then?"

I laughed at my sister's ceaseless chatter. "As long as the rain holds off." Striding through to the kitchen, I relished the warmth and comfort that can only be found within your childhood home. The plume of rich smoke hit us as soon as we entered, just as Mother slammed the oven door closed again, wiping her brow on her apron.

At the sight of us, her face lit up, like an oil lamp rising to flame.

"There you both are," she said, arms outstretched. "Come in, my loves, come in. Fred should be along any moment."

Eleanor glanced at me.

"And his lady," Martha drawled, as she gathered the glasses from the dresser. "If we can call her that. She's utterly dreadful, you know."

Mother whipped her briskly with her tea towel. "Martha, you mustn't say such things!"

"Come on, you know what she's like, she was absolutely awful when we met her, and—"

"—That's quite enough, young lady." Mother peered anxiously down the hall, as though expecting to see Fred and his fiancée already there, listening in on the conversation. "I'm sure she's perfectly pleasant when you get to know her."

"She's terribly rude and hostile," Martha whispered, perching on the nearest stool, beckoning for us to come closer. "I think she looks the sort who—"

"Are you prattling again, Sister?" Arthur appeared at the back door, a smart flat cap resting on his oiled hair. "Goodness me, poor Miss Elizabeth Stride, and to think, she's set to marry into this family."

"No one's forcing her," Martha grumbled, fiddling with her plait.

I shook my younger brother's hand warmly, observing the cravat at his neck, which was a particularly soft silk. He caught the line of my gaze, then patted it down self-consciously.

"I know, I know, paisley's considered a little out of fashion these days, but I simply couldn't resist it. I found it in Liberty's last weekend."

"It looks very fine on you." I instinctively touched my own naked neck, feeling somewhat underdressed by comparison. But then, Arthur always did have a taste for fine clothing. Fortunately for him, he now commanded a good enough salary to indulge it.

"Is that someone I hear coming through the door?" Mother trilled, opening the oven again and releasing another cloud of fragrant smoke into the room. "Arthur, would you be a dear and greet them? I don't trust Martha to be well-mannered, you know what she's like."

Eleanor stiffened. I could tell by the set of her jaw that she was preparing herself for the inevitable encounter. Her anxiety brought forth a fresh wave of nerves in myself, and I smoothed my waistcoat down, wondering what to say to the brother I hadn't seen for so long. Would

Fred be civil? Or was he still holding a grudge against me? It was impossible to predict.

We heard chatter and footsteps, clattering in the hallway. I braced myself.

"Good afternoon, everyone." Fred strode into the room, thumbs tucked into his braces, looking every bit as self-assured as I remembered him. If he was uncomfortable with my presence, he gave no sign of it, though seemed reluctant to meet my eye, looking at all corners of the room apart from the one I was standing in.

He's grown a moustache, I noticed, observing his profile, which was sharp-jawed and tense. The facial hair looked well on him, gave his face a sense of gravitas. I felt an unreasonable stab of jealousy and hastily pushed it from my mind. Now was not the time for ill feeling, after all.

"Hello, Fred, it's wonderful to see you again." I held out a hand. After a pause, he took it, then without warning, pulled me into him. I gasped with surprise, then tentatively returned his embrace.

"Less formal, little brother," he whispered into my ear.

I grinned, pulling away from him. "Very well, Fred. It is good to see you again."

The woman beside him coughed, surveying us with open interest.

"You must be Elizabeth," I ventured as warmly as I could, though in truth, I was shocked by the sight of her. Although Martha's comments had prepared me to some degree, I hadn't anticipated the *reality* of such a woman. Her hair hung, tousled and tangled, to her collar, and her face was unusually long, with protruding cheekbones. Aside from her grey eyes, which were currently sparkling with amusement, there was only roughness about her, and none of the usual feminine charms associated with the fairer sex.

Whatever does he see in her? I wondered, then averted my eyes, aware that I was staring more than was appropriate.

"Yes, that is me," she replied, in a voice that was thick with accent, perhaps Northern European or German. "And this is your wife, I presume?"

Eleanor stepped forward, extending a hand. I noticed it was trembling slightly.

"It's very nice to make your acquaintance, Miss Stride."

"Stride's not her real surname," Fred said, leaning against the doorframe. "No one can pronounce her real name, so she's made one up to suit her." He glanced around, with challenge in his eyes.

This is going to be every bit as painful as I anticipated, I realised, sighing inwardly.

"I meant to ask last time we met; where are you from originally, Elizabeth?" Mother wiped her hands on her apron.

Elizabeth surveyed the kitchen with an expression that was somewhere between aloofness and interest. "I am Swedish," she replied. "I came to England when I was fourteen, after my father died."

There was an uncomfortable silence. Fred sighed, then slapped the table. "Enough about all that now. When's food going to be served then, Mother? I'm starving and no mistake."

She chuckled, relishing the change in subject. "Not too much longer, dear. You all go on outside. Enjoy the sun. Martha can help me serve up."

"Why me?" Martha squeaked, leaping off the stool. "Why can't one of the others do it?"

"Because it's only right and proper that you learn to be useful in the kitchen," Mother replied, as she nudged her aside to reach the carving knife from the drawer. "Isn't that right?"

"No," Martha muttered ominously, but held her arms out to receive the serving plates, nonetheless.

"I shall return to the deck chair," Arthur announced, sweeping out the back door. "If only the neighbour's dog would stop its incessant barking, then I could rest my eyes for a while. I'm ever so tired."

"Try doing my job, then," Fred growled, as he followed. "You have no idea what hard labour is until you work at the Docks. Never a moment goes by when my back doesn't ache."

We emerged into the balmy sunlight. The garden was tidy as ever, the roses neatly pruned, the table already laden with cutlery and plates.

I could just about detect the vague buzz of the bees within their hive at the bottom of the garden, concealed by the buddleia bushes. It immediately soothed my spirits, taking me back to happier times spent here, playing marbles on the patio, or hide-and-seek among the shrubs and plants. I could tell from glancing at my wife's face that she was thinking the same; of all those days she'd come over to play as a child, while her aunt and my mother gossiped in the kitchen.

How fortunate we were, I thought wistfully. I hadn't really appreciated it back then; only noting how cramped the house had always felt, how much smaller it was than the elegant buildings in the city. How wrong I had been, to focus on those things, when true contentment had always been within my reach.

"What a beautiful day!" Eleanor announced, startling me from my thoughts.

To my horror, Elizabeth Stride sat without waiting to be asked, assuming the position at the head of the table, despite Fred's unsubtle nudge at her elbow.

A blackbird chirruped noisily at the top of the apple tree. Somewhere in the distance, a cow lowed uneasily. We all waited for one another to speak.

"So," Eleanor said finally, in a too-bright voice, tilting her bonnet to shade her eyes from the sun. "When will the wedding be, Elizabeth?"

"I do not know." The other woman yawned without covering her mouth. Her two front teeth were grey.

"We've got to save money first," Fred said, shifting uneasily in his seat. "It's not like we're free to do as we wish, like you and my brother here."

Ah, there it is. The note of resentment, buried deep, but evident nonetheless. In some strange way, it reassured me that he still felt *something* about it all and hadn't just forgotten us completely. Still, the bitterness in his tone disturbed me, hinting at further unpleasantries still to come. I sighed. The last thing I wanted was to fight with him, especially not on a day like this.

"Perhaps you'll marry in the autumn?" Eleanor suggested, scrabbling for words to fill the silence. "It's such a glorious season for weddings, don't you think?"

Elizabeth Stride shrugged, then picked up a fork, passing it from hand to hand.

"Wake me up if I fall asleep," Arthur said, stretching like a cat in the deck chair. "I don't want to miss the food." He promptly tugged his cap over his face, ignoring the rest of us. I resisted the urge to roll my eyes. *Typical Arthur,* I thought. *Never mindful of social niceties, far too interested in enjoying himself.* Still, his laid-back manner served to calm the rest of us, easing the tension from the conversation like an iron over cotton. I leaned back against my chair, feeling my stomach start to untighten.

"So." Fred poured himself a glass of cordial, oblivious to the splash of fluid over the side, which landed on the napkin. "You two are enjoying married life, then? I heard the wedding was very pleasant."

The edge to his voice was unmistakable. I glanced at Eleanor and reached for her hand across the table. "It was a beautiful service," I replied evenly, meeting his eye. "It is a shame you couldn't be there."

Elizabeth snorted, eyes lit with poorly concealed contempt. I bristled. Who did she think she was, anyway? To come into our home, and to be so scathing and dismissive? Up close, I could see she was older than Fred, the lines around her eyes poorly concealed with powder. It made perfect sense why Martha had been so rude about her earlier. Still, I wanted to rebuild my relationship with Fred, and if that meant enduring this harsh-faced woman, then so be it.

"Whereabouts do you live, Elizabeth?" I asked, with as much sincerity as I could muster.

"Here and there." She looked up, her expression twisted in defiance. "I was in the workhouse until recently."

Eleanor winced. "You poor thing. I've heard that they're very hard on people."

I felt a rush of love for her. Typical Eleanor, to pity this woman, despite her hardness and poor manners. No doubt it had been her own actions that had landed her in the workhouse in the first place. She looked the type.

Elizabeth's face softened, and for a moment, I caught a glimpse of the girl she'd once been; vulnerable, lonely; a stark contrast to her usual closed-off expression. "It wasn't a good life," she admitted. "But I'm out now. Fred's been kind to me, despite the hardships he has to endure."

"That's wonderful to hear," I said warmly. "Though I'm not sure Fred's life is *that* hard. Plenty of people have employment down at the Docks, don't they? At least it's a job, with a steady salary."

"I'm not sure you'd know much about it," Fred growled. He met Elizabeth's eyes, then looked away.

To my relief, a clatter of plates interrupted the quiet, breaking the strange atmosphere. A moment later, Mother and Martha appeared, laden with serving dishes and plates, and both rather red in the face.

"That silly sister of yours has managed to spill hot fat all over the floor," Mother huffed, placing the rabbit in the centre of the table. It steamed restlessly, still hissing from the heat.

"You passed it to me when I wasn't ready!"

"I specifically asked, '*Are you ready to take the rabbit for me,*' and you said—"

"—Well, this looks splendid," I interrupted, keen to avoid yet another round of bickering. I seized the carving knife, watched Fred's expression darken, then realised my error. *He's the oldest brother,* I reminded myself, cursing my forgetfulness. *It's his job, now Father's not with us.*

"Here," I said swiftly, as I passed the knife across. "You do the honours."

"No, you've started it now. You may as well carry on." He leaned back, arms folded, and guilt rose in my chest; not just guilt about the carving, but about *everything.* How he'd fallen, how the only woman he could attract now was a hardened harlot from the workhouse.

Arthur yawned loudly, then ambled over to join us, patting Eleanor on the shoulder as he passed.

"What did I miss?"

Fred sighed, then wiped his mouth with his sleeve. "Nothing, little brother." He looked at me, and something passed between us, something dark and unhealthy. "Nothing at all."

SIX

— 1969 —

THE GHOST DOES not understand this song the woman keeps playing, over and over, late at night. It sounds distasteful, with a plodding, grinding rhythm that sounds distinctly suggestive. Strange, given the almost ecclesiastical church organ thumping in the background, while a male and a female whisper to one another in an unfamiliar language.

The woman plays it on a round black plate, scratched ceaselessly by a small needle within a strange flat box. After she is done, long after the sun has set, she places the plate back in a paper case, which is blue. The ghost has read the wording several times in the past. *Jane Birkin. Serge Gainsbourg.* The names mean nothing to him, but that's not unusual. Little means anything to him these days.

Her face glows by the lamplight, a lumpy cigarette smouldering in the ceramic dish beside her. The smoke trails aimlessly to the ceiling, which is already stained. She is unhappy, but then, that is how she always is. Her heart is suffused with sad, despairing love, made all the more desolate by the knowledge that her man does not love her back.

I have forgotten her name, the ghost realises, feeling guilty. He knows he should remember, they've been with her for a long time now. *It begins with B, I'm sure of it. Or is it D?* He looks around the apartment for clues, but fails to find any.

He thinks that she will smoke more of her strange cigarette, then pass out on the cushions that cover her living room floor. However, tonight she surprises him by staying awake. Her anxiety is evident from her continual fidgeting, the way she keeps loosening her dark hair from its bun, then gathering it up again. Finally, she looks at her clock; a polished wooden and glass box above her fireplace. Her man is not coming tonight, that's very clear. Watching her mood plummet further, the ghost feels himself falling with her, dragged in on the wave of her emotion. It is always this way, which he supposes is why he stays with her. Otherwise, why else would he?

The Fortune Teller is in her usual position by the armchair, idly watching over them both. Sometimes, he forgets she is there; her quiet presence blends effortlessly into the surroundings. He knew her name, once. The essence of it slips over his tongue from time to time, before sliding away. *Perhaps I should ask her to remind me,* he thinks.

"You know we should move on soon," she suggests, noticing his stare. "I understand your need to be here, but she's only making you more distressed, not less."

Yes, he thinks, a vague hint of a memory toying with his mind. *I do have reason to be worried about her.* He looks back at the woman, who has started to cry, leaving trails of black ink down both cheeks. Her sobbing wilts him, because it is a defeated sound; the grief of one who has already given up.

"I do not think we can leave her," he replies flatly.

The Fortune Teller shakes her head. "There's nothing we can do. She isn't even aware that we're here. No one ever is."

That isn't true, he thinks. There have been times when the woman has stiffened, peered earnestly in their direction, as though sensing their presence. And once, she mentioned it to her man, when they lay on the mattress on the floor, smoking and draped over one another like puppies. *I think this place is haunted,* she'd said, her naked skin shining in the light. He suspected that in his living days, he would have found it an erotic sight. Now, he only looks on with a vague, disconnected interest.

He tells the Fortune Teller about his memory, and she edges closer.

"That's interesting," she says carefully, the spectre of her shawl glittering in the dimness. "See, you do remember some things still."

He nods, though the truth of it is that his memory fades with every passing moment. Images pass through his head like steam trains, whistling through with vivid brightness before vanishing again. Before, it frightened him badly. Now, he is beginning to accept it as an inevitable slide into nothingness. Perhaps he even welcomes it. It's a chance to sink beneath the waves, to let everything go, and to simply forget.

"I remember my wife," he says carefully, though even the memory of her is growing distant. *Eleanor.* He knows her name, and must hold it close, for if he loses that, he'll lose everything.

The Fortune Teller groans. "Yes, but you don't remember how she—"

A clatter breaks through her words. The woman has dropped one of her strange black musical plates, and it rattles on the floor like a discarded coin, before finally falling silent. He sees the cover, tucked neatly under her arm. *Sgt. Pepper's Lonely Hearts Club Band.* Another favourite of hers, particularly one mournful song in the middle, about a girl leaving home. It's another song that she likes to play again and again, whilst leaning back against her endless velvet cushions, crying quietly.

"Why don't we go down to the river?" the Fortune Teller suggests, pointing at the door. "We can talk more about your memory, and how we can help you."

Her concern makes him smile, if only for a moment. He admires her optimism and resilience, how she remains positive, despite the drudging depression of their existence.

"I do not think I can be helped."

"That's not true."

"Besides, I want to stay here." He's reluctant to leave the woman. Her energy, bleak and draining as it is, stirs something within him, and he wonders if by staying with her, he'll retrieve something of himself.

A hint of a smile plays at the Fortune Teller's lips, before fading. "You always cling to lost souls, you know that, don't you?"

"So you keep reminding me." Aside from a dim recollection of the last person he'd stayed with, a sad-faced woman who kept staring at a photo of a man in uniform, he can't remember any others, only occasional memories of faces, glimpses of personalities. An energetic teacher, married, fighting for some cause or other. A foppish man who drank too much. A hard-faced lady, with a strong, Scandinavian accent. Other people, swimming in and out of his mind like fishes through weeds. He doesn't know who they were, but knows that he knew them once, not that it matters now.

The music has stopped. The silence of the apartment challenges the balance of the atmosphere, threatening to tilt it off-kilter. That's why the woman plays the melodies, no doubt, to swell through each corner and block out the sadness. The ghost watches as the woman eases her arms into a coat, a tan-brown garment with oversized lapels, which she ties carelessly at the waist. She has cleaned her eyes, he notices, wiping away the streaks of black, repainting her lashes so they appear thick, brittle, and insectile. It is a strange fashion, but then, he has seen others do the same. Times have changed.

He follows her into the wintry night, not understanding why anyone would choose to be outside, when the wind bites like a snapping dog. A dusting of fine rain immediately clings to the woman's hair, sending strands upwards in a frizzy halo. She turns away from the Thames, heading west along Lower Thames Street. He knows the route well; it leads towards St Magnus the Martyr; a church he remembers vaguely from his past. He avoids it wherever possible, there's something about the whitewashed walls that makes him feel uncomfortable. *Cursed creature,* he thinks, without knowing why.

For a moment, he wonders if she is going inside, whether she seeks respite in the house of God, though such a gesture would surprise him. It seems most people these days have forgotten religion. Sure enough, she passes the church, then turns down a narrow side road, pressing a hand against the wall to balance herself in her towering shoes. Music throbs in the distance, muffled by the wind. *Yet more music,* he thinks wryly. *This era seems unable to survive without it.*

The ghost wouldn't have noticed the black door, had the woman not stopped directly in front of it, rapping smartly before waiting, arms folded. The door's surface absorbs the light from the street lamps, in a manner that's vaguely threatening. A minute later, it opens, and a large-bellied man steps out, neck constricted by a too-tight collar.

"You on the list?"

It's a strange way to greet a lady, the ghost thinks, waiting patiently. He's noticed that impertinence seems almost acceptable nowadays, especially among younger people.

The woman keeps her gaze to the ground. "I need to talk to Frank," she mutters. "Frank Tanner."

Ah, he thinks. Now it makes sense. She has come in search of her man. He'd sensed her growing impatience, her need to be with him, back in her dwelling. And she believes he is here, concealed somewhere within this dark, threatening building. *She shouldn't go in,* he thinks, feeling oddly protective of her. *It isn't a good place.*

"Frank's in a meeting." The man rests both arms on the top of his stomach, implacable as a statue.

"It's okay." She scrabbles in the small bag around her neck, then pulls out a handful of scrunched notes, which he realises is modern money. "Here, have this. I won't be any trouble, all right?"

How the ghost wishes that the man would shake his head and send her on her way. Yet he knows humankind too well, how easily they're swayed by material wealth. Already, he can see the telltale gleam in the man's eye; the fingers tensing around the money, ready to pull it to the safety of a jacket or trouser pocket.

"You've got ten minutes. Any more and there'll be trouble. You got it?" She nods, pushing gratefully past him. The ghost has no other choice than to follow, drifting up the narrow stairs behind her. It's dark, but the darkness is thicker, more syrupy than the ghost would like. It has a dense, watchful quality that suggests nihilism and dangerous intentions. It's one of the worst aspects of his existence, these mists of torment that he experiences, laden with the promise of danger and unhappiness to come.

It is worse upstairs. The walls pulse with projected lights, which blob and shift with water-droplet ease; and people arch, bend, and fold, reminding him of reeds in a stiff breeze. Their eyes are wide, blank, oblivious to the world around them. Music pulsates, muting all other sound, an overpowering cacophony of drumbeats, wailing, and chanting voices. It is unholy, depravity made into sound, and the ghost fights the urge to leave this stubborn woman to her inevitable misery.

A glaze-eyed man, hair scraped back in a bun, grasps her by the waist and drags her to the dance floor. The ghost feels her panic, flitting just beneath her skin; but also her weary acceptance. *She has been touched like this before,* he realises. *Roughly, and without love.* The vague warmth of anger floods over him, before sinking away again. Emotions are becoming increasingly difficult for him to summon these days; it's as though they're drifting on a tide, being pulled further and further out to sea.

"I'm Frank's girl, Bernadette," she hisses, extracting herself from the man's octopus grasp. The words work; his eyes widen and he drops her immediately, only to melt back into the crowd.

Bernadette, that was her name, the ghost tells himself, relieved at how familiar it sounds to him. How could he have forgotten? He is sure it won't happen again. *Bernadette. And she is looking for Frank,* he reminds himself, keen to establish the facts. He remembers Frank's face: Angular, with stone-carved, harsh cheek bones. Full, cruel lips. Almost feminine in certain lights, though perhaps that's because of Frank's long, straggly hair, which so many men of this age seem to favour. He does not like Frank. As for the Fortune Teller, she shrinks whenever Frank is near. She claims he reminds her of *her Strong Man,* though the ghost is never quite sure who she's referring to. *Another of those old memories, now rotted to nothing,* he thinks sadly.

But now is not the time for reminiscing. The woman has already pressed on, shoving past sweaty body after sweaty body, until she reaches a door at the back of the room. The music seems louder here, vibrating off the walls, drenching everything in madness. He has never heard such noise before, nor seen such darkness. It is a bad place. A *terrible* place.

And she is about to step into it, he realises, just as the woman prises the door open.

Beyond, the passageway is dim, the walls rough, plasterless, dirty. She has been here before, that much is clear as she presses towards a closed door at the end. It is a place of *horrible* things; the ghost can feel it oozing from every angle. For some reason, he feels as though he has been here before too, following someone else up this very corridor, before it became a place of vice and nastiness. *Harry's office,* he thinks, without knowing who he's thinking of, or why. *A long time ago. Not anymore, though.* And just like that, the memory is gone.

Without knocking, the woman pushes the door open and storms through. It is a simple enough room, not much in it besides a plain desk and a few battered plastic chairs surrounding it. He marvels briefly at the shiny black object on the desk, the thing with all the round buttons, each with a letter or number upon it. *A typewriter.* An innocuous enough item, and a seemingly nonthreatening space to accompany it. Yet it is not as innocent as it seems. The ghost can sense blood, hidden under the faded rug, scrubbed to a pinkish tinge. The walls shriek with violence and desperation.

Three men stare at the woman, at *Bernadette.* Silence prevails for at least ten seconds, if not longer, each of them motionless as a statue. The only thing that moves is the coil of smoke from one of the man's cigarettes, trailing uneasily to the ceiling.

The ghost recognises Frank immediately, one hand resting on the desk, the other clenched in a tight, unforgiving fist. "What the fuck are you doing here, Bernie?" he snaps, without greeting her. This is how their relationship is, harsh tones and violent gestures, followed by moments of sweetness. A dangerous form of love, in his opinion.

Bernadette blinks, stupidly as a sheep. "You said you'd come over at nine o'clock, I waited *hours* for you, Frank, just like I do every time, and—"

He rolls his eyes. The other men laugh.

"Jesus Christ, woman." Frank runs a hand over his hair, then glances at the other men. "I've got business here. Now go home, make yourself a drink, calm down, and—"

"—I won't calm down, I'm sick of calming down! We're meant to be getting *married*, Frank. Doesn't that mean anything?"

The man sitting behind the desk, the one in a suit, presses his fingers together, forming an arch towards the ceiling. "You need to go home now, love," he says, and though the words are softly spoken, *love* lingers like a hammer in the air, full of threat.

She folds her arms, eyes already brimming. In a moment or two, the ghost knows she'll cry, then those fat rivers of black will fall over her cheeks again, just as they always do. It fascinates and frightens him in equal measures, how monstrous and pitiful she looks.

"I'm only going home if he comes with me."

Frank snorts, slams his fist down. "Don't be so fucking ridiculous. You leave now, or I swear I'll—"

"—you'll do what? Hit me? Because that makes you the big man, doesn't it? Hitting a woman."

The two other men mutter, then stand. Neither are tall, but their presence bloats as they rise, swelling and filling the available space. The ghost retreats instinctively, watching as the shifting cloud of darkness twitches, settling more evenly around the woman's head.

She is in trouble, he realises, keeping his eyes on her, afraid to look away. *She has to leave, or risk taking a path she shouldn't go down.*

"Sweetheart," the man behind the desk drawls, stretching each syllable with serpentine ease. "I asked you once, nicely. I won't be so nice the next time. Frank needs to talk through some business, and you need to learn your place."

Don't answer back, the ghost begs, daring to edge closer, hoping to distract her with his presence. She doesn't see him, he knows that much, but she shivers sometimes when he drifts too close. *We have to leave,* he communicates silently, praying she'll notice, at least on a subconscious level, *otherwise it'll end badly.*

"Frank?" she says instead, laden with pain, uncertain as a child.

Frank shakes his head. "Go home. I'll speak to you later."

Finally, the tears come, as the ghost had known they would. The woman's shoulder hits the doorframe on the way out, sending her off-kilter into the hallway, reeling like a spinning top.

I'm useless, I'm useless, I'm useless, she chants softly, eyes sightless, until she staggers to the room with the music. *I'm a useless, dumb bitch. That's what everyone says.*

It is hard to cope with the emotion. The ghost pulls back, hating himself for his weakness. The woman spirals out of sight.

Later, he finds himself on a wide street, still busy with people, despite the late hour. He watches them pass; after all, what else is there to do? He can't return to the woman's apartment, not until she's tethered her misery to more manageable levels. And he cannot brood on her, it is too painful to think about. Instead, he surveys the late-night crowds around him. The men and women wear strange trousers; tight around the upper leg, widening to triangles at the bottom. Their shirts are bright, gaudy, sumptuous as Indian royalty. It is a world that fascinates him, because it is so opulent, and so seedy.

Yet there is still chivalry among this chattering chaos. A man holds a door open as his wife passes through. Another wraps his arms around his beau, and the ghost hovers near, welcoming the glow of their love, which radiates out like an aftershock.

Why do I not attach myself to people like this? he wonders, with the hint of a smile. After all, he remembers love. He knows the pleasure of kissing a pale shoulder, of simply holding a lover close, feeling the lover's chest rise against his own. Why is it that he is so attached to those who are in pain?

Perhaps it's my purpose, he muses, drifting homewards on the breeze. *To help them in some way.* He wishes he understood his greater meaning, other than to try to find *her. Eleanor,* he reminds himself, struggling to pull her face into his memory. Above all else, he must grasp hold of her name, her face, the *feel* of her whenever she was near. If he loses that, there will be no point in carrying on.

He returns, eventually. The woman has lit the candles, the strange ones that ooze over her empty wine bottles like erupting lava, a vibrant display of purples, reds, and oranges. She is calmer, glassy-eyed, fingers stroking the sheepskin rug beneath her. The ghost looks to the plastic thing beside her, the transparent, cylindrical thing with a long needle sticking from the top. There's a stained spoon beside it, blackened underneath by repeated heating, and a metal contraption, from which flame spurts if you strike it correctly. And the welts at her elbow, the marks she usually goes to great lengths to conceal. But not tonight. Tonight, there's no one around to see them.

The Fortune Teller is already here, watching sorrowfully from her corner. Her eyes gleam with compassion.

"Is it the opium again?"

"They do not call it opium," she reminds him, easing closer, making sure to keep a wide berth of the woman. "Remember? I told you only a few nights ago. They call it heroin."

Heroin. It is a grandiose name for something that only causes pain. He tests the word in his mouth, trying to drill it into his memory, to ensure he does not forget it again. Except he knows he will, at some stage. His mind is deteriorating, he knows that, and each day, it seems a little worse.

The woman's head eases slowly around, as though coasting on a gentle breeze.

She senses us, the ghost realises. Although the woman appears a million miles away, there is an alertness to her, a sensitivity to their presence that the *heroin* has heightened. For all its ill purpose, it brings her closer to them, and this moves him in a way that he doesn't quite understand.

"Who are you?" she whispers, eyes saucer-round, then, slowly as a swan gliding on water, she collapses to the floor.

The ghost waits a while, studying her motionless form. "Has her man been back at all?" he asks, flitting to where she is lying. He fears death will find her, if she is unable to find herself in time.

The Fortune Teller shakes her head. "No sign of Frank at all. She was filled with rage when she first came in, then she did *this*."

"She went to see Frank and asked him to come home. But he refused."

"You shouldn't have gone."

The ghost feels indignant at this misunderstanding of his good intentions. "Why shouldn't I? I may have been able to help her."

"You can't help her," she corrects him. "No one can, living or dead. You have to realise that, you're not here to save anyone. You only wanted to come here to see what she was like, don't you remember?"

No, I don't, he answers silently. The realisation stings. What is his purpose again? It is to find his wife, he is sure of it. But he doesn't know how to locate his *Eleanor,* he can't even remember where she died, let alone where she might be drifting now, without him.

He chooses his words carefully. "If you could be of more help with locating my wife, then—"

A single look, and he wilts on the spot, cowed into silence by the force of the Fortune Teller's glare.

"You *know* why you can't find her," she says, her anger sharpening her, bringing her into focus. "We go through this all the time. You never used to forget so frequently; what is happening to you?"

The ghost frowns. Her rage rattles him, not least because he *does* have a vague recollection of discussing this before, but cannot remember what was said. He knows it was something to do with a boat, but then, that makes no sense to him. Why should a boat have anything to do with his wife? As far as he's aware, he wasn't a seafarer, and neither had she been.

"I think my memory is worsening," he says eventually, then looks back to Bernadette. Her breathing is deep, melodic as a rising tide. The candles shed wax over the hearth tiles.

The Fortune Teller sighs, then comes closer, reaching for him, passing through him like the wind. "I know," she says simply, standing beside him. "I shouldn't lose my temper with you. It must be terrible."

There it is again, her overwhelming kindness, which he both appreciates and rejects, like a child with a blanket on a warm night. She offers comfort, solace, but also a sense of smothering.

Of drowning, a voice adds, deep within him.

Perhaps, he agrees. *Perhaps that too.*

They wait, as the seconds tick loudly on the mantelpiece clock. The candles sputter out, one by one, and the room is left in darkness. The woman fails to move; sprawled across the rug, still wearing her heeled shoes, with their elaborate straps.

He does not know what time it is when the Fortune Teller twitches beside him, startled into movement. Her gaze travels to the door, alert as a dog, just as Bernadette's eyes flicker open.

"He's here," the Fortune Teller says warily.

"Who?" the ghost asks, though he already knows the answer.

"Him. *Frank.*"

Before he can answer, the door flies open, crashing into the wall with animal force. The man is drunk, that much is obvious before he even staggers through the door; and his eyes are pig-small, puffy, and furious, roving around to catch her in his sight.

She doesn't even flinch as he wrestles her upwards, throwing her against the sofa, clutching her chin between his fingers. The glaze of her expression shows that the heroin still holds her, and the ghost hopes it will numb the pain of what's to come.

"You stupid *bitch,* how dare you come to my place of work when I'm doing business!"

A slap, resounding as gunshot. Her head flies to the side, before falling on her shoulder. The ghost cannot see her face, which is a small mercy.

"Do you realise how fucking stupid you made me look?" Another slap, harder than the first. "Do you?"

He hauls her face to his. Rage, torment, dislocated fear, they all congregate, forming the all-too-familiar cloud of darkness. The ghost and the Fortune Teller instinctively melt back against the wall.

The woman murmurs something and holds out an unsteady hand. Her cheek bears the livid mark of his hand.

"What? What did you say?" Frank turns, sees the evidence of her *heroin* taking; the needle contraption, the heating device, the tortured spoon. He sighs, then slumps to the floor. "Oh, I see. *I see.* You're using again, is that it? Jesus Christ, woman; where did you get it from? Did you steal it from me? Because if I have to tell Davey that I'm short on stock, you know what he'll do to me, don't you? What he'll do to us both?"

The woman shakes her head, dazed as a newborn lamb, then starts to sob. To the ghost's surprise, so too does Frank; a silent, wrenching heaving that causes him to collapse in on himself, like a discarded puppet.

"Oh God, you stupid woman, why do you do it?"

"I don't know, Frank; I don't know . . ."

They crawl together, two beetle-like forms on the rug, and coil around one another, seeking some meagre comfort from the other's form. The ghost sighs. He has seen this before, it's always the same. The building rage, the overstepping of the mark, the violence, then finally the bittersweet, despairing reunion. It is what keeps the woman tethered here; those minor moments of tenderness, when Frank erodes, when she can be the strong one instead.

Because then, she feels as though she is needed, the ghost realises. *And that is all that matters to her.*

"He'll kill her one day, if she's not careful," the Fortune Teller comments. It's obvious that she's as relieved as he is at the dissipation of the darkness, even if it's only temporary.

The words send a shiver of memory through him. *I have seen a killing before,* he realises. *A woman, alone at night. And a man, with a moustache.* He knew that man, he's confident of it. It was someone close to him, someone he once cared about. As for the woman, he's not so sure, but he recognises her face; that combination of harshness and vulnerability.

A slit throat, he remembers, then as anticipated, the memory fades. It is probably for the best. Some things should not be recollected, and he suspects that is one of them.

The Fortune Teller takes him by the hand, not that he can feel it, but he senses the intention of closeness, and that is warmth enough. "You know we should move on soon, don't you?"

The ghost smiles. "So you keep saying." He looks to the woman, still clutching her man, welded to him as tightly as the wax on those empty wine bottles. *They've melted into one,* he realises, then feels a hollowness within him, a deep longing to be held again.

Perhaps she's right, he thinks, looking at the Fortune Teller, at the steadfast glint of her eyes. *Perhaps it is time to move on. Perhaps it's all this negativity that's making me forget myself.*

"We should find some new people," he says mildly.

She raises an eyebrow. "We should try simply being *alone,* and moving forwards."

SEVEN

— 1877 —

ARTHUR CAME FOR us at midday on the dot, just as he'd said he would. His brougham was a fine sight, though the polished sides and red wheels were looking a little unpolished, much like my brother himself, whose cravat was askew. We laughed to see his head poking above the reins, grinning from ear to ear as he brought the horse to a stop.

"Goodness me, what a day for it, eh?"

"It certainly is, Brother," I replied, smiling as he leapt from the driver's seat, then gallantly bowed to Eleanor, who giggled like a girl. "This infernal rain, it never seems to stop, does it? It's hardly shopping weather."

"Yes, but we must go," Eleanor said, taking my hand and stepping up into the carriage. "I have so many Christmas gifts to purchase, and if I leave it too late, I'll have no time to wrap them all."

Arthur and I exchanged a look.

"You can blame the Queen for this," he muttered, with a wry grin. "That German husband of hers, bringing all these odd customs into the country."

"In all fairness," I corrected him, "people were giving gifts before them."

"Yes, but not to these excessive levels." Arthur rolled his eyes, then leapt back up to his seat. "Goodness me, do you remember Christmas when we were children? We thought ourselves fortunate to get some fruit and nuts in a stocking."

"I remember that year my aunt and I joined you for Christmas," Eleanor added. "After poor Auntie's sweetheart left her high and dry, do you remember?"

Arthur chuckled. "I should say so. Your aunt was in a terrible mood, all day long. Mother had to dose her up with plenty of gin to cheer her up."

"That was the same year that Fred pushed me over in the snow and I cracked my chin on the step," I said balefully, wincing at the memory of the blood hitting the whiteness below. It had ruined the day for me, as I remembered; my chin throbbing with pain for several hours after.

"Yes, because you called him some awful name or other," Arthur reminded me. "You could be terribly harsh to him sometimes, you know. Just because our dear Daddy called him those things didn't mean that you needed to as well."

"Well, let's leave that in the past, where it belongs," I said sensibly. "Now, are we going to go or not? Eleanor is absolutely desperate to spend some money."

"Gosh, I'm thankful I have no wife to bankrupt me."

"I heard that," Eleanor said pertly, leaning over and rapping him on the shoulder. "I'll have to spend even more now, just to spite you both. Honestly, what a pair of Ebenezer Scrooges you two are!"

We laughed at the reference, and I settled beside my wife as Arthur got the horse moving again. It was a brisk, gloomy day, the threat of more rain looming in the distance, yet my spirits were high. After all, Christmas was approaching, and best of all, Eleanor suspected she may be with child, though it was too early to be certain. I longed to confide in Arthur, to see the smile on his face, but I'd given my word that I'd keep it a secret until Eleanor was certain. It thrilled me, the thought of a child, *our* child, nestling deep within her, growing even as we sat here, readying itself for the world. What sort of parents would we be? Would I be more like Mother, kindly and fussy, or severe and firm, like

Father had been? Fred had always teased me that I was unbearably like our father in temperament, which was ironic, given how much he had taken after him in appearance. We'd almost certainly need a nanny to help Eleanor in the house, though I scarcely knew how I was going to afford it. I'd have to find a way, if necessary.

Eleanor caught my eye and smiled, resting a hand on her abdomen. It never ceased to delight me how we could read one another's thoughts. She referred to it as 'psychic energy', no doubt an expression she'd learned as a younger woman, when we used to visit the circuses when they came to town. She and Arthur had always had a fondness for the unusual, which was surprising, given how even-tempered and moderate they both were. I usually only accompanied them as a means of getting closer to Eleanor, though as we had grown older, Fred had put a stop to that, with his barbed comments and surly stares.

Still, I liked to humour her in her little oddities. They were part of what made her so wonderful.

"So," Arthur shouted over his shoulder, collar turned up against the wind. "Where are we headed to first, eh?"

Eleanor edged forward. "I should very much like to go to Fortnum and Mason, if that's all right? They've got the best selection. And perhaps Whiteley, and Harrods too?"

"I see." Arthur cast a quick glance at me, chuckling. "I'll be carting you two all over the city, is that right? I should charge by the hour, I'd make a fortune."

Eleanor slapped him on the shoulder. "It's mainly Fortnum's that I need to visit. I presume you'll be dandifying yourself up in Liberty?"

"They do have the best selection of fabrics."

I laughed, then settled back against the seat. Arthur was certainly becoming the well-to-do gentleman these days, but then, why not? He worked hard at the bank, and had been promoted twice in quick succession. He deserved all of this, even if his rapid ascent was something of a shock. But then, that was how he'd always been. Good old Arthur. Hardworking, ambitious, yet eternally good-natured. How could I begrudge him his success, when he'd striven so hard for it, in such an amicable manner? Though deep down, I wished some of his fortune would rub off on me. No matter how many times I pressed for promotion, I always seemed to be overlooked. *One day, I'm sure,* I told myself, glancing again at Eleanor's stomach. *I just need to be patient.*

"How's Fred?" I asked, more out of courtesy than anything else. The last time I'd seen him hadn't ended well, mainly thanks to his unpleasant strumpet, Elizabeth Stride, who'd entirely ruined poor Mother's luncheon party. By the end of the afternoon, we'd all been more than delighted to see her leave. Her presence had been much like a cloud, ruining the good mood of the party; and Fred's behaviour hadn't been much better.

Arthur tutted, then rapped the horse's rump with his whip, sending the brougham into a sudden spurt of motion. "Fred's morose, as always," he replied. "The wedding's off, by the way. Did Mother tell you?"

"No." I looked at Eleanor. We were always the last to know these things. "What happened?"

"Not quite sure, though I suspect Fred uncovered some rather distasteful things about Elizabeth's past, by the sound of it."

"Heavens, what sort of things?" Eleanor leaned over the seat, oblivious to the biting breeze.

Arthur shifted in his seat. "Oh, I don't know. Mother only said that Fred had heard some rumours from friends, about his Long Liz and her previous employment."

"Gosh." I scratched my chin. The news didn't surprise me. If anyone ever looked like a woman of ill repute, it had been her. *Long Liz,* I thought with a smirk. What a strange nickname. I wonder how she'd earned it?

"Mother was rather horrified."

"I can imagine." Mother was remarkably liberal, but the thought of welcoming such a creature into her house was probably a step too far. It mortified me too, the memory of us sitting in the garden, casually talking to a woman of that nature. What had Fred been thinking? Especially with Martha present, not to mention my wife. They were impressionable; they should not have been exposed to such a woman.

We rattled towards the heart of the city, through the busy streets, past crowds of people, all wrapped up warm against the chill air. London never ceased to fascinate, carriage after carriage bouncing merrily down the main thoroughfare, shop awnings quivering in the wind. It was the sheer variety of people that astounded me; elegant gentlemen passing beggars on street corners, all shades of society blended in a single, simmering pot.

Still, I was glad we didn't live too close to the centre. Our little house, close to the Thames, was ideal, apart from the bells of St Magnus the Martyr chiming at all hours, which did get rather wearing on occasion. In our cosy home, Eleanor and I felt a part of the excitement of the city, without being submerged in it. Living in the very centre must feel a little like drowning, I suspected; too much noise, stimulation, and the suffocating press of so many other people.

Finally, Arthur pulled to a stop, leaping nimbly to the floor, then opening the door for us both.

"How's that for service?" he declared, offering his hand for Eleanor to climb down.

"You're very kind, good sir," she replied, smoothing her skirt. "And thank you ever so much for bringing us in, it's certainly the way to travel."

"Ah, that's nothing. Have you tried that underground railway yet?"

I shuddered, clambering down to the street, then closing the brougham door. "Absolutely not. I've heard the tunnels are choked with smoke and gas."

Arthur laughed, before patting me on the back. "You're so very cautious, Brother! You should give it a go, it's exhilarating. Whistling through the darkness, arriving at your destination in a matter of minutes. It really is an experience."

I knocked the side of the brougham. "I think I'll stick to what I'm familiar with, thank you."

Eleanor smoothly slipped her hand through my arm, leading me gently to the pavement. "Do you know," she said to Arthur, who was trotting dutifully behind, "I've been trying to persuade him to take me on a pleasure cruise for months now. Yet he won't. He says he's worried about the water."

"Ha, and you live by the Thames. What a thing!"

I coughed deliberately. "It's not that I'm scared, I simply fail to see the advantage of sailing down a muddy old river, seeing all the sights that we're familiar with already. That's all."

"I think it would be marvellously romantic," Eleanor said, eyes sparkling. "Perhaps I can get you to change your mind one day, darling."

I groaned.

Arthur winked. "If you don't take her, I will. The poor lady deserves to experience at least one cruise along the Thames in her life."

"If you say so." I thought of the river, the thick, brown waters, the way they oozed and sucked at the muddy banks, and I shuddered. I'd never understood the fascination with the Thames. Although there were moments when gazing out at the waters calmed my senses, for the most part, I found it an unsightly behemoth, lazily slicing the city in two.

"Was that a yes, then?" Eleanor asked, squeezing my arm.

"Perhaps." After all, I reasoned, as the doorman welcomed us into the inviting warmth of Fortnum and Mason, it was only a river cruise. And for my wife, I would have gladly done anything.

EIGHT

— 1940 —

IT IS THE end of the world; the ghost is certain of it.

For hours, the sky has been teeming with silver contraptions that he knows are called *aeroplanes*; wheeling and diving above the city, dropping their cargo on the docks below. The city had been filled with screaming, footsteps pounding this way and that along the streets, but even the shrill panic of people had not drowned out the constant, grinding whine of those aeroplanes above, nor the crash as their cargo, their *bombs,* had hit the ground.

An inferno, that is what London is now. The ghost wanders along the dockside, watching the firemen as they direct their jets of water at the solid walls of flame; already busy ripping warehouses to pieces, reducing elegant buildings to rubble. They are fighting a futile battle, but he respects them nonetheless; their grim determination to do *something* to counterbalance the hell that surrounds them.

The sirens shriek, a toneless wail that causes fresh groans and wailing from the people around him. "More bombs on the way," one shouts, hurrying her smoke-shocked toddler down an alleyway. "There's more of the bastards coming."

The ghost understands that the country is at war, though the reason is a mystery to him. During his time with Helen, in her cosy terrace with her two children and elderly mother, he's listened in on their conversations; their musings on a person called *Hitler,* his possession of Denmark, Poland, France. Who this Hitler is, he cannot imagine. How can one person conquer an entire continent? Such a thing should not have been possible. But then, this is a new era. *Every* era is new to him, though times keep getting stranger and stranger; and none yet as strange as this one.

He searches the streets, bewildered by the despair that surrounds him. For the living, still racing here and there in the streets, the sky is darkening, the sun beginning its slow retreat over the horizon. For the ghost, the blackness has already settled in far earlier; the dark waves of fear and hopelessness radiating from every person in this once great city. It is cloying, suffocating, almost unbearable.

My city, he thinks sadly. He knows he once lived in this area with his wife, and that their house is now nothing more than a mass of charred wood and broken stone. *The bombs have robbed me of another piece of my past,* he thinks bitterly, though suspects his own memory is already doing a good job of erasing his living days. Try as he might, he cannot recollect things as clearly as he once could. It is alarming, and he prays it will stop soon, or risk tugging him under an endless ocean of forgetfulness.

The whine in the distance grows louder; it is the aeroplanes, re-turning once more. The answering screaming comes soon after, the running feet, the panic. It whirls around him like a storm; buffeting him left and right. He wishes he could find Agnes, his Fortune Teller. But she's been away a lot recently. He suspects it's due to his habit of for-getting her name, though it only happens on occasion. And of course, she has a natural distaste of situations such as these. She loathes need-less death, especially when caused by human cruelty.

Someone shouts beside him, a man with more whiskers than visible skin. "Look lively, they're coming!"

More screams. The ghost looks up, squinting through the hot smoke, the swirling darkness.

It seems there are more aeroplanes than there were before; a perfect formation of shining silver killers, tearing towards them. It reminds him of a swarm of bees, and he thinks, *I kept bees once, or my mother did. I'm sure of it.* He remembers their dull drone, not dissimilar to the high-pitched whine of the aeroplanes overhead.

Then the bombs fall, drop after drop after drop; a relentless spew of metal, shrieking through the air before exploding on the ground. The surrounding buildings light up like lightning, turning the roads to a series of crazed flashes and erupting fires.

Perhaps this is Hell, the ghost thinks. A bomb detonates only a foot or so away, but has no effect on him. He remembers a vicar, many years ago, preaching of the Devil, of a place where sinners burn for eternity. Surely that vision of Hell must have been like this; heat, confusion, pain, hopelessness?

On the ruined pavement, a woman weeps, a guttural, animal sob that clangs discordantly against the hoarse shouting and screaming. In her arms, she cradles a child; a girl, her head bleeding freely. The ghost can sense already that the child won't make it, he can feel her vital energy draining from her, as swiftly as water from a breaking dam.

Should I wait for her ghost to appear? he wonders. *Would it give her comfort, to know that she wasn't the only one here?*

There isn't much point. Most ghosts only linger for a moment or two, dazed, wide-eyed, then they disappear into nothing. He doesn't know why this happens. A few remain for longer. Perhaps some wander around for years, as he has done. But he remembers enough to know that he is the anomaly, he and his Fortune Teller. *Agnes,* he reminds himself firmly. *Do not forget her name.*

As he wanders through the streets, he sees death on every side. An elderly couple, crushed beneath a pile of bricks. One man, or what he thinks was once a man, blown in two, his blackened midriff still smoking. And children, several children. Two boys lying on the road, fingers still entwined. They'd been running away, he can tell; he still senses flight upon them, even after death. The weight of it is as strong as a blow to the stomach. *Such a waste,* he thinks, *to lose their life before it had even begun.*

He wonders if he'd once lost a child, in the past. Details escape him now, his memory dims a little more with every passing day. *No,* he tells himself, flinching as the building beside him explodes into flame. *I would remember if I had been a father. I'm certain of it.*

Helen's house is further along the riverbank, close to where his own house had once stood. It's a modest, workingman's home, with a broken back window and missing tiles under the doorstep, but nonetheless, he hopes it is still standing. Despite Helen's loneliness, despite her aching sadness in her husband's absence, the house is a happy one. He can't stand the thought that it might have been detonated to the ground.

Why am I with Helen? he wonders. But then, he's never sure why he remains with anyone these days. It has something to do with the area she lives in, he knows that. He remembers an elderly face, a frail, vein-lined hand; then hastily pushes the memory away. *Focus on Helen, and no one else,* he tells himself firmly, and focuses his efforts on reaching her street as swiftly as possible. It is unwise to think of that other person, he is certain. It will only bring pain, and plenty of it. *Best to forget,* he reminds himself.

Thankfully, Helen's house remains stoically in place, though the skyline surrounding it is unnaturally altered. Aside from a haze of smoke staining her windowpanes, it looks almost uncannily untouched; a haven of safety in a wilderness of terror.

He drifts in. The sound of the sirens, the explosions, the whine of the aeroplanes; all become muted the moment he enters the narrow, meagre warmth of the living room.

Helen is on the settee, her son on one side, her daughter the other. The ghost has difficulty remembering their names or their ages. They seem young enough to still need their mother, though old enough to bear themselves with defiance. *Good for them,* he thinks, approvingly. *They won't take this assault lying down. That's courage for you.*

Helen's mother is out in the kitchen. He can hear her clattering in the cutlery drawer, and the soft pad of her slippers against the linoleum floor.

"Do you think they'll stop soon?" the boy asks. His shorts are badly darned at the knee.

Helen shakes her head and pulls him closer. "No. I think they're going to keep this up all night. Don't worry, though. We'll think of something."

They stare at the small, tiled fireplace; so simplistic and humble compared to the fireplaces he remembers from his living days. A small clock ticks on the bookshelf. *They don't know what to do,* the ghost realises, suddenly worried for them. *So they choose to wait here instead, for now.*

Another bomb detonates from somewhere behind the house, perhaps in the neighbouring street. The children don't even flinch. They have become used to this appalling onslaught, even after only a few hours. Like their mother, they are resilient.

Finally, Helen's mother appears, clutching the doorframe with twisted fingers, cup of tea in the other hand. The ghost smiles. In spite of everything, in spite of Death itself raining down upon the city, the woman still has the good sense to brew herself a drink. Her calmness in the face of adversity astounds him.

"I still think we should pop along to Ivy's," she suggests, "see if there's room in her shelter for us."

Helen's face takes on a pinched, pained expression. "I'm not asking her, she'll only say no."

"Not to the kids, she won't. Nobody would turn away a child."

"Unless there's no more room in there. The shelter's not exactly the Ritz, is it?"

The ghost thinks he remembers Ivy; a buxom, wide-faced woman who lives close by, with hair scraped into an unforgiving bun. If it's who he's thinking of, she hadn't seemed like the sort of woman to welcome anyone into any shelter of hers, no matter how desperate the situation.

Helen's mother teeters to the settee and places a hand on her daughter's shoulder. "Helen, dear, we need to do *something*. We can't stay here, everyone else has gone to find safety, this is—"

"I know, I *know!*" Her eyes wander to the mantelpiece, to the photograph in the centre. It's grainy but truthful; a narrow-shouldered man, decked in uniform, jaw set tight for the camera. *Helen's husband,* he reminds himself. Not a handsome man, but a likeable, open-faced man nonetheless. He can see why she loves him.

"What about Monument Station?" Helen's mother continues, undeterred. "Getting underground's what we need to do, love."

"But if we go out in the streets now, we—"

"—no excuses. We need to do something, we can't just wait for . . ."

She falters as her daughter starts to cry. Someone shouts in the street outside, accompanied by racing, unseen feet, which clatter and fade into the distance.

Helen's mother sips her tea, but the ghost can sense her growing panic, hidden like a child under a blanket. "I think we need to take the risk," she continues gently. "It's only a quick walk, and it's better than waiting here like sitting ducks. We'll need to check up on poor old Ellie though, sitting in her bed, there's no chance she'll be able to get out to safety, not in her condition, poor old girl. As if she hasn't lived through enough."

The ghost flinches. They've mentioned their old neighbour Ellie before, and it *bothers* him on some level, though he doesn't know why. He puts it out of his mind and turns back to the living.

Helen shakes her head, already standing. "Mother, I can't worry about Ellie. We've got enough on our plate."

"Well, then. Let's get moving, shall we? We'd best get on our way quickly."

She is right, of course. There's growing threat in the air, the sensation of danger edging closer and closer, like a prowling lion. The ghost has witnessed the bombs and their indiscriminate destruction. It could just as well be this house as any other, and they would do well to get to safety.

Helen inhales deeply, defeated. "Let's gather some things, then," she says, then without waiting for a reply, slopes off towards the stairs.

The ghost knows why she's reluctant to leave. It is because this is *their* house, hers and her husband's, bought and paid for, and fought hard to keep. That bed upstairs, it's the same one in which her two children were born, and where they were conceived. Every room in this house, small though it is, leaks out the joy and contentment of their marriage, and Helen cannot let it go. She's already had to let *him* go, after all, and she hasn't heard word of him for weeks.

The ghost drifts after her, wishing he could settle her pounding heart, which seems to him as loud as a soldier's drum. She pulls a suitcase off the top of the wardrobe and starts stuffing it with clothing, toothbrushes, a pair of ribbons for her daughter's hair, though the ghost suspects they'll be too preoccupied to worry too much about personal appearance. He's always found it strange, how women are so concerned with such things, even in times of danger.

I may have said that to Eleanor, once or twice, he thinks, following Helen back downstairs. *She worried about her appearance too, I remember that.*

And then, in a rush of action, they depart. The door slams shut and silence settles over the rooms like dust. The house seems infinitely larger and lonelier without them in it.

The ghost resumes his position beside the mantelpiece. It occurs to him to follow them, to join them in the underground station, but he's been in places like that before, he's certain of it; and he hasn't liked it. Even the thought bothers him; the stuffiness, the lack of fresh air. *It's too much like drowning,* he decides, and roots himself more firmly into position. He will guard the house instead, though he knows he won't be much use if a bomb hits it.

He waits. Waiting is something he has become good at over the years. Occasions often call for it, aimless days that feel filled with purposelessness, where he simply does not know where to place himself. He vaguely remembers being *busy* in life, always working, always rushing around. How did he become so still and so passive?

Outside, the sky turns black, yet the city is still lit by a myriad of fires, burning brightly through the night. The planes leave, until they're nothing but a vague hum in the distance, before returning, bringing chaos back to an already brutalised landscape. The ghost wonders how much more they can take, the people out there, bravely trying to bring about some control. Their desperation seeps through the walls, the exhaustion building in every muscle of their straining bodies. Life does not prepare people for events such as these; yet it is in these moments that men and women can become something more, something astounding.

The ghost wonders if he ever achieved anything astounding when he was alive.

A subtle strike of a bell. The mantelpiece clock, it must be midnight. It's only then that he realises the Fortune Teller is beside him. *Agnes.*

She's smiling crookedly, and he can see the outline of the teeth that were once there, gleaming in the darkness. "Why are you waiting here?" she asks, sidling closer. "Can't you see there's a war going on?"

The ghost chuckles. It is good to see her, despite everything. In truth, he'd been starting to panic that she'd chosen to leave him for good, that she'd perhaps *disappeared,* like all the other ghosts seemed to do. *Then I'd be entirely alone,* he realises, and shudders at the thought. This existence is unsettling enough, without having to endure it on his own.

"I was enjoying the peace and quiet," he mutters, at exactly the same moment a bomb explodes, somewhere in a neighbouring street.

"Helen and her family have gone, then?"

"To the underground station."

She nods. "That's a sensible idea. Why don't you come out with me, down to the Docks? They're unrecognisable, just a mass of rubble and fire."

"I've been there already." The destruction holds no fascination for him.

She looks at him shrewdly. "Perhaps we should see *Ellie*?"

The ghost doesn't like the suggestion, nor the way that she empha-sises the name, laden with a meaning that he's obviously supposed to grasp. Refusing to rise to her bait, he shakes his head. "Why don't we wander the other way instead?" he suggests. "Away from all the chaos?"

Agnes drifts closer, shimmering slightly before sharpening into focus. "It's chaos *everywhere*. Those aeroplanes, they've been up and down the length of the Thames, dropping their bombs. I've never seen anything like it."

She waits. He doesn't answer. Sometimes, he is like this. His thoughts start to fray and untangle, then quite suddenly, he forgets what has happened only a moment before. The worsening of his memory frightens him, makes him wonder if he is slowly losing him-self in the passage of time. *Surely not,* he reasons to himself, quelling the nagging fear within him. *It's perhaps a temporary state of affairs. And there are many things I remember. Eleanor. Helping her dress in the mornings. My two brothers, though I can only recollect one name; Fred. The deep, throaty chuckle that my mother produced, whenever any of us made a joke. My sister, Martha, and how her face was always grubby. I know these things, so I can't be losing my mind entirely. And that is a comfort.*

"Sorry, what were we talking about?" he says finally.

Agnes sighs. "It happened again, didn't it?"

"What?" he asks, although he knows exactly what she's referring to.

"You keep forgetting things." Her expression darkens, and she drifts into mistiness. "Don't think I haven't noticed; it's obvious. You've been forgetting my name too. I sometimes wonder if you remember how we met."

He thinks, long and hard. The vague details are there; her gaudy tent, the shining glass ball on her table. He remembers talking to her, long into the night, after she'd been crying. And he knows that a man had hurt her. A *Strong Man*, he thinks, incomprehensibly. *In gladiator boots and a leotard.*

"I do remember."

"I think you're remembering less." Suddenly, she dives towards the door, gesturing outside. "Come on. We can't lurk in here all night. It doesn't seem proper with the owners of the house away."

The ghost smiles at her unexpected propriety. "I suppose you're right."

Together, they venture out, emerging like tentative mice from a hole. The aeroplanes have gone, for now, and the street is empty. It's unnaturally dark, and for a moment, the ghost wonders why, before realising; *they've put all the lights out.* Presumably to make the area harder to see from above.

"How many people died tonight, do you think?" he asks, then is immediately horrified by his casual tone. This is one of the problems of having died oneself; death suddenly becomes very mundane and unexceptional. He knows he should show more respect to the living.

"Too many to count, poor souls."

They pass street after street; some torn apart by the bombs, others incongruously undamaged, as though belonging to another place in time. St Magnus the Martyr, to his great relief, is still standing, its spire jutting defiantly to the sky.

"My old house is down there," he says, pointing down the narrow road. "Well, it *was,* anyway. It was destroyed earlier today."

Agnes gives him a strange look. "You've told me where your house was before, you know. In fact, you've taken me there a few times in the past, don't you remember?"

He thinks hard. In truth, he can't recollect doing so, but he doesn't want to admit it. "Perhaps," he says eventually, aware that he's not fooling her. She can read him unnervingly well.

"How has Helen been?" she asks, after a while. "And her family?"

The ghost ponders the question. Helen has been the same as she always seems to be; strong and unflappable to others, slowly crumbling away inside. Sometimes, he watches her, sitting up in bed, holding a book but not reading it, and he worries about her; about the silent turmoil that wrenches her in two. Her fear for her husband is a palpable, bloated thing, a silent, awful pressure that she bears every day.

"She is frightened that her husband is dead," he says simply.

Agnes nods. "The same can be said for every wife in this city. I don't know how they carry on while bearing such a weight."

"Where do you suppose the men have been sent?"

The Fortune Teller shrugs. "To fight the Germans, I suppose. That's all I keep hearing, whether I'm at the market, or the Docks, or the schoolyards. It seems strange, that the country is fighting them again, after the Great War."

The Great War? he wonders, then remembers. There had been another war, not so long ago, only it had been nothing like this one. There had been no bombings, no devastation and destruction; or at least, not on this level. The country, which had once been so stable, so certain of itself, had been reduced, bullied into submission. *Will it ever recover?* he questions, looking around. How on earth can they rebuild all of this?

"At least Helen has her children at home," Agnes continues, as they turn the corner. "Some women have had to say goodbye to their husbands *and* sons."

They wander onwards, past the more respectable dwellings, towards the shabbier, less welcoming streets. Here, houses huddle like plotting men, their black windows staring at passersby like a series of hostile eyes. A man leans against a wall, cigarette in hand; as though it were any other normal night, and not a time when all hell broke loose upon the city. The ghost admires this quality in Londoners; the ability to simply stiffen one's resolve in the face of adversity, and calmly continue regardless.

"These streets are familiar," he notes suddenly, observing the corner shop nearby, its windows crammed with posters and handwritten advertisements. He has walked here before, many times, he thinks.

"It's Whitechapel," Agnes says patiently. "You used to work here, when you were alive. Don't you remember? Even I remember you telling me that."

The ghost tests the name. *Whitechapel.* It seems familiar, and an image springs to his mind of a desk, a neat tray with correspondence in it, a ledger. Similar desks around him, each occupied by earnest, suited men; some bespectacled, others with balding heads that glinted in the dusty sunlight.

"Yes, I can recollect that," he says, fighting to conceal his happiness, as it seems somehow unnatural on such a bleak night. Yet it is such a joy to him when these memories come to him, fully formed and accessible. Once, he would have taken such a thing for granted, but these moments of clarity are too rare not to be appreciated now.

But there is something else, a darker, more frightening memory, layered just behind this one; a memory he can't properly access. He stops beside a school, its brick façade a mass of shadows.

"This isn't right," he mutters. "This wasn't here back then."

Agnes sighs, then flickers to a halt. "Lots of things are different now."

He knows that, but this is more significant. Something important happened here, something *terrible,* and he was witness to it, he is sure. A name passes through his mind, *Dutfield's Yard,* but there's no sign of any yard around here, only this solid, incongruous school, sat primly on the street, defying him to disagree with its existence.

"Perhaps this was the place I once worked," he mutters, though the words ring hollow. He *knows* it is something more than that, but he can't grasp the details. A figure, sidling away. A woman on the ground. Blood, and lots of it. *His brother. Fred.*

The Fortune Teller waits patiently, then nudges him, her cloak glittering for a moment, like the reflection of stars on a distant lake. "Come on," she says. "It doesn't do to dwell too much on the past. We should keep moving forward."

Moving forward to where? he thinks. What is it exactly that they're pressing towards, and is there any point?

They drift for miles, through parts of the city that are ravaged and burning, and parts that have survived entirely intact. It fascinates him, how the bombs have changed the landscape, how their impact will resonate with bell-like clarity for years to come. For these old buildings, these monuments, landmarks and pieces of the past; they'll never be reclaimed. A single explosion has levelled them out to nothing. *Sometimes, time eases things away slowly,* he thinks, as he continues. *Then at other times, it eradicates everything in a single moment.*

Morning comes, the sun rising with inappropriate brightness, hazy through the smoke and floating ash. The fires burn on, some with continued fervour, others tiring to smouldering heaps of embers. The aeroplanes return, a mass of whining drones above them, deposit another barrage of bombs upon the already defeated city, then finally race into the distance. People return, hollow-eyed, smudged and worn, and the ghost can feel their loss, their mute, disbelieving sense of horror. It is an attack that none of them saw coming, even though they had been warned. And it is an attack that has left many without a home to return to.

He floats back to Helen's home, Agnes beside him. To his pleasure, it still stands, as resolute and pragmatic as it had been the night before; one of London's survivors. Another window has been smashed, no doubt by the force of a neighbouring bomb, but aside from the crumbs of glass scattered across the kitchen floor, the house is entirely intact.

His heart lifts. He knows this will mean everything to Helen.

"When do you think they'll return?" Agnes asks, taking her position by the mantelpiece.

"Soon." He is sure of it. Helen won't be able to stay away for long. *If they return at all,* he thinks, then hastily pushes the thought away. Of course they will. As Helen's mother had said before, the station was only a short walk away. They would have made it, and they'll make it back, he is certain.

Sure enough, an hour later, just after the clock has dinged a quiet rhythm marking the passing time, the door handle turns. The door thuds open. The family returns in a cacophony of excited chatter, heavy footsteps, and breathless wonder.

"See," Helen's mother exclaims, propping her walking stick in the corner. "I told you everything would be all right, didn't I, love?"

Helen's relief is painted across her face, washing over her like warm water. "Thank heavens, eh, Mother? I don't know what we would have done if—"

"Hey, Ma," her son shouts, head protruding from the kitchen door like an overeager puppy. "The kitchen window's got all smashed up. Come and have a look."

They bustle into the cramped space, yet the ghost can feel their happiness, concealed under a vague veneer of concern.

"Yes, we'll have to get someone to replace that quickly, what with October around the corner," Helen's mother declares, rolling up her cardigan sleeves. "And the other one, it's about time, really."

"October's not here yet, Mother, September's only just started—"

"You know what I mean, dear."

Helen chuckles, places her hands on her waist. "We've got nothing to complain about, considering what's happened to other parts of the city. Let's get this cleaned up. Benjamin, move away, will you? Last thing we need is you cutting yourself."

"Can I have a bun first? I'm starving."

The ghost smiles, revelling in their contentment, even though he suspects it's only fleeting. This war isn't over, he can sense it, the impending danger, the protracted hostility over the years. It looms over London like a dirty fog, seeping into corners, tainting the brickwork. And still, he has the notion—no, the *knowledge*—that this will not end happily for Helen, nor for her children or mother. He suspects that

Helen knows it too, otherwise why would she cry herself to sleep each night, while clutching one of her husband's old shirts?

Agnes sidles over, slipping comfortably into the space beside him.

"You're thinking about the darkness here, aren't you." It's a statement, not a question.

The ghost nods. "It seems so *unfair*. Helen is a good person."

"Well." Agnes waits, watching as the glass shards are hustled onto the dustpan. "That is life, isn't it? Bad things happen to good people. You and I should know that, more than anyone."

He feels the truth in her words, but cannot verify it in his mind, for the truth is, he has forgotten what happened to him when he died. There are only loose, floating segments of memory, indistinct images that make no sense. He sees Eleanor's hand, reaching to him, but it is wet, and glistening in the moonlight. Why is that so? What happened? And why, when he remembers his brothers, does it feel like a visceral punch in the gut? None of it makes any sense, but he's reluctant to force it. *If the truth chooses to remain buried, perhaps it is for the best*, he thinks.

"What do you remember of your life?" he asks her, eager for distraction.

"All of it," she says simply. "Laid out behind me like a quilt. I haven't forgotten a single detail."

He looks away, hearing the barbed accusation, simmering beneath the surface of her words. It isn't his fault he's forgetting things, he's sure of it.

"What about the man who was strong?" he asks.

"You mean the Strong Man? Ernst?" Agnes looks at him in disbelief. "Surely you remember Ernst, and what he did to me? You were there, after all."

I was there, he tells himself. *Only, I don't remember the Strong Man's face, or his name, until a moment ago. As for what he did to Agnes, I haven't got a clue.*

"Did he hurt you?" he says uncertainly. "Ernst wasn't a good man, that's correct, isn't it?"

The Fortune Teller only shakes her head. "You really are forgetting things," she says, with infinite sadness. "And who knows when it will stop? How can I stay here with you, when your memory of who I was is draining away?"

Draining away. Those words, they are apt. It feels like a slow, gradual decline, and for a moment, he sees the future as it may be for him— endless days of dreamlike forgetfulness, an existence in which nothing makes any sense. It is a horrifying thought.

Then he realises. She is threatening to leave, if he cannot change. And then he will be alone, drifting aimlessly from decade to decade, a lost, sad soul without a single person to talk to.

"I will make sure I get my memory back," he says, watching as Helen and her family retreat to the living room. "I promise."

Agnes looks at him sadly. "You've said that before. I wish you would let me help you."

The ghost says nothing, only shrugs, because he doesn't believe *anyone* can help him. Not now, anyway.

The next day, he notices that she is not there. She has slipped away, as she did before, without a farewell or even a warning. Was it to teach him a lesson? To make him appreciate her presence by emphasising the misery caused by her absence? He worries that this time, it is for good. Then where will he be?

The bombs keep falling. Day after day, the grating buzz of the aeroplanes fills the skies, until the people of London scarcely register the noise. It has become a part of their existence, an airborne disease that they tolerate, whilst fearing its effect. As for the people themselves, they have become grey, half-dead things; and even the London humour is fading, the characteristic twinkle of the locals' eyes dimming to weary stoniness.

The ghost stays with Helen and her family, remaining in their house on the nights they flee back to the underground station, wondering if his presence somehow protects the surrounding walls, makes the bricks impervious to attack. He contemplates where the Fortune Teller might have gone. *Agnes.* He must keep saying her name, as it is important.

The darkness still lingers in the house. Each time they retreat to the safety of the underground station, he wonders if they will not return; if their destiny is already neatly sewn up, and the days are just waiting to play out, like a scripted performance. Yet each time they come back, a little more worn and dishevelled than the last; and he is happy that they have survived one more day.

Helen's mother suggests sending the children to the countryside. The ghost can see how much pain even the idea causes. Helen fears the death of her children, but she fears their absence more; he can sense it coming from her, rich and pungent as vixen scent. *She believes something terrible will happen if they leave her sight, the ghost realises. She senses the darkness too, and she's preparing to fight it, with everything she's got.*

But London is no place for children anymore. Even Helen knows that, and as her neighbours send their children to Devon, to Somerset, to Sussex, she knows she must too. Only for her, it feels more like losing another part of herself, crumbling into solitude until everything she loves seems like a faded memory. It is an emotion the ghost understands only too well.

The son and the daughter are sent away. The daughter looks solemn as the train pulls away, but the son is already staring in the opposite direction, the new adventure pulling him away before his physical self has even fully departed. Helen's mother pats her eyes with a rumpled handkerchief. Helen refuses to cry, but the tears are there, suppressed just below her throat, and shoving against her eyes. She is a geyser, ready to erupt; but when she does, it will be a silent explosion, a detonation that blasts no one but herself.

The house is larger without two young people racing from room to room. The sounds echo without the soft press of a child's body to bounce from. Without children to give the home meaning, it becomes little more than a stage, every movement a little less driven, a little more performed. Helen's mother settles by the gas fire, knitting an endless, mud-brown scarf. Helen bites her nails and listens for further news on the metal box with the dials, the thing she calls a *wireless*.

The ghost waits too. Sometimes, he thinks he senses the Fortune Teller, the warmth of her essence flitting somewhere close by. But then, before he can verify the sensation, it is gone, leaving him wondering, and doubting his own senses. And all the while, the war thunders around them. Death envelops the city like a dirty mist, and it is impossible to imagine life ever thriving here again.

Finally, the day comes when the darkness within the house, *Helen's little home*, where happiness was once a daily experience, not a half-forgotten memory, thickens to a soup. The ghost knows, before the door knocker is even rapped, that Helen's time has come.

Every second that her hand hovers over the door handle stretches into agonising eternity. She chews her lip, and her heart quickens.

The telegram boy, whom the locals have already nicknamed *The Angel of Death*, stands waiting on the doorstep, holding the card in his hand. She already knows what it says.

The Air Ministry regrets to announce that your husband, Sebastian Skinner, has been killed in action. Letter to follow.

"No," Helen mumbles, knees already giving way.

"I'm sorry, I'm so sorry," the boy replies.

This scene, filled with such pain, has with it the terrible sense of inevitability. The dark swirls above Helen's head sink over her like a shroud, and the ghost notices, as he has in the past, that it is much like a wild beast claiming its victim after a patient, deliberate wait.

He feels constriction where his chest once was, a deep, hollow ache for Helen and for her silent, shaking suffering. And for the suffering of every other soul in this cursed city; mothers mourning their sons, grandparents still reeling with disbelief that such a thing could happen in their lifetime. Children made into orphans each and every day. And all for what?

What is life really for, anyway, if we're so happy to squander it? he wonders. *Why are humans so willing to end the life of another?*

He remembers, with sudden vividness, a body, face down on the cobblestones. A throat, slashed open. And a name, from the very depths of him. *Long Liz.*

Then just as soon as it comes to mind, it is gone again. For the moment, the ghost's mind is mercifully, yet torturously blank.

NINE

— 1878 —

IT HAD BEEN torture, witnessing Eleanor in that state. Everything about the last day had been intolerable, but seeing my wife laid so low was undeniably the worst of it. I hadn't realised how pink her cheeks were normally, until I'd seen them like this; ghost-white, haggard with resignation.

Poor Eleanor. That impotent phrase kept rolling through my mind, ineffectual as a feather in a storm. *Poor, poor Eleanor.*

And poor me, I supposed. We were both worldly enough to know that such things happened to women, that the loss of an unborn child was a common thing, regardless of one's social standing in life, or one's health or age. Yet we'd dared to imagine, as her stomach started to swell, that she may be one of the fortunate, one of those who carried a child without complaint.

I'd been excluded from much of it, as was to be expected, and she'd asked to be left alone afterwards. No physicians, she'd insisted, despite my protestations. She merely wanted *time*. Time alone to mourn, time without me beside her, which stung more than I cared to admit. Still, I had to give her that, at the very least. I owed her that much.

I'd offered to strip the bedsheets, to wrap them carefully, even to burn them, had she so desired. But she insisted upon undertaking the task herself, and I'd watched, rigid with sadness, as a tear dropped from her chin and hit the dried blood, forming a watery blotch of regret.

I'd told Mother, of course, who'd promptly passed the news on to the rest of the family. News never remained still for long amongst us, but always travelled, untethered, from parent to sibling. Fred had presumably made no comment, or at least, none that Mother had reported to me. Arthur, on the other hand, had raced to our house the moment he'd heard. *Dear old Arthur.* Yet it really wasn't what I needed at present. Like Eleanor, I craved solitude; a chance to allow my emotions to accommodate reality.

"Come now," Arthur said, hanging his jacket on the coat hanger, in a manner that was rather overfamiliar. "Surely I must be able to assist with something. Mother said you needed some help." He followed me into the kitchen, his eyes boring uncomfortably into my back.

"I don't see why she would say that," I said curtly, pulling out a chair for him. "There's nothing that can be done."

"Yes," he acknowledged, sitting down, then taking his pipe from his pocket. "But good God, don't you want to *talk* about it?"

I glanced towards the stairs. Aside from the dull click of the grandfather clock, the house was silent. I presumed Eleanor must be asleep, still resting after the ordeal. "What on earth is there to talk about?"

"I don't know. How you feel? I mean, losing a baby is a common enough thing, but that doesn't make it *easy,* does it?"

I nodded. He was right there, I'd had no idea how much it would hurt. "You know I'm not one for talking," I replied uneasily.

"No, you're very like Father in that way."

"I'm not the one who's really suffering, though," I clarified, ignoring the barbed tone of his comment. "Poor Eleanor is in a terrible state."

There it is again, I thought. *Poor Eleanor.* As if my sympathy could change anything.

Arthur leaned back in the chair, surveying the landscape outside the window; the murky waters of the Thames just visible on the other side of the road. It was a gloomy evening, charcoal clouds clogging up the sky, the last dirty remnant of winter. He sighed. "Why don't we have a drink somewhere? It'd do you good to get out for an hour or so, and you'd give Eleanor the peace she needs."

I shook my head. "It's hardly appropriate to go to some tawdry inn while my wife recovers from such an ordeal."

"Yes, but you're no use to her, are you? Women are well equipped to deal with this sort of thing, and it is female business, after all. Besides," he added with a gleam in his eye, "it's not a tawdry inn I had in mind. My gentleman's club isn't far away, we could go there."

"I hardly think I'd fit in." I gestured to my waistcoat, which was looking decidedly shabby, though I was reluctant to let it go. The promotion I'd hoped for at the office hadn't been forthcoming. It seemed as though I was destined for a life as a middle-ranking clerk after all. *Well,* I thought, surveying Arthur. *Not all of us can be high achievers.*

"You'd be absolutely fine. Just put a tie on, you'll be right at home."

I shook my head. "No, really, Arthur. Not tonight. A walk might be a fine thing, though. I could do with some fresh air."

"Dear me, you sound like Mother." Arthur chuckled, then tapped his pipe on the table, before patting down the tobacco. "Very well. If that is what you need, then that is what you shall have."

I realised my winter coat was still in the bedroom, draped across the chair where I'd discarded it, after thinking I'd need to run out to fetch a physician. Each staircase squealed as I edged upwards, and I felt wretched, creeping towards such a vulnerable, miserable creature.

The door was ajar. I could hear her breathing, thankfully deeper and more serene than before. The shape of her body curved beneath the sheets, hourglass smooth, softly rising and falling. I wanted to touch her, to smooth the curls from her forehead, which were matted with dried sweat. It broke me, somewhere deep inside, to see her looking so small and so defeated. *Life is brutal,* I thought. *And it chooses its victims without discernment.*

I quickly penned Eleanor a note in case she awoke in my absence, then crept back downstairs. Arthur had already opened the front door and was waiting patiently.

"How is she?"

"Sleeping, thank goodness."

"Be thankful for small mercies. Now, shall we?"

We stepped out into the cold. A fine mist of rain troubled the air, settling immediately over our hair, our coats, our exposed faces. I glanced back at the house. The bedroom window was dark, empty as a horse's eye, glaring over the river beyond. The sight of it disturbed me in some profound way, and I shivered, thinking *I've seen this house, crushed to the ground. I've stood here, years from now, and seen its destruction.*

"Are you all right?" Arthur nudged me, frowning. "You look rather spooked, as though you'd seen a spirit or something."

The words pulled me back into the moment. "I'm perfectly fine," I replied, pulling my collar up to my chin. "I just had one of those moments. You know, when you have a certainty that something bad will happen?"

Arthur chuckled. "Sounds like nonsense to me. That's your wife's influence, that is; with her love of fortune tellers and the like."

I nodded. Eleanor was strangely preoccupied with that sort of thing, and always asked Mother to read her future in the tea leaves. Perhaps it was a womanly attribute, a desperate desire to believe there was something more than what we experienced around us. Whatever it was, it certainly wasn't something I related to. My beliefs were decidedly more secular, though perhaps the upset of the last day had unseated me, made me more prone to fanciful thoughts.

"You may be right," I agreed, as we made our way down the street. "I just had this sudden, strange notion that I was viewing my home, years from now, and that it had been blasted to the ground. Isn't that a peculiar thing?"

"Blasted to the ground? That certainly is a strange thing to think up. I should think you'd be more at risk of flooding here than anything else." He gestured to the Thames. "I envy your astounding views, but not your position; flood damage is a terrible thing to put right, you know. Makes your house reek for weeks on end afterwards."

We trudged along the path, which was already pitted with puddles. It truly was a miserable night, and quite unthinkable that it could be March already. Arthur slipped in some mud, then cursed under his breath.

"Damned muck. Honestly, why can't you live in the centre of the city, as I do?" He studied his shoe, then gave me a rueful stare.

"I have no desire to live amongst all the noise and chaos," I replied, nimbly jumping over a sizeable puddle. "Though it would be nice to be a bit closer to the office, I suppose."

"See? Though you wouldn't want to live in Whitechapel. I'm surprised your company hasn't moved premises yet, they've got a good reputation these days."

"Steady on, we're not in the heart of Whitechapel, are we?" I bristled at the perceived slight. After all, it was employment, and not badly paid either.

"You're in the Jewish area."

"And what of it? Honestly, I fail to see why so many people take umbrage against the Jews."

Arthur grinned, then patted my shoulder. "My apologies, I didn't mean to offend you. I can see that tonight is not the night for teasing."

"No, it really isn't." My thoughts drifted back to Eleanor. Perhaps leaving the house wasn't such a good idea after all. What if she awoke and was frightened that I wasn't there? What if, heaven forbid, the bleeding started again? It had been several hours since it happened, and she'd seemed recovered enough afterwards, but then, I was no medical expert.

I expressed my concern to Arthur, who wrapped a sympathetic arm across my shoulder.

"I believe your good wife will be *fine*. After all, I don't mean to belittle your experience, but this is commonplace, isn't it? She will recover, she will get with child again, and she will be a mother in good time, I am sure."

We continued walking, wandering peacefully as the quiet streets gave way to crowded urban terraces, red-brick house after red-brick house, all piled atop one another like children in a schoolyard. I'd veered unintentionally towards my place of work, driven no doubt by some instinct; the habit of many days of repetitive action.

It was a different place by night. A man in a tattered top hat studied us coolly, before slipping back into the shadows. Two women, their stained corsets visible underneath roughly draped shawls, smiled invitingly, whispering sweet offers, which carried hauntingly on the breeze.

"Good Lord, why did you bring us here?" Arthur glanced over his shoulder, then at me.

I shrugged. "Curiosity, perhaps. It's not like this when the sun's up."

"I should hope not. Look, there is a woman there with nothing on her—"

I followed the line of his gaze, then looked away sharply. Whitechapel was more depraved than I'd realised. The woman's breasts were fully exposed, hanging loosely to her waist like two half-full sacks of flour. She laughed when she saw us.

"A couple of mollies, I'll be damned!"

"He's my brother, thank you very much," Arthur protested.

She laughed again. Even in the dim light, I could see she was missing more than a few teeth. "That's what they all say, love. Come and spend some time with me, I'll turn you."

"I think we should go," he muttered to me.

I agreed, though there was something liberating about being here, walking among a street of perversity and ill repute. It freed my spirits, taking me away from the weight of the last day, and for a moment, I was tempted to delve deeper into the filth, to explore the darker, seedier side of the city I thought I knew so well.

"Come on, let's head back," Arthur said firmly. "You've had enough fresh air for one night."

We stopped just outside Dutfield's Yard. It looked eerily dark, quite unlike the cheery, busy place it usually was in the daylight, with its sack-makers shouting across the courtyard, and the cart-builders hammering at their wood. An old man leaned beneath the mounted cartwheel on the wall, pipe glittering with every inhalation. It reminded me of an oil painting; unreal, vague, and somehow beautiful.

"I feel a little like I'm under a spell," I whispered, as we turned to leave. "This place is quite captivating, don't you think?"

"No, not in the slightest." Arthur frowned, then lightened at the sight of my expression. "You are odd, you know. You always were the peculiar one."

"I thought that was Fred?"

"No, he was the ill-tempered one. He'd fit in far better here than we ever would."

I grimaced. That was probably true. It was strange, how things had turned out. Fred had always done all right, until Father died. But then, something had been said, and it had changed him, stripped him of his easy-going charm, and replaced it with sullenness and suspicion. It had been alarming, how swiftly he had become the creature he was today.

"'Ere, you two. What you doin' round here, eh? Come for a snoop, have you?" The man with the pipe glowered, arms folded across his chest.

The hostile sentiment shocked me out of my reverie. "Let's leave," I suggested. The old man was still watching us, eyes fierce with intent. He looked older than Mother, but I still believed he could inflict damage upon us both; even worse if he called on concealed friends, if a mob emerged from the shadows and set upon us.

Arthur tutted. "I've been saying that for the last ten minutes!"

The old man stepped forward. I held my hands up placatingly, then hastily dragged Arthur down the street. Laughter trailed us; deep, guttural amusement, with more than a hint of menace lacing the edges.

Not so entrancing now, is it? I reprimanded myself, as we hurried away. As usual, I'd found myself the outsider, neither welcomed nor actively rejected. I found myself reflecting on our own strange position in life; one foot placed in the comfortable middle classes, the other positioned more awkwardly in the lower echelons of society, thanks to our humble upbringing, not to mention our prevailing connections to the Docks. *Yet look at us now,* I thought, glancing at Arthur, taking in his smart woollen coat, the sharp cut of the collar. *Some of us have gone up in the world, others have fallen. What a strange lot we are.*

"Do you ever feel guilty about your success?" I blurted suddenly, as we rounded the corner. The rain was now falling in earnest, fat, weighted drops that dragged my hair into my eyes.

Arthur coughed. "No, of course not. Why should I?"

Indeed, why should he? It was a fair point. Yet here he was, a man living a life of comfort, while his eldest brother resided in dank, broken rooms and was paid a pittance for breaking his back each day at the dockyard. "I don't know why I said that," I said. "After all, it's—"

"—after all, I worked hard to achieve what I have," Arthur interrupted. "And although it may seem as though I live a charmed life, it hasn't all been a bed of roses."

"How do you mean?" I had to shout to make myself heard over the pounding rain.

"Well, look at your life." He gestured down the road, as though my entire existence lay before him, a carpet of possibilities on the ground. "You have a happy marriage, children on the way . . ."

"Not anymore," I reminded him, the truth of it hammering against my chest.

He waved my comment aside. "But you will have. You'll have more children, you and Eleanor; and you'll be happy. And what do I have? A large, empty house, with no one but myself, the maid, and the cook to rattle around in it. I know which type of life I'd rather have."

This wasn't like Arthur. The moisture on his face gleamed in the lamplight, highlighting the tension in his jaw. I reached across, forgetting the horrendous weather for a moment.

"You will find someone to be happy with," I promised him. *How could he not?* I thought. *He is handsome, friendly, generous; what more could a woman want?*

He gave me a dark look. "What, someone like your Eleanor? I can't imagine there are many women like her. Most are so dashedly empty-headed, it defies belief."

Overhead, the clouds rolled uneasily, the moon flitting between them like a secretive thing. I felt a moment of worry, a resounding gong of alarm, somewhere deep within me, which dissipated almost as soon as I'd become aware of it. *I need a good night's sleep, next to my wife,* I thought, wishing I were there already, tucked up in the warmth of our bed.

I nudged Arthur with my elbow, giving him a wink as he turned. "As long as you don't choose a woman like Long Liz, you'll be fine."

It worked. He grinned, then nudged me back. "Dear Lord, if I *ever* bring home a creature like Elizabeth Stride, do have a stern word with me, won't you?"

"Or was that woman right earlier, when she called you a *molly*?" I laughed, pointing at his bright cravat, which poked from his collar like an impudent child.

He rolled his eyes. "I personally prefer the female of the species."

My house was a welcome sight at the end of the road, tucked neatly beside the beech trees, waiting to envelop me into its pleasant interior. The rain had soaked us both, seeping through our trousers, moistening our faces so they appeared liquid in the dim moonlight.

"Won't you come in and get dried off?" I opened the door, waiting for him to follow.

Arthur shook his head. "No, I'm going to return home, it's late." He glanced through the door, to the stairs. "I'll leave you to get back to your wife."

His words hung deliberately in the air, laden with something I couldn't quite discern. Was he jealous? He'd certainly never seemed it before, but I couldn't tell. It was most unlike him; normally he was as easy to read as a children's book.

"I'll bid you good night, then," I said, uncertainly.

Arthur waited, then smiled. "You'll be all right, you know. Everything will be fine."

"Yes, I'm sure it will," I replied. He'd meant it kindly, but I wish he hadn't said anything at all. That same strange feeling surged through me, as it had done earlier in the evening; the sense that something terrible was about to happen. I remembered the vision I'd had of my house, lying on the ground in a crumbled ruin, and shivered.

"Good night," Arthur said quietly. "Give my regards to your wife."

I watched him go, then closed the door with a quiet click. The house loomed around me, rich with anticipation and foreboding.

Pull yourself together, I told myself sternly. Now was not the time to fall apart, not when Eleanor needed someone to support her.

Superstition was never something that had bothered me in the past, and I would do well to remember that.

TEN

— 1922 —

THEY KNOW THEY should be used to all of this now, but it's still shocking. The ghost sees his own horror, mirrored on Agnes's expression like curdling milk. This is an era he will never acclimatise to, and he can tell she feels the same.

People call it the *roaring twenties,* and he can see why. Everything is brash, ostentatious, designed to stun and titillate. Watching them all, these young, hedonistic revellers, limbs jerking to the crass bellow of the brass instruments onstage, he cannot stop himself from comparing to the behaviour of his own past. *How times have changed,* he thinks with dismay. In his time, even touching an unmarried woman's hand would have been indecorous. Now, they grope and stroke without care, exposed legs, unbuttoned collars, sweat glittering on every forehead.

"It is a pit of depravity," he mutters, wishing he could order himself a drink. Indeed, the barman is scarcely able to keep up with the shouted orders, the calls for more champagne, more cocktails, more wine. The alcohol flows like water from a smashed dam, and none of them care. It is excessive, in every sense of the word.

Agnes laughs. "You said that yesterday. And possibly the day before."

"Did I?" He can't remember now, but does recollect being here last night, glued fast to the gentleman who captivates him so much.

Georgie, they call him, or *Georgie-Porgie,* from time to time. Limp, flop-haired, with heavy-lidded eyes that struggle with focus. Not a character the ghost cares for much, but then, he seems to have no control over whom he becomes attached to anymore.

"Your memory is becoming quite terrible," Agnes comments, and he cannot tell if she is in earnest or not. She has a fair point. His ability to recollect things, particularly events that happened while he was alive, is becoming unreliable. Memories enter his head, linger for a brief time, then slip away, and it's not always guaranteed that he can seize them back.

A shrill laugh, barely inches from where they float, makes them shrink away instinctively. The woman in question looks like a child, a voluminous headscarf trapping her curls. Her hair reminds him briefly of Eleanor's, but that's where the similarity ends. The painted lips, the low-cut dress, it is the attire of a harlot, he thinks; and wishes the girl would cover herself.

"Look," Agnes says, pointing over the woman's shoulder, to the other side of the dance floor. "It's Georgie. You were wondering where he was."

The ghost looks and immediately sees. Indeed, it is impossible to miss the man, with his dislocated gait and clumsy footsteps. Georgie has already consumed most of the contents of the wine bottle in his hand, if his glazed expression is anything to go by. He saunters into a dancing man, apologises in entirely the wrong direction, then staggers onwards, laughing, then wiping his lips.

The ghost feels the sense of his own imagined lips tightening in disapproval. *A drunkard,* he thinks. He remembers working with a man who couldn't hold his drink, before he'd been unceremoniously dismissed for being late to work on one too many occasions. It had caused a scandal, or at least, he thinks it had. It is difficult to recollect the precise reactions at the time; all he has a sense of is a generalised atmosphere of disapproval. *Or perhaps it had been a dream,* he wonders. These sorts of thoughts disturb him, in a way he cannot quite pinpoint. It concerns him that he no longer seems able to grasp the truth of his memories; that they have become slippery as fish, sliding through his fingers.

"Look at him now," Agnes says, drawing his attention back to the dance floor.

The insufferable Georgie has stumbled and is already close to hitting the ground as the ghost turns. The noise of the impact is muffled by the ruckus, the disturbing sight softened by the surrounding feet, stamping and twitching ceaselessly around Georgie's head.

He will feel the pain of it tomorrow, the ghost thinks, watching as the man hauls himself to his elbows, reaches for his bottle, then rolls to the floor again, laughing.

"Poor creature," Agnes mutters.

"In what way? All I can see is a useless man who seems intent on drinking himself into the grave."

She gives him a strange look, but says nothing. He sets his gaze to the man on the floor, wishing fervently that he would pull himself together, that he could somehow find some shred of dignity within himself, and rise to his feet. *Why do I feel somehow responsible for his actions?* he wonders. The urge to scold Georgie is strong and unexpected, and impotent, of course. His ability to chastise *anyone* disappeared a long time ago.

"Good heavens, Georgie old boy, do get up!"

Thank heavens, the ghost thinks, watching as a familiar face strides through the throngs, reaching down and seizing Georgie firmly under his armpits. This man they have seen before; dapper and rat-smart, with beady eyes and a pointed moustache, but a not-unkind expression. *Harry,* the ghost reminds himself. *His name is Harry. And he owns this nightclub.* The nature of their relationship is perplexing; almost like father and son, rather than companions. They talk often, in hushed tones, away from prying ears. The ghost senses that these conversations don't bring happiness to either of them.

Georgie continues to laugh, even as the man hauls him to his feet. "It's only a jape, Harry, nothing to concern yourself with . . ."

"This *isn't* a jape. And I don't believe for one second you're enjoying yourself. Now, come into the back office, let's get you cleaned up." Harry glances anxiously around them, not that he need worry. Most of the dancers have already forgotten about Georgie's existence, and are too busy resuming their complicated dance steps, or giggling inanely at nothing in particular.

"Don't be a *bore*, Harry. You're always such an infernal stick in the mud."

"Now isn't the time. Come on, let's get you sobered up."

Georgie stumbles, lurches to the side, and laughs; a superficial, too-high trill that ends in a cough. "What if I have no desire to sober up, eh? What then?"

"I won't take no for an answer, I've a responsibility to your father. Now please, come with me."

Georgie sighs in defeat, and they make their way through the crowd, before disappearing through a door at the back of the room. The ghost turns to Agnes, who shrugs.

"We may as well follow them," she suggests, then gestures to the crowd surrounding them, the beads of her shawl momentarily catching the light of the table lamps. "It's not like we've anything better to do."

The door is covered in velvet; a sumptuous yet ostentatious gesture, in the ghost's opinion. But then, this is the attitude of the time, everything in a glut of abundance, without care for humility or restraint. It amuses him that the other side, the side that's unseen from the dance floor, is plain wood, without adornment. *All for show,* he realises. *It's all meaningless.*

At the end of the corridor, Harry holds open the door to his office, hurrying Georgie through. His jaw is rigid, and his expression humourless. In this featureless, businesslike space, Georgie seems even more out of place, flopping into the chair like a discarded sack. Thanks to the warm glow of the desk light, the ghost can now see the moisture on his shirt, a vague, beige stain of wine and grime from the floor.

"The man has no shame," he mutters, to no one in particular. "He is an embarrassment to his family."

"He is unhappy," Agnes replies.

"How can you tell?"

She looks at him, before saying simply, "All drunken people are. They drink to forget, or else to forgive themselves. You of all people should be more kind towards him, don't you think?"

"I don't see why," he says, though the comment niggles him, stirring up emotions that he'd rather keep buried. Sometimes, forgetting is better; he does not wish to recollect the full details of his association with this shameful man. "Anyway, excessive drinking is a sign of weakness, surely?"

"I suppose some weaker people may use drink as an excuse to blot the world out."

Like Ernst, he thinks, understanding her thoughts. Her Strong Man. Whiskey had been his choice of drink, if the ghost remembers rightly. Or had it been vodka? Ernst had been Russian, he's sure of it, so vodka would have been the natural choice. He cannot ask her, he's embarrassed to admit to his lapses of memory.

A slap of fist against the desk draws their attention back to the living people in the room.

"Georgie, this has got to stop," Harry begins, working himself into a full-blown lecture. "Every night you come in here drunk, and every night—"

"—It's not *every* night, old man. Come on, don't exaggerate. I only come on—"

"—Every night that you're here, Georgie, you're completely inebriated. There's only so long you can keep doing this to yourself. You can't simply drink away your father's money!"

Georgie waves his hand, before sinking lower into the chair. "Ah, Father. Why bring him into this, eh?"

"I happen to be a friend of your father's, and I naturally feel some responsibility towards your welfare, and—"

"Is *that* what you call it? I'd hardly call what you did to me responsible behaviour."

Harry's cheeks are reddening. The ghost feels for him; after all, he's only trying to help. "That's damned unfair, Georgie," he splutters, "and you know it. I—"

"—You seduced a young boy, and—"

"—You were nineteen, for goodness' sake, don't make this sound more sordid than it is!"

The ghost winces. Their emotions are whipping at the room, tearing it to shreds. There is darkness here too, soft but full of menace, lurking close to Georgie's head. *The man is on a path to self-destruction,* he thinks. *And, of course, he is a sodomite.* He remembers hearing of men like that, back in his living days. *Mollies, the people called them. But I knew this about Georgie already. How could I have forgotten?*

Agnes touches his arm briefly. "I can tell what you're thinking. But times are different, you know; and love is still love, regardless of who does the loving. Don't be so stern in your judgement."

Can it be love? he wonders. Perhaps it can, maybe Agnes is right. But certainly not like this. This reeks of secrecy, deception, seduction. The older man, Harry; his love stains the room like tobacco, it's overwhelming, painful to behold. His love is certainly not reciprocated, for Georgie idolises a very different sort of creature. As far as the ghost can tell, his beau is not a gentleman that deserves any sort of love, especially not the desperate desire that Georgie has for him.

He waits patiently, curious to see where the conversation will end. Harry rustles the papers on his desk, arranging them into a neat pile on the corner. Only the flit of his eyes reveals his anxiety.

"Harry," Georgie says finally, "what do you want from me?"

"I don't want *anything* from you. Can't you see that?"

The sound of the wine bottle, slamming against the desk, echoes flatly off the walls. Harry winces, then continues. "I'm *worried* about you, that's all. You used to have a respectable position at the school, a place to live, now look at you! And there's your health to consider, you know what the doctor said about your heart."

The ghost senses the sincerity of Harry's concern, but doubts the truth of the statement that he doesn't want anything from his former lover. Harry wants a great deal, that much is obvious. He wonders at the school comment; he wouldn't have taken Georgie for the type to be a teacher, or indeed capable of holding any position of responsibility over children. But now it has been spoken aloud, it sounds familiar. He strains to recollect; but aside from a vague memory of a musty classroom, he arrives at nothing.

"For heaven's sake, what are you wittering on about?" Georgie stands, teeters, then falls back into the chair, graceless as an upended tortoise. "This is intolerable. You're not my father, Harry. You're *nothing* to me. Stop all this . . . *controlling*. I'm not your puppet, and you don't own me."

"Christ, I never once suggested that I did—"

"You do! Every word you speak, every move you make, it indicates ownership. It's *disgusting*. I don't love you anymore, Harry. You were a bit of *fun*, that's all. An escape from the dreariness of living with my parents. How many times must I tell you this, before you get it through that thick skull of yours?"

Harry does not reply. The air is thick with the unsaid; recrimination, guilt, misery. It is agonising, being surrounded with such emotion, and the temptation is to simply depart, float through the door and leave the two men to it. The ghost is certain that it is getting worse, that he's becoming more sensitive to negativity; though he can't recall what it was like straight after he died. Perhaps it has always been this painful.

"Oh, dear," Agnes murmurs, and edges closer to the wall, before fading out of sight. He can see why, as Harry has started to weep, and it is embarrassing to witness. In his time, such a flagrant display would be unthinkable. Yet the emotion moves the ghost, despite his mortification. *I know what it's like to suffer from unrequited love,* he thinks, then wonders why. He doesn't remember Eleanor ever not loving him, and he's fairly sure he'd not been in love before her. Why had such a thought come to him?

"Shall we leave them?" Agnes suggests, drifting back into view. "There seems little point remaining."

"I suppose so." He studies Georgie, whose face is as pursed and blotched as a petulant child. For a man in his forties, there is something surprisingly immature about him; a quality that can be appealingly playful at times, and horrendously childlike at others. *He has innocence,* the ghost thinks, as they pass back through to the corridor, towards the bar. *But that innocence is spoiled with privilege and overindulgence. Goodness knows how his parents raised him.*

"How about we visit your old house?" Agnes suggests. "You might find it restorative, after witnessing all of that."

Is it near here? the ghost wonders, then reprimands himself. Of course it is near here. They are close to the Thames, not far from the Docks, and that is where his house was, the home he'd once shared with Eleanor. Sometimes, he feels he needs to repeat these facts to himself, to ensure they don't slide away from him.

"Why do you want to see my house?" he asks, curious.

She shrugs. "Perhaps it's good to remind yourself of happier times." And so, they pass through the door, back into the deafening chaos of the dancing, the pungent odour of spilt alcohol and sweat. "It is interesting to see something of your living life," she replies finally. "And besides, there's nothing more for us here. Georgie will be unconscious soon, as he always is. And Harry?"

"Harry will no doubt continue crying," the ghost finishes, then adds, "but at least Archibald isn't here tonight." *Archibald.* Even the name is vaguely repugnant, he thinks. Georgie's lover, a hulking ape of a man, who looks peculiarly squeezed into his suits, as though ready to erupt out of them at any second. Although he's younger and more handsome than Harry, he's less *human* somehow. More instinctive, brutal, and mindless. The ghost doesn't approve.

They move silently down the stairs and out to the street below. A man and a woman are conversing outside, heads nearly touching. The ghost cannot tell if they are fighting or whispering sweet words to one another. It is often the way with relationships in this era; there is none of the restraint or dignity that he remembers from his own time.

"It's a nice night," Agnes comments. A hint of a smile twitches the corners of her mouth, glittering in the dark.

He laughs. "You say that as though it affects us, which it doesn't."

"Why not? We can still appreciate a full moon, without feeling its glow on our skin. The warmth of the night might not touch us anymore, but we can still imagine the sensation."

The ghost says nothing. He believes she has a far more fanciful notion of their existence than he does. "Shall we carry on?" he suggests instead. The idea of seeing his old house has grown on him, there's something about being back there that triggers memories for him, makes them flow like liquid, rather than coming in halting fits and starts.

"I wonder if that family still live there?" Agnes says.

For a moment, he's confused, then remembers. *A family,* he reminds himself. *A man, his wife, a baby, young enough to still be at his mother's breast, but old enough to walk a little.* But when had they been living in his old house? He cannot recollect if it was a mere year ago or a decade, and he doesn't like to ask.

The street looks as it always has, lined with beech trees, stretching parallel to the sluggish river. He can remember pacing the road, briefcase in hand, on his way to work, and strolling along at a leisurely pace, with Eleanor's arm linked in his. He also recollects a rainstorm, soaking both him and his brother, on the way back from goodness knows where. The memories return, as clearly as photographs, and it reassures him, because it means his mind is still functional, and can still operate as it should.

There is a sign outside the house. *For sale. All enquiries, contact Fraser and Sons Estate Agents, Berner Street, Whitechapel.*

"I suppose that answers our question about the family." Agnes points to the black windows.

The ghost looks instinctively to the window at the top of the house, just above the porch. *Eleanor would have slept there,* he reminds himself. *That was our bedroom.*

Inside, the house looks different. Every time it is different, a little more distanced from the home he remembers. The floorboards are now covered in carpet. There's a stain by the living room door, only faint, but the spectre of a spilled glass of red wine, by the looks of it. The kitchen cupboards have been replaced; they're simpler, starker, less personable. He looks around and feels a sense of loss, for yet another part of himself has been erased. This may once have been his home, but it isn't any longer. Now, it's just an abode for others to inhabit.

"Modern fashions are strange, aren't they?" Agnes drifts to the centre of the living room, staring up at the light fitting. It is made of some sort of frilled glass, stained an unnatural colour, suspended by chains. In his opinion, it looks like some sort of aquatic creature, hung out to dry.

"I cannot picture myself here anymore."

"I'm not surprised."

But it is worse than that. He cannot picture *Eleanor* here either. Where has their old fireplace gone to, the one she used to sit beside, reading her books in the evening? Why have they replaced the glass in the windows? Is it a deliberate attempt to distance the property from its roots? And if so, why?

Agnes continues, glancing back at him as she glides up the stairs. "I can't imagine living in a house like this," she says, smiling as he follows her. "But then, I cannot imagine living in a house at all."

A caravan, he reminds himself. When he'd first found her, she'd lived in a caravan, one of those Romany creations, decorated with gaudy paint and peeling letters. Part of the circus troupe.

"A house can be very pleasant if you have a family to share it with," he says, then wishes he hadn't. She makes no reply, only moves towards the master bedroom. It has a new door, he notices, far plainer than the old one, and painted a cold, brutal white.

Her hand hovers close to the doorknob, and the word falls from his mouth almost of its own volition.

"Stop."

"Why?"

"Because I don't want to go in there."

She pauses. "You said this last time. What is the problem with this room?"

He shakes his head. He doesn't know exactly, the only thing he's sure of is the confusing flood of memories that hit him when they stand here, out in the lonely corridor. Blood. Plenty of blood. Eleanor, crying. And his brother. *Why my brother?* he wonders. *What business would my brother have in my matrimonial bedroom?* "We mustn't enter," he says urgently.

Agnes sighs. "It may be good for you to go in. Perhaps you *need* to face whatever memory you have of that room."

"No." The protest comes out sharper than he'd intended. "I don't. Let's leave, there's nothing here for me anymore." *They've finally spoilt it,* he realises, and is surprised to find the knowledge doesn't hurt him as much as expected. The house has moved on, but that is acceptable. That is what time does, after all, carrying everything along with it like detritus in a flowing river, and it is pointless to rail against it.

An owl whistles as they leave; a mournful wheeze that reminds them of the late hour. Aside from the ruffle of breeze through the trees, it is a still, silent night, devoid of human life, a world away from the commotion of Georgie's club.

"Have you finally given up searching for Eleanor?" Agnes asks. The moonlight shines through her, illuminating the ancient remnants of her skirt, her beaded shawl, the unruly mass of curls on her shoulders.

No, he thinks, with sudden ferocity. *I will never stop searching for her, even though I have no idea where to find her.*

Agnes waits, then links a wisp of an arm through his. "You know," she says, "you have to let Eleanor go. I keep reminding you of this, your desire to be with her is—"

"—Don't say *pointless,*" he interrupts. "You only say that because you don't understand. Eleanor's love . . . that alone would have kept her here, searching for me. Don't you see?"

The moon passes behind a cloud, and Agnes's face likewise dims. "It isn't like that, I can promise you. You've got it all wrong."

"What would you know about it?"

She gasps, exasperated. "Because of what we've seen, and because you *told* me things! Back when I was alive, and since then. Not all of it, admittedly, but enough to suggest that—"

"Stop!" He holds out a hand, and is not sure whether it's to silence her or to hold her at arm's length. Certainly, her words are creating a gulf between them, a chasm of unsaid words, of unresolved emotion. *She has no right,* he thinks, surprised at his own sudden fury. *They are my memories to pick through, not hers.*

He can tell she wants to say more. There's a torrent of accusation and confusion, bitten back behind her lips, and he cannot bear it. The only thing to do is move away, towards the river; the thing in this city that draws and repels him in equal measures.

The water is flowing slowly, the waters edging along surreptitiously, dragging the occasional branch on a ceaseless trajectory. *I swam in it once,* he thinks, then shakes his head, as that cannot be right. Some people used to swim in it, among the oil and the mud, but he was not one of them. The mere thought of being submerged in that dirty, oozing water makes him shudder. *Perhaps it was Eleanor?* He sees her hand, moist, dripping, then sighs. He *knows* where that memory comes from, and it is not from a cheerful paddle in the river. But what led to that moment, when her hand reached for his, when her eyes disappeared beneath the tossing line of the water?

It's true, he realises. *I am losing my memory. I can't delude myself any longer. Things are slipping away from me, as surely as those twigs, bobbing out to the sea.*

"I'm sorry."

He turns. Agnes is beside him, a hand hovering close to his shoulder, reluctant to commit to touching him.

"No, it's me who should be apologising," he replies. "I know you are only trying to help me."

"I shouldn't have pressed you. The past is painful, I know."

Isn't it for both of us? He remembers something of her experiences with Ernst, the distant twist of his eyes after drinking, the brutishness of his fists. She'd feared Ernst, and the ghost had told her to leave; that much is certain. But he hadn't meant for her to do what she'd done. *Leave him,* he'd said, without considering the consequences. Guilt rises, swelling in what once was his throat. *How I wish I could take that conversation back.*

"You're a good person," he says finally, and squeezes the ghostly remnant of her hand. "Even though I sometimes feel my mind is going, I will not forget that."

Together, they drift back to Harry's bar. Though the hour is late, they know the music will still be playing, the people still dancing; though with less coordination and even more abandon. Alcohol will have taken hold and become the ruling force, as it does every night. A fight may break out. A woman might weep, pushing a man from her with damp, sticky hands. It is the time when depravation is at its height, and they know that Georgie will be amongst it, drowning in the chaos.

It is worse than expected. A lamp has been smashed, flecks of coloured glass glitter the floor like drops of water. There are two people, slumped across the stage, though why, it is impossible to tell. They are breathing, they seem unharmed, but their expressions are pained, eyes pressed tight against the surrounding mob.

And there is Archibald, Georgie's beau; hulking by the bar, pouring himself a generous measure of whiskey. The barman has wisely edged away, leaving the bottle to the man's mercy.

Where is Georgie? the ghost wonders, then sees him, slumped awkwardly on a stool, back propped up against the mirrored wall. His misery is evident, radiating from him like turpentine fumes. *They have fought,* he thinks. Always, he and Archibald fight, before falling into one another's arms. It is the pattern of their relationship. Again, he finds himself wishing that Georgie had stayed in love with Harry, who, though older, has none of the visceral cruelty that Archibald possesses. *But that is the nature of love,* he thinks. *It is never balanced, never fair, and seldom ever sensible.*

"Pour me a drink," Georgie whines, a reed-thin sound above the noise.

Archibald ignores him and pours the remains of his whiskey down his throat. The slam of the glass echoes above the screech of the brass band.

"I said, pour me a drink. Why won't you pour me a drink?"

"I'm not pouring you another drink, you damned fool."

The ghost winces, glances at Agnes. It is painful to watch.

Georgie's lip curls, even as he almost slips off the bar stool. "I'm asking for just one more damned drink, Archie. It's not a lot to ask."

The ghost cannot stand the wheedling tone, nor the plaintive plead of his gaze. It is the expression of a man with no pride left, who cares nothing for appearances or the opinions of others. *He will end up on the streets if he isn't careful,* he thinks, and remembers those poor souls who skulked around Whitechapel, late at night. The drunkards, the criminals, the destitute; all muddled together in a featureless, broken heap.

Archibald lurches closer, bringing the whiskey bottle with him. "I'm not giving you another drink," he hisses, face pressed close to Georgie's own, "because you're *disgusting,* you hear me? You're revolting. Look at yourself."

There is a vague darkness, troubling the air around them. The ghost has seen it before, he recognises it as the accumulation of pain, rage, and misery. At present, it's centred over Georgie's head, a personal cloud of shame and sadness.

"Don't say that," he bleats. "You know I love you."

Don't be so weak, the ghost wants to shout, then wonders why it matters so much. After all, this man is nothing to him, only another person to attach himself to.

"Well, I don't love you. At the moment, I can't even bear to look at you."

Agnes sighs. She knows this cruelty, it transports her back to a place she'd rather not revisit.

"Why are you with me, then?" Georgie straightens. "Why is it you'll come home with me tonight, even when you hate me?"

Archibald pours himself another drink, raises the glass in mock salute, then consumes it. "I have no idea," he says finally. "I really don't. Probably because I worry about you, which does me no good at all." He turns, leans against the bar, surveys the room with an unsteady, furious eye. "I say," he announces suddenly, in a tone quite different to before. "Why is your father here, Georgie?"

Georgie's chin rises like the prow of a ship, and his hands instinctively rise to his chest, pulling his jacket defensively across his chest. "Where?"

"By the door, see? He doesn't look happy."

The ghost follows the line of their gaze, but cannot see who they're talking about. There are too many people, leaping and spinning and laughing before him; a brash swirl of dress-suits, sparkling skirts, and waxed hair.

"I don't believe it." Georgie rises, teeters, and grasps the bar. "Of all the nights to come here . . . Christ, Archie, why didn't you give me that drink when I needed it?"

"You'd best go and speak to him; he's obviously looking for you."

"I refuse to!" The febrile fist against the bar does little to emphasise the sudden, bright rage within him. "I *refuse* to let him run my life for me! I'm a grown man, for goodness' sake!"

Archibald smirks. "Go on. Run to daddy. I'll catch up with you later, no doubt."

And then he is gone, sliding through the crowd with serpentine ease, surprisingly graceful for a man of his stature. Georgie watches him leave, and the ghost watches Georgie, waiting to see what will happen next. This is new to him. The father has been referenced many times; portrayed as draconian, controlling, yet so far, he's been nothing more than a fiction; a much-derided character in Georgie's spiralling narrations. Unless he has encountered him before, and forgotten. It's hard to be sure, these days.

He can tell Agnes is as curious as he. She flits close to him, trying to see beyond the crowd.

"This is completely bloody unfair," Georgie mumbles, and waits like a condemned man, turning his back to the world. The crowds ease apart, making way for the man approaching the bar, and finally the ghost catches sight of the man Georgie dislikes so much, the one who fathered him.

The sight is like a blow to the head; shocking, all-encompassing, and it sends him reeling.

I know him, he thinks. *My God, I know him so well.*

"Are you all right?" Agnes is beside him as always, eyes turned to his. "What happened?"

"The father," he croaks. "I cannot believe it. I know this man."

"Who, this man here?" They watch Georgie's father, dapper in his well-cut suit, as he rests a disapproving elbow on the bar beside his son. "Of course you know him. Why? Had you forgotten who it was?"

Yes, the ghost thinks, with growing desperation. The music sounds tinny, ringing with tunnel-like fluidity, and suddenly, none of it seems real. *I could peel back this scene,* he thinks, sensing the room start to spin, *and there would be nothing behind it. Nothing. We're all of us completely meaningless.*

"You surely can't have forgotten this man," Agnes presses him, wrapping a spectral arm around his shoulders, trying to anchor him in the moment. "Or if you have, things have become worse than I thought."

The ghost studies the older man carefully; the trimmed grey beard, the hint of a paunch straining over his belt. *Those eyes,* he thinks. *I know those, I've seen them countless times before. Though the rest of him has changed, I'm sure of it.*

He strains to remember, knowing how important it is that he recollect this man, who he is sure was once a vital part of his life. But he has no recollection of who this person might be, only the impotent knowledge that he *should* know, and that his lack of knowledge shows how much he is fading.

"I cannot tell you who he is," he says finally, and drifts across the room, away from them all.

ELEVEN

— 1878 —

"YOU MUST GO and see him."

The tone of Mother's voice was final, absolute. She wasn't going to let this drop.

The mantelpiece clock chimed; a single melodious note, disturbing the silence. We'd only arrived at Mother's cottage an hour ago, but it felt like longer. *How the hours drag in times of disharmony,* I thought, wishing things were different. "Mother," I said gently, not wishing to agitate her further, "I fail to see what good our presence would do there, especially at present. Why don't we—"

"—Fred needs to see his family, for goodness' sake! We can't just leave him in a cell to rot!"

Arthur and I sighed simultaneously. From her cosy position in the armchair, Eleanor gave me a sympathetic look, then wandered to the kitchen, presumably to make some tea.

Fred's arrest was still something of a shock, even though we'd had over a day to dwell on it now. The news still defied belief. Fred was many things; belligerent, arrogant, as mulish as any man I'd known, but extreme violence was something new. Certainly, beating a fellow dock worker, then stealing his money, was a novelty. *Thank goodness Eleanor got away from him when she did,* I thought, then chastised myself for my lack of charity. Fred hadn't even been tried in court yet, and here I was, his brother, casting judgement upon him. Shame fired through me, though perhaps not as strongly as it should have done.

"I've heard it's a terrible place," Mother continued, eyes wide, fingers wrestling in her lap. "I can't comprehend it. A son of mine, in a prison like that . . . what would your father have thought?" And then the tears started again, more earnest and abundant than before. Arthur and I glanced at one another, both discomforted by the tension in the room.

"Clerkenwell probably isn't too bad," Arthur said eventually, straightening his tie. "I mean, it's only while he's awaiting trial, isn't it?"

"It's a *gaol!*"

"I know that, Mother. But if he's innocent, he'll be out soon, I can guarantee it."

She sniffed, dabbing her eyes with her handkerchief. "But you know what trials are like. It won't be fair, they'll—"

"Look, Mother, if you're worried, I can afford to get him a solicitor, it's only a guinea."

"Only?" I said with a dry chuckle, then straightened my expression at the sight of Mother's face. "But yes, quite. Arthur can afford to get Fred some assistance, so you needn't worry."

Mother gulped, clasping a hand against her chest. "It isn't just that. It's the shame of it. What will the neighbours think? It's already mortifying enough that Mrs Heddingley knows about Fred working at the Docks. When this gets out, they'll—"

"—They'll probably prattle about it for a few days like all good villagers, then forget about it," Arthur finished. "Come on, Mother, you know what they're like. The people of Battersea, they're decent enough at heart. They're not going to mock you."

"Only talk behind my back," she said gloomily.

Curse Fred, I thought, leaning back against the plump cushions. *Even if he didn't do it, what was he up to, lurking around the Docks late at night? I always suspected he was in with the wrong crowd.*

Martha's head popped around the doorframe, curls more tousled and unkempt than usual. "Eleanor's made some tea," she announced, looking solemn. "Do you want to take it in the garden? It's ever such a nice day."

She was right. Spring had finally arrived, bringing with it one of those delightfully balmy, mellow Sunday afternoons, which seemed almost divinely designed to luxuriate in. *Except not for us,* I thought ruefully, standing up and straightening my trousers. *No, we've got to worry about Fred, yet again. Always the same old story, though this time, he's gone even further than usual.*

"Oh, I don't think so," Mother said, rising to her feet. "How can I enjoy my tea, knowing that my eldest boy is locked up in a dreary cell somewhere, wondering if he'll ever see the light of day again?"

Arthur rolled his eyes. "Mother, even if he does get sentenced, he won't be in prison for that long. Please, let's try to keep things in perspective."

"It's not as bad as it seems," I added helpfully.

"It's probably quite exciting," Martha added, then hastily ducked back behind the doorframe at the sight of Mother's expression.

"Exciting? What a preposterous thing to say!" She snorted, then rose from the armchair, tugging her skirts back into place. "I'd feel a lot better about it if you two would agree to go and visit him."

Arthur gave me a look, then nodded. "Very well," he said, easing his arm over Mother's shoulder and guiding her out to the kitchen. "If it would put your mind at rest, we'll do it."

"Today?"

"I doubt they'll let us see him at such short notice," I said quickly, catching Eleanor's eye. She winced, then started setting the tea tray.

"They will if you pay them, won't they?" Mother said, with a deliberate nod in Arthur's direction.

Poor old Arthur, I thought. *Already, he's become the family's personal bank. I wonder how long it will be until the role irks him?* Knowing his generous nature, it probably never would. I personally had never been comfortable asking him for financial assistance, though Mother seemed to have no such problem.

Martha skipped around the table, her stockinged feet sliding on the tiles. "Can I go too?"

"Absolutely not!" Mother squawked. "Whoever heard of such a thing?"

"Why can't I go? I won't make a fuss or anything."

"It's indecorous for a young lady to enter a gaol."

"Oh, *everything's* indecorous when you're a girl. It's so dull, why do men have all the fun?"

"That's a very good question," Eleanor muttered quietly, eyes twinkling. She handed me the tray, which was stacked to the brim with cups, saucers, a teapot, and a pile of buns.

Arthur nudged his sister. "If it was up to me, you could come like a shot," he said, as they headed out into the garden. "But it isn't, I'm afraid. I'll tell you everything about it, though, how about that?"

"No, you will not!" Mother trailed after them, her voice trailing out into the sunshine. "There's absolutely nothing she needs to know about gaols, thank you very much!"

I grimaced, waited for my wife to step out, then followed, tray in hand. I didn't anticipate being able to spend much time enjoying tea in the sunshine. Past experience had taught me that if Mother wanted us to do something, she'd keep on at it like a terrier with a rabbit, until we caved in. Sure enough, less than half an hour later, Arthur and I eventually conceded defeat, headed out to the main street, and hailed a hansom cab to take us to Clerkenwell House of Detention.

"So much for a relaxing weekend," I grumbled, as the driver whipped the horses to a canter. The carriage jolted into action, before settling into a comfortable, rattling rhythm. "I was quite enjoying resting in the garden, listening to the bees and the sparrows."

"I know," Arthur replied, patting his brow with his handkerchief, before folding it delicately back into his pocket. He surveyed me carefully, before adding, "So, do you think he did it?"

I leant back, considering. "Who knows? I don't feel as if I know Fred at all these days. He's sunk low, Arthur, he really has."

I thought back to that last disastrous time I'd seen him, when he'd brought the odious Elizabeth Stride into our family home. She'd certainly seemed like the type to drag a man down into the gutter. I supposed we should be thankful for small mercies that their relationship had ended when it did.

"I wouldn't mind so much," Arthur said, with a twinkle in his eye, "if Clerkenwell wasn't such a deucedly unpleasant place to visit."

"Worse than Whitechapel," I added.

"I wouldn't go that far. But still. It's a den of ill repute. We shall have to be on our guard for cutpurses."

The hansom cab finally pulled outside the gates of the prison, the horse hoofs clattering to a halt over the cobblestones. It was a suitably grave, ominous gate; oak-heavy and flanked by cold grey stone.

"'Ere you are," the driver croaked through the hatch door. "You just visiting, then?"

Arthur paid him, then rapped on the glass. "Yes. That will be all, thank you."

With a grumble, the driver released the catch on the door, letting us climb out. It was even warmer here than in Mother's garden; the air was more stagnant, and far less fragrant. A group of filthy children gazed on with eyes that were too big for their heads, and a beggar rested against the wall, fingers clasped around a bottle. *Arthur wasn't wrong about this place,* I thought. *Let's hope this doesn't take too long.*

"Shall we?" To my surprise, even Arthur looked rather hesitant, his usual confidence sliding beneath an expression of concern.

We raised our fists and knocked smartly on the gate door. Then, we waited. The children edged closer, eyes widening at our clothes, our shined shoes, the cleanliness of our skin. I felt like a foreigner, gawped at by strangers, even though my own home was just a few miles across the river.

Finally, with an ear-splitting creak, the gate swung open. A stiff, austere man peered out, uniform buttoned to his neck, a boxlike hat atop his head.

"Yes, gentlemen?" He scratched his muttonchops, a raspy, insect-like noise, then folded his arms, looking down at us from the length of his not inconsiderable nose.

Arthur stepped forward. "We're here to visit a prisoner. It's urgent."

The guard shook his head. "No visitors permitted."

"We have money."

"Hmm." The guard paused, then studied us carefully. "How much do you have?"

We glanced at one another and shrugged.

"How much does it take?" Arthur asked.

"Ten shillings."

I snorted. "Surely not."

"That's what it is, gentlemen. Take it or leave it."

Arthur pressed against the gate before the man could close it. "How about five shillings?"

"Eight."

"Seven?"

The guard sighed, an elaborate noise that suggested he'd engaged in this ritual many times before. "Very well. Come in and tell me which prisoner you'd like to visit. You haven't got long though. That's the rules, I'm afraid."

We entered the courtyard and tried not to flinch as the gates slammed shut behind us. The main building was an elegant yet forbidding affair; brick-built and flanked by pillars, but the surrounding buildings were far starker. These, I presumed, must be where the prisoners were held captive.

"Come on, come through. We haven't got all day." The prison guard ushered us through to a grimy-looking room with a large, unwieldy desk, plus several other guards, all wearing matching expressions of weariness and ill-concealed contempt. I felt my skin crawling beneath my shirt.

"Right, Frederick, you said his first name was?" The prison guard rifled through some papers on the desk, then prodded a finger against one of them. "Ah, yes, here he is. Cell eighteen. I'll take you there now."

We followed him down the narrow corridors, which stank of damp, crumbling brick and human misery. It was a hovel of a place, poorly kept and badly designed; even worse than I'd imagined it. After a time, we began to pass cell doors, grim metal affairs with grilled windows. I spied the occasional face, peering out at us with interest, but kept my head down. I had no wish to interact with these people. *Come to mention it, I hardly have any desire to interact with Fred,* I thought bitterly.

Cell eighteen was on the left, at what must have been the end of one of the wings. It felt darker here, perhaps a little colder. Certainly, this wasn't a place that sunlight ever reached. In fact, it was as far removed from the beautiful spring day outside as could be imagined.

Pity rose in my chest, tremulous as a bird. *No creature deserves to be trapped somewhere like this,* I thought. *Especially not my eldest brother.* Fred was a hard man to understand, and even harder to like at times, but he wasn't a bad person, I was certain. How had it come to this? A memory came to mind of the three of us, running across the fields after church, Martha wailing in the distance, her plump little legs unable to keep up with us. We'd been laughing, breathlessly panting, intent on reaching the woods before Mother could call us back.

How things have changed, I thought, as the guard pulled open the cell door.

Fred sat within, hunched and diminished on the spartan single bed, as though the walls themselves had drained him. He raised his head as we entered, then broke into a coughing fit, which may have started as a laugh.

"What are you two doing here?" he growled, thumping at his chest.

"That's a fine greeting," Arthur replied, entering the cell reluctantly. "A *good afternoon* or *hello* would have done the job, you know."

The guard clicked his fingers in our direction. "You've got five minutes, you hear?" Without waiting for a reply, he slammed the door behind us.

Let's hope he remembers to let us out again, I thought, laughter rising nervously in my throat. I looked around. There was nowhere to sit, only the bed, and it didn't feel appropriate to perch next to Fred, especially in his present state.

A blackbird warbled from outside, a distant trill that sounded vaguely forlorn, or perhaps it was the dank ambiance of the cell that made it seem so. We waited patiently for Fred to speak.

"Well, here you have it," he said eventually, gesturing around the room. "My palace. It's a step up from my room down at the dock, to be honest."

Arthur leant against the wall, exhaling heavily. He appeared surprisingly comfortable with his surroundings, given how incongruous he looked. "Mother's out of her mind with worry, you know," he said.

"I'm sure she is. She always frets about everything."

"She's got fairly good cause to fret this time. I mean," Arthur said, looking up at the meagre window, with its thick iron bars, "this is *terrible*, Fred. It really is."

"I didn't do it, you know," Fred grumbled, shifting awkwardly. The sheets crackled under him, sounding more like paper than fabric.

"Why were you even there?" I asked. "Surely you can see that it looks suspicious, walking alone at that hour?"

Fred bristled. "Oh, you think I'm guilty, do you? Well, thank you very much, Brother. Thank you for your faith in me. Not that I'm surprised. You and Father always saw the worst in me, even when I hadn't done anything wrong."

Arthur raised his hands placatingly. "That's not what he said, Fred. Come on, we've only got a few minutes, we need to work out how we can get you out of here. Let's not waste the time bickering."

Fred shot me a dark look, then leant back against the wall. "I was out looking for someone. That's all. I saw the man on the floor, all bloodied up, but it wasn't me who hit him. I didn't steal his money either."

"Who were you looking for?" Arthur asked.

"No one you'd care about."

"Not Elizabeth Stride?" I guessed.

"It's none of your business."

I sighed. This was getting us nowhere, and I wished, more fervently than ever, that we hadn't come. I could tell from Arthur's expression that he was thinking the same.

"Perhaps you should forget about Elizabeth," I suggested gently. "That sort of woman will only drag you down, and—"

"—You don't know her, so don't start with all that. She's just got herself mixed with some bad folk, that's all. She's had a damned hard life."

"I wasn't saying she hadn't, I merely said—"

"—This isn't getting us anywhere," Arthur interrupted, tapping at his wristwatch and giving us both a pointed look. "Fred, did you see the person who did hit him? The man who'd been attacked, I mean."

Fred shook his head. "No, they were long gone. I heard the man groaning, he was by the side of the river, his head bleeding. I was trying to help him, but look where it's got me!" His cynical laugh sounded flat and muffled against the dense brick walls.

"Look," Arthur said slowly, smoothing his hair down. "I can afford to hire you a solicitor, one that will—"

"—Oh, I'm not accepting your charity, little brother. I need to keep some scrap of dignity."

"Don't be ridiculous, Fred, you'll stand a far better chance of being released with a legal expert fighting on your behalf. You can't defend yourself in the court, you won't stand a chance."

"No." Fred crossed his arms and glared at us both.

"If you won't do it for us," I snapped, "do it for Mother. Think about how this affects her. Everyone in Battersea is gossiping about it."

Something in Fred's expression softened for a moment, like the sun filtering through a bleak cloud. Then he met my eye and hardened once again.

"I can't be held responsible for the idle prattle of villagers."

"I suppose that's true," Arthur said with a sniff. "God, the air in here is diabolical, isn't it? No wonder you've got a rotten cough."

"Yes, that's why people die in places like this."

"Now, there's a cheerful thought."

Fred's eyes narrowed, then he chuckled. "Look at you two," he said slowly, leaning back. "You look about as out of place as can be. Especially you, Arthur, with your fancy clothes."

"Yes, what a funny trio we make," Arthur commented with a grin. "A dandy, an office clerk, and a felon awaiting trial."

Fred laughed, just as the door swung open with a protesting squeal.

The guard peered in, eyes shadowed by the peak of his hat. "Time's up, gents."

"That wasn't five minutes!" Arthur stuttered.

"It was by my watch."

Seven shillings for that, I thought, then followed Arthur out into the corridor. *What a waste of money, not to mention time.* We'd achieved nothing from our visit, apart from verifying that Fred was alive and mostly well.

"Don't you worry," Arthur muttered, as the prison guard locked the cell door carefully behind us. "I'll get him that solicitor, whether he likes it or not. We won't see this family shamed any further."

I nodded, all the time wondering when it was that Arthur had become as preoccupied as I about preserving appearances. We'd always laughed about Mother's pretentions when we'd been younger. How had it happened that we'd gradually inherited those same pretentions ourselves? *I always thought Father would be ashamed if he knew how low Fred had fallen,* I thought, walking back along the corridor and out into the relief of the sunshine. *But perhaps he'd be just as appalled by Arthur's and my rise into snobbishness.*

We exited the same way we had entered, through the weighty, unforgiving prison gates. As they clanked shut behind us, I took a deep breath, relishing the open air, pungent and sewage-laced as it was. *We must get my brother out of there,* I thought, with sudden ferocity. *Whatever he is, and whatever he's done, he doesn't deserve to stay in a place like that.*

"Let's hail a hansom cab," Arthur suggested, tugging at his collar. "I don't know about you, but I'm rather keen to get back to Mother's.

Look, there's one over there; quickly, come on, before someone else gets it."

Out of the corner of my eye, I noticed a bonneted figure, watching us with brazen curiosity. Before I had a chance to observe her properly, she turned, heels clicking along the uneven road as she departed. Her dress was muddied at the hem, ill-fitting around the shoulders, and there was something about her posture that was familiar.

Long Liz? I wondered, but couldn't be certain. The figure disappeared around the corner. *Surely it can't have been her,* I reasoned, tempted nonetheless to go after her, just to make sure. *Why would she be hanging around outside, when she and Fred are no longer engaged?*

"Come on," Arthur said, nudging me out of my stupor. "I have no desire to stay here longer than necessary."

"Yes, yes," I replied distractedly. "Arthur, did you see that woman? The one who was here just a few moments ago?"

"No, why?"

I opened my mouth, then closed it again. There had been something unsettling about the incident, though I couldn't perceive exactly what had bothered me so. Perhaps it had been the bright, unflinching nature of her gaze, before she'd scurried away.

"It doesn't matter," I said finally. "Let's return to Mother's."

TWELVE

— 1912 —

A SMASHED WINDOW.

It's something the ghost has seen before, many times. But on this occasion, with a group of baying women surrounding the scattered glass, it's somehow more shocking, more *absolute*. The glass captures the sunlight in an almost celebratory manner; like dangerous confetti.

Agnes chuckles. She finds his horror amusing, he can tell. He chooses to ignore her, and, instead, follows the crowd of females down the street, sensing their energy, their jubilance and defiance, combined with more than a little anxiety. Soon enough, they start to pick up their pace, no doubt searching for the next shop window to smash, and he hastens his own pace to keep up with them; horrified and fascinated in equal measures.

Suffragettes, he thinks. That is all they have heard about for the last month or so, staying with Daisy and her husband, who bears it all with weary tolerance. Daisy is here now, they can see her red hat, bobbing among the crowds. How such a thing could be tolerated, he doesn't know. He remembers women used to be happy for men to make all the important decisions, but it seems that, once again, the world has moved forward and left him behind.

"You really don't like this, do you?" Agnes says. Her eyes glitter with amusement.

"You know perfectly well that I don't. It's highly improper."

"Oh, you stick in the mud. Don't you think it's rather wonderful?"

He frowns. "What, smashing windows? Vandalising property? No, I think it's rather awful, to be honest."

"I don't mean that." She pauses, casting her eyes back to the women, her eyes glittering momentarily in the sun. "I mean, fighting for equality. Wouldn't you say it's about time?"

He doesn't answer. Another crash spills through the air, followed by more cheering. Glass peppers the street like raindrops. The ghost shakes his head. It is quite beyond his understanding why anyone would want to act so rashly, so violently. It is especially unnatural to see the gentler sex behaving in such a manner.

"That'll show Mr Selfridge!" one lady bellows, hands waving in the air. "That'll show all of 'em!"

Again, the women roar, leonine huntresses every one of them, baying for blood. Daisy cries out with the rest of them, and the ghost does not know whether to be awed or repulsed. These women are warriors, such as those he remembers reading about, long ago; those Amazonian females with spears in hand, war-cries crashing from their lips. He never imagined he'd see such a thing on the streets of London.

"I only wish I'd been that strong," Agnes said wistfully, gliding down the street after them. "Things might have been different, then."

No, they wouldn't have, he thinks, remembering the viciousness of Ernst's attacks. Even after several vodkas, he always managed to connect fist to face, never missing his mark. Had Agnes stood up to him, all she would have received was more beatings, perhaps worse. Ernst hadn't been a man to rise up against, only to bow down before, like wheat beneath a scythe.

"What if her children see her?" He does not mean her own children, for Daisy doesn't have any, or at least, not yet. Rather, he means the children she teaches at the local public school. There, the girls are educated in needlework, cooking, alongside rudimentary skills in writing and reading; which he believes far more suitable. They have separate gates, separate classrooms. It makes better sense, he thinks; and there is certainly none of this nonsense about *equality*.

He can tell Agnes is smirking, even though the brightness of the day dapples her, makes her more transparent than usual. "Isn't it right that women start to challenge inequality?" she comments, pausing as another woman clambers on top of a wall, shouting yet another rousing speech to the masses. "If Daisy's students witness this, perhaps it will be a good thing."

"Or perhaps she'll lose her position at the school," he mutters.

"That would be a shame, she's an excellent teacher."

He concedes the point. Daisy has a way with children, a knack of focusing them, drawing their faces towards her like flowers to the sun. He and Agnes have often sat at the back of the classroom, listening to the screech of chalk, the clatter of wooden chairs, and Daisy Taylor's voice, unfailingly cheery, rising above the childish chatter. Sometimes, the sound saddens him; reminding him of the children he never had. He wonders if he would have been a good father, whether his sons and daughters would have loved him. The devastation is in knowing that he will never get to find out.

Finally, the crowds disperse. Oxford Street is tattered, tugged apart; its usual milling shoppers still gawping in horror at all the glass, at the discarded rosettes and placards. The suffragettes have marked their territory, and the ghost senses things will never be the same again.

They follow Daisy back to her home, only a few doors from the ghost's own house, which is now owned by a couple and their toddling, squalling child. He visits occasionally, simply to take in the ambiance of his former life; though it seems to dwindle daily, the essence of his life with Eleanor seeping out of the walls, like a gradual, final exhalation.

Daisy's home is vital, perky, the mirror-image of its owner. Bright geraniums flank the porch, and the door knocker, an iron woodpecker, gleams in the sun. It is a house that the ghost approves of; well-kept, tidy, nothing within that is superfluous to requirements.

Daisy's husband, Michael, places his newspaper down at the sight of his wife, then rises from the sofa. The ghost adopts his favoured position by the fireplace and waits patiently. He enjoys listening to them; their easy way of talking reminds him of times spent with Eleanor, and the similarity of their home to his own makes their conversation even more poignant.

"So, how did you get on, love?" Michael asks, smile already in place.

She sighs, unties her bonnet, then positions it neatly on the hat stand. "There was a good turnout, plenty of people there to make some impact. I was a little worried about the vandalism, though."

Good, thinks the ghost, though at the time, Daisy hadn't seemed concerned at all, cheering and waving her hands like the rest of them.

"Gosh, what sort of vandalism?"

Daisy shrugs, looking abashed. "I expect you'll read about it in tomorrow's papers. Some of the ladies were throwing rocks through the windows of the stores."

"Good heavens, you didn't say there would be anything like that! You could have been arrested!"

Agnes rolls her eyes, then settles beside the ghost, listening intently.

"Yes, but I wasn't," Daisy concludes, wandering to the kitchen. "And at least it's a powerful message, don't you think? It's what we need to make people sit up and listen."

Michael sighs, and the ghost pities him. He can sense the man's concern, his panic that his wife has got herself into something larger, darker, and more troublesome than she initially thought. *He loves her so much*, he realises, feeling the familiar warmth spread over him. *So much, that he'll support her in this, even though he has his doubts.*

"What if someone from school had seen you?"

"That's what I said," the ghost murmurs. Agnes smiles, following Michael through to the kitchen.

"Yes, but nobody did." Daisy places her hands around Michael's waist, and pulls him towards her. It's a little like watching a tugboat bringing a larger ship to harbour, but Michael doesn't protest, instead, allows himself to be eased along, until he's entwined in her arms. "So, it was perfectly fine, you see?"

He nuzzles into her neck, breathing in the scent of her. The ghost eases, recollecting similar moments in his past; a stolen kiss on a bared shoulder, fingers laced around a narrow waist. It all seems frighteningly distant now, the memories slipping into one another like eels, forming tangled, impenetrable knots. He guessed that his living days would start to slide away from him, but hadn't realised it would happen so swiftly.

"Do you think we should retreat somewhere else?" Agnes suggests, nodding to the couple.

"Yes." The ghost steals one more lingering look at the two of them, then nods. Propriety insists that they give Daisy and Michael the privacy they deserve. *Young love,* he thinks wistfully. *It consumes all, like floodwater.*

The thought makes him shiver. He freezes, taking a moment to calm himself.

"Are you all right?" Agnes pauses, noting his discomfort.

"Yes, I'm fine." And he finds that he is; the moment gone, almost as soon as it had arrived. *Water,* he thinks, as they pass out of the house. *Why is it always water?* Outside, the dreary length of the Thames rests before them, its surface sparkling in the sun; an open taunt to his dwindling memory.

The next day, they follow Daisy to her school, buried in the heart of Whitechapel. The area has changed, the ghost finds. The streets are cleaner, the alleyways less dark. He spies his old offices, the windows just the same as they had been in his time, though the nature of the business has changed. They belong to a publishing company now, judging by the smart sign next to the door.

It was partially this proximity to his workplace that drew them to Daisy in the first place. He and Agnes had spotted her, walking home from work, and been drawn to her energy, her restlessness, and the urgency of her desire for change. And the sadness within her, that magnet of pain that always seems to pull him. *The loss of a child.* Daisy does not talk of it, but he can sense it within her, caged deep inside, and he sympathises, remembering similar pain from his own past.

They've accompanied her to school many times, though the location still troubles him. He remembers that there used to be a yard here, Dutfield's Yard, where wheelmakers worked; and that something terrible occurred, something he had seen, though he doesn't recollect the details.

Sometimes, it feels more like a half-remembered dream. A woman, face down on the cobblestones, blood puddling around her head like treacle. It had been dark, he can remember that much. And a man had sidled away from the scene, skipping from shadow to shadow like a spectre. He believes that he witnessed this in the early days of his ghost existence, shortly after his own passing, though he cannot say for certain. Things had been confusing back then, which is why he suspects that he cannot remember properly. *Perhaps it will come back to me one day,* he thinks, as they approach the school, the innocuous, turreted building, with seemingly no knowledge of what once happened on its grounds.

The school gates are shut; it's still early. Daisy slips silently through the side entrance, nodding at the caretaker, who lets her into the building. The hallway is lofty, cool, the dust-covered windows filtering soft sunlight to the floor. She doesn't notice, only paces to her classroom, shoes clipping against the tiled floor, as she does every day of the week. They drift after her, sensing already that this day will be different. The air is thick with anticipation.

The cough that interrupts her from her thoughts echoes flatly from the walls. Daisy turns. The ghost and Agnes turn too, already knowing that fate is wheeling into motion.

"Ah, Mrs Taylor, might I have a word, please?"

Daisy's anxiety is palpable, even before she detects where the voice is coming from.

"It's the headmaster," Agnes comments, pointing to the open door.

The man's balding head gleams dully in the light. Personally, the ghost cannot understand how he rose to such a lofty position; his slope-shouldered, flabby physique seems incapable of representing authority. He casts a feeble shadow on the floor.

"Yes, Headmaster, can I help?" Daisy's voice sounds reedy, mouse-like in the long, cavernous hall.

"In my office, if you please." He nods inside. "This won't take long."

Agnes glances at the ghost, and he can tell they are thinking the same thing. *Yesterday's suffragette march. He knows.*

The office is suitably academic in nature; walls lined with leather-bound books, the desk outfitted with a variety of important documents and pens. Behind it all, the headmaster seems swamped, a short, squinting figure dwarfed by the furniture of those who owned them before him. He waits, fingers laced, while Daisy perches on the only other available chair.

"Mrs Taylor, there's something I'd like to discuss with you privately. Something quite urgent."

She squirms. The ghost can tell her thoughts are running along the same lines as theirs; that same panicked voice chanting *he knows, he knows, he knows.*

"Yes, of course. What is it?"

The headmaster pauses, then rubs the side of his nose. "It's a rather sensitive issue."

The ghost can see Daisy steeling herself. It is etched in the tautening of her muscles, the straightening in her spine. *She is waiting for the inevitable dismissal,* the ghost thinks, and despite his reservations about her actions yesterday, he pities her anguish. *She is good at her job,* he wishes he could shout. *Don't let this one incident stop her from teaching.*

"You see," the headmaster continues, oblivious to the woman's growing panic, right before his eyes, "it's about a benefactor of ours. Or rather, I should say, his son."

"Oh?" Daisy's relief is palpable, filling the room like warm air.

"Yes. A very generous local benefactor, you may be aware of him, Mr Arthur Dinnock?"

"I've heard of Arthur Dinnock, sir."

And so have I, the ghost thinks, reeling backwards. Agnes grasps him, motioning for him to listen.

"Yes, I rather thought you might have." The headmaster clears his throat, then rifles through some papers on his desk, more to keep his hands busy than for any practical purpose.

"He's referring to my brother," the ghost hisses, incredulous. "Arthur, that's my brother, do you see?"

"Yes, I know the name of your brother," Agnes answers patiently. "Listen, in case we miss anything."

Arthur, the ghost thinks, gazing in wonder around the room. *It must be. How many other Arthur Dinnocks live around here?* He wonders how old his brother must be; late forties, perhaps over fifty? It seems incomprehensible that his younger, easy-going brother should be so aged. *I remember Mother being forty,* he thinks. *Arthur cannot be older than that, it simply isn't permissible.*

"Anyway," the headmaster continues, placing the papers neatly down again. "Mr Dinnock has requested that we find some form of employment for his only son. Confidentially speaking, Mr Dinnock's son is something of a gadabout, rather an embarrassment to the family from what I can tell."

"What has this got to do with the school?"

"Our benefactor believes that his son might benefit from undertaking some teaching. Give him a role in life, you know the sort of thing."

Daisy eases back in her seat. The ghost can already see her mind at work, grasping the possible outcomes with lightning quickness. He respects her intelligence. "I see," she says slowly. "So what do you need me to assist with?"

"I'm glad you asked." The headmaster leans forward, keen to come to the heart of the matter. "I would like you to work with him initially, let him observe your lessons, so he might pick up the ropes, as it were. Your class are the youngest, which will be easiest for him to start with."

"Wouldn't it be better for him to observe Mr Faircott, with the first-year boys?"

"For some reason, his father has specifically requested that George learn the trade with a woman, not a man. I have no idea why, perhaps he feels your gentler approach might be better suited to him."

My nephew, coming into school to train to be a teacher? The ghost stares at the desk, overcome with a succession of questions, all competing for precedence in his head. *Arthur's child is a gadabout? I'm going to be able to see my nephew?*

"You know it might not be the same Arthur, don't you?" Agnes says, floating back towards the wall. "It might be an entirely different person, just with the same name."

"I doubt it." The ghost doesn't believe in intuition, but nonetheless, there is a firm knowledge within him that his brother *is* the person in question. *Perhaps it is fate,* he wonders, then shakes his head. He's always avoided such superstitious notions, left them instead to Eleanor, who was rather involved in such things.

"Will that be all?" Daisy stands, smoothing down her skirt.

"Yes, thank you, Mrs Taylor. You can expect George Dinnock today, at the start of class."

"Today?"

"Yes, his father wishes for him to make a prompt start. He believes it will be character-building."

The ghost's emotions leap, somewhere where he once had a heart. *George,* he thinks, with something close to ecstasy. He remembers the name, knows that he's already seen the boy before, when he was younger. *What was he like?* Loosely formed memories spring to mind; a short, dark-haired boy, trimmed collar peeping over a buttoned jacket. A baby, gurgling in a cot.

"Do you remember George?" Agnes asks, curious, as they follow Daisy out of the office.

"I believe so." He catches sight of her eye, then hastily amends his words. "Yes, I think I do."

"So, you'll recognise him, perhaps?"

The ghost ponders. He doubts that his memory is good enough to match the child George with his adult counterpart, but suspects some feeling within him will guide him. *I'll know if he's a relation of mine*, he thinks, excitement rising within him. *I'll be able to feel it.* "I think I will know him," he answers, smiling.

Daisy looks less happy at the prospect, but her relief is still evident as she heads towards her classroom, grateful that her position is safe for now. The ghost waits at the back of the class, watching as she arranges chairs, checks her books, makes sure she has enough chalk for the board; and all the time, he wonders what his nephew will be like now, if indeed it is him. The word *gadabout* lingers, like a hint of bad odour. Why would any member of his family be a gadabout? Arthur had a good work ethic, so good that he managed to make himself a wealthy man. How could his son possibly be the opposite?

Outside, the dim rumble of children's chatter starts to grow, swelling into a crescendo of noise. The bell is rung. Daisy sighs, smooths down her bun, then opens the classroom door, ready to greet her pupils.

The ghost always enjoys this moment, the tidal wave of youth crashing into the room, tossed and turned by their own exuberance. He's even begun to remember some of their names; Jane, with the two tightly pulled plaits, Nancy, with cheeks as red as strawberries, Ada, who looks rather feline, with her long face and aloof expression. They surge to their seats, a sea of heads, all focused on their teacher.

"It's a shame they don't get to learn what the boys are learning," Agnes comments mildly.

"Don't start with that again," the ghost replies, with a hint of a smile. "You're as bad as Daisy."

"Good morning, class," Daisy begins, eyes alight with pleasure.

"Good morning, Mrs. Taylor . . ." They falter, confused, as a man steps into the door. His panting is so loud, it reaches over the girls' whispering.

"Gosh, I'm late, aren't I? It was that damned cab, I told the driver to head to Berner Street, and . . ."

Daisy steps forward smoothly, hand extended; more to quieten him than greet him, perhaps. "You must be George Dinnock? Do come in, I was—"

"I know, I know, I'm frightfully sorry at being late, I . . ." the man falters, as though only just noticing the numerous eyes, fixed upon him with open interest. He straightens his boater, then grins. "Hello there, everyone."

Daisy stifles a smile. "Class, say good morning to Mr Dinnock."

Agnes nudges the ghost, studying his expression for a reaction. "Well, is it him?"

"I . . . I think so." He isn't completely sure. There is something in the man's face that reminds him of Arthur; the childlike amusement, the easy smile, but everything else about him is off-key. *He is foppish,* the ghost thinks, taking in the spats, the bold pinstripe of the suit, the elongated cut of the collar. *Somewhat irresponsible-looking. Not what I was expecting.*

In truth, he is a little disappointed.

"Give him a chance," Agnes advises, as George sidles to the back of the room.

As the lesson progresses, the ghost can tell that George is taking no interest. Rather, he seems preoccupied with his left shoe, fiddling with the laces until the ghost wishes he had hands to bat the foot off the man's knee.

If Daisy is aware of his discourteousness, she shows no sign; only devotes her full attention to her girls, helping them to practice their handwriting.

Why not offer to help? the ghost thinks, frustration rising within him. *Rather than sitting there, plucking at your ridiculous footwear and looking as though you'd rather be anywhere else but here?*

The humming is simply too much to bear. Even Daisy registers his disinterest at this point, and surveys him, one eyebrow raised.

The bell rings for morning break. The girls walk out demurely, before racing into a run across the playground. Daisy closes the door behind them, sighs, then waits.

Finally, she coughs. The sound resonates in the now empty space, highlighting the shift from childish endeavour to adult solitude. "Excuse me?"

George twitches.

Has he fallen asleep? the ghost wonders, glancing at Agnes incredulously. She looks as though she doesn't know whether to laugh or wince.

"Er, excuse me? Mr Dinnock?"

"Yes?" He raises his head, and it is impossible to tell whether he'd been fully conscious or not. "Is that it, then?"

"The children are currently in the playground," Daisy explains patiently, fighting to keep her expression neutral. "Then we'll start our next lesson, which is needlework. Would you like to be more involved this time? Perhaps you could look at some of their work, or offer some words of encouragement?"

George snorts. "I'd rather not, thank you. Needlework isn't my strength at all. No, I'll just sit here, don't you worry about me. Pretend I'm not here."

Daisy inhales deeply, then starts to pace along the classroom floor. Her agitation is evident. "Mr Dinnock," she begins, focusing on the floor, "I was given to understand that you wanted to learn how to teach children, so—"

"—Ah, I think you've got the wrong end of the stick there. My *father* wants me to learn how to teach. I personally have no interest whatsoever."

The ghost splutters. He is lost for words. *What an ungracious, impolite man,* he thinks, horrified that this creature is a relation of his. *Whatever would Arthur say, if he knew his son was speaking to a lady like this? Certainly, if Mother were alive to hear it, she would have given him a piece of her mind and no mistake.*

Daisy looks likewise ruffled, her usual composure shaken. "Then, if you don't mind my asking, what exactly do you hope to achieve by being here? The headmaster informed me that—"

"—Look." George rises, taking great pains to smooth his jacket down. "Father is desperate to find me some form of meaningful activity. As long as he believes I'm doing something useful, everything will be fine. All you have to do is forget I'm here. Honestly."

The ghost can sense Daisy's confusion. She is at a loss as to how to proceed. He fully sympathises with her, for what can one do with a man like this, who seems not to care about societal expectations or polite behaviour?

Finally, she rests on a desk, and meets George's eye. "I have been ordered," she begins, in a louder voice than before, "to train you how to teach, Mr Dinnock. And that is what I intend to do. I appreciate you may not want to be here, but now that you are, I think it's appropriate if you make yourself useful. So, would you help me lay out the girls' samplers? Their lesson starts in five minutes."

George chuckles. "Gosh, this is a rum deal. If only my friends could see me now, Harry would be in fits."

"Why is that?" Daisy asks, challenge alight in her eyes. "Surely they can see that teaching is a respectable profession."

"Yes, but it's not really the sort of career that suits my personality, I'm afraid. Harry often says that I—"

"—what does this Harry do for a living?"

George frowns at the interruption. "He owns a nightclub; not far from here. Perhaps you've heard of it, it's a dashedly grand place for a—"

"—Well, putting Harry's nightclub aside for a moment, shall we get to work?" Daisy's steely expression suggests that he would be foolish to consider any refusal. Wisely, George nods, and traipses to the front of the class, looking every bit like a scolded schoolboy himself.

"Good for her," Agnes whispers, hiding a giggle behind the hint of a hand.

The ghost nods grimly. "Quite."

By the end of the day, it is apparent that George is exhausted, both mentally and physically. Daisy's polite insistence has not wavered, even when met with increasing mulishness and surly tones. The ghost's respect of the woman grows, and he wonders, *perhaps she is a female who deserves the vote after all.* Certainly, she has proved herself more mature than his feckless nephew, who, though in his thirties, has the spoiled demeanour of someone far younger.

Daisy waits for the last of the pupils to leave, then purposefully closes the door, blocking out the noise of the playground.

"You didn't enjoy that one bit, did you?"

George glances up, surprised, then chuckles. "Not much. Did you?"

"Not really." With a grin, she sits on the nearest desk, tucking a stray hair behind her ear. "So, do you want to tell me why you're *really* here?"

"My word, you're a forceful woman, aren't you?"

The ghost notes that the sentiment was meant as a compliment, not an insult.

Daisy nods. "I can be, from time to time. If I'm to have you in my classroom, I need to understand what's going on, does that make sense?"

George sniffs, selects the desk beside her, then rests upon it. "Yes, I suppose that's fair. My father has decided I'm a useless good-for-nothing and has threatened to cut me out of his inheritance if I don't change my ways. He believes teaching is a suitable profession, so here I am."

"But surely it's rather beneath your family, isn't it?"

George shrugs. "Not really. My grandfather was only a clerk at the Docks, and my uncle works there still, I believe. We come from relatively humble stock."

Not so humble, the ghost thinks, bristling. Mother's Battersea home, though small, had been charming enough; and was one of the better residences in the village. *Still,* he thinks, *if George is used to the finer things in life, then I suppose a cottage in a village is rather downmarket.*

Daisy looks at George shrewdly. "Your father must have worked hard then, to get where he is in life."

"Yes, I suppose he has," George answers bitterly. "That's all he really enjoys doing, working. Mother is impervious to it, of course. As long as he keeps buying her expensive dresses and jewellery."

"You really shouldn't speak of your mother like that."

"You should stop telling me what I can and cannot do."

They sit in silence, glowering at one another. The ghost wonders what George's mother is like; his sister-in-law. Presumably, Arthur must have married well, and given his handsome appearance, he must have attracted someone similarly pleasant to look upon. *I must have seen his wife,* he realises, knowing that he's seen George before, some time in the past. *But I don't recollect it.* The thought disturbs him. He treasures his memories, though they are becoming more difficult to grasp, and is petrified at the thought that they might slide away from him entirely.

"You remind me a little of my mother," George says eventually, a smile twisting the corner of his mouth. He stands, scoops up his boater from the table at the back of the classroom, then turns to face her. "She has the same sort of forthright manner, especially when she wants me to do something."

Daisy smiles. "Do you get along with your mother?"

"She loves me well enough." He shrugs. "She's got a past, though; one that she won't share with me. But then, we all have secrets, don't we?"

For a moment, Daisy's smile freezes. Her eyes harden and the ghost can tell she's musing the words, thinking of her own secrets, which glow within her.

"Yes," she says, as she stands. "We certainly do."

Outside, the weather is still fine; the gentle spring sunshine lightening the monotone grey of the playground. George bids Daisy farewell, half-respectfully, half with irritation, then strides towards the gate, whistling a faded tune beneath his breath.

The ghost watches him, and wonders.

"Did you want to follow him?" Agnes asks. The air stills, and she becomes more visible, her shawl mottled and worn in the light.

"No." He shakes his head. "I don't think it would be a wise idea."

"Why not?"

I do not know, the ghost thinks. He just believes it to be true; that facing his brother would be the worst thing he could possibly do. But he cannot tell Agnes that. She couldn't possibly understand.

Instead, he drifts away, allowing himself to be carried on the subtle breeze.

THIRTEEN

— 1878 —

I'D NEVER HAD any great fondness for circuses. However, Eleanor's begging soon wore me down. How could I say no to her, after the turmoil she'd been through recently? Although she'd recovered well after losing the baby, I could see it still tormented her; especially on those quiet nights, when she was sewing by the fire. If a circus could help remedy that, then so much the better.

I was prepared to admit that the procession had been an impressive spectacle. The people of St Katharine's Docks and beyond had poured from their houses to witness the succession of gaudy caravans, strutting horses, and dancing performers, gambolling, leaping, and juggling as the circus continued its relentless march into the city.

Arthur accompanied us, as he so often did, and the open excitement on his face amused me. Here he was, a full-grown man, lit up like a schoolboy at the sight. I told him as much, and he laughed, pointing at the great beast that lumbered at the back of the procession. An elephant, no less, trunk ambling from side to side like a branch in a breeze.

"Surely even you can't fail to be thrilled by *that*." Arthur poked me in the ribs, as though daring me to disagree.

I rolled my eyes, remembering similar experiences from our youth. Eleanor and Arthur had always been the most excited to see the arrival of a circus or funfair in town, and had taken great delight in ensuring that we all accompanied them, whether we'd wanted to or not.

"I never imagined an elephant would be so large!" Eleanor gasped, clutching my arm. "It is quite monstrous!"

"Yes, it is a remarkable creature," I admitted, giving her a smile. We waited until the last of the circus had passed, then retreated to the house.

"So," Eleanor said, smiling in Arthur's direction, a complicit grin that left me in no doubt as to what was coming next, "can we go to the circus tonight?"

"Yes, let's!" Arthur beamed, hands on hips.

I looked at the pair of them, then laughed. How could I resist the two people I loved most in the world? "Goodness me, it's just like the old days," I said, linking arms with them both. "Go on then, you've talked me into it."

That evening, Arthur sent his brougham as promised, complete with the driver he'd hired recently, a taciturn chap with an impressive drooping moustache, who went by the name of Higgins. As we clambered inside, Eleanor giggled, her excitement evident. It was a relief to see her looking so much like her old self again.

"So," Arthur declared, rapping at the glass. The brougham lurched into motion. "Are we all ready to enjoy an experience we'll never forget?"

"I certainly am," Eleanor replied, settling into the leather seat.

"My word," I exclaimed, "you make it sound as though we're travelling to the moon or something."

"Don't be a sourpuss, Brother. It'll be marvellous fun." Arthur winked at me, then added, "Don't you remember how we used to beg Mother and Father to take us to the circus, when we were young?"

"I remember you begging them," I retorted.

"And you too, don't pretend you didn't," he laughed. "You were fascinated by the Strong Man, if I remember correctly. You wanted to know if he could really bend steel with his bare hands."

"I'm looking forward to seeing the lions," Eleanor said.

I scratched my chin. The prospect of seeing the animals wasn't one I entirely relished, especially as they always appeared so miserable in their tiny cages, but I was happy to overcome my reservations for this night, at least.

Soon, the carriage reached the green. The sight of the big top was awe-inspiring; a soaring behemoth of red and yellow, illuminated by several surrounding oil lamps, mounted on poles in the ground; their pungent smoke curling trails into the darkening sky. A painted sign at the entrance, complete with a rough illustration of a rotund ring-master, declared *Captain Otto's Circus of Wonders,* though I thought the name seemed rather grandiose for what appeared to be a rather standard circus. Already, the field was crowded, and I stared at the sight of so many people, their silhouettes milling around the smaller attraction tents. Beside me, Eleanor rubbed her hands in glee.

The smell hit us as soon as we stepped out the brougham; roasting chestnuts, burning oil, and the heady tang of the animals. We immersed ourselves in the crowd, giving ourselves over to the noises, the sights, the strange and unusual at every turn. Arthur immediately made a path for the coconut shy, then afterwards, he protested that they'd been nailed to the posts, though I personally believed he was a rotten aim. He always had been, even when playing cricket back at school.

"Look!" Eleanor tugged at my elbow, pointing through the crowd. "There's your Strong Man!"

"I think I should have another go at the coconuts," Arthur grumbled, looking mutinously over his shoulder.

"You really shouldn't." I pulled him towards us, trying to divert his attention. "I know you don't like losing, but you've already wasted over a shilling."

"Keeping count, were you? You should come and work at our bank if you're so good with numbers."

Eleanor batted us both. "You two are like children! Come on, let's go and have a look."

The Strong Man had already attracted a sizeable crowd. Although his plinth was small, the sign over his head was not; a richly decorated plank declaring him to be *Ivan, the Strongest Man in the World.* I was somewhat disappointed by the reality of the man himself; not much taller than I, with muscles that were sinewy rather than bulging. However, his chest was an impressive girth, and currently straining out of what looked like some sort of leopard-skin vest.

"My friends!" he shouted suddenly, in a guttural, unfamiliar accent. "In a moment, I shall take this iron crowbar and bend it, using only one hand and my teeth. If you would like to see this, please, drop a penny in the pot. My son, Ernst, will be bringing it around."

A boy dutifully emerged through the crowds, energetically shaking what looked like a small bucket. He glared as I handed over the money, as though my coin had personally insulted him, before disappearing through the crowds.

He's a charming little chap, I thought, still able to hear the rattling of his pot, as he made his way back to the stage. *Still, I suppose he's never been educated, nor raised in the ways of polite society.* I couldn't imagine a worse sort of life; always on the move, never settling; it wouldn't suit my temperament whatsoever.

"You look deep in thought," Eleanor commented, just as the performance began to start. I smiled, shook my head, then turned my gaze to the stage.

True to his word, the Strong Man took his crowbar in hand, then made a performance of repeatedly hitting it against the side of his plinth, calling on members of the audience to test it for him. I began to grow bored. Arthur yawned, then caught my eye and grinned.

"Now, it will be done!" With a roar, the Strong Man took the bar between his teeth, and after a series of elaborate eye-rolling and grunting, proceeded to bend the metal. The crowd clapped rapturously. I looked at my brother and shrugged.

"Not quite as exciting as I'd been expecting," I murmured into his ear.

"No, I rather agree. I'm sure it was much more thrilling when we were younger. Let's go elsewhere."

We wandered through the throngs of people, and all the while, I kept my eyes on my wife, noting the gleam in her eye, the renewed energy of her step. This was what she had needed, I could see that now; something to refresh her senses and help her to feel alive once more. I vowed to take her out more often, into the city, to galleries, exhibitions, museums, regardless of whether we could afford it or not. Everything I had, I would gladly give to her, just to see her smile.

She noticed my gaze and bit her lip. "What are you looking at me like that for?"

I leant across and whispered in her ear. "Because I love you. Is there any better reason?"

"You are sweet." Kissing me on the cheek, her eyes fixed on something over my shoulder. "Oh, look over there! They've got a Fortune Teller!"

I turned, then groaned. "No, really, Eleanor. Anything but that. It's all stuff and nonsense, you know."

"I know, but it will be fun, won't it?" She looked at Arthur, who nodded enthusiastically. "Please?"

As long as she doesn't take it too seriously, I thought, following as she and my brother surged restlessly towards the narrow tent. The last thing I wanted was for some charlatan to give my wife false hope about another pregnancy, or worse, dash her hopes further.

"Gosh, this looks fun, doesn't it?" Arthur stopped just outside the tent and peered into the semi-darkness. A single, mostly molten candle flickered on the table, just visible between the swathes of the tent entrance.

"Is that what you'd call it?" I studied the dim interior of the tent, wondering where the Fortune Teller was. If she was inside, she was certainly doing a good job of concealing herself.

To my surprise, a young, dark-eyed girl emerged from the shadows, only a few feet from where I stood, looking every bit as sinister as a spirit, slinking through the night. At closer inspection, I could see she was a striking little thing, with large, knowing eyes, and a mass of curly hair wrapped loosely under a shawl. "Sixpence a fortune," she muttered, kicking at the grass underfoot. "Payment in advance."

"Will it be you reading our fortunes?" Arthur asked, as he rooted in his pocket for some change.

The girl shook her head. "My aunt. She's a world-famous psychic, she's read the fortunes of royalty."

"Has she really?" I replied dryly, already regretting my decision. I knew I should have declined to partake in this nonsense while I had the chance.

The girl counted the coins carefully, then closed her palm over them, tightly as a sealed oyster shell. "One at a time, if you please. Ladies first."

Eleanor beamed, and without a second glance in our direction, stepped into the tent. We heard the dim rumble of a voice, asking her to sit down, then the entrance curtain was fully drawn, shutting us out.

"Well," Arthur said finally, after the girl had disappeared behind the tent again. "This is all rather thrilling, isn't it?"

"It was a silly idea," I replied, folding my arms. Across the field, a man in a tailcoat and top hat was shouting from a podium, though what he was hollering, I couldn't tell. If the milling crowds were anything to go by, it seemed as though the circus performance was about to commence. I hoped Eleanor wouldn't be too long.

"Come on now, where's your joie de vivre? Don't you find it amusing?"

I shrugged and looked away, reluctant to meet my brother's eye. In truth, I was finding his enthusiasm exhausting, not to mention mildly irksome; especially as I sensed it was for show, to rouse a sense of nostalgia in us all. But then, that was Arthur; ever the crowd-pleaser, and it probably wasn't fair to judge him harshly for it. Instead, I studied my shoes intently, hoping that Eleanor wouldn't be too long.

Thankfully, she emerged after only a few minutes, smiling widely. I smiled back, despite my reservations.

"Well?"

"Apparently, I'm going to be rich when I'm older," she said, moving aside. "Though she mentioned unhappiness, which isn't surprising, given what's happened to us recently."

Sounds like the usual guesswork and rubbish, I thought, with relief.

"So, shall we go?" I asked, extending my arm to her.

"Not yet," Arthur interrupted, pointing into the tent. "I paid for all of us to have a go, and that includes you. Come on, get on with it, otherwise we'll miss the performance."

With a sigh, I ventured into the tent. I knew there was no point protesting, my brother would only cajole and wheedle until I gave in. It was even darker inside than I'd anticipated, perhaps because my eyes had grown accustomed to the bright pools of light created by the lamps outside. I looked down to see a minute woman sitting behind the table, watching me with alert, birdlike eyes.

"Hello," I said awkwardly, unsure where to put myself.

She nodded, her voluminous shawls rustling with each movement, then gestured for me to sit beside her. Without waiting for me to settle, she began shuffling at her cards, shutting her eyes, and muttering under her breath. I fought the urge to sigh.

"Are you looking for a simple reading, or do you have a specific question?" she asked. Her voice was rich and velvety as a glass of port, surprisingly deep for such a small person.

"Keep it short, please." I glanced at the curtains covering the exit. *What a ridiculous waste of time,* I thought, wishing that etiquette didn't insist that I remained here, rather than simply getting up and leaving, as I wanted to.

"Very well." With a nimble flick of her wrist, she dealt three cards, face down upon the table. Their geometric patterns gleamed dully in the candlelight. "The first card represents your past," she announced, then without waiting for my response, turned it over.

I gazed down. It showed a man with a crown, sitting on a throne.

"The Emperor," she continued, eyes squinting in concentration. "You had a contented childhood. Solid foundations in life. A comfortable upbringing, I suspect."

Anyone could tell that, just by looking at me, I thought, but nodded nonetheless. "And the next?" I asked, anxious to push on.

"The next card represents the present." She flicked it over, then nodded; the beads of her shawl tinkling delicately with the movement of her head. "The Wheel of Fortune."

"Sounds a bit more interesting, what does that mean?" I was becoming curious, despite my reservations.

She pondered, drumming her fingers across the table's surface. The candle flickered in response. "It can mean a number of things," she said finally, touching the card lightly with her thumb. "It's reversed, which means your life hangs in the balance. Things may change soon, and swiftly. Your peaceful existence may be under threat."

I snorted, unable to stop myself. "I presume the final card foretells my future, then?"

"It does." She glanced up at me. "Do you want me to turn it?"

Not really, I felt like saying, but some morbid interest drove me to nod instead. "Go on," I muttered. "Let's see what fate has in store for me."

The image on the third card was unmistakable, even to someone like me, with no interest in this kind of thing. *The Hanged Man.* I observed the card's image, the resignation on the man's face, as he hung suspended by the ankle. *Ah well,* I thought, feeling unsettled and relieved in equal measures. *At least it wasn't Death, I suppose.*

The Fortune Teller looked more concerned than I was comfortable with. I waited for her to speak. Finally, she raised her eyes and took a deep breath.

"A sacrifice will be made," she said simply, then without waiting for a reply, scooped the cards back up. "Then, stasis. You'll be lost at sea, cast adrift forever."

"Hang on," I said, quite without meaning to. "Whatever do you mean by that? That doesn't make any sense at all."

She shook her head and refused to meet my eye. Indeed, there was something about her posture that indicated fear, though quite what she had to be afraid of, I had no idea. Certainly, my presence didn't usually inspire fright in people. "Sometimes," she said quietly, realising I wasn't going to leave until I had an answer, "it is better not to explore the cards too deeply."

"What on earth does that mean?" I rose, confused.

She sighed. "Sometimes it is better *not to know*."

An involuntary shudder ran through me. *Damned superstition*, I thought, feeling suddenly angry with Eleanor for suggesting it, and with Arthur for paying for it, despite my having showed no interest whatsoever.

"My friend?" The Fortune Teller's voice caught me, just as I'd lifted the curtains to depart.

I turned, reluctantly. "What?"

Her hollow face looked ghoulish in the low light, yet there was a concern there that reminded me, inexplicably, of my mother. "Please be careful," she said. "And do not show your friend in, I will not be telling any more fortunes tonight."

Without another word, she blew out the candle, leaving us both in darkness. I shivered as I remembered her words, despite the warmth of the evening. *You'll be lost at sea. Cast adrift forever.* I knew that it meant nothing, but nonetheless, they niggled at me, persistent as an ice-breeze through my body. Stepping outside, I was relieved to breathe in the reassuring fumes of the oil lamps, not to mention the sight of my brother and wife, as they waited expectantly for my return.

"What was said?" Arthur asked immediately, sidling up beside me.

"Absolutely nothing," I said curtly, still cross at him, though I knew it wasn't really his fault. He'd only been doing it for a lark, with no malice intended. "You can't have a turn though, she said she's finished for the evening."

Arthur grimaced. "But that little girl took my payment, I was rather looking forward to having my fortune read. I wanted to find out if I was going to meet a ravishing beauty tonight and make her my wife!"

"Shall we try to find her, and get her to give your money back?" Eleanor stepped closer to the tent and scrutinised the shadows behind.

"No, let her have it," Arthur said, with typical generosity. "She probably needs it more than I do. Come on, we should hurry, most of the people have gone into the big top now, and we don't want to miss the show."

As we made our way towards the tent, following the trail of lamps, I couldn't help but muse over what the Fortune Teller had told me. It was all hogwash, of course, but nonetheless, her words played over my mind, even as we took our seats on the rough benches inside. The horses, resplendent in their bells, ribbons, and feathers, started to canter around the ring, and the music began.

I was angry at myself. After all, I was a rational man, why should I be perturbed by a silly playing card? Yet her comment echoed flatly in my head. *Sometimes it is better not to know.*

Still, at least Eleanor was having a wonderful time, pointing and gasping at the spectacles before us, and that was all that mattered.

"This is jolly good, isn't it!" Arthur shouted, over the rapturous applause. The horses trotted lithely out of the ring, and a set of clowns, faces thickly daubed with paint, raced on. "I'm ever so glad we came, aren't you?"

"I certainly am!" Eleanor said, leaning into me. "We should come out more often, don't you think? It's been just what I needed."

And that's what's important, I thought, trying to ignore my own reservations. In truth, however, there was nothing I wanted more than to return home, settle in the living room with my newspaper, and pour myself a quiet drink. The circus simply wasn't for men like me, it was too bright, too brash, designed only to inflame and ignite, when my spirits tended to prefer being settled and soothed.

The crowd roared with laughter, though at what, I wasn't quite sure. The music twinkled higher; one clown tripped and fell, red nose landing on the sawdust. I made an effort to smile.

"You could at least *look* like you're having fun," Arthur whispered eventually, with a nod in Eleanor's direction. "You've got a face like a washed-up trout."

I smirked. That had been one of Father's favourite expressions, and I hadn't heard it in a while. "I would, only it's not terribly funny," I whispered back, taking care to avoid being overheard. The last thing I wanted was to come across as a killjoy.

"That's your problem, you see." Arthur's expression grew solemn as the crowd erupted once more into laughter. "You *think* about things too deeply."

It is better not to explore the cards too deeply, she'd said. The memory sent goosepimples running up my arm.

"Let's just drop the matter," I said firmly, sitting up straighter on the bench.

Arthur's eyebrow raised. "Gosh, you're cantankerous tonight. You should try to be in a better mood, you really should."

"Really?" I bristled at his tone. It was unlike my younger brother to hector me. *Perhaps he feels he's more important, now he's got his new promotion,* I thought uncharitably.

The clowns had formed a tower, teetering on one another's shoulders like badly stacked playing cards. It was obvious what the outcome would be, but the audience whooped and cheered regardless, like over-excited children.

Arthur coughed. "I should say so. It wouldn't hurt you to enjoy life a little more, would it? For Eleanor's sake, if not your own?"

Eleanor turned towards us, expression quizzical. "Are you two all right there? You're missing the fun."

"Yes, we're fine," I said, placing a hand on her arm. I glanced back at Arthur, then added quietly, "I enjoy life very well, thank you very much. And Eleanor's happiness is my concern, not yours."

"Steady on, there's no need to be like that." Arthur's expression hardened for a moment, then he held his hands up in mock-defeat. "I take your point, though. Let's carry on watching, shall we?"

I nodded, forced a smile, then took Eleanor's hand and squeezed it slowly and deliberately, ensuring that my brother saw it.

FOURTEEN

— 1901 —

AGNES HASN'T SPOKEN to the ghost in two days.

He understands why. The suffering of living humans has always affected her, and none more so than one of her own kin, particularly this aunt, who had cared for her as a child. He observes the dying old woman, noting her readiness to ease out of this life and into the next.

If only it had been like that for us, he thinks, envying the simplicity of the process for every other ghost they come across. All they experience is a moment's confusion as they slip out of their body, a gleam of recognition, then *plip,* they fly from existence like a flame extinguishing in water. He doesn't know why it is different for him and for Agnes. *Perhaps we did something terribly wrong in life, and we're now paying a penance for it,* he wonders.

Occasionally, they come across other ghosts, lurking miserably in ancient buildings, skulking in churches. Generally, these creatures flee at the sight of another like them, leaving no clues to hint at the nature of their existence. And so, he and Agnes remain alone, together, oblivious to why they remain, and what the future holds for them. It is an intimidating, frightening thought.

Agnes's aunt looks rather like a walnut shell, he thinks; small, brown, and leathered, narrow eyes blinking in and out of consciousness. It cannot be long now; her breath grows raspier, the rising of her chest more laboured with every inhalation. The circus women gathered around her sense it too, and clasp her hands more tightly, willing her to stay, whilst preparing her to go. Crammed into the caravan, the concentration of their life-force seems almost a taunt to the dying that is happening before them.

He thinks he remembers this aunt. There is something about her that strikes a note deep within him; a chime of a distant memory. He can see her at a table, a series of tarot cards in front of her, and for some reason, one particular card clangs loudly as a bell within his mind; *the Hanged Man.* However, he doesn't know where this vision originated. Perhaps from his time spent at the circus, shortly after he'd died. Strange, how his memory fails him at crucial moments like this. He hopes it will not worsen with time; after all, his memories are all he has left.

"Agnes?" He approaches gently, as one might a skittish mare.

She shakes her head, then dwindles into invisibility, though he knows she is still here. *Very well,* he thinks, understanding her need to be alone. This aunt was obviously close to her, this pickled old creature who seems nothing more than loose bags of flesh to him. *We have no choice over who we love in life,* he realises, and feels a vague tang of bitterness at the thought.

Still, he pities the old woman, on her narrow bed. She looks lost beneath the stained old blankets, her skin mottled in the weak light that filters through the tiny caravan window. Presumably, she'd once been young, beautiful, travelling from town to town with the circus, seeing the sights of the world. Agnes has told him a little of her childhood, growing up in the gaudy confines of a caravan, telling fortunes in exchange for money. He can imagine how it might have been.

This is miserable, he thinks, wishing he could leave. The cramped space reeks of forthcoming death, but he can't depart, not without Agnes. They are now linked, tied to one another like ropes in a storm, though for exactly what reason, he's not sure. Details tend to escape him these days; making his memories somehow soggy at the edges, like a landscape seen through misted glass.

The woman coughs, an agonising, exhausted splutter, and the ghost thinks, *This is the moment.* He can sense death, easing closer, ready to claim her. Sure enough, her chest flutters, then stops, and at last, after days of suffering, she is free.

He watches, fascinated as always, as her spirit forms; her misty features gradually fusing into focus. She blinks, then stares at the living women around her, who still hold firm to her empty shell of a body. Agnes returns to the corner and waits, motionless.

"Agnes?" The voice has a richness to it that the ghost was not expecting from someone so short and narrow-shouldered.

Agnes drifts forward, arms outstretched. "Aunt Esme, you recognise me?"

The ghost smiles. It is a relief to hear Agnes speak again. He'd missed her comments, the reassuring murmur of her voice as they travelled from place to place. He makes himself as unobtrusive as possible, aware that this is a private moment, an occasion that he has no active role in.

The aunt's mouth twitches; a conflicted motion of confusion and pleasure. Then, she notices herself, the transparency of her body, her sheer lack of physicality. He can see the realisation dawning, the gradual disbelief. The ghost feels for her. It must be painful to know that life has come to an end, that all you held dear has been stripped from you, as carelessly as bark from a willow branch. He personally cannot remember what it was like; the experience of dying has all but faded from his mind now, as all troubling experiences inevitably do. He only remembers the sensation of not breathing; the wide-eyed gaze at the sky above, and how distant it had looked.

And I remember Eleanor's hand, reaching for mine, he thinks. How they'd locked fingers, before death had wrenched them apart.

"Aunt, I'm so glad to see you again," Agnes says, moving forward. She, like the ghost, is amazed that the old woman has remained so long. Normally, they vanish long before this.

"Agnes?"

"Yes, it's me, don't worry, Aunt Esme, everything is—"

A frown shadows the hollowed remnants of her aunt's face. "Agnes, you did a *terrible* thing."

Agnes's expression crumbles.

Her aunt extends her hands, and to the ghost's horror, he realises that she is warding Agnes away, as though frightened of her. "You did an unforgivable thing, my girl. How could you do that? *How could you?*"

And then, just like that, she is gone. One moment there, finger poised in accusation, the next, vanished. Now that she has departed, the ghost is aware of the living women again, their quiet sobs filling the room. He looks across to Agnes and sees the sparkle of a tear upon her cheek.

"Agnes?" His voice wavers, uncertain.

She shakes her head, then flees from the caravan; the air rippling in her wake like a restless mirage.

He spends the rest of the day searching for her, ignoring the commotion that surrounds him; the rustle of heavy fabric as the tents are assembled, the continual thud of hammer on peg. The circus men seem to shout ceaselessly through the day, a tirade of stoic camaraderie and hoarse, jocular insults, but he scarcely notices. Finally, he concludes that wherever Agnes may be, she doesn't want to be found, or at least, not at this moment.

At around lunchtime, Aunt Esme's corpse is carried from the caravan by two men, one weeping openly. It seems that Agnes's aunt was a respected member of the circus, and several people stop their work and observe, solemn-faced, as she is taken to a large open cart, over to the other side of the field. He wonders what they will do with her body. Do circus folk have funerals? Will they take her to a local church for burial, or do they have their own ways of disposing of her?

For the first time, he finds himself thinking about Agnes's living body, or at least, the remains of it. *How old must it be now?* he wonders. More morbidly, he wonders what state it must be; how forcefully the worms have done their work. When did she even die? He can't remember the date, but doesn't believe it was that long ago. But who knows? The years have started to bleed into one another, and it is difficult to keep track of the passage of time.

And mine, of course. He feels strangely removed from the thought of his old physical form. After all, it is nothing, only an empty vessel to house what he is now. *All those times I peered into the looking glass and believed I was seeing myself,* he thinks, ruefully easing aside as a crowd of workers set about erecting another tent. *And all I was seeing was an artful arrangement of cells and fluid, nothing more.*

As the sun sets and the crowds start to arrive, he moves to another part of the field. It is difficult to bear the volume and vitality of so many people, and their exuberance is draining. Also, he doesn't like remaining here. He's never liked circuses, even in the days when he used to hover close to Agnes, back when she'd been alive. They leave him unsettled.

Finally, Agnes finds him, long after the people have surged into the big top to watch the show. She appears at his side, as the muffled calliope plays on, somewhere within the bowels of the tent. The frenetic notes, skating upwards and downwards like racing rodents, nettle him, and he wishes for quiet, a world without such endless motion and noise.

"How are you?" he asks, scarcely daring to look at her.

The silence is answer enough.

"They took your aunt's body away," he offers.

"Yes, I know."

Somewhere in the distance, a dog barks. The ghost smiles ruefully. He forgets there are houses just beyond this park, that they are still in the heart of the city, even though the surrounding trees blot out most of the evidence.

"Agnes," he begins, falteringly, "your aunt didn't mean what she said."

She shakes her head. "I think she did."

"It was just the shock of seeing you again. She blurted the first thing that came to mind, then—"

"—no, she *meant* it." The severity of her voice forbids him to press the issue. Agnes waits, surveying the silhouettes of the neighbouring beeches, before adding, "She was right, of course."

"That's not true." He's quick to jump to her defence, because he remembers how it was for her, how unendurable life had become whilst she was alive.

"It *is* true. It's considered an unforgivable sin by my people."

The ghost nods reluctantly. He understands that travelling folk are steeped in deep-rooted beliefs, and that their philosophies are often unshakeable. Staying with them in the past taught him that.

"But you were a good niece," he guesses, wishing he had more than words to comfort her.

"Was I?" She shakes her head. "I always felt trapped with her; she must have known that. You realised it, when you first found me. It was one of the first things you said. *You don't belong here. This place is too small for you.*"

He has no memory of this, but nods all the same. "Do you want to leave?" he asks. There's nothing left for her now, not after this; only a scattering of distant cousins, a couple of aunts and uncles who are equally as infirm as her Esme.

Agnes sighs. The roar of the crowd filters through the thick fabric of the big top, like a crashing wave on a distant shore.

"Aunt Esme was the only one who was ever kind to me," she says, and her eyes grow dim.

He remembers her talking about Aunt Esme before, how she'd raised Agnes after the death of her mother. Agnes had laughed when she'd told him, at the irony, of how she might have been a trapeze artist like her parents, had fate not stepped in and made her the protégée of the Fortune Teller instead.

However, she had a natural talent for reading people, just as her aunt had. It ran in their family, she'd told him, the knack of looking past a person's face and seeing their path, laid out before them like an unfurling ribbon of inevitability. She'd favoured the tarot cards, as Aunt Esme had done before her.

Even now, in death, Agnes still has that ability to read those around her. And she knows more about the ghost than he is comfortable with, especially now his memory is less reliable. He suspects she may know more about him than he does himself.

"But surely," he continues, trying to draw her attention back to the present, "there's nothing to hold you here now?" In all honesty, he'd be pleased to move on from the circus. They've been here too long, and he yearns for something different; new people, a new way of life. He *needs* something to tether himself to; to stop himself from drifting.

She shrugs, reaching to her shoulder and drawing the mists of her shawl across herself. A half-remembered gesture, no doubt, from her living days. He finds himself doing similar actions, from time to time. Shivering against a breeze, even though he can no longer feel it. Stroking his stomach, even though there's no stomach there to touch anymore, only the transparent echo of what once was.

"What do you remember about the first time you came to me?" she asks.

He says nothing.

"I was staring at the candle," she says, filling the silence. "I stared for so long that I couldn't see anything else. It must have been a trance, I think, and that was how I was able to hear you. You found me, one night after Ernst had beaten me badly. At first, I thought I was imagining you. Then I wondered if you were the ghost of one of my ancestors." She laughs, a bitter sound. "That's how desperate I was for someone to protect me. Pathetic, I suppose."

"It's not pathetic to seek comfort from others."

"A living person, perhaps. But a ghost?" Her gaze slides to meet his. "You became my only friend, and you weren't alive. I couldn't even *touch* you."

"I'm sorry."

"Why? It wasn't your fault. None of it was."

He doesn't reply, sensing that she is wrong. He is partially to blame for it, he is certain.

"How long do you think we can go on like this?" Agnes asks eventually, almost conversationally.

He ponders. "I don't know."

"I mean," she continues, shimmering faintly in the dim light, "when will it be our turn? To disappear, as the other spirits do? Why are we still here?"

Ah, he thinks. *The big question.* An issue they skirt around regularly, too nervous to explore the answer. Why do most ghosts vanish immediately, often with an expression of relief or contentment on their faces? Even those who linger for a while tend to disappear eventually. Only the tortured ones, the sad, twisted figures in lonely places; only those poor souls remain. *So, we must be like them.* "What do you think?" he asks.

Her aunt's death has made her fearless; freed her tongue. "I think we are *cursed.*"

The word makes him shudder.

"We're not cursed," he reassures her, unconvincingly.

"Why do you dismiss the idea so quickly?"

"Because . . ." He falters, looks to the sky for inspiration. A flock of swifts duck and weave in the gloaming light, and he envies their freedom. "Because we've done nothing to be cursed for," he concludes, then catches her eye. *Or at least, I haven't,* he thinks, then feels guilty to think such a thing.

"Do you know," she says, as they start to drift back to the circus tent, "I've never hated Ernst. Not once. And what I did . . ."

"Yes?"

"That was never about hatred. I didn't do it for revenge."

He nods. He knows this to be true, because he was there; though not in the final moments. Had he been, he would have done everything in his power to stop her. "I know," he agrees. "Revenge has never been in your heart." He wishes he could hold her for a moment, do *anything* to ease her anxiety. "You are a good person." *A better person than I ever was,* he finishes silently.

"Are Ernst's family still here?" He'd thought it indelicate to enquire before, but now that Agnes has broached the subject, it seems acceptable.

She nods. "Not that I ventured too close. A part of me was terrified that his father would sense me. Ivan *never* liked me. He thought I was weak. I think he wanted Ernst to marry Greta, but he'd already arranged the betrothal with my father, years before." Her eyes wrinkle; a trace of her old humour returning. "*Everyone* wanted their boys to marry Greta. She married Bernard instead; the clown. Do you remember him?"

"I think I remember Greta," the ghost murmurs, straining his mind back to those times. A big-boned, full-lipped girl, he seems to recollect. Sensuous, broad-jawed, with a laugh like an emptying drain. "Didn't she used to dance with the horses?"

"Yes, standing on their backs, with her red and lilac leotard." Agnes smiles. "She was a sight. I always liked her, despite everything."

"Why don't you visit Ernst's father, before we leave?" he suggests. "It might bring you some peace."

She considers, then shakes her head. "No. Ivan will bring me nothing. That's all he ever did."

Later, when the show is finished and the crowds have trickled to just a few remaining people, the ghost leaves Agnes; understanding her need to be alone, to take the time to bid this place a final farewell. It was her life, but now she has a new life, such that it is, and this circus can no longer provide for her.

He wanders past the smaller tents; the various hastily erected stages with their signs, promising all manner of exotic sights. *The Incredible Bearded Woman of Burma. The Most Tattooed Man in the World.* It makes him smile, inwardly. He knows Eleanor would have loved all of this; the intoxicating scents, the clanging music, the *feel* of so much anticipation and excitement.

A blurred memory stirs him; of an evening at the circus; he, his wife, and Arthur. *Elephants,* he remembers. *Lions. A man, bending a bar of metal with his teeth.* For some reason, the thought of it makes him frown.

The Hanged Man, he thinks again, then remembers Aunt Esme, pointing an accusing finger at Agnes, before dissolving into nothingness. The thought makes him freeze, strain to recollect more, but the memory refuses to be grasped too tightly. Rather, it remains elusively distant, teasing him, just beyond his reach.

Agnes finds him in the end, as she always seems to be able to do.

"Are you ready?" she asks, eyes shining against the brash light of the surrounding oil lamps.

"I should be asking you that question." He gestures to it all, inviting her to look at it one last time; the soaring mountain of the big top behind them, the circus folk, still milling around, chatting, relaxing after another hard night's work. "Are *you* ready to leave all of this?"

Her form quivers in the air, before solidifying. "Yes." The answer is resolute, final. *She's given thought to this,* he realises. *The decision has not come lightly.* "Besides," she says, almost carelessly, "they will be packing up and leaving soon, anyway. As they always do."

"Where will we go now?" he asks, attempting to sound lighthearted, even though he doesn't feel it. "After all, it is a new century. The world is our oyster."

She laughs. "We cannot leave London. We are chained here, for better or for worse."

"Perhaps we should seek out happier experiences." *Maybe that is what we need,* he thinks, *to move forward. Perhaps it's our misery that tethers us here, weighing us down like ballast.*

"We really should." Agnes's expression lights up with sudden fierceness; a glimpse of the beauty she once was, back when she had skin to be beautiful in. But her words sound hollow to him, and he knows that she is not convinced.

"Though I need to keep searching for my Eleanor," he reminds her.

"Really?" She darkens. "We cannot keep doing this, you said so yourself."

Did I? Perhaps that is true, though he cannot recollect it.

"Yes, you said it was better not to think on it. You *must* remember that."

He says nothing, and they fall into step with one another, leaving the circus for the final time. But all the while, the same words run through his head, loud and chiming as a church bell. *I will never stop searching for Eleanor. Never.*

If he stops, he will have no purpose. So, he must carry on. Because love is all he has left, really. And if he gives up on that, he loses his hold on the only thing that matters anymore.

FIFTEEN

— 1878 —

THE AIR HAD been as thick as syrup all afternoon, the ominous roll of thunder cutting through the hubbub of the streets outside. It hadn't put any of us clerks off our work, of course; we were paid to concentrate and ensure the figures stacked up, regardless of what was going on around us. However, when Mr Harrison announced that it was five o'clock, I was relieved. Our tiny office was oppressive on days like this, especially with the windows sealed shut.

I bid my colleagues farewell for the day, then stepped outside, just as the first fat drops of rain started to fall. Fortunately, I'd come prepared that morning with my umbrella, which I gladly pulled up over my head, saving my hat from a soaking.

Berner Street was unusually quiet, most likely because of the inclement weather; which was exactly as I liked it. Although it was a somewhat downtrodden area, the pavements were pleasantly wide, and the road blissfully empty. Sometimes, in moments like this, it even felt less like London, and more like the peaceful streets of my childhood.

The quiet also gave me the opportunity to brood on Mr Harrison's words regarding my promotion. Always, it seemed just around the corner, but certain company setbacks were preventing it, all the more frustrating given Eleanor's latest spate of spending, which was threatening the bedrock of our meagre savings. This morning, the latest word had been that they were 'discussing' the option of promoting me to senior clerk, a position I'd been yearning after for over a year now. How I wished they would just get on with their decision, rather than drawing it out in this painful, protracted fashion; especially given my concerns about our dwindling funds.

Still, if spending gave Eleanor pleasure, how could I deny her? In all honesty, the purchase of a new purse or dress had never seemed like a cause for excitement to me, but then, I was not a female, and I acknowledged it may be different for them.

Sure enough, as I arrived home, the first thing I noted was the large hatbox, sitting beside our sofa, decorated ostentatiously with gold rope and fringing. Scarcely had I shaken my umbrella out and placed it by the door, than Eleanor had rushed down the stairs, cheeks flushed, eyes bright. She'd had an enjoyable day, I could tell.

"There you are!" she chorused, helping me out of my jacket and placing a kiss on my cheek. "I was worried you'd get soaked to the skin!"

I kissed her back, glad to see her healthy glow. She was back to her old self again, thanks largely to Arthur's and my efforts to keep her entertained. I'd never been out so often in all my life, but it was worth the additional expenditure, just to see her like this.

"I remembered to go prepared," I said, pointing to the dripping umbrella, then gestured to the hatbox. "I presume you didn't get wet whilst you were out shopping, then?"

Eleanor's face flushed, and a hint of defensiveness crept into her expression. "No, I was perfectly dry. And I had a wonderful time. I met with Genevieve on Regent Street; do you remember Genevieve? She used to live near me when I was a girl. She's married exceptionally well; her husband is a—"

"—Lucky Genevieve," I interrupted, trying not to feel irritated. "And poor you, getting stuck with a lowly clerk, eh?"

Eleanor laughed. "Oh dear, don't say it like that! You earn an honest living, and that is all that matters. Guess who else I happened to see, though? You'll never guess."

I sighed. "May I sit down first, my dear? It's been a long day."

"You can sit down and guess at the same time, can't you?"

I could see her determination, etched in every muscle of her face. *Very well*, I thought with a smile. *If this is the game she wants, she shall have it.* I strode to the sofa and kicked off my shoes, resting my feet upon the footrest. "Let me see," I began, patting the sofa for her to join me. "You saw Father Christmas?"

She slapped my arm playfully. "You are silly. Guess properly."

"An old school friend?"

"No."

"Oh, I don't know, Eleanor, do just tell me."

"I saw your brother, Fred."

Fred? The name surprised me. Since Arthur's solicitor had managed to get him out of prison, Fred had all but disappeared. The last I'd heard, he'd lost his job at the Docks and was taking on some casual work with an ironsmith in Southwark. I didn't even know if he was still renting that sad, dank room by the Thames, or whether he'd moved to a new abode. Even Mother hadn't heard from him, which was highly irregular.

"You look shocked."

"I suppose I am, a little." I straightened, loosening my tie, which suddenly felt rather tight. "What on earth was he doing on Regent Street? Did you speak to him?"

Eleanor blushed. "Yes, I had to, didn't I? I mean, he is my brother-in-law."

No, you didn't have to, I thought meanly, then scolded myself for it. Eleanor was absolutely right, of course. Fred was her family now, regardless of their history. "Very well," I said slowly, still struggling to acclimatise to the thought of Fred in such a well-to-do shopping district. "What did he say to you?"

"He said he was looking for a gift."

"A gift? For who?"

"He said a lady, but wouldn't go into details."

I snorted. "Well, it can't be Mother, her birthday was last month. And Martha's isn't until November. What's he up to, I wonder?"

Eleanor smoothed her skirt carefully, easing out each crinkle in turn. "Aren't you going to ask me how he looked?" she said casually.

"Presumably just the same as ever," I scoffed. I felt guilt for my lack of charity towards my brother, but then, when had he ever shown me any kindness? Any brotherly gesture he showed towards me was usually ruined by a dark look or hostile comment.

She shook her head. "No, not at all. He looked quite smart, believe it or not."

"In what way?"

"He had a well-made top hat, plus a long coat. If I hadn't have known him better, I would have thought he was comfortably off. In fact, he reminded me rather of your late father."

"Really?" The notion made me bristle, though I did my best to swallow my misgivings down. I thought back to when I'd last seen him, languishing in his dirty cell at Clerkenwell. I couldn't marry the vision of the man I'd seen there with the one my wife was describing, it didn't make sense.

Eleanor studied my face carefully, then leaned into me. "He didn't look as handsome as you," she murmured in my ear.

I shifted uneasily. "That wasn't why I was pulling a face. It's just . . ."

"Yes?"

I couldn't put it into words. Was I suspicious of Fred, concerned that he'd managed to find money through dishonest means? Or worried that he'd somehow known Eleanor was shopping today, and had deliberately attired himself smartly to attract her? *Don't be silly,* I told myself firmly. Fred and Eleanor had only courted briefly. My response was ridiculous, pure and simple.

"Did he say anything else?" I asked, forcing myself to sound more cheerful.

"Only that he'd found new employment, over in Shadwell. And was living in a new place too, much nicer than the previous one, apparently. I said good luck to him; he's had a rough time of it, hasn't he?"

"Yes, I suppose so," I said, musing on the information. Shadwell was close to Whitechapel. Perhaps he found employment near to my offices. I wondered what sort of position he'd managed to acquire, and how on earth he'd found someone to take him on without any reliable references. Though it made me guilty to think it, I couldn't help but suspect he'd become involved in some sort of shady endeavour, otherwise how would he find decent employment with no credentials?

My suspicions must have been etched across my face, as Eleanor prodded me in the ribs, fairly hard.

"You should be pleased for him."

"I am," I protested weakly, then repeated, "honestly, I am," more to convince myself than her. If Fred had managed to improve his lot in life, then all the better. Whatever he got up to was scarcely any of my business these days. It saddened me, though. I remembered the brother he'd been in my youth, jovial, protective, energetic; before Father had died and changed his demeanour irreparably. *Who knows what might have been, had Father lived,* I thought, wondering.

To lighten the mood, I pointed to the hatbox. "Go on," I said, "show me then."

Eleanor smiled, and reached down willingly enough, discarding the lid with a flourish. What emerged was an elaborate affair, with a silk ribbon wrapped around the brim, not to mention several ruffles and feathers. *She really doesn't need such adornment,* I thought, watching as she positioned it on her head. *She's far more beautiful in her simple bonnet, or better still, with nothing covering her hair at all.*

Still, I didn't say anything. She posed coquettishly, then laughed. "You don't like it, don't you?"

"Absolutely not. It's very . . . fine."

"Fine?" She laughed again. "You do know I can tell when you're not being sincere?"

I pulled her back down on my knee, wrapping my hands around her waist. "If you like it, I like it. Is that good enough?" I kissed her cheek, trying not to imagine how much the milliners might have charged for it. Our financial situation was my concern, my responsibility to fret over. Not hers.

"I know you think it's a bit frivolous. But I can't help liking things like this, you know. It's because I never had much growing up with Auntie Nora, you see."

"I understand that," I said evenly. It hardly seemed the time to remind her that I hadn't grown up in a wealthy household either. "And I am happy for you to have the hat, my love. It's just that we do need to keep an eye on our financial situation, and—"

"Yes, but that's your job. You like working with numbers, you told me so yourself." She glanced out the window. "Look, it's stopped raining now. Shall we go for a walk?"

"Really?" It was rather late, and I wasn't much in the mood to head out again, after only having just returned.

"Yes, I've been cooped up in the house for hours, I should like to take some fresh air. What do you think?"

Her pleading expression was too much for me to resist. With a sigh, I rose to my feet, hoping that a short stroll would be enough to appease her restless spirits. I didn't dare ask what dinner might be, or even if anything had been prepared yet; the kitchen was lacking any pleasant aroma, which indicated it might be rather late until my appetite was satisfied. *Father wouldn't have stood for no dinner,* I thought unkindly, as we wrestled ourselves into our overcoats. *But then, times are different, I suppose. Eleanor is far busier in the day than Mother would have been, back then.*

"Shall I wear my new hat?"

"Aren't you rather worried it might get rained upon?"

Eleanor shook her head. "I'm sure it will be fine. How else will I be able to show it off, if I never wear it?"

"That is a fair point, my love." Sweeping the door open, I stood aside to let her pass through, then shut it reluctantly behind me.

We soon fell into a rhythm, instinctively taking the route we often took when out for a walk; along the river path, away from the main docks. It was quieter there; the birds could often be heard chirruping from the neighbouring trees, and the air felt cleaner somehow, less tainted by the continual smoke of the passing steamboats.

An elderly couple passed us, bidding good evening as they went. Eleanor tilted her head to them, then grinned at me. "That was Mr and Mrs Macready, wasn't it?"

"Gosh, I have no idea."

"Yes, they moved into the house along the road, the large one with the fine pillars outside? He made his money from whiskey, believe it or not; he's opened a distillery across the river."

"However do you know these things?" I was genuinely bemused; my knowledge of the neighbourhood was vague at best.

She patted the side of her nose. "I have my ways. And Arthur is of course a fountain of information."

Good old gossiping Arthur. She was right, my youngest brother always seemed to have the latest news from town. He made it his business to discover every new event and uncover every secret. "Yes, he has his uses," I replied blandly. "So, how long did you want to keep walking?"

"We've only just started!"

"I know, but there's a fine mist to the air, it will surely start raining soon."

"Don't be a bore, darling. Let's keep going for a while longer, yes?"

I nodded and felt the warm press of her hand slipping through my elbow.

"Look!" She pointed down the river. "It's one of those pleasure cruises. Doesn't it look fun?"

I squinted, following the line of her finger. Sure enough, a large ship was navigating the waters, its chimney prodding into the grey sky like a solitary finger, belching smoke. We waited, watching as it drew nearer, its paddles cutting haphazardly through the water. A few people on board waved at us, and Eleanor waved back enthusiastically, holding onto her hat to prevent it blowing away in the breeze.

"It's such a romantic thing to do," she said, as the ship ploughed its way past us, driving inexorably forward to the centre of the city. "Don't you think?"

I scratched my chin thoughtfully. She'd mentioned this before, each time with greater intent, and I knew how much she yearned to experience it herself. "I'm not sure it appeals to me," I said eventually. I couldn't quite say why. Was it something to do with being out on the river, vulnerable to the force of nature? Or was it the machinery itself; the vague repulsion I felt for the ship's enormous tossing paddles and its foul-smelling fumes? *Probably it's more the fact that I can't swim,* I thought, with a dry grin. As children, my brothers had always teased me for my reluctance to join them in the lake for a splash around. *If I fell overboard,* I thought, with a grim smile, *I'd sink like a stone.*

Her face fell at my answer. "I don't understand why you're so negative about it," she said eventually, biting her lip. The mist around us thickened, as the first raindrops settled on our shoulders. "After all, it's just a boat trip, nothing more."

"Yes, I know," I said patiently, tugging her arm gently, to indicate we should turn to go home, "but I can think of far better ways to spend our money. How about—"

"—is that what this is about? Money? I thought you said we were comfortably off?"

"We are, but frivolous activities such as a pleasure cruise really are a bit much."

"This again?" She frowned. The rain fell harder, casting widening circles across the surface of the river beside us. "Why does everything have to be about our finances? It's rather crass, don't you think?"

The comment made me flinch. There had been several occasions where I'd bitten my tongue about her spending; though perhaps she hadn't realised. *Maybe I've concealed my financial concerns a little too well,* I thought. *Perhaps I need to be a little more honest with her.*

"My love, the thing is—"

"—The thing is, you want me to stay at home and produce children. Is that it?"

I stopped walking, momentarily stunned into silence. "Eleanor," I said eventually, "that's not the case at all. I've never made you feel as though—"

"—You have. After the . . ." She swallowed hard, and wiped her face, freeing the moisture from her skin. "After *what happened,* I feel as though you blame me for it, that you're just waiting for me to get with child again, to make everything better."

"Good heavens." Her comments left me feeling winded, raw; not least because they seemed so unjust. I'd done my damnedest to make her feel loved, protected, and entertained, yet still, she blamed me. She saw the hurt in my expression and softened immediately.

"I don't mean to upset you," she said quickly. "It is only that these last few months have been difficult for me. Do you understand?"

"Of course." The wind lashed at the treetops above us, sending fresh droplets of rain upon our heads. Fortunately, we'd not ventured too far out, and our house was almost in sight.

She nodded, relieved. "That is the only reason I'd like to have a bit more fun. To try to put all that behind us, make life more pleasurable again. Don't you think that's worth spending a little bit of money on?"

I eyed the river with apprehension. Sometimes, it seemed to me more beast than fluid; a supple, serpentine creature, winding a path through the capital; its murk and muck leaching out into the banks beside it. "Could we perhaps choose an activity that doesn't involve water?" I suggested, with a laugh that emerged more of a hoarse croak than a sound of amusement. "Perhaps a trip to the theatre? That would be pleasant, wouldn't it?"

Eleanor sighed. "Yes, of course. That would be wonderful."

Rough thunder pealed somewhere in the distance, a vague murmur of the storm to come. I waited for the lightning, but none was forthcoming. *Perhaps too far away,* I wondered. Taking my wife's arm more tightly, I drove the pair of us forward, head ducked to avoid the worst of the weather. The feathers in her hat had wilted and curled, like dying ferns.

We strode in silence for a short while, keen to get home. I still hadn't the courage to broach the topic of dinner, especially after her earlier outburst. *Perhaps I could roll up my sleeves and have a go myself,* I thought, glancing at Eleanor's set jaw and downcast eyes. *After all, I used to watch Mother in the kitchen all the time, how hard can it be?*

"Here we are," I announced cheerfully, inserting the key in the lock. "Thank goodness. Look at us both, we're wet through!"

She entered the hallway, removing her hat with the tenderness of a parent carrying a child. "Perhaps it wasn't such a good idea after all," she admitted, as another roll of thunder cut through the air, sharper this time, and with more menace.

"If it gave you the fresh air you needed, then that's all that matters," I said, shaking the worst of the rain off my coat before hanging it up. "And I meant what I said earlier, you know. Let me know what performance you'd like to see at the theatre and I'll book it. I promise."

Eleanor smiled weakly, before heading out to the kitchen. "That's very sweet of you. And don't worry about the pleasure cruise."

I followed her, dutifully as a pup wandering after its master. "Really? I mean, we can do it if you'd—"

"—No, it's fine," she interrupted, a little more sharply than anticipated. "After all, your brother said he'd take me if you weren't comfortable with the idea."

For a terrible moment, I thought she was referring to Fred. Then I realised she meant the younger brother, not the elder. A surge of irritation rose in me. Arthur was a wonderful chap, but what right did he have to offer to take my wife on an evening cruise, without my accompanying them? It was improper and undermined my position as her husband. I made a mental note to address the issue with him when we next met.

"That won't be necessary," I replied, pulling the kitchen chair out more roughly than I'd intended. It shrieked across the tiles, causing Eleanor to wince, perhaps more theatrically than was appropriate for the situation.

"What do you mean?"

"I mean," I said seriously, as I sat down, "that if it really matters that much to you, then I will take you. There will be absolutely no need for Arthur to accompany you, or anyone else for that matter." I waited, watching as her face broke into an open smile. "As you say, it will be romantic. I'm sure I'll overcome my reservations once we've set sail."

"Oh, thank you!" She flew at me, wrapping her slender arms, which were still damp, around my neck. "You are a dear. I'm sure you'll enjoy the experience."

I stifled a sigh, and patted her hand, which felt reassuringly heavy against my throat. "I'm sure we shall."

I shall just have to enquire about that promotion again, I thought, more sombrely. *Or else take on extra hours to pay for it.*

But then, I'd always said I'd do anything for her. And I was prepared to stand by that, no matter what. What is the purpose of loving someone, if you aren't prepared to sacrifice all to make them happy? So that was what I would do, despite the prospect being somewhat daunting.

I watched her busying herself in the pantry, and wondered, *why is it so much harder to make her smile than I'd anticipated?*

Then I swallowed the thought quickly and rose to help her.

SIXTEEN

— 1890 —

THE BROKEN MIRROR sends moonlight upwards; shards of light that cast orbs across the brightly coloured walls of the caravan, and the base of the wooden-panelled bed. It was Agnes's late mother's mirror, the ghost knows this because Agnes has mumbled it once before, on a quiet, bright night much like this. Now it is gone; yet another strand of her past smashed to oblivion.

She sits by the little oven, knees pressed together, eye already swelling. She is undeniably one of the most painfully vulnerable living creatures he's seen in a long time, especially now, so bruised, so tormented that she seems scarcely able to draw breath.

It is unlike Ernst. He usually takes more care with his beatings, aiming for the stomach, the chest, the back; areas that cannot be seen by others.

She is so unhappy, the ghost thinks, and wishes he could reach out to her. But they are two different entities; he dead, she alive, and their communication lies only in the snatched moments when she's focusing on her candlelight, when her mind splits open and allows his voice to enter. He treasures these conversations, even though she is in pain. It isn't just the acknowledgement that he exists. It's the richness of *her,* the force that flows from her every word. Although her misery drew him first, it is her inflamed soul that keeps him here, longer than he'd initially planned.

The ghost knows that she cannot keep going like this. Her life is untenable, unsustainable, and with every bit of brutality inflicted upon her, she shatters a little more. She is alone, solitary despite the ceaseless din of the circus surrounding her. Her aunt Esme has some knowledge of what Agnes endures, but chooses to stay out of it. It is the circus way, he understands that. What occurs between a courting couple is nobody's business but their own.

Eventually, Agnes climbs to her feet, unsteady as a colt, and starts to collect the pieces of mirror; pressing each to her heart as though willing it to weld itself back together. He senses her urgency; her aunt will return soon, she only grants limited private time for Ernst and Agnes, enough as is appropriate for a pair of young lovers.

Aunt Esme could put a stop to this, the ghost thinks bitterly. *She could end the relationship, and let Agnes be free.* However, that is the nature of betrothal. Ernst's father and Agnes's father made an agreement many years before, and their word remains unbreakable, in spite of everything. Agnes and Ernst must marry, and it must be a circus affair.

The mirror shards are discarded into the bucket next to the oven. Agnes touches her eye, winces, then smooths down her skirt. The ghost notices that it has been ripped at the bottom, possibly after snagging on something after she fell to the floor. He doubts Agnes will care, though; she is only intent on escaping the tiny confines of the caravan and stepping out into the cool autumn evening.

Most of the circus folk are gathered by the fire, eating from tin plates, deep in conversation or laughing at some bawdy joke or other. The ghost can see Aunt Esme's silhouette even from this distance away; a small, slope-shouldered back, hair tied neatly in a high bun. She doesn't notice her niece, stealing down the stairs of the caravan, heading out to the dark of the surrounding trees.

He follows, unable to stop himself. Though his focus is on finding Eleanor, he is concerned about this waifish, shawled creature. In the years that he has remained with the circus, he has grown fond of her.

After all, she is the only one who has ever spoken to him, since his death.

And her eyes are beautiful, he thinks, then chastises himself. As a married man, or at least, a man who was married before he died, he shouldn't be thinking such things. However, it is undeniable, from a purely aesthetic point of view. Agnes's dark eyes are fathomless, deep as wells; sometimes sparkling with amusement, at other times, filled with the misery of the world. He doesn't think he's ever seen such emotion contained in one person. It moves and distresses him in equal measures.

She heads to her favoured spot, as he suspected she might; a park bench beneath an aged oak, almost entirely shadowed by the over-hanging leaves. Weeds clump around the base; this is not a place that is visited often, much less tended to. Humans have given up here and let nature take over. As Agnes settles amongst it all, she looks almost organic herself; her curls mingling with the surrounding undergrowth, her shawl as mottled as the soil beneath her bare feet.

For a long time, she says nothing. Minutes stretch, falter, and die, and still she waits, eyes fixed on her hands, placed neatly in her lap. He sits beside her, and without quite understanding why, lowers the ghost of his hand on hers.

"It will be all right," he whispers, knowing she will not hear him. Her mind is elsewhere, wearily ploughing through the tatters of her life. And worse still, he believes his statement to be a lie. Agnes will not be all right. There is no future for her like this, or at least, not one worth looking forward to. He senses it; that tragedy clouds before her, smothering out any chance of happiness like a damp cloth over a candle.

Hatred for Ernst, with his mercurial nature, his lack of control, flares within him; combined with hatred for himself and his inability to change things. It is the worst aspect of being a ghost, he finds; the emotional responses to those around him are the same, but he no longer has the physical presence to be able to make a difference. He's nothing more than a dim echo of a bell, a feather in the wind, a picture drawn in the sand. *Fleeting and useless,* he thinks, and takes his hand away.

The next morning, Ernst finds her, though has the decency to blush at the sight of her darkening eye. The ghost notes how he flexes his fists instinctively, as though the previous night's actions still reverberate through his fingers. *It always starts with his fists,* the ghost realises. This is the man's language, the words that he understands. Brute force. Strength. Feeling through touch. By contrast, his eyes see virtually nothing of the reality of things; much less the pain he's caused the woman he's supposedly meant to love.

"Are you set?" he asks, nodding across the field, which is filled with the sound of hammers, men shouting, the voluminous thud of tents being dismantled. "The horses, are they fed and watered?"

Agnes shakes her head. "I'll do that now."

"Let me do it for you."

"No, it's best if I do it, they prefer it."

Ernst stiffens, sensing the slight. He looks somehow diminished in his flat cap and faded sepia-brown shirt, as though someone has deflated him, taken the battle out of his body. And again, his emotion descends to those fists, flexing involuntarily, before being stuffed into baggy pockets, placed in storage for a later date.

"At least we are not travelling far, eh?" He kicks at an imaginary pebble on the ground.

"No, that's true." Agnes looks up, shielding her eyes from the sun. "I remember Battersea well from last time. It's a pretty little village."

It is, the ghost agrees silently, warming at the mention of his childhood home. It will be good to go back, to visit his mother's old house, even though she's no longer in it. He wonders who lives there now; it has been a while since he's visited.

Ernst coughs, then spits on the ground. "It will not be a village long, let me tell you. This city, it is growing by the day. One day, all those villages, they'll be swept away by it."

Agnes laughs, and for a moment, there is a spark of *togetherness* between them; a sense of what could be, if only Ernst would stop corroding their relationship with his abuse, and she with her protracted silences. "I don't think that would ever happen," she says softly. "A city will only grow as big as people let it, won't it?"

The ghost isn't so sure. In fact, he rather agrees with Ernst on this occasion. Already, London is a different place to how it was; it sprawls lazily outwards like an ever-unravelling rug. And other things have changed too. Automobiles have become a more common sight; though of course, only the wealthy drive them. Now, some households even have remarkable machines called *telephones,* polished black boxes with numbers on the front, and a strange, handheld contraption on the top. He's heard people talking into them, and believes their voices are transported to other places, far away. It astounds him, how much is shifting. *Humanity never rests*, he thinks. *And it is never satisfied.*

She leaves Ernst to other chores, then finds Aunt Esme, who is carefully packing her candles and crystal ball, even though they both know the items are only for show. For them, the truth of the future lies in tarot cards and nothing else, though they both know without the appearance of more, they wouldn't earn the trust of their customers.

The caravan is dark. Aunt Esme prefers to keep the door closed, even on a bright autumn morning like this. Only the barest hint of light creeps through the tiny window, lighting a pale path across the top bunk. She looks up as her niece enters, then grunts.

"You need a cold compress on that."

Agnes touches her eye reflectively. "It's too late for that now."

Esme sighs, then closes the lid of the box, smoothing her fingers over the polished wood. "You shouldn't let people see you like that. It is unseemly."

You make it sound as though it's her fault, the ghost thinks furiously. He's never warmed to Aunt Esme, even when he first met her, back when he was alive. He'd asked her to tell him his fortune once, not that he remembers exactly what she said. Only that one card, turned over hastily at the end. *The Hanged Man. Why can't I recollect more about that meeting?* he wonders, not for the first time. It seems odd, to have so hazy a memory of such an event. Sometimes, it worries him, this lack of memory, though it's comforting to think it only occurs sporadically.

"Shall I feed the horses?" Agnes stands by the oven, fingers pressed against one another over the smooth planes of her skirt.

"I've done it already." Esme looks up, then pats the stool beside her. "Sit for a while. You look as though you haven't slept."

"I slept well enough."

"You were tossing and turning as though you had the Devil inside you. Now sit."

Agnes pauses, then obediently rests by her aunt. She seems too tall for this caravan, yet the ghost notices, as he has done before, her knack of merging with her background, fading into the shadows almost as successfully as he does. *She would make a superb ghost,* he thinks, with a wry smile, then wishes he hadn't. The thought of Agnes dying disturbs him greatly, more than he'd like to admit.

"What occurred between you and Ernst last night?" Esme eyes Agnes shrewdly, then places some bread on top of the oven to warm it through. "What made him angry?"

Agnes looks down at her lap. "He is always angry, Aunt Esme. All it takes is the slightest spark to ignite him." Although her eyes are downcast, the ghost can see the sudden blaze of impotent rage within them, before it is gone, concealed behind her usual unreadable expression.

"You don't think your father made the right choice for you?"

"You know what I think." This time, the accusation is clear.

Her aunt tuts, rearranges the bread to heat it better. "It's not your place to think, my dear. That's not how it's done. We women must know our place, after all."

"Yes, Aunt Esme."

Silence. The ghost shifts awkwardly, aware that this is a private moment, yet unable to tear himself away. He finds himself magnetised to this dark, shadow-eyed woman, more than any other living creature. *Perhaps I am just attached to misery,* he thinks, flickering somberly in the dim light. *And her despair is greater than most.*

Esme looks up, eyes squinting. She's done this before, suddenly focusing on him, as alert as a hunting dog. It seems likely that she senses his presence but doesn't know what to make of it.

Be kind, he whispers. *Otherwise, I don't know what will happen to her.*

Agnes breaks the quiet, leaning forward, making herself visible once more. "Shall I make some broth for lunch? We have some potatoes and carrots left over."

"I've prepared something already, girl." Esme casts a final, suspicious look in the ghost's direction, then smiles. "You tend to that eye, quickly now."

"I will, Aunt. Not that I think it'll do any good."

"You must try." The bread, when poked, leaks a path of acrid smoke, which dissipates into the air. "After all," she adds, reaching for the butter, "we wouldn't want Ernst to lose interest in you, would we? You need to keep your looks and keep our family from shame. Yes?"

The ghost's spectral chest constricts with loathing, for the one person in Agnes's life who could make a difference, were she just a little less blind to the despair that rages in her niece's heart.

Agnes only nods, then looks away.

The day passes. The sun rises softly, then falls. At last, the circus is ready to move; a slow procession of bright caravans and rickety animal enclosures. The elephant follows last, leathery in the afternoon light. The ghost wonders if the poor creature remembers Africa, or whatever wild continent it was born on, and whether he mourns for his old homeland. *Things always become more valuable after you've lost them,* he thinks, and falls into step with the tired beast.

It is a relatively short journey to Battersea, and the crowds are already lining the main street, waving and cheering; small children weaving through adult legs, straining for a better view. The ghost sees faces, familiar faces; Mrs Makepeace from the post office, the reverend, so much greyer than he remembers. A few names evade him, a fact he finds frustrating. As a living man, his memory was sharp as cut glass, now it feels dulled at the edges. Perhaps it is a side-effect of being dead. *Probably nothing to worry about,* he reassures himself. *It will come back in time, I am sure.*

Agnes sits behind the reins, whispering to the horse. She shrinks from the attention, as she always does; people in abundance cause her distress, he can tell. That is why she's well suited to fortune telling. It's only ever one person at a time, in safe, predictable surroundings.

The ghost plods on in time to the sway of the elephant's trunk. It is not far now, he knows the field that they're heading to.

It doesn't take long for the circus to establish itself, taking root and sprouting around the nucleus of the garish big top. Poles hoist fabric to the air, colourful signs rise like flags, shouting their wares. Agnes assists her aunt, assembling their humble tent, placing all ornamentation in the correct positions; the crystal ball, the battered table, the monkey skull, showcased on a couple of musty books.

It is Agnes's shift tonight, a chance for her aunt to rest in the caravan, in the dark, clutching her chest, as she so often does. The ghost presumes she has some sort of respiratory problem, but as Esme has never mentioned it, it is difficult to confirm. Her attitude to health is like the rest of her clan; tight-lipped, close-eyed, self-stern. *Whatever she's got, it'll probably kill her,* he thinks, without much compassion.

The calliope trills into a tap-dance of soaring notes. Darkness wraps the circus in its own private realm; an alternative reality of amber light, bellowing voices, the crack of rifles from the shooting range. Business as usual, it would seem.

Agnes goes through the motions, sitting quietly behind her table as customer after customer tiptoes hesitantly through the flaps of the tent; eager yet repelled by the prospect of knowing what's to come. The ghost can see that her heart is not in it. She barely shuffles the cards, reading pasts, presents, and futures in the same monotone. By the time the third dark stranger is mentioned, he even detects the hint of a weary smile, flickering across her face. *She no longer cares about this,* he thinks, standing at her shoulder, resisting the urge to move closer, to feel the warmth of her body. The realisation alarms and excites him in equal measures, because it shows that Agnes is *changing*, though quite how, he isn't sure.

At the end of it all, Ernst pokes his head through the entrance, a red-faced slab of meat, invading an area of quiet contemplation.

"What a night, eh?"

Agnes nods slowly, then returns the tarot cards to their weathered box.

"It's always the provincial folk though, isn't it?" Ernst continues, scrutinising her closely. "They're the ones hungriest for a bit of excitement."

Again, she doesn't answer. She wants him to go away, the violent desire oozes from her like smoke. The ghost wishes he would disappear too, simply vanish without trace, and leave them both alone. His presence is disturbing and unnerving, like a bull in a small field. It's impossible to know when he will next charge.

"Well," Ernst says finally, pushing a shoulder through the opening, forcing further entry. "Why don't you join the rest of us, eh? Bernard has got the guitar out, Greta's already started dancing. You could even have a drink or two, Esme will never know."

"Esme will know." The words ring flat, deterring further response.

It seems Ernst is oblivious to the hint. His brow drops, and the ghost notices how tiny his eyes are; deep-set and shining, like currants pressed in dough. *Like a rat's,* he thinks, and instinctively moves closer to Agnes, who shivers, as though sensing his presence.

"You cannot live like a little girl all the time. You are soon to be my wife, that means growing up, you know."

She nods, and each movement of the head is sadder than any gesture the ghost has ever seen. "I know that," she says quietly.

"That means you giving me more than a kiss too."

"So you say."

Ernst glares, then sighs. The air seems to heat with every breath he takes, as he hogs the available air and boils it in his combustible lungs. The ghost recoils in loathing, wondering how such a creature can continue to exist unimpeded, when people like himself die young every day. *This world isn't fair,* he thinks bitterly.

"You will learn to like me. Your father would want it that way. Why can't you be like the other girls?"

The ghost is close enough to see the shimmer of a tear, hidden in the corner of Agnes's eye. "I don't know," she whispers. "I am sorry."

Don't you dare apologise, the ghost thinks furiously. *You owe him nothing, least of all that.*

Ernst studies her a while longer, then shrugs. "Suit yourself," he mutters, fingers tightening around the fabric of the entrance. "Other women can do what you can't."

And so he departs, with the cruel words dawdling in his absence, like stench on a still day.

The ghost waits. It seems that the atmosphere has darkened, that time has rushed past them both, letting decay settle in without them noticing. He imagines them suddenly, him and her both, remaining still and silent, while the earth changes and dies. *Why is it that we seem to have a sense of permanence, while everyone around us is so fleeting?* he wonders, then questions why such a thought would come into his head. It is strange, unreal, like so much of his existence these days.

She reaches to the candle and draws it nearer, hugging its base like an old friend. The ghost freezes, knowing what will happen next. It has been so long since they have conversed, he had started to worry that Agnes no longer valued their discussions, stilted and discordant as they so often are. His heart leaps at the prospect, of having someone to *hear* him, and acknowledge his existence. He waits, breath held, as her pupils engorge and unhitch themselves from the world around them. Her breathing deepens. The tent constricts, tightening around the two of them, warm as a lover's embrace.

"Are you there?" Her whisper is nervous, yet desperate. *She needs me as much as I need her,* he realises, both thrilled and weighted by the responsibility.

"I am." He hears his voice as she must do; thin, distant, fuzzy. They stand together, yet life forms a chasm between them, forcing them apart.

A hint of a smile touches her face, though there is no happiness in it.

"I wanted to see if you were still with me."

"Of course," he replies, hoping she can hear the fondness in his words. "I won't leave, not if you need me."

"You're a kind person," she mutters. "Or were, perhaps I should say?"

He chuckles. "I hope I still am."

"I sometimes think you are the only person I can talk to."

"What about your husband-to-be?"

"Stop it. You know what he's like."

"Why are you marrying him?" He cannot understand why Agnes doesn't leave; anything other than stay here, letting her life fall into tatters.

"I have to, I've told you before. It's not the same for us circus folk as it is for others." Agnes draws a deep breath, leaning forward on her elbows, eyes still glued to the tall flame. "Are you still looking for your wife? Or have you finally decided to let it go?"

The bite in her voice is unmistakable; the snap of a wounded animal protecting itself. "I can't let it go," he replies.

"But after what you've told me . . ."

"I need to find her and I wish you would help me."

"But I can't. I read tarot cards, but they only work if you touch them. You're dead, so—"

"—I know that. But there are other ways."

She lifts her head, eyes still fixed on the steady flame of the candle. "It's not healthy for you to be like this, you know."

He doesn't want to discuss this, even though the yearning within him is as strong as ever. He has a thought, a vague, dislocated notion that it would not be good for him to think more about his wife at present, that dwelling upon her would bring about sadness. *Why is that?* he wonders, frustrated by the meagreness of his memory. *It's her that I long for the most, yet I'm terrified of finding her. What am I frightened of?*

"What are you going to do?" he asks instead, diverting his thoughts from subjects that discomfort him.

To his distress, she starts to cry. Not silent tears, but full, weighty sobs, which ripple through her shoulders like turbulent waves. He's never seen her like this before, so raw, so exposed. It is flattering and disquieting in equal measures, that she should trust him like this, but also rely on him so heavily.

"I'm sorry," he says impotently. "I didn't mean to make you sad."

At last, a vague smile twitches her lips. "Don't you see? You're the only person that *doesn't* make me sad. I wish . . ."

"Yes?"

"I wish things were different."

But they can't be, he finishes for her. He was born several decades before and died when she was just a girl. Everything separates them, societal expectations, conventions, time itself. There is no escaping the futility of it all.

"You need to leave him," he blurts suddenly, surprised at himself.

"Who, Ernst?" The pupils widen a fraction. The candle sputters briefly, a reaction to her intake of breath.

"Yes. He is no good for you." *There, I've said it,* he thinks, feeling both exhilarated and concerned that he's overstepped the mark.

Agnes chuckles. "I *know* he's no good for me. But in the circus, you obey your parents, your family. And Ernst has been chosen for me."

"He's a brute." The ghost finds that the words tumble out, quite of their own volition, like water spurting from a broken dam. So long he's harboured these thoughts, it is a relief to finally give them voice. "He's not a good person. You deserve more. Why don't you escape from it?"

That tantalising word, *escape*, it fills the small space like an ever-expanding bubble, and he can see her mulling it over, envisaging the results of taking such a step.

"How could I escape?" she mutters bleakly. "There's no way out for people like me. What other life could I possibly build for myself?"

He shakes his head and wishes he could shake her, make her see how much possibility there is in the world, when you have two living lungs to breathe with, and a heart that still beats, and still cares. "You can leave all this," he says firmly, knowing that if he's ever going to persuade her, now is the time to do so. "You can be free."

Agnes's eyes soften. "Now there's an idea. Would I be with you? Would you stay with me?"

Again, that burden of responsibility, combined with the excitement that someone *needs* him, after all this time. Someone he cares for, with whom he likes spending time. It is intoxicating. "Yes," he says softly, "I would be with you."

"Do you promise?"

"I do."

She nods, satisfied, and turns from the candle. At once, the communication is gone, the line severed. He retreats to the shadows, hoping that he's said enough to make the difference, because she *is* worth more, more than all the others put together, and if anyone deserves to be happy, apart from his Eleanor, it is her.

After a while, she stands, pats down her skirt, and returns to her caravan, where Aunt Esme lies snoring in the darkness. The ghost waits by the step, watching the slow passage of the moon as it presses through the night sky. *I have done something good today*, he thinks. *I have eased Agnes's pain, and that makes my existence more worthwhile.*

The night passes. Stars glare fiercely then sigh into dimness, silenced by the oncoming sun. The ghost takes it all in, wondering why he never appreciated such beauty whilst he was living. The senses are wasted on those who have life, and only death brings true wonderment at the world. Somewhere in the distance, a cockerel crows, hoarse and broken in the dawn light. He wonders if it is still the same farmer who owns it, over by the inn on the outskirts of the village.

From within the caravan, a body finally stirs. Feet settle on the floorboards, and a creak announces the awakening of a previously sleeping person. *Aunt Esme,* he guesses, turning instinctively to the door. He hears a murmur, the low groan, presumably grimacing at the stretching of ageing muscles.

Then, a gasp. A breathless shriek. Silence, hasty and rushed as a stab wound.

The ghost feels dread, tomb-dark, blossoming within him, though doesn't know why. He rises, alert. Then the scream comes, as he feared it would, a terrible, hollow sound that rents a passage through the peaceful morning air, followed by a low howl, bovine and bereft.

He knows what has happened. *He knows.*

"Agnes," he whispers, and rests the memory of his fingers against the cool wood, wishing he could draw strength from the solidity of the surface. "No, I didn't mean for you to do that, I didn't."

He ventures inside, though every part of him rails against it. He doesn't want to see, he would give anything not to witness this. But he *needs* to know.

Within the dim interior, he spies Aunt Esme, collapsed on the floor, still screaming into her shapeless nightdress. Then, hanging over the top bunk, he sees the hand, outstretched, blood congealed across the wrist. That is all; a single hand, but such a sorry sight, along with the puddle of blood beneath it.

My fault, he thinks blindly, retreating instinctively from Esme's ferocious unburdening, and the sight of that lifeless arm. *I told Agnes to leave all this. But I didn't mean in this way.*

"What have I done?" he wails, knowing that his misery will be heard by nobody but him.

A spectral hand passes before him, then rests gently on the mists of his forearm. He looks down, knowing immediately who it is, but too ashamed to meet her gaze.

"You can look at me."

"I can't," he whispers back, filled with horror at the sight that awaits him.

"It will be all right."

"Why do you say that?"

"Because I am with you now," Agnes's ghost whispers.

SEVENTEEN

— 1878 —

IT WAS A fine evening, the sky still pleasingly light, especially after the otherworldly darkness of the theatre. I offered Eleanor my jacket, though there wasn't much need; the air was still balmy, with only the hint of a summer breeze.

Martha scampered past me with a shove that was bordering on impertinent, and seized Eleanor's arm. "What did you think of it, then?"

"What, the performance?"

"Of course the performance, silly! I just loved Josephine and Ralph, didn't you?"

Arthur trotted to catch up, with Mother following closely behind. "Martha, I knew it!"

"Knew what?" She stared at her brother, perplexed and irritated in equal measures.

"That you're growing up to be a romantic," Arthur replied, eyes twinkling. "Did you think the man playing Ralph Rackstraw was dashing?"

"Of course I didn't, what a ridiculous thing to say!"

"Methinks the lady doth protest too much."

I chuckled at the sight of Martha's face, reddening by the second. She was far too easy to tease, always had been, even as a toddler. *Poor her,* I thought, giving her shoulder a sympathetic squeeze. It must have been challenging, growing up with three older brothers.

"What did you think of it, Mother?" I asked, falling back to keep her company. Her hip was aching, I could tell by the slight limping of her left foot.

She smiled, sidling her arm through mine. "I wasn't sure I'd like it at first, I'd heard *HMS Pinafore* was rather bawdy, but actually . . ."

". . . You enjoyed it?"

She laughed. "I did. It was a splendid idea, we've all had such a pleasant evening, though I do wish Fred could have joined us. My only concern is at you paying for it all, my love. Are you sure the expense wasn't too—"

I held up a hand, stopping her mid-sentence. It was as much to prevent myself from having to think about our financial situation as anything else. "Don't worry about any of that," I replied, with as much sincerity as I could muster. "It was my pleasure."

"Can we go to the theatre more often, Mother?" Martha raced back, skirt billowing around her. "Every month or so?"

"Absolutely not, you silly girl."

Arthur grasped Martha by the arm and spun her around, oblivious to the disapproving looks of the crowds milling around them. "I shall take you, little sister," he announced, before whirling her to a halt. "Because I am a truly marvellous brother, am I not?"

Eleanor stifled a giggle behind her glove. "Arthur, you are funny."

Passing Mother over to Arthur's waiting arm, I caught up with my wife, and placed a hand around her waist. "Well, the *HMS Pinafore* was hardly Shakespeare, was it?" I whispered, giving her a wink.

She gave me a look that I couldn't decipher. "Not everything has to be highbrow, you know."

That wasn't what I'd meant, but I wasn't sure how to explain. It seemed that Eleanor had been especially brittle towards me as of late; keen to misinterpret my words, no matter how kindly they were meant. I wondered if perhaps she might be with child once more, and the exertion required had tested her nerves. Mother had explained to me, in delicate terms, that this was what happened, when women fell pregnant. However, Eleanor had said nothing to me on the matter, and I felt it imprudent to ask, in case the question caused her suffering.

"Why don't we take a stroll through Westminster?" I suggested, gesturing to the street before us. "Arthur can take Mother and Martha home. It might be nice to take in the evening air, just the two of us."

She softened immediately. "That's a wonderful idea. We could walk to Oxford Street and have a look in the shop windows."

It wasn't exactly what I'd had in mind, but if it made her happy, then so be it. I nodded, then conveyed our plans to the others. Martha's face immediately fell. I could tell by her expression that she was hoping for an invitation to join us, but the prospect of her exuberant chatter whilst I tried to converse with my wife wasn't terribly appealing. I appeased her as best as possible, then left it to Mother to take over. Mother always knew what to say to make things better, thank goodness.

We bid them farewell, waiting as they disappeared into the crowds in the opposite direction.

I patted Eleanor's arm affectionately. "Are you happy to walk? It's some distance, you know."

"Nonsense, it's no distance at all, a brisk twenty-minute walk, if that."

I felt sure she was incorrect, but chose to let it pass. It wasn't worth bickering over, not on a calm, warm night like this. "Did you know the late Dickens used to live around here?" I said, gesturing to the elegant buildings that surrounded us.

"Did he really?" Eleanor looked up, smiling. "He wrote about the poor so much, I presumed he lived in a less well-to-do neighbourhood, like ours."

"Ours isn't that bad," I protested, guiding her across the road. A hansom cab swerved to avoid us, wheels clattering against the pavement. I ignored the expletives and fist-shaking that ensued from the driver, wishing that the good people of London weren't always quite so eager to lose their temper over such trivial matters.

"Oh, come now," she continued, stepping neatly in time with me. "If we were better positioned in life, we'd live somewhere like your brother, wouldn't we?"

"I quite like our little home."

Eleanor sighed. "So do I," she said softly, pressing her head briefly against my shoulder. "But we won't be living there forever, will we?"

I didn't quite know what to say. I'd imagined that we'd reside there quite happily for several years, and her reluctance was unsettling, leaving me feeling somewhat anchorless. Anxiety gnawed inside my stomach, panic that I wasn't living up to her expectations, fear that she might consider that she'd selected the wrong brother, that she should have stuck with Fred after all.

"Darling," she said gently, waiting for me to meet her eyes. "Why the long face? This is meant to be a lovely evening out, let's enjoy it properly, shall we?"

I nodded, then stepped aside for another couple to pass us. To the rest of the world, we were a well-heeled pair; she with a grand velvet hat and full-skirted, well-tailored dress, I with my smart suit and cravat, which she'd recently purchased for me from Liberty. So why was it that I felt a failure; a charlatan, dressed in attire that didn't reflect my true nature?

We walked in silence, each deep in our own private thoughts. After a while, Eleanor laughed nervously. "I think you were right."

"About what?"

"About it taking longer than twenty minutes." Her giggle was infectious. I couldn't help noticing that as she laughed, she held a hand over her stomach, just as she had done before, when there had been a baby there, growing within her. My hopes soared, though I knew it was unwise to let them.

"You weren't *that* wrong," I replied gallantly. "Perhaps only by quarter of an hour or so." I paused, then raised my eyebrows. "Or maybe half an hour."

A playful slap on the elbow was the reward for my comment. The sun eased gently behind the buildings next to us, forming a hazy halo that cast long shadows across the street. I felt happier than I had done in weeks. Months, perhaps. *What more could a man want?* Here I was, with a beautiful wife, a steady job, a comfortable home; admittedly not as grand as desired, but still, what else did one need in life?

"You seem deep in thought," Eleanor said eventually.

"Deep in happiness," I replied. "I am a lucky man."

We reached Oxford Street just as the sun had finally set. The sky was a myriad of colours; rich navy, spreading to a peaceful blue, with pink clouds settling in the distance. *Red sky at night, shepherd's delight,* I thought instinctively. Father had always said that, believing it to be an unshakeable truth, no matter how many times the weather proved to the contrary. It had been a red sky in the morning on the day he'd died. Arthur and I had been present. Fred had refused, unsurprisingly. Strange, how such a detail should remain with me, though in all honesty, I didn't dwell on his death much, nor any person's death, for that matter.

"Look at this display," Eleanor said, pointing at the nearest store. "What fine fabric, don't you think?"

"I suppose so." It looked much like any other velveteen material I'd ever seen, though admittedly, the waning light cast a soothing gleam across it. "Why, are you considering it for—"

My attention was suddenly diverted by a commotion, further down the road. Someone cursed, a raucous, shrill voice that jarred with the surroundings. Squinting, I immediately identified the source of the disturbance, a man angrily gesturing at a single woman, his wife nervously hanging on to his arm. Likewise, Eleanor's grip upon me tightened.

"I say, what's going on down there?"

"Some sort of argument, perhaps?" Eleanor peered down the street, jaw clenched. "Whoever it is, she looks rather out of place. That bonnet is at least three seasons old."

"Hang on a moment." I narrowed my eyes, focusing on the woman as she marched urgently towards us. "That lady, she looks an awful lot like—"

"Goodness, it can't be, can it?"

But it was. Elizabeth Stride, unchanged from the last time we'd seen her, chin still as defiantly set as ever. Eleanor hadn't been wrong about her attire; her skirts were faded and rough with washing, her bonnet crooked on her head.

She met my eye, and to my horror, stopped before us, brow lowered in a manner that was positively simian.

"Were you looking for me?"

"Excuse me?" I stuttered, thrown by the strangeness of her question. I'd forgotten how heavy her accent was, glottal and rolling, the English vowels weighting her tongue like ball bearings.

Elizabeth Stride snorted, then straightened her bonnet. "Don't bother denying it. Fred sent you to track me down. Well, you tell him that—"

"—Really, I must protest," I interrupted, hand raised to silence her. "We were merely taking an evening stroll, I had no notion that you would be here, and—"

"My foot you didn't. I know how persistent your brother is. It's harassment, that's what it is. Regardless of my standing in life, he has *no right,* no right at all, do you hear me? It's frightening, and I've got enough to be concerned with, without him stalking after me like that. I'll go to the police, tell him that I will. He'll get thrown back in gaol again, where he belongs."

"Now, hang on a minute," I said, confounded by her words. "What are you trying to say? That Fred has been bothering you? Why would he do such a thing to someone like you?"

The words came out more scathingly than I'd meant them to. A brief flicker of hurt crossed the woman's face, before her expression hardened again.

"I may be poor, but that doesn't mean a man can mistreat me as he likes," she muttered, glaring at us both as though daring us to disagree.

"Dearest Elizabeth," Eleanor said, choosing her words carefully, "why don't you come with us, let us buy you some food or something? You look half-starved, you're much thinner than when we last saw you. And I don't like to see you looking so alarmed. You keep glancing over your shoulder as though someone's going to attack you at any moment."

My heart warmed with the kindness of the sentiment. It was so like my wife, to think of someone's welfare, no matter how disreputable or unpleasant they may be. And she was correct. Elizabeth Stride's posture was tense, alert, much like a terrified animal, ready to flee at a minute's notice. *What on earth has Fred been up to?* I wondered. I felt ill-equipped to deal with a situation such as this.

Unfortunately, Eleanor's generous offer failed to have the desired effect. Instead, Elizabeth Stride's mouth tightened, lips narrowing to a single harsh line. "Is that your trick, then?" She sneered, taking a step back. "Take me somewhere where Fred's waiting for me? Is that right?"

"No," Eleanor protested, looking at me in alarm. "Of course not. I only meant it kindly."

"Very well. Whether you did or not, I'll decline your offer. You tell Fred that he needs to leave me be, do you hear? I'm back with Thomas, I'm *married* to Thomas, and that's all there is to it."

Heavens, she's a married woman, I thought, groaning inwardly. *That idiot brother of mine, he was courting another man's wife.* How had it happened? Had Fred known, or had this woman deceived him? What sort of life had Fred been living, to end up in a situation like this?

"Mrs Stride," I said, sensing that she was about to depart, and swiftly too. "Please, before you leave, could you tell me where Fred is at present? We hear very little from him, contrary to what you might believe. And your words cause me concern."

I met her gaze evenly, watching a range of emotions flit through her grey eyes; suspicion, confusion, doubt. Perhaps even a hint of compassion, concealed somewhere in the depths.

"Last I heard," she said quietly, leaning closer, "he was in with a bad crowd."

I grimaced at her words. "What, criminals, do you mean?"

She shook her head. "Worse than that. There are people in this city that do terrible, evil deeds. Do you understand?"

"I understand the notion of evil, but not what you mean by it." Her words alarmed me. What were her implications? That Fred was involved in something unspeakable? It didn't tally with the brother I knew. Fred could be thoughtless and ignorant at times, but he wasn't a bad person, and he certainly wasn't capable of serious wrongdoing, unless time had changed him in ways I couldn't conceive of.

Eleanor tugged at my arm, nodding to the people around us. "I'm not sure we should be having this conversation, especially not here, out in public. Can we—"

"—No, I need to know." It was true, though I hadn't meant to remove my arm quite so brusquely. Eleanor looked hurt, but said nothing. "Mrs Stride, can you tell me where Fred is? I need to try to find him, it sounds as though he may be in danger."

She stared at the ground, then finally shook her head. "I can't. I won't be a part of this, it's too risky. You find him on your own; I'm sure you'll manage, with all your money and fancy acquaintances."

"Please, just a few more questions, I . . ." My sentence trailed into nothing as I watched Elizabeth Stride shake her head, then continue her determined march up the street. We stared after her, waiting until she'd disappeared around the corner, then turned to one another.

"How peculiar," Eleanor commented, biting her lip. "What on earth do you make of all that?"

I raised a hand to my cheek, feeling somehow bruised by the encounter. "I don't know," I mumbled eventually, watching as the lamplighters started the business of illuminating the darkening street. "But I didn't like it, not one bit." The words *terrible* and *evil* ran through my head, insistent as clanging bells, daring me to probe further, to imagine the full weight of their implications.

Eleanor tapped my arm, trying to rouse me from my thoughts. "She was probably speaking falsely."

I wasn't so sure. Although Elizabeth Stride undoubtedly was not a woman to be trusted, there had been something about the urgency of her expression, the force of her claims, that made me believe her. Behind that blustering, aggressive façade, I'd caught a glimpse of a frightened female, and that worried me more than anything.

"What do you suppose she meant, about Fred being involved with people who were worse than criminals?"

Eleanor shook her head firmly. "I don't think we should be having this conversation, darling. After all, this is the ranting of a low woman we're talking about. Why not confide in Arthur, if you're concerned? He'll know what to do."

I frowned at the comment, offended by the suggestion that my younger brother would have better ability to address the situation than I, despite the fact that she was probably right. *Money has an uncanny knack of uncovering the truth,* I thought bitterly, thinking of my own dwindling funds. *And Arthur has plenty of it.*

"I'll look into it myself," I said firmly, then nodded back the way we'd come. A couple of hansom cabs were lined beside the pavement, waiting to return weary people to their houses. "Come on, let's go home, shall we?" The whole experience with Elizabeth Stride had soured the mood, leaving me oddly disquieted.

Eleanor peered down Oxford Street, her gaze flitting from window to window, before sighing. "Yes, I suppose so," she agreed. "It's getting rather late, and Miss Stride has proved that this area can attract rather unsavoury types."

"*Mrs* Stride, you mean."

She covered her mouth, stifling a horrified laugh. "Gosh, yes. Isn't it terrible? Whatever was Fred *thinking*?"

"As long as Mother never finds out." I clicked a finger at the nearest driver, who whipped his horse obligingly, trotting it along to meet us. "The shock would kill her, I'm sure."

"Not your mother, she's invincible, isn't she?"

I smiled, welcoming the flippancy after such a shocking encounter. "I rather think you're right, my dear. Though my goodness, had Father still been alive, he would have had something to say about it." The driver flipped the lock on the door, and we climbed aboard gratefully.

Surely Elizabeth Stride can't have meant what she said, I thought, scanning the street for signs of the unfortunate creature. She could have gone anywhere, down any narrow alley, through any door. I realised that I knew virtually nothing about her, only a vague mixture of rumour and the occasional fact. Who was she? Where did she live? If she was married, did she have children? Was she a woman of the streets, as I had long since suspected? She certainly had the look about her.

She's sure to come to an unfortunate end, I thought, and shivered. I caught sight of Eleanor's expression and guessed that she'd been thinking much the same thing. But then, was there any point worrying over such a person, when there was nothing to be done to help her?

Still, I worried all the same. And I worried about Fred too; and for some strange reason, which didn't make any sense, I worried for myself too.

Sacrifice, the fortune teller in the tent had said, staring down at the image of the Hanged Man card. *Lost at sea. Cast adrift forever.* Why was it that that particular encounter still haunted me, when it should have been regarded as a trifling matter, of no importance whatsoever?

But still, her words often tormented me, and now, more so than ever.

A sacrifice will be made, she had said.

I shivered, despite the warmth of the evening, then firmly forced the memory from my mind.

EIGHTEEN

— 1888 —

THE GHOST CANNOT think. No, that is not entirely true. He *cannot bear to think.*

He saw George again today, tousle-haired and dirty-kneed, feeding ducks by the pond with Mother, who is older now, of course, her spine starting to noticeably hunch and twist. He'd stayed with them all afternoon, watching George, watching his mother, plus Martha with her new beau, a thin-faced man with kind eyes and red hair. And Arthur too, who is stouter now, but somehow wearier, his eyes less affable than before.

My family, he'd thought, and the words had caught in him like a fishhook, twisting his insides, causing his vision to blur. It had been too much for him, and he had departed, blind to his surroundings, desperate to silence the agony in his heart.

Now, he wanders, and his only instinct is to escape, to get far away from the pain of it all. They have forgotten him, they have all continued with their lives. Martha, still a girl in his memory, has become a woman in his absence, with a prospect of marriage on the horizon. *Does she ever think of me?* he wonders, and knows that he would weep, had he eyes to cry with. *Does she ever lie awake at night and think of the brother she lost? Does Mother still tend to my grave? And Arthur? How does he feel?*

George, he says to himself sadly, knowing the boy will never think of him, that his name is merely a distant mist in the darkness, a blot on an otherwise joyous young life. For young George has everything a child could ever want; toys in abundance, a governess to teach him, the finest sweets to tempt him. He is coddled, humoured, adored. *What more could a boy possibly need in life?* Bitterness swamps him like mud, along with the knowledge that Arthur has the ability to provide his son with everything. He is the father every child deserves, and this only makes the ghost feel more of a failure. He thinks back to Eleanor, and to her first miscarriage. *So much blood, so many tears,* he remembers. *And nothing to show for it after.* He thrusts the memory away, rejecting it, consigning it to the darkest, most unreachable recesses inside himself.

What use is memory, anyway? He curses, drifting from street to street, heedless of where he is going. *It only causes me pain, remembering these things, when the living have already forgotten.*

It comes as no surprise that he ends up in Whitechapel. He often finds himself here, among the ruffians, the beggars, the lewd women with their loosened stays and shabby dresses. He passes The Ten Bells; a notorious public house even when he was alive, which is crawling with people, their combined breaths misting the windows.

How welcome it would be, to drink myself into an oblivion, he thinks, imagining the rich warmth of wine at the back of his throat, or a cool ale on a summer's day. He remembers himself and Arthur, toasting one another at his wedding. Hastily, he stifles the memory down, thinking *not now, not while I am like this.* Forgetfulness is *everything* at present. And so, he strives to keep his mind blank, focusing only on the here and now; the surrounding street, the people passing him by. It is a poor way to survive, but it will have to do.

Quite how he finds himself in the next public house, the Princess Alice, he does not know. The name itself is enough to make him shudder, the irony not lost on him. *The perfect place for a dead person such as I to linger,* he thinks, and eases himself onto a bench, beside a whiskered old man and a woman with few teeth left in her head.

If I try hard enough, I could almost imagine the press of the wood against the back of my thighs, he thinks, biting back a dull laugh. *I could smell the cheap alcohol and pipe-smoke, feel the heat of all this human flesh, compressed into one space. I could dream I was really here, breathing, sweating, and laughing like the rest of them.*

How he wishes he could forget it all. He would give anything to forget. *God, grant me the gift of memory loss,* he thinks, leaning into the old man beside him, sneering as he shivers. It gives him pleasure, to see that he can still affect people, albeit on a meagre level. He still *matters,* a small amount. He is *still here.*

A glass shatters, cutting through the drone of voices, glittering tiny shards across the floor. A violent act it appears, judging by the shouting that follows, then the shoving, the leery bellow of drunken, swaying men. Someone laughs, grating and guttural as a raven. The worst of humanity is here, it would seem, and that is exactly what he needs; to be surrounded by aggression, commotion, and confusion.

Indeed, there is more tension in the atmosphere than usual; a sense of apprehension and poorly concealed suspicion. It is due to the recent spate of murders, or so he believes; prostitutes, either stabbed or mutilated in some terrible manner. Not that he follows the news much anymore, only the snippets of hushed conversations that he hears as he drifts through the city; the mutterings of street-traders, the frightened prattle of women, pushing their babies in rattling perambulators. *Leather Apron,* they whisper, no doubt referring to some miscreant in the area; or more lately, *Jack the Ripper,* though goodness knows where the name has come from. Some fanciful journalist or other, no doubt.

He watches the brawl, keen to absorb it all. A man stumbles, then falls across a table, only to be shoved unceremoniously to the floor. Somewhere in the crowd, a woman shrieks a name, over and over, *John, John, you silly beggar, pick yourself up, John!* Perhaps a wife, a sister, a mother. *A woman who hasn't forgotten a loved one,* he thinks darkly, studying them all.

Then he sees her by the bar, a woman he hasn't set eyes on in years. It is undoubtedly her; she has the same long face, wide-jawed, though the hair is greying at the temples, just slightly. As for that steadfast, dispassionate gaze, he'd remember it from anywhere.

Elizabeth Stride. Fred's woman. No, not his woman, he's remembered that wrongly. She was married to someone else, she'd once shouted the information at him on a busy London street. He peruses the men surrounding her, wondering which one is her husband, if he is with her at all. *If he ever existed,* he thinks cruelly. She hadn't been a woman to be trusted then, and he doubts she is now.

The chaos subsides. John, whoever he may be, picks himself off the floor, rubbing his back. Someone passes him an ale. Normal conversation resumes. The ghost rises, gliding closer, magnetised by the prospect of hearing Elizabeth Stride's heavy, rolling accent after all this time.

She is talking to a man; she speaks with a stutter that he doesn't remember her having before. Her black jacket and skirt are incongruously dark in the lively surroundings, giving her hawkish form a severity that suits her fierce expression. He edges closer, though why he's attempting surreptitiousness, he's not sure. It's still instinctive, even after so much time spent being dead.

They do not know one another well, that much is obvious. It is an arranged, yet awkward meeting; her posture is largely uninterested, going through the motions, the man's nervous, agitated even. He wonders what the nature of their relationship is. The man continues to raise a hand to his short moustache, tweaking the sides as though seeking solace from it. He clutches a parcel against his lapels.

Finally, she leans into the bar, fixing him with a look that means only one thing; raw, defensive, and inevitable.

"Shall we go somewhere more private?"

The man coughs, then looks over his shoulder. "Pray tell me," he whispers, moving closer, lit up with anticipation. "How much might this encounter cost me?"

She hisses a price under her breath, the exact amount lost under the general hubbub. The ghost shakes his head, horrified and fascinated.

He'd always suspected her of this low sort of behaviour, and here it was, tangible evidence. Distaste rises within him like bile.

"I've a room, over in Berner Street. Shall we?"

The man drains his glass, then jumps visibly at the sudden hand on his shoulder; a large, strong hand, laced with protruding veins. The ghost glances up, intrigued at this sudden turn of events, then freezes.

Fred. He finds himself face-to-face with the brother he thought he'd lost in the swathes of time; now here before him, leaner, hollow-faced, and ferocious as a wild animal. For a moment, the ghost is frightened, even though no harm can come to him. The echo of a long-forgotten conversation returns to him. *Terrible. Evil.* Is this what his elder brother is? Certainly, he cannot reconcile this rage-filled, sinewy man with the amiable boy of his youth.

"Elizabeth," Fred mutters without blinking.

The ghost can see that she has paled, turned an odd shade of green, even. He wonders if she is going to be sick.

"I thought your name was Anne?" The moustached man pipes up, grasping his parcel more tightly.

"Fred," Elizabeth whispers, pressing herself against the bar. Her body language worries the ghost, because it is the frightened movement of a creature trapped by a predator; not the self-assured stance she normally adopts. He wishes, as he has so often before, that he had a physical form to use, that he could influence the situation, rather than impotently watching it unfold before his eyes.

"I told you the other day not to run from me."

"Not here, not now. We'll t-talk later, honestly, but this isn't the t-t-time . . ."

"She's with me," the other man says grandly, though his hitched breathing reveals his anxiety.

Fred sneers, then pushes the man aside. "Not anymore, she isn't. You'll talk to me *now*, Elizabeth, or I swear I'll murder Michael Kidney, I'll find him now and gut him like a fish. I'll throw him in the docks."

The ghost shudders to hear his brother talk so callously. It is as though something has possessed him, taken ownership of his body and driven him to madness.

"You leave Michael out of this, I'm n-not with him anymore—"

"—Not what I heard. I heard you were living with him."

She takes a deep breath, straightens, then threads a thin hand through the moustached man's arm. "Do excuse this man," she says deliberately, glaring in Fred's direction. "He's an . . . an old acquaintance." Pressing a finger on Fred's waistcoat, she hisses, "We'll talk later. Don't you d-dare follow."

Fred watches, open-mouthed, as she pushes through the crowds, dragging the man with her. Then she is gone, the door swinging wildly in her aftermath. The crowds resettle, as though the path she walked through them never existed.

My brother, the ghost thinks, scarcely daring to move any closer. This man is achingly familiar, yet frighteningly alien. Strings of memories dance before him; making a wooden sleigh in Father's shed, sliding in the mud on the little path behind their house. He remembers Fred then, a handsome boy, tall for his age, dark eyed, swarthy as an Italian peasant. Always ready for a jape, eager to laugh at a situation, rather than let it get him down.

Then Father died, and that changed everything. He remembers the day well and wishes he didn't. Mother's solitary wail, vulnerable as a child, muffled as she pressed her face against the bedsheets. His father's hands, folded too neatly across his chest. Fred had left the house, simply opened the front door, and walked into the distance. He'd returned late in the evening and had refused to speak to anyone.

What did Father say to him, before he died? Fred had never said. It's certain that he'll never find out now. The secret will stay within his older brother, for better or worse.

Now, Fred's features have somehow depleted, folding in on themselves, like poorly risen batter. Years of smoking and drinking have started to weather him already, turning his skin to tanned leather, though his eyes remain as shrewd as ever.

He wonders if Eleanor has seen him like this. If she could reconcile the wretched, haggard figure here with the good-looking, irascible young man he'd been back then.

Oh, Fred, he thinks, wishing he could touch his brother. *I wronged you. I didn't know it at the time, but I did. If it's any comfort, I'm suffering for it now.*

They remain like that for a time, brother beside brother, though the fibre of life forms a chasm between them. It is comforting, on some level; the pair of them, washed with misery, fighting to run from their memories.

Fred drinks an ale, then another. His eyes glaze, and for a moment, the ghost is certain that his brother *senses* him, that he is aware of his presence in some vague, semi-drunken manner. He reaches across tentatively, and touches him.

His brother's expression softens, for a second or two. The ghost dares not move. Then, without warning, Fred pulls his hand away, slams the empty glass on the sticky bar, and presses his way to the door, just as Elizabeth Stride had done before him. The ghost wonders where he is going. Home, perhaps. Or just to pace the streets, as he himself does so often. *Maybe it runs in the family,* he thinks with a rueful smile. Hastily, he follows, remembering how fast Fred is when he sets his mind to it. An elderly couple lurch through the door just as he's exiting, and he moves aside instinctively, before chastising himself for forgetting. Old habits die hard, it would seem.

The pavements outside glow with the warm light from the pub, before reaching into darkness. He scans the street, gaze moving from one pool of light cast by the street lamps to the next, but none of the figures look like Fred; they're either too stout, too short, or too feminine. Finally, he makes out a silhouette in the distance, pacing furiously, shoulders hunched. *It must be him,* he thinks, swiftly drifting closer. *There's no possibility that he could have walked any further in such a short space of time.*

The figure moves alarmingly fast, head down, hands shoved deep into trouser pockets. Wherever he's going, he's going there with purpose, that much is clear. The ghost wonders if Fred is heading towards Elizabeth Stride's dwelling. Where had she said she had a room again? Berner Street, that was it. The same street he used to work on. Funny how the passing of time seemed to tie him so often to this place, almost like it had been scripted long ago, and he is merely a player in a larger piece, acting out his turn.

The man turns a corner, and the ghost hurries to catch up. Anxiety is building within him, though he doesn't understand why. After all, what is the worst that Fred could do? Find his old flame and shout at her again? Try to locate this Michael Kidney, whoever he may be, and beat the living daylights out of him?

He's not a violent man, the ghost reminds himself, even though he's unconvinced. He remembers Fred as a child, holding his head a fraction too long underwater in the river. Or pushing Arthur against a wall after an argument, so hard he'd dislocated his shoulder bone. *He has the potential to hurt people,* he admits. *But never maliciously. Never intentionally. He's not a bad person, regardless of what Father said that day.*

The ghost reaches Berner Street and cannot see his brother anywhere. *Perhaps he went a different way,* he thinks, looking behind him, though deep down, he knows this is where Fred is. The only question is, which abode is Elizabeth Stride's? She made no mention of a house number.

A group of skull-capped men pass him, loudly discussing something to do with the rights of Jews. He watches them pass, then notices the quiet after they have gone. By day, the street echoes with the bangs and thuds of the cartwright's hammer, or the steady footstep of a businessman, on his way to work. By night, its inhabitants stick to the shadows; nothing but gleaming, watchful eyes from alleyways and doorsteps. Occasionally, the ghost has moments when he is glad he isn't alive, when death provides him the gift of invulnerability. This is one of those times.

The Cartwright. He looks up. The familiar cartwheel still hangs on the wall, marking the entrance to Dutfield's Yard. The ghost stops, then wonders. After all, there's nowhere else that Fred could have concealed himself on the street, unless he's darted down one of the alleyways, though no one in their right mind would do so in this area.

It's the darkness that he notices first. Not the natural shadows created by the surrounding buildings, but the *blackness,* the soupy mist that he's come to associate with danger, misery, and despair. This is a *bad* place, something terrible is happening, and instinctively, he moves close to the reassuring solidity of the wall, reluctant to peer too far into the deserted yard.

He doesn't notice anything out of the ordinary at first, only the stairs to the workshop, casting staggered shadows on the cobbled ground; and the door to the outhouse, swinging half-open like a slack mouth. Then his gaze travels naturally downwards to the bundled shape, haphazardly strewn on the floor beside the iron grating.

Feet, he observes dumbly, noting the protruding shoes, pointed primly to the wall. Then, he spies a hand, fingers outstretched. Something about that naked palm, still touching a paper bag, spilling what looks like nuts across the ground, is more pitiful than he can stand. The darkness shifts around the body, palpable as a living creature. Despite himself, he looks to the face, knowing that he *must* see. For him, it is as unavoidable as existence itself.

It's her, as he knew already that it would be. *Elizabeth Stride.* He notices the silk handkerchief at her throat, a strange pattern decorating the fabric, which he realises is spreading blood. The gash at her neck glistens in the low moonlight.

Instinctively, he scans the area, though it takes him a moment to appreciate what he's searching for. *Her ghost.* For she is undoubtedly dead or dying fast; no one could survive a wound like that. The puddle around her head still spreads, casting a halo of darkness around her splayed hair.

He does not have to wait long.

Her spirit rises from her body, hollowed and greyed by death. He watches, fascinated, as she pauses, studying her own lifeless form with clinical disinterest. *How unsurprised she seems,* he thinks, amazed by her composure. *Almost as though she anticipated this moment.*

She looks up, the thin light catching what was once her strong nose, her low brow.

"You?" Confusion wrinkles her features. "Why? Why *you*?"

"Why am I here, you mean?" The ghost is lost for words, uncertain how to explain his presence. He can detect her quick mind making the links, connecting himself and Fred, and suspecting the worst.

"Did he do it?"

"No." The ghost replies before he allows himself a chance to think. "No, he never would."

She sneers, and he shrinks back.

"It doesn't matter now, anyway. I knew I'd get it in the end."

And with those words, she vanishes, shockingly passing from existence to nothingness.

Goodbye, Elizabeth Stride, he thinks, studying the sky with something like sadness; not because of any warm feeling towards her, but for the sense of what she could have been, had she lived a different life. But now it is too late. She has gone, and like him, her life has ceased to have any meaning anymore. *How swiftly it is all over.*

Now, he searches for something different; for *someone*. The deed was done only a few minutes earlier, the murderer may still be here, lurking in the shadows, or concealed behind the lavatory door.

It wasn't Fred, he tells himself, still haunted by Elizabeth Stride's final, defeated words. He remembers the rumours, the mumbled stories of murderers lurking in dark shadows, gutting unwary women like helpless fish. *No,* he reassures himself, wishing he could summon more conviction. *It can't have been him. Some other man did this, I'm certain of it.*

He ventures further down the yard, knowing that he's safe, that he cannot be seen, but filled with fear, nonetheless. It's because of the *evil* that is here, a sharp spice that thickens the air around him. He's reluctant to turn his back on the body, even though he understands well enough that it's only a vacant shell now, nothing more.

The stables at the end of the yard are empty. The dark space beneath the wooden stairs is deserted. *No one's here,* he reassures himself. *The murderer, whoever they may be, has fled.*

A shout, some distance away, freezes him. He hears a clatter of metal, a tool being disturbed perhaps, then sees a silhouette, racing away, out of the yard. The shouting swells, a suspicious voice that turns to alarm. *Someone has seen her,* he realises, rooted in place like a guilty creature. *The crime has been discovered.*

He is relieved when the man appears at the entrance to the yard, illuminated by the neighbouring lamplight; even more relieved when he starts to shout more loudly, braying for attention. And relieved most of all that he is no longer solely responsible for watching over her body, for in truth, he cannot bear the sight of it. It's not only that the murdered body belongs to someone he briefly knew, nor that the foul darkness still swirls around her. It's the misery of knowing that her life was unhappy, and her death even more so.

There is no justice in this world, he thinks, staring at the night sky overhead, willing it to take him, to rid him of the strain of feeling like this, day after day, night after night. But he understands that wishing is useless. Prayers are futile.

Unlike Elizabeth Stride, whose sadness has now come to an end, his seems likely to continue. It is an unendurable thought.

NINETEEN

— 1878 —

THE NOISE WAS intolerable, the crush of bodies even more so. Although the *Princess Alice*'s ticket-men were doing their best to manage the crowds, the surge of person after person was proving too much for them, resulting in a continual press of warm hands, shoulders, and bellies against us.

Eleanor seemed not to notice. Every time I glanced down to her, I noticed how bright her expression was, how she was absorbing every moment of this, storing it for future memories. I also noticed the loving clutch of her hand against her stomach. I'd asked her, tentatively, a few days ago, whether she was with child again, but she'd only shook her head, casting her eyes coyly to the kitchen sink. From her expression, I'd presumed the answer was negative, and hadn't liked to press her on the matter.

"I had no idea there would be so many people joining us," I muttered, as we shuffled closer to the gates.

"Whatever did you imagine, then?" She pointed at the deck, which was already filling with those fortunate enough to have already clambered aboard. "We often watch the ships go past, and they're always heaving with people, aren't they?"

I conceded the point with a non-committal shrug. Just because it was to be expected didn't mean I liked it. I detested the invasion of my personal space, and found it hard not to push back against those who surrounded me. Sometimes, I wished Mother hadn't raised me so well, that I might jostle and shove like the rest of them.

Finally, we reached the front of the queue, such that it was. The poor ticket-officer looked half-dead, his eyes appraising the people behind us with open exhaustion.

"Two, is it?"

Eleanor smiled at me. I grinned back. "Yes, that's correct. How much?"

"Four shillings."

Not as much as I'd suspected, but still enough to make me inwardly groan. I paid, and we shuffled our way through, tiptoeing along the gangplank. The muddy waters glugged and lapped at the bank beneath us, clearly visible through the wooden slats. Eleanor strode forward confidently, oblivious to my anxiety, and I had no choice but to follow, herded sheep-like onto the boat by the trail of passengers behind me.

We ventured inside first. The interior was impressive, even I was forced to admit it. Polished panelling lined every wall, and already, the plush seating was filled with people, all wearing near identical expressions of excitement and merriment.

"Isn't it lovely?" Eleanor exclaimed, beaming at the couple next to us, who were far more shabbily dressed than us. Indeed, the ship seemed to attract people from all walks of life; from waxed-moustachioed gentlemen to women with drab shawls and even drabber dresses.

"It is very fine indeed," I agreed, momentarily enchanted by the décor. I peered out the window to see a few people still scuttling up the gangplank, then pointed. "They really do pack them on, don't they?"

"Well, if you wanted something exclusive, you'd have to pay far more."

"This was costly enough." I gestured to the door. "Did you want to stand on deck and take in the sights? Or did you want to visit the dining area?"

"I'd imagine the dining room will be full to bursting at this time, wouldn't you?" We looked around, bewildered and enthused by the sea of faces that surrounded us. I'd only been on board for a few minutes, and already I was longing for the moment we could disembark at Gravesend, and take a turn around the Rosherville Gardens, which had been highly recommended to us by Arthur. By night, they were illuminated with hundreds of brightly coloured lights, which was quite magical, or so he'd told us. Regardless of whether he'd been exaggerating or not, the description was enough to send Eleanor into fits of excitement, and to double her efforts to convince me to take her.

"Shall we look for a place to sit down?" Eleanor said, clutching me tightly. "I'm quite eager to rest my legs, aren't you?"

"Perhaps later?" The last thing I wanted was to jostle with people for a seat.

"How about exploring the rest of the boat, then?"

Before I could answer, a loud roar cut through the hubbub, followed swiftly by a ponderous thudding noise, which I soon realised was the paddles, whirring into action through the water. Sure enough, a moment later, the boat lurched into motion, cutting through the river like a prehistoric beast wading through a swamp. It was magical and disconcerting in equal measures, though despite my reservations, I couldn't help but appreciate the experience. It felt safer inside, somehow; completely removed from the watery world that enveloped us. I wondered how many people aboard could swim.

"Do you think they have lifeboats?" I asked nervously, much to the amusement of the elderly woman beside me.

Eleanor shook her head in disbelief. "Oh, darling, everything will be fine. Don't worry. And yes, for your information, I saw a lifeboat attached to the side."

"Just the one?" I nodded around the room. "There are hundreds of people on board."

"Stop worrying. Nothing bad will happen. Now," she continued playfully, waving a hand at the door closest to us, "shall we take a turn around the boat, see what other rooms there are?"

"I'm not sure," I replied, peering through the bevelled glass. "It looks awfully crowded in there. Why don't we stand outside?" I gestured out of the window to the banks beyond. Already, the boat was maintaining a good speed in the water, with houses, trees, and people passing us at a rapid rate. A lone man walking his dog waved at us, and Eleanor waved back, her satin glove gleaming in the autumn light.

"Go on then," she said generously. "Let's have a breath of fresh air."

I peered out of the main doors. The decks were already filled to the brim with passengers pointing at the passing landscape, or conversing with those around them. "I doubt we'll be able to see anything, though," I said, ensuring that Eleanor and I kept close to the reassuring solidity of the boat's wall, rather than the flimsy railings. "We'll never get through the crowd."

She groaned. "Come now, don't be a spoilsport. We'll just do what everyone else does."

"What's that?"

"Push our way to the front."

Before I could protest, Eleanor had launched towards the rows of backs lining the sides of the deck, muttering 'excuse me' and 'I do beg my pardon' so many times, I couldn't help but laugh. I followed in her stead; ever her quiet shadow, willing to bathe in the gloriousness of her sunny demeanour. Eleanor was at her finest when she was like this; exuberant, daring, and joyous.

The wind hit me full in the face, reeking with the scent of the Thames; rotting seaweed, muck, and sewage. Indeed, the river was full of the latter, which immediately made my eyes water. Eleanor seemed not to notice, only clutched the railings until her knuckles whitened, eagerly leaning out to take in as much of our surroundings as possible.

"Please," I muttered, squeezing next to her, "do be careful. I don't want anything to happen to you."

She turned to me, then without warning, kissed me on the cheek. The moisture of her lips chilled in the breeze.

"Don't worry, nothing will happen to me," she replied, snuggling into my shoulder.

"How can you be so sure?"

She smiled. "Because you'll always be there to protect me, won't you? I mean, that's what you do best."

I considered her statement. Was that how people saw me? As a protective figure, first and foremost? I supposed there were worse things I could be.

She took my silence for agreement, and stood beside me, silently enjoying the experience. Around us, passengers chatted, laughed, and moved around, some retreating to the interior because of the autumnal weather, others keen to endure the wind and make the most of the unique view of the outskirts of the city.

"Why did you ask your mother if she wanted to join us?" The question was sudden and unexpected. I scanned her face, trying to determine the root cause of it. In truth, I'd only invited her last weekend as she'd been complaining about being stuck in the house all the time, but at the time, I'd noticed a twitch on Eleanor's features, as though she hadn't quite approved.

"Well." I rubbed my nose, struggling to think of the right words. "I suppose I just feel sorry for the old girl sometimes, that's all."

"Yes, but it's strange that you'd invite her and not Arthur, when you knew how much he wanted to come."

I stiffened at the comment. "If I'd invited Arthur along," I said eventually, "then it would hardly have been a romantic trip, would it?"

"What, and it would if your mother had been with us?" She laughed, causing the family behind us to look over with open curiosity.

"No, of course not. But if I'd invited Arthur, I would have ended up inviting everyone else anyway." *And it would have cost a small fortune,* I finished silently. *Or even worse, Arthur would have offered to pay and I would have been entirely humiliated.*

"At least Arthur is always good fun."

"What do you mean by that?"

"Nothing, of course." Her gaze sidled away from me like snow sliding off a branch. "Only that you do take things terribly seriously all the time. There's nothing wrong with enjoying life, you know."

"Isn't that what we're doing now?"

"I suppose so."

Awkwardness lingered between us, where there had only been affection before, jarring us apart, making me feel dislocated, cast adrift. I studied her out of the corner of my eye and was surprised to see her smiling.

"Let's not bicker," she whispered. "After all, this is meant to be a special occasion for us, isn't it?"

I nodded, though the feeling of disquiet remained. The river suddenly seemed threatening; a living thing slithering beneath us, waiting for an opportunity to pounce. I loosened my collar, sweating despite the coolness of the air.

Eleanor nodded across the deck to a group of women, laughing gaily and pointing to the other side of the Thames. Their skirts were slightly too short to be decent, and I could even detect a glimpse of bare ankle. Hastily, I looked away.

"I say," Eleanor whispered, leaning close to my ear. "Do you think those women are . . ."

I waited, but she let the full meaning hang silent, instead raising her eyebrows and nodding.

"You mean of ill-repute?" I studied the women more closely, making sure to keep my gaze limited to the head and shoulders only. "Surely not, not on a boat like the *Princess Alice*."

As though to contradict me, one of the women cackled loudly, slapping her companion's back. Her hair was a garish shade of red, which contrasted sharply against her pale, pasty skin. I cringed.

"They let absolutely anyone on this boat," Eleanor said, still in the same low voice. "You can tell by the clientele."

One of the women, whose back had been to us, turned so her face was in profile. I gasped, scarcely able to believe it. "My goodness," I hissed, nudging Eleanor a little too hard in my surprise. "Look, that's—"

"—Good heavens, you're absolutely right, it's Elizabeth Stride." Eleanor's eyes widened. "Isn't it uncanny to see her again, twice in one month?"

"Well, I suppose we must live in the same area. Those must be her friends," I said, keeping my eyes fixed upon them. Fortunately, we hadn't yet been noticed.

My wife chuckled. "Or her work colleagues."

"Eleanor, really. It isn't decorous to say such a thing."

She sniffed. "I think we're both perfectly aware what sort of creature Mrs Stride is. After all, she was *married,* and said nothing to poor Fred."

Poor Fred, I noted bitterly. *Why the sympathy for him? He's hardly a saint either.* "I rather think Fred deserved everything he got," I said, aware how unkind the words sounded, but unable to stop myself.

Eleanor looked at me with alarm. "Really?"

"Yes. He's proved himself to be a wastrel, beyond redemption." The sentiment choked me, shutting up my throat, but I continued, nonetheless. "He's a different person to the one that used to court you, you know."

"My goodness, is *that* what this is about?" Eleanor's eyebrows raised to two perfect peaks. "Are you jealous of your brother?"

"Absolutely not."

"You have no reason to be jealous of Fred. It was only a brief romance, it never would have led anywhere."

"Are you certain?" Again, my words sounded harsher than intended.

She sighed, smoothed a stray hair, which had escaped from under her hat. "Of course. Fred would not be the brother of my choice. He's positively beastly at times, so filled with anger and righteous indignation."

Really? It wasn't how I'd envisioned him, but it was interesting to hear her opinion expressed aloud. Her comments also reassured me, soothed the envy that had been bubbling in my chest for far too many years.

"Well, I wasn't jealous anyway," I said for clarification, then caught her eye and beamed, aware of how ridiculous it must have sounded.

She giggled and reached for my arm. "You did a very convincing job of pretending."

I patted her back, then glanced back over the other side of the deck. Elizabeth Stride and her companions had disappeared, which was probably for the best. The last thing I wanted was another awkward encounter with her, especially after the last time. *I wonder if I will continue to meet her in the future?* Surely twice in one month was enough of a coincidence for anyone, let alone a third time. No, I was confident this would be the last time I saw the unfortunate woman. She'd cast enough of a dark shadow on our family as it was.

"How do the other boats pass us?" Eleanor said, startling me out of my thoughts.

"With great care, I hope," I replied, looking at the width of the river. It scarcely seemed wide enough to accommodate one large boat, let alone two.

"Perhaps they have special passing places, do you think?"

I smirked at the thought. "I doubt that very much, having seen some of the boats that travel this river. It's more a case of blaring one's horn as loudly as possible and hoping the other vessel moves out of the way."

Eleanor laughed. "I suppose they know what they're doing. These are men that have been sailing the Thames for years, aren't they?"

"I'm certain of it. We've absolutely nothing to fear."

She giggled, covering her mouth. "That's exactly what I've been trying to persuade you of for *months,* my love."

"Well, you were absolutely right," I replied, with more conviction than I felt. I cast a final, hesitant glance up the river. An enormous boat was lumbering along in the other direction, its hull gleaming dully in the setting sunlight. *It really doesn't seem possible that it could squeeze past us,* I thought, then shivered as a strong breeze flared from the north. *But then, as Eleanor said, I'm sure it will be fine. I need to be less serious, if only for one night, show my wife that I too know how to have fun.*

TWENTY

— 1889 —

THE GHOST IS lost. Not geographically speaking; in fact, he'd wager few people knew this area of London as well as he did. Rather, he's become anchorless, a creature without a home, like an abandoned dog, left to roam free. Only a few years as a ghost, and look at him now, what he has become.

There is no pleasure in freedom, rather, this liberty is a burden worse than any chain or restraint. And how he loathes this spirit form. As a living, breathing human, he might have fancifully imagined there to be a certain freedom to not being tethered to a body. The reality is far different. As a ghost, he has no power, no voice to express himself. Situations unravel, and he cannot change them. People move on, and he cannot prevent them from doing so.

And how they have all moved on, he thinks bitterly. *How short that period of grieving seemed to be.*

The Thames revolts him, with its syrupy, stinking waters, its cloying banks. He watches two dirt-splotched children wading through the mud, searching for goodness knows what; urchins ready to be swallowed up by the fetid mess of the river, of the greedy city itself. No matter how closely he follows them, they remain oblivious to him. He is of no importance, a redundant being that casts no shadow and leaves no echo in the air.

What is the point of all this? he wonders, feeling more wretched than before. And that is perhaps the worst thing of all, that a human always has the ultimate method of escape, whereas he has nothing. He can only drift aimlessly, think futile thoughts, and hate his own paltry existence.

He wanders, forcing his thoughts into a vacuum. Because that is what he desires, more so than anything else. *To forget.* To not feel this pain anymore. To not have these memories, raging through him, one after the other, like whiplashes across his back.

Billingsgate Fish Market is busy as ever, people surging in and out of the arched entrances; flat-capped, frowning men wheeling carts of crates, the silvery shimmer of fish upon fish, piled up for sale. He remembers the building being constructed, standing on the road, watching with fascination as the builders teetered on shaky scaffolding, shouting orders at one another. It's still relatively new, only a few years old now, though already, the thick fumes of passing boats and the stench of the river have tainted the brickwork, given it a weathered, weary appearance. It seems more fitting like this, somehow. After all, selling fish shouldn't be glamorous. It involves slippery guts, slimy scales, and glassy, staring eyes; the baldness of death itself, staring back at every customer.

This is good, the ghost thinks. Amongst these surroundings, he can lose himself. The ceaseless motion, the urgent heat of all these people, it dulls his thoughts, stops them wandering where he does not want them to. He winds further into the cavernous space of the market, instinctively following certain figures; those who seem more morose than their jovial, raucous comrades.

Their sadness reassures me, he realises, with a sense of shame and exhilaration. *Their misery somehow softens mine, makes it more bearable.*

He spies an old woman, leaning heavily on a gnarled stick, back twisted as a light-starved seedling. Immediately, he is drawn, magnetised by the sense of *darkness* that hovers above her. He doesn't understand what it is exactly, only that it lurks over some people and not others, and that a few attract it more strongly. This woman's darkness is so thick it's almost solid; churning the air, boiling with something like rage around her bonnet.

It isn't wise to get too close. The ghost knows this from experience; stray too near to these afflicted people and it results in disorientation, nausea, even blackouts. Instead, he follows at a distance, focusing on her faded pink hat, bobbing haphazardly through the crowds. Interestingly, the crowds seem aware of her darkness too, instinctively veering away from her, like water bubbling around a troublesome rock.

Her fish is already purchased, he can tell by the paper-wrapped slab protruding from her basket. *A single fish,* he notes, observing the one small loaf of bread, the modest cabbage. A small meal for two, or perhaps just for one, it is difficult to tell.

Yet she lingers, perhaps relishing the comforting press of other bodies, the noise of conversation. If he ventures closer, he can sense a hint of her existence; a lonely, threadbare armchair by a fireplace, the painful *missing* of others in her life. She's lost her husband, that much is clear, though he also suspects she's lost more; children perhaps, and friends. Either way, her grief is palpable. *She wishes only to die and be done with it,* he realises sadly, then winces at the irony. *For some of us, it never ends,* he mouths, filled with desire to warn her. However, she may be one of the lucky ones. He's witnessed a couple of deaths, one of them being Mother's old neighbour Mr Harding, who simply vanished with a beatific expression on his face.

And how I hated him for it, he thinks with sudden ferocity. *How I wished that I'd had his life and death, and he'd had mine.*

From a neighbouring aisle, a man drops a crate of fish, sending a slippery wave of salmon over the floor. The swearing and shouting bring the ghost back to reality, and he swerves to avoid the mess, forgetting that it wouldn't affect him in the slightest. The crowd close around, keen to survey the chaos, and he loses the old woman behind a wall of curious faces. This matters more to him than he imagined it would, for he *needs* to follow her, to find out what has caused her so much distress. He suspects that it has become an appetite, a need to consume sadness, in order to maintain his own feeble existence. *If that is the case, what a pathetic creature I have become,* he thinks.

Finally, he senses her; the bloom of bad feeling, now close to the exit, like a noxious gas escaping a room. Sure enough, above the milling heads, he spots her tiny, shrunken form, now out in the open, the wintry light hitting her hunched shoulders.

She moves faster when out in the open, scuttling crablike along the side of the river, stick rapping in time with her disjointed steps. Her basket rattles on her hip, the contents jostling within, but she seems not to notice. Whereas before she'd seemed comforted by the crowds, now she seems only to want to escape them, to create as much space around her as possible.

The sky is leaden, a dead weight set to drop on the city. The ghost wagers that there will be snow before the day is out. The old woman's only defence against the cold is her ancient shawl, and the thick cotton top beneath it. *No overcoat, no scarf to protect her,* he thinks, and reflects on his own wardrobe as a living human, how he'd thought it paltry at the time, and how mistaken he'd been. His old collection of jackets, waistcoats, shirts, and trousers were abundant, humiliatingly decadent, and he'd been too much of a fool to appreciate it.

Yearning for his old life bites him, hard as winter frost. He pushes the thought aside, concentrating only on the woman. *I have to focus on her and not my own miserable existence,* he thinks, floating behind her. *There is no alternative.*

Laden carts clutter by, wheels bouncing on the road. Bowler-hatted gentlemen jostle for space against a continual press of aproned tradesmen, pushing piles of crates. The occasional beggar lurks in shaded alleyways, one clutching a weeping baby, attempting to rock it to silence. The city's heartbeat seems to throb down Lower Thames Street, yet the old woman fails to notice any of it, only teeters forward, head pressed down, stick clacking mercilessly at the pavement.

It is no surprise that she veers left, towards St Magnus the Martyr. He could sense the devout on her from the start, the staunch faith that radiates from her like steam from porridge. *This is all she has left,* he realises, looking up at the brick tower, topped with its thready pillars and needle pinnacle, poking at the clouds above.

She bows her head, tightens her shawl, then presses through the wooden doors. Inside, it is much as he remembers it, and the *ache* of it strangles him, dragging him down to the nearest pew. How he wishes he could feel its solid, reassuring smoothness beneath him, or breathe in the calm, cool air. *We used to sit at the back,* he thinks, choking on the memory. *Whispering, whenever we thought we could get away with it. We never were the most devout of worshippers, Eleanor and I.*

He wonders if Eleanor ever finds herself here, resting on the pew, remembering those days. *Does she ever search for me, as I did for her? Or has she forgotten too, like the rest of them?*

In his misery, he's misplaced the old woman, but soon spies her at the front; a hunched sack of fabric, motionless as a statue. The darkness surrounding her has eased, retreating to a vague fuzz, hovering a distance above her head. It is because this is where she knows some sort of peace, the ghost suspects, if only for a short while.

Compelled by a sudden force, he rises, quite without realising it, and wanders towards the altar, the two gold candlesticks, the wooden angels, heads tilted to the ceiling.

He settles beside her, ignoring the swirling darkness above them both, and reaches for her hand. *Perhaps we can offer one another comfort,* he thinks, *even though one is dead, the other alive.*

The old woman's reaction is startling and immediate. Her hand stiffens then retreats, with rodent speed. Her head spins, and for a moment, her eyes meet his.

She sees me! the ghost thinks, with exhilaration and terror. Her pupils seem fathomless, empty holes that capture and pin him in place, helpless as a butterfly. But what does she see, exactly? Can she make out a vague form of the man he once was? Does he appear as mist or disturbance in the air? Or is it just a sense of death that she detects, clinging to her with limpet determination?

Whichever it is, he will never have the chance to discover, as the woman rises, more swiftly than a person of her age and stature should be able to.

"Cursed creature," she mutters.

That word, *cursed*. It rings through him, rendering him frozen and silent. *Perhaps she meant herself,* he thinks desperately. *She cannot mean me. She does not know me. She may not even know I am here, it may all be a fancy of mine.*

But she repeats it again, this time more loudly, with a twisted finger crooked in his direction.

"Servant of Satan, I sense you. Be gone."

The ghost reels, not at the accusation, but the venom in which it was spoken. The darkness descends, the previous peace shattered with brutal, agonising force. He wants nothing more but to retreat, to push this woman from his memory, but he *can't*. He must stay, must let the scene play out, if nothing more than to find out just how much she understands of him.

"I have no business with Satan," he whispers, but can tell by her unchanging expression that she does not hear him. It would seem that she is only dimly aware of his presence, and that her actions are largely instinctive; an animal protecting itself against potential predators. *If only she realised how harmless I truly am,* he wishes, repelled by his own insufficiency. *Even Satan wouldn't take it upon himself to work with a lacklustre creature like me.*

The old woman probes her loose collar and draws forth a simple cross on a chain. The ghost sighs, and realises that this is the way it will always be. Most will never even note his existence, and the occasional few who do will perceive him as a ghoul, to be expelled from the vicinity as swiftly as possible.

She is right, he thinks. *I am cursed. I was cursed a long time ago, before I even died; I just didn't know it.*

A dull click startles them both. The woman lowers her cross and peers to the back of the church, to the plain door hiding in the shadows of the corner, which is now open.

Footsteps emerge into the church, firm and purposeful, before pausing.

"Good afternoon, is everything all right?" It's an honest voice, firm and reassuring. The ghost glances back to see its owner; the priest, narrow-shouldered and earnest, his white collar the only interruption to the otherwise sombre black of his outfit.

The old lady slumps, the fight slipping from her like mud from a broken bucket. The ghost sighs and moves quickly away.

I need to be gone, he tells himself, with the word *cursed* still ringing through him. *This is no place for me.* He catches drifts of their conversation as he heads towards the door.

"I am well, Reverend."

"Really, Mrs Thackston? This is the second time you've been in today, are you sure that—"

"—I am certain. I only come here for solace. I trust that's not a problem?"

"No, no problem, of course not. Did I hear you speaking with someone, a few moments ago?"

The ghost pauses, halfway in the building, halfway out. He waits, as does the reverend.

Finally, the answer; slow and uncertain. "No. I wasn't talking to anybody."

"Mrs Thackston, that's not the first time I've heard you muttering in here. It's always the same worrisome words, about the devil. Would you like to pray with me, perhaps that might help?"

The ghost shakes his head and leaves the building; relief and bitterness jostling for place within him. *So, she sees devilish creatures all the time,* he realises, ignoring the bustle of people around him, the noise of horse hoofs and carts on the road. *She is mad, and prone to seeing spirits around every corner. She didn't sense me at all. Only the fictitious creations in her head.*

Loneliness swells, harsh as a winter tide. The ghost lets it carry him, pushing him forward to goodness knows where, because he has no destination, no home to return to. This is life for him now, this terrible, pale existence, where he is unknown to everyone, and increasingly unfamiliar even to himself.

He drifts, for how long, he doesn't know, winding through familiar streets that are made strange by his physical detachment. He passes old haunts; past pleasant theatres where he once enjoyed shows with his family, through well-trodden paths where he used to stroll with Eleanor. Every sight wounds him, every sound sirens a reminder of what he has lost. But agonising as these places are to behold, they are harmless in comparison to the sadness that rips through him. The pain is unbearable, yet he *must* bear it. He has no other choice.

Oh, Eleanor, he thinks, stopping his pacing, for just a moment. *Arthur. Mother. Martha. Little George. How you all torture me.*

Night comes and the streets adopt a different nature; less lively, more watchful. Now is the time for shadows and the people who operate in them, but also for the wilful, the wild, the lost souls seeking to sweep themselves away under the cover of darkness. Still the ghost wanders. Indeed, he dares not stop, because he doesn't trust himself. He can only keep going, until some sort of solution presents itself.

The moon rises, gleams, then eventually falls, and still he paces, seeking oblivion in continual motion. Weak sunlight peeks over the tops of the surrounding buildings, like a nervous child. It settles on a poster, pasted haphazardly to a brick wall.

Captain Otto's Circus of Wonders, he reads.

The ghost remembers that circus. It is contained within yet another memory; he and Eleanor, walking from stall to stall, watching the Strong Man bend a bar with his teeth. Arthur paying for him to get his fortune told, though he hadn't asked for it.

The woman who'd turned over the Hanged Man card, he thinks, and stops for a moment, and wonders. Had she known? Might she be the one person who could sense his presence, who could actually speak to him?

And if so, could she help me get back to my wife?

He notes the current location of the circus. It is a desperate plan and he knows it will probably end in failure. For all he knows, the Fortune Teller may have left a long time ago, or even died. But it is worth trying, because there is now nothing else left for him to do.

She said a sacrifice would be made, he thinks, picking up his pace, a vague tendril of hope igniting his movement. *And so it was. A far larger sacrifice than I'd ever imagined.*

Let's see what else she knows.

TWENTY-ONE

— 1878 —

ROSHERVILLE GARDENS, AS Arthur had told us, were charming. Eleanor and I had watched, enrapt, as Signor Gellini took to the tightrope, high above the crowds, his oiled torso shining in the firelight. Later in the evening, they had let off the fireworks, a profusion of sparkling showers and racing lights, which charged through the darkening sky. I had to confess, I spent much of the performance admiring my wife instead, and the way the illuminations set alight her tilted cheek each time a rocket soared upwards.

Her joy was palpable, an emotion so intense it seemed to colour the air around her, brighter than any firework. I don't think I'd ever loved her as much as I did then, seeing her upturned chin, the smooth line of her neck, the gleam in her eyes.

She is beautiful, I thought, surveying the other men around us, and their partners. None gleamed with such light as Eleanor, who outshone them all. I pulled her closer, protective of my hard-won prize, proud of how I'd managed to secure her love.

After the fireworks had finished, we took a turn around the gardens. Some people were resting in deckchairs beneath a tree, although the sun had vanished some hours before. It made us laugh to see them, reclining lazily, faces open to the sky as though enjoying the heat. *What a curious race we are,* I thought, nodding at them all. *And yet our idiosyncrasies are truly wonderful.*

Of course, the evening stroll, delightful as it was, couldn't last forever. The *Princess Alice* was due to set sail again in a few minutes, which brought about the natural close to our evening. I had to admit, Eleanor had been right about the trip. It had been a delightful time, and for a moment or two, I'd been able to put my worries aside and take simple pleasure in being with my wife, just as I used to do.

The boat loomed by the bank, bovine and squat in the water. It jarred with its surroundings, this mass of industry; all metal, paddles, and belching chimney. It was a hard-edged, man-made monstrosity, overshadowing the tranquillity of the natural surroundings.

Still, I clambered aboard, eager suddenly to return home. The river was ink-black between the slats of the gangplank. I kept my chin up and scrabbled to the safety of the deck.

"That was simply divine, wasn't it?" Eleanor exclaimed, adjusting her hat. The muffled shouts of the men releasing the ropes that tethered the boat to the bank echoed behind her; a rough sound that contrasted with her gentle voice.

I wrapped an arm around her shoulder and pulled her close. "I really rather enjoyed it, you know."

"I told you that you would."

"You did." Before she could reply, I pressed my lips quickly against hers. She stiffened, no doubt aware of the impropriety of the gesture, then relaxed against me.

It was a simple kiss, a mere meeting of the lips, yet something about the moment resonated within me. *I will remember this moment as long as I live,* I thought fervently, then, *I hope I will, anyway.*

"What brought that on?" she whispered, glancing around us.

I smiled. "The sight of you. That's all. I'm so glad you had a lovely time, my dear."

The bellow of the horn startled us both, not to mention the people around us. The last boatsman on dry land leapt aboard and pulled the gangplank away. A moment later, the paddles began to turn and the chimney resumed its relentless spew of smoke into the night sky. It was time to head home.

I longed for the warmth of our bed, for a chance to have Eleanor in her completeness, not tethered by corsets and endless fabrics. I wished for things that were not appropriate for a gentleman to yearn for, yet was unable to prevent myself from doing so. An image flitted unbidden in my mind; pulling the pins from Eleanor's hair, letting the curls tumble upon her bare shoulders. Touching those curls with a hesitancy that verged on worshipful. Stroking that smooth, unblemished skin. All of it for my gaze alone, and no other man's.

Eleanor's veiled expression suggested that she knew my mind. She smiled, then looked away. I sensed she had some awareness of her power over me.

I am helpless before her, I realised, warmed by the notion.

In the semi-darkness, we could make out strange, lumpen shapes; the silhouettes of passing houses, bushy-branched trees, hedgerows, and even a horse chewing in the blackness, its long face pitched stoically over the fence. One could imagine, being out here at this time, how the ancient people were inspired to create their folklore. There was something magical yet menacing about the nighttime landscape, as though all the secretive creatures had emerged at the sight of the moon, and were skulking the banks, watching us as we powered past.

It was an unusually fanciful thought for me, but then, on an evening like this, it was impossible not to be affected.

"Look," Eleanor said, jolting me from my thoughts. "That's a large ship. It looks almost too large to squeeze along the river, don't you think?"

I followed her line of sight. She was right, there was a behemoth of a boat coming the other way, no doubt laden with timber or coal, and off to some far-flung place. We often witnessed ships such as these when we took our walks along the riverside, but somehow, from our position on the boat, it seemed much larger than usual; a hulking mass with a sharp, snout-like stern.

A stray curl had escaped from under her hat and was bouncing merrily in the breeze. I tucked it gently back, then touched her cheek with the back of my hand. "I'd rather take in the view in front of me," I whispered, "than watch an oversized ship plough along the Thames."

"It's producing a wretched smell too," Eleanor said, her gaze still fixed on the boat. "Do you think that's the engine?"

"I couldn't say, I'm no expert on these matters."

She shivered, an involuntary action in the chilling air.

I gestured to the saloon. "Shall we go inside?" In truth, I'd have rather remained outside, but I knew that, as a member of the fairer sex, her constitution was weaker than mine. Through the windows, I could see people milling around within, deep in conversation.

Eleanor shook her head. "No, I think I'd much rather stay out here."

"By the way," I added, pointing to the river below, "I think that might explain the smell. Look at the state of the water, isn't it dreadful?"

We both gazed over the edge. The Thames was clogged with sewage, its scent ripe and acrid. The surface of the water gleamed like oil with the effluence.

"That's ghastly." She shook her head. "You'd think they'd find a better way of disposing of such things, wouldn't you? Think of the poor fish in there."

"I suspect there aren't many fish in this part of the river."

"I say," Eleanor said suddenly, head snapping up like a cat awoken from a nap. "That other boat is right in our path, look."

I glanced up. She was right; the large ship was making a course directly for us. I frowned. Presumably the captains both knew the ways of the river, but it seemed needlessly reckless to veer towards one another in such a manner.

"I'm sure it will be quite safe," I said reassuringly, sensing the tension in Eleanor's posture. The irony made me chuckle, that she should be the nervous one now, and not I. "There you go, I think it's steering to the right now, see?"

We both watched. The boat was steering to the side, but didn't seem to be moving quickly enough. Behind us, an unearthly green lantern began to shine, no doubt lit to ensure the vessel was aware of our location.

"I'm sure the situation is under control," I muttered. The sight was disconcerting, though I refused to let myself worry about it. The men steering these boats were undoubtedly of good repute, who encountered other vessels on the river on a regular basis. Presumably this was some form of common nautical practice, nothing more.

A cynical chuckle startled me, from somewhere behind me. "Lord, it looks like it's coming straight for us, don't it?" For a dreadful moment, I thought the voice belonged to Elizabeth Stride, who surely must have boarded the boat for the return journey. But turning, I saw that it belonged to a much older, shorter woman, who was clutching the railings and staring wide-eyed at the water beyond.

I gave her my most appeasing smile. "I'm sure everything will be perfectly—"

But my remaining words were cut off, interrupted by the sudden shouting of the boatsman, standing on the crew deck above the saloon. I didn't like the sound one bit. His bellow was raw, unrehearsed, and full of panic.

The crowd around us began to murmur; a growing sound of apprehension and concern, before a single voice cried out, shrill and wild. "We're going to crash into it!" Instantly, pandemonium broke out, like a river breaking its dam. Passengers pressed against us, momentarily sending me off-balance, and I grasped the railing, hastily reaching for Eleanor.

"What's going on?" she gasped, staring at the chaos around us. "Do you really think we're going to collide?"

I didn't know what to say, only held her tightly and watched as the boat continued to glide inexorably towards us. Its grinding, roaring noise ceased, and I realised they had cut the motor in an attempt to slow the speed.

My God, I thought, unable to comprehend the manner in which the evening had turned. It was unthinkable, *unimaginable,* that we should have a collision. Things like this simply did not happen, not least to people such as ourselves.

What will happen if it hits us? Would it merely graze the side of the *Princess Alice,* or tear it apart like a knife through butter? Then another thought occurred to me, a darker, more dreadful thought that, once lodged in my mind, was impossible to shift.

I cannot swim. If we end up in those waters, I will not be able to swim to safety. And I won't be able to help Eleanor.

I swallowed hard, my collar uncomfortably tight against my Adam's apple. *It will not come to that,* I thought, pulling my wife closer. *The other boat will miss us, I am certain of it.*

But a minute later, I knew my assertion was wrong. Impact was inevitable, evident from the harsh line of the ship's prow, now bearing directly towards the side of our boat. Though it had cut its engine, the speed at which it progressed was still terrifyingly fast. From somewhere in the midst of the panicking crowd, a lady screamed; an unearthly noise that tore through my nerves. And as though a gate to Hell had been opened, the rest of the passengers soon followed; a cacophony of shouting, wailing, some rattling at the saloon doors in an attempt to get in, or perhaps let people out, I couldn't tell which.

Eleanor moaned, a low, animal noise that frightened me more than any of the screaming. "I won't let anything happen to you," I whispered in her ear. "I promise you, my love; whatever happens next, you will be fine."

She opened her mouth to reply, but her answer was lost as the ship finally reached us, slamming into the boat with inexorable force. In a single moment, the entire deck tilted, wrenched upwards by the impact, and we tumbled with the rest of them, our backs crushed against the railings. To my horror, the boat continued to rise, as the larger ship bit deeper and deeper into the deck, splintering wood, causing metal to shriek in protest. A young woman screeched, lost her footing, then tumbled over me, before disappearing into the darkness below. It took me a moment to realise that she'd fallen into the water, and that the muffled, pitiful cries coming from the darkness were hers.

In the chaos, I saw Eleanor's face, eyes wide with panic. Still, she gripped on to me, much to my relief, and I clasped her tightly, fighting to keep us from toppling over the edge. The larger vessel was now halfway through the deck, and I saw one of their crew, in a moment of peculiar clarity, throwing ropes towards us, shouting something that I could not discern over the noise.

It will be all right, I thought, amongst the sea of terror, the people thrown overboard, the relentless grinding of metal on metal. *We will be safe, I am sure.*

Eleanor screamed. She tumbled backwards, perhaps pushed by the press of so many other bodies, perhaps not. I reached for her, and in those last, desperate moments, I thought I had ahold of her, her forearm within my fingers, before my feet slipped from beneath me.

And then we fell together, Eleanor and I. The world flipped, cascaded, and dropped before my eyes, then came the inevitable slap of the river, forceful as a rifle-shot. Water bubbled at my ears like chattering, gobbling birds, then all was darkness; cold, dreadful darkness, as I sank further and further. My fingers slipped from Eleanor's and I scrabbled them back again, desperate to find her amongst the black.

Somehow, I managed to break the surface. Although I'd taken care not to inhale under the water, my chest was on fire, my breath ragged with the shock. To my relief, Eleanor was beside me, curls smeared across her forehead. Her hat bobbed a little distance away, an incongruous flash of colour, mocking us with its frivolity.

I cannot swim, I remembered.

At the realisation, I felt myself start to sink. No matter how hard I kicked my legs, I couldn't keep my head above the water, and down I went, up, then down, then up again; a helpless cork bobbing in the water.

"You need to use your arms!" Eleanor screamed, then choked as a wave of fetid water hit her in the face. "Paddle with your hands!"

I tried, but the turbulent waters made it near impossible. We drifted closer to the *Princess Alice*, which was now impossibly high above us, as though soaring from the water, ready to take flight. *Because it is.* Even greater panic hit me. *She's rising, because she's about to capsize entirely.*

I tugged at Eleanor's hand, then went under again, losing myself in the rank murk of the river. Confusion became my only sense of being, as my world tossed and spilled. Swirling water bruised my ears, filth flew past my eyes, and all of it filled my mouth.

Don't breathe, I told myself furiously. But the desire, as any man knows, is always going to win in the end. I inhaled, just a little, and water burned through my throat.

Is this what it's like? I wondered, still fighting, despite my growing hopelessness. *Is this what it means to die?*

I closed my eyes and waited. Then sound erupted around me, a hellish burst of crying, splashing, and desperate screams.

"Stay afloat! Don't go under again!"

I bobbed under, then back up. Noise, no noise, then noise again. It disorientated me more than the cold, making my reactions slow and stupid. All the while, the boat rose higher, towering above us both. I stayed afloat for a minute or two, though how, I wasn't quite sure. My chest was livid with needle-pain and I could scarcely breathe, but I was alive, for now. Eleanor's face was only inches from mine, smeared with filth, her hair fanning the water around her.

"Did you hear me?" she screamed, spitting out water. "Keep kicking! You *must* keep kicking and paddling, don't let yourself sink!"

I clutched to her, helpless as a baby, knowing that in this terrain, she was the strong one, not I, although her swimming wasn't proficient. A few feet away, an elderly woman cried out, held a hand to the air, then went under. She did not emerge again.

This is about surviving, I told myself, trying to ignore the agony in my chest. It felt as though a torch had been lit within, burning me from the inside out. *That is all we must focus on. Surviving. Nothing else matters now.*

The river roared behind us, and the boat finally flipped, its underbelly naked to the sky, streaming rivulets of water. Then, without warning, it fell to the other side with an unearthly crash. The Thames heaved and surged, resisting this unwieldy object, and battering us, its passengers, with vengeful force. Eleanor and I were swept further up the river, along with the multitudes of others struggling to stay above water.

"They're throwing ropes!" a man hollered, from somewhere in the distance. But no matter how hard I strained my eyes, I couldn't see a single helping hand. Our landscape had become a scene from a nightmare; a sea of desperation and dying.

I saw a woman, her bonnet still clinging to her head, paddling urgently for the banks, and realised at once who it was. *Elizabeth Stride.* Her strokes were powerful, confident, and sliced through the water with ease. Anger swelled within me, that she should somehow survive this terrible ordeal, and we should not. To my satisfaction, a man beside her, struggling to stay above water, lashed out a foot and caught her in the mouth.

When did I become such a mean-minded spirit? I chastised myself, watching as she went under. To my relief, she emerged only a second later, clutching at her jaw.

"We need to reach the bank!" Eleanor shouted, grasping my hand more tightly. "Do you think you could kick your arms and legs, if I led the way?"

In truth, I wasn't sure. Already, my limbs were aching with exertion, and no matter how hard I increased the intensity of my thrashing, I still found myself continually bobbing under the surface. Without her hand to raise me back up, I knew that I would have undoubtedly sunk much earlier on.

A sense of hopelessness washed over me. "I do not think so," I gasped back.

"But we must try!" She looked at the underside of the *Princess Alice,* which protruded from the water like a monstrous belly. "It is too cold, I cannot keep us both afloat for much longer!"

"Someone will help us, surely!" I said, then choked as my head went under again. More water roared into my mouth and I retched, bile and foulness pouring over my chin.

"They won't, we're too far away. We must do something!"

The next moment only lasted a second or so, but it seemed to stretch for an eternity. Her wet face shone in the dim moonlight, and it was as though I was seeing *her* for the first time; not the friendly, joyful creature I'd married, but the *real* her, full of beauty and resilience.

You will survive, I thought. Because I knew it to be true. *I knew.*

Because a sacrifice will be made.

As though answering my thoughts, the tossing waters of the Thames closed over me again, sealing me up in the dark. And what darkness it was. Blacker than any winter night, bleaker than any tomb. But this was how it had to be. For the first time since falling into murky water, I could see clearly, as though the script had been written centuries ago, with the only thing remaining being my part in the performance. This time, instead of clutching her tightly, I released her.

I let Eleanor go.

Her hand slipped from mine, as easily as a child's, and she was gone.

TWENTY-TWO

— 1878 —

LITTLE GEORGIE IS aware of him, the ghost is convinced of it.

For close to an hour, he has drifted closer to the crib, then retreated. In and out, as soft as the tide. And all the while, Georgie gurgles, hands outstretched, eyes focusing as the ghost hovers above him.

"You see me, little one," he whispers.

Georgie chuckles in response, a fulsome, throaty sound that reminds the ghost painfully of Arthur, even of his father, when they were all young lads. *The family laugh,* he thinks ruefully, and wonders if his had sounded the same, when he'd been alive.

This baby fascinates him. Such bright, flickering eyes, surveying every inch of the nursery, reluctant to miss a single moment. The room seems apt for him, somehow; with its rich cornicing, velvet drapes, and thick, welcoming rug. Like a little prince's room, almost. *He is destined for great things,* the ghost thinks, and reaches down to touch him.

Of course, he feels nothing, only the dull sense of his fingers slipping through something, in another place and time. Georgie, on the other hand, seems to relish the feeling, clawing his hand up quickly, keen to grasp the ghost if he can.

I'm afraid that's impossible, the ghost thinks, and moves sadly away.

The reality of death still torments him, even after several months, or over a year now, perhaps. He cannot tolerate the futility of it, the sense that he is *nothing* of any consequence, and that every moment spent floating aimlessly from room to room is another moment wasted.

And of course, being here is torment too, though where else can he go? He knows no one else and has no other place to wander to. So, he must remain. Each day, hope ignites, that they might notice him, or even briefly feel his presence. And every evening, it is snuffed out as unceremoniously as a candle.

Still, they talk of him occasionally. Stilted, laboured conversations, where the silences seem frequently richer and more meaningful than the words that are spoken aloud. So much is left unsaid, so many sentiments remain hanging. He longs for them to speak them aloud, but they never do. He is starting to think that they never will.

Georgie cries out, just once. His gaze is still fixed on the ghost, chin tucked tightly against his pudgy chest, peering down the length of his helpless, kicking body. The ghost considers returning, continuing their endless game of back and forth, but there seems little point. Besides, the child needs his sleep. *Babies must have rest,* he reminds himself sternly, as though this is a fact that should concern him.

Arthur's house is grand, even in the dark. The ghost slips through the nursery door, along the hallway, with its rows of watchful portraits. The rug is luxuriant, Persian, and he wishes he could sink his toes into it, just once. He would give anything to feel something again, even if it was as mundane as a piece of material against his feet.

The door to the master bedroom, at the front of the house, is far more grandiose; a set of double-doors in fact, each with its own shining doorknob. The ghost pauses, the lingering mists of his fingers hovering above the wooden surface.

It is tempting to enter.

Don't do it, he tells himself. *Don't cause yourself more needless pain.*

A noise downstairs makes him pull his hand away sharply; a sharp clatter, something metal striking the floor perhaps. He hadn't realised anyone else was awake with him, aside from little Georgie of course.

The staircase sweeps to the entrance hall, and the ghost sweeps along with it, letting himself drift downwards like a falling feather.

He immediately identifies the location of the noise, as the door to the study is ajar, and a soft light casts a long strip of amber across the floorboards.

Arthur is in there. He knows this before he enters. After all, who else would be? No one else has the key, and besides, it has been firmly identified as his space, and his alone. His *inner sanctum*, he's referred to it before, to Mother, to Martha. To him too, he believes, a long time ago. Arthur's inner sanctum. *Whatever is he doing in there?* the ghost wonders, curious. The face of the grandfather clock shows that it's already past midnight.

Arthur is at his desk, much as the ghost anticipated. The oil lamp lights his cheeks, catching the sheen of sweat. An empty whiskey glass rests beside him, and a half-empty bottle. Judging by his glazed expression, he's already drunk a considerable amount.

The ghost glances at the paperwork without much interest. The numbers are mostly gibberish to him, complicated columns filled with sums; something to do with work, it would seem. Arthur himself doesn't seem to be reading them either, though keeps tapping at the documents with his pen. His thumb is covered in ink, as are his first two fingers, but Arthur seems oblivious.

They make his hand seem diseased, the ghost thinks with fascination. *This is not the Arthur I remember.*

Of course it isn't. The Arthur he recollects is someone different, almost a fictitious character. This individual here; this pallid, vacant mess of a man, *this* is the real Arthur.

You are more like Fred than I'd realised, the ghost thinks bitterly.

Arthur coughs, raises his hand to his mouth, then groans quietly. He pours another drink. The ghost watches, motionless in the corner, as his brother tips it cleanly down his throat, then places the glass carefully back down again.

Why are you anaesthetising yourself with whiskey? the ghost wonders, watching with interest. After all, Arthur has everything he wants. He has made sure of it.

A muffled cry echoes from somewhere upstairs, muted by the sheer excess of space in the house. *Georgie. Georgie is calling out for me to return,* the ghost thinks irrationally. *At least somebody wants me.* Silence resumes, then the baby's cries start in earnest, first hesitant, as though testing out the sound in the darkness, then louder, more insistent.

Arthur groans, buries his head in his hands, then mutters, "I cannot give you any more of myself."

"Whatever do you mean by that?" the ghost replies, though he knows his brother cannot hear him. It is often like this; him responding to Arthur, quite without the other being aware. It is a way to pass the time, and it gives him some sense of belonging.

It had sometimes been the same when they'd been children, ironically; when the ghost had lain awake, scared of the shadows, and whispered to Arthur in the darkness, despite knowing he was fast asleep. *I always trusted him more than Fred,* he thinks, *even back then. If only I'd known.*

Georgie's screams increase in volume. The ghost can imagine his face only too well, the reddening rage at the knowledge that no one is coming. He's seen it before, and respects the baby's anger, his decision to choose vitriol rather than sadness. *It's far wiser to fight against the world than to miserably accept it,* he thinks. *I should know.*

Finally, Arthur rises and drops the pen to the desk, ignoring the splash of ink on impact. He teeters, staggers, grabs the back of his chair for support. The ghost can tell it will take a few seconds for him to find himself again, to stop the room from swaying this way and that, like a boat at sea.

"Why can that woman not hire some help, like I told her to?" he mumbles, to no one in particular, before advancing to the door. "Why must it be I who has to deal with this?"

The ghost frowns, irritated by the self-piteous tone to his brother's voice. "Go to your baby, you drunken fool," he murmurs.

Arthur departs, still muttering under his breath. The ghost can almost convince himself that it was a gesture of obedience. Slowly, he follows, curious to see what his younger brother will do. One thing is certain, Arthur's no natural with children. It's surprising, given his affable, enthusiastic nature. The ghost would have wagered good money that he would make an excellent father.

Maybe it's the manner of the child's conception, he thinks bitterly. *The guilt must weigh on him dreadfully. The snake.*

Arthur is in no hurry to reach Georgie, though it's possible the alcohol coursing through his system is slowing him down. The ghost finds it difficult to keep composure, watching him stagger this way and that, all the while fumbling for the bannister, using it to anchor himself to an upward trajectory. His footsteps are surprisingly silent, though. It seems Arthur is well practiced at moving quietly through his own home, regardless of how many tumblers of whiskey he's consumed.

The upper hallway is darker than before. The moon has stealthily edged behind a cloud, and the delicate glow that previously lit the rug is now gone. An unseen body rustles in the master bedroom, before settling again.

A deep sleeper indeed, the ghost thinks wryly. *Like the dead. She should attend to her baby instead of lying in there, all alone.*

Georgie's howls have softened to the occasional whimper; either because he's aware of their approach, or has given up hope of anyone coming. Arthur hovers outside the door, hand poised against the wood, frowning.

"You should let me go to see him instead," the ghost says aloud. "I sense that his uncle might have better luck than his father."

It's a cynical, brutal comment, and one he regrets, even though no one can hear him. He knows he should be more gracious. He understands that his brother, that *all of them* must move on with their lives. And he appreciates that he is dead, and that there is nothing that can be done about it.

But still, it stings. Every moment that he exists, it stings.

"The little fellow's asleep," Arthur whispers. For a breathless moment, the ghost believes he's addressing *him*.

The soft whining from within contradicts the comment, but the ghost can tell by his brother's expression that Arthur *wants* to believe it. He *needs* Georgie to be asleep, because he is unable to cope with a crying child at present, so that is the version of events that he will select. The one that works in his favour.

"You were never this selfish when I was alive," the ghost mutters, and brushes through his brother's body, right through the door. He fancies that Arthur shivers a little as he passes, though it could just be the chill of the night.

Georgie's room is warmer, cosier than the austere corridor outside. The cot is jerking slightly with the force of the baby's kicking, the blankets in a tangled heap at the bottom. The ghost smiles.

"You're not asleep at all, are you?" he coos, and the baby looks at him, alive with interest.

He can see Arthur in Georgie's face, or at least, he thinks he can, though Arthur is fairer than this child here. *Perhaps he takes after his uncle instead,* he thinks, remembering Fred's swarthy colouring, or indeed his own dark brown hair, as it had been in life. It is perhaps a shame that the baby didn't inherit Arthur's blond locks. He was always fussed over as an infant, thanks to his rosy cheeks and curly, buttery hair.

"Still, I think dark rather suits you," the ghost whispers, then regrets it. The sentiment sounds far more ominous than he'd intended it to. Despite everything that he's discovered since his death, he wishes the child no harm. He is an innocent, and furthermore, he's part of his family, for better or for worse.

And nothing matters more than family, he thinks sadly, smiling as the baby reaches a hand towards him, desperate to grasp at him.

He remains with the child for a while, an hour, or perhaps two. Georgie seems reluctant to settle, thrashing out suddenly every time his eyelids droop, and whimpering again if the ghost attempts to move away. It is touching that Georgie is so comforted by his presence, but exhausting too. Such neediness, it's beyond the ghost's ability to respond to it. He cannot be relied upon, because he is unable to rely on himself.

Finally, he drifts to the door and stays there, sensing the child keenly searching for him in the dark. Georgie gurgles, raises his legs upwards, then thumps them down in protest. The ghost sighs.

Children are insatiable, he realises, and for a moment, is thankful he never had the chance to be a father. He is not sure he would have been terribly good at it, not after seeing the reality of what is involved; the endless crying, the eagerness for stimulation, the refusal to be satisfied. *Or perhaps that's just you, little man,* he thinks, as he gazes across the room. *Maybe you're harder work than most.*

As he passes back through the door, Georgie's moans immediately rise to a wailing crescendo; first uncertain, testing the air with their potency, then rising in volume to a full-throated screech. The ghost winces and glances instinctively down the corridor, towards the master bedroom.

"It's your turn now, Arthur," he mutters, gliding closer, trying to ignore the lusty bellows behind him. "I've already done my fair share for this night."

At first, he believes they will not emerge, that they will wilfully ignore their son until he resigns himself to his lonely fate. Then finally, with a tumultuous rustling of bedsheets and muttered expletives, he hears heavy feet, plodding across an unseen floor. A moment later, Arthur emerges, hollow-eyed, hair sticking unflatteringly towards the ceiling like a cleaning brush.

Then *she* follows, a few seconds after. As ever, the sight of her pulls the ghost inwards, shrinking him in upon himself, like melting ice.

Eleanor.

Admittedly, his former wife is not looking her best. Her eyes are red and swollen, her mouth pinched. He wonders if she's been weeping about something, and for a moment, dares to hope it's about him. She does, on occasion, when she believes no one else is with her.

But I'm always with you, he thinks fiercely, following her up the hallway. *Except in that bedroom. I cannot enter there, not even if I wanted to.* Even the thought of it rips into him, a visceral, violent ache that almost brings him to the floor.

Eleanor and Arthur both pause outside Georgie's door, studying one another's expression in a manner that the ghost finds disconcertingly intimate. *How well they understand one another,* he thinks savagely, lingering beside them both, wishing he had fists to strike out with. *Were they always like this? Was I simply too blind to notice it?*

Finally, Arthur taps on the doorframe, a fraught gesture. The ghost notices his wedding band, gleaming dully in the dark. "I do wish you'd let me arrange for a nanny to help you," he whispers, agitation clear from every clipped word.

"I said you didn't have to get up with me, Arthur. Go back to bed if you like."

"I can't sleep with that intolerable noise going on."

Eleanor tuts. "Well, go and drink more whiskey then. That should do it."

Or why not stop bickering and go and attend to your child? the ghost thinks, though he cannot deny the pleasure of seeing them argue. *You'd settle Georgie far more quickly if you actually went in to comfort him.*

"Just hire a nanny. That's all I ask," Arthur retorts darkly, then pushes the door open. The ghost can see that the baby's face is ruddy and damp from the howling, his expression unnervingly livid, more like an adult than a helpless child.

Eleanor reaches down, then places the child to her shoulder. Immediately, he settles, nestling his head against her neck.

She is a natural mother, he thinks, though it hurts him to do so. *I cannot deny that she was born to do this.*

She shushes Georgie, rocking gently to and fro until the baby calms, only uttering the occasional haphazard sniffle. Arthur sighs impatiently, leaning against the wall, looking every bit the exhausted, defeated new father.

"What now?" he says finally, arms folded.

"I wait until he's fully asleep, then put him back down again." The mocking tone is unmistakable.

"I mean what about the future? We cannot continue like this."

Eleanor sighs, stroking Georgie's hair. "Very well. Get a nanny if it will bring you joy. Get whatever you want."

"That's not what I meant."

The ghost stiffens. He's noticed fractiousness between them before, but this seems more earnest, less trivial. Suddenly, it feels inappropriate to be here, listening to their private conversation, despite their treachery towards him. He wonders if he should leave.

"What did you mean, then?" Eleanor places Georgie gently into his cot, pulling the blanket up to his chin.

Arthur sighs, then rubs his cheek. It's a gesture the ghost remembers well, the helpless stroke of the face, a sign that he'd rather avoid confrontation if possible.

"Let's have this conversation another time," he says finally, inching the door back open.

"No," Eleanor says, joining him. "Now is as good a time as any." Her tone permits no refusal. The ghost should know, she used it on him enough times. *I'd feel sorry for Arthur,* he thinks, *were I not so filled with fury at him.*

"I scarcely know where to start," Arthur mutters, as they return to the hallway, shutting the door quietly behind them. "You know that things haven't been easy for us."

The ghost notices that Eleanor's hand strays involuntarily to her own wedding ring, twirling it nervously round her finger. *It must have cost far more than the one I purchased for her,* the ghost thinks gloomily. *Though she didn't seem to object to my ring at the time.*

"It isn't surprising, is it?" she replies, jaw taut with emotion. "I did tell you, when you proposed, that it would take me a while to recover myself."

"For heaven's sake, Eleanor, you're not the only one who misses him!" Arthur's voice breaks, and for a moment, the ghost is moved, before remembering himself again. "You lost your husband, but I lost my brother and greatest friend!"

"Shh, do keep your voice down. The last thing we want is for Georgie to awaken again."

Arthur breathes deeply, reestablishing himself in the present. "Very well," he says finally. "I just—"

"—Just what?"

"I just want to make you happy. I want to make Georgie happy too, believe it or not."

Eleanor shakes her head. "I wish I could believe you."

"I do my best, you know."

"I know. But," she pauses, fighting to find the right words. "But I can't help thinking that you resent him—"

"Eleanor, that's unfair. Come now, I've made every effort to shower that boy with everything a child could possibly want."

"Apart from love?"

"Surely you can understand why it's so difficult for me?"

"Arthur, I've been understanding. But the boy needs a *father*."

The ghost couldn't agree more. During his time in this house, lurking in the shadows, watching his wife and brother commence their romance in his absence, he's been frequently surprised by Arthur's lack of fondness for his son. *Presumably guilt,* he thinks again. *Because he knows he had no right to produce a child so soon after his brother's death, especially not with his widow. Still, it's harsh on poor Georgie. No child deserves to feel unwanted.*

Eleanor and Arthur reach the master bedroom. The door is already ajar, and the ghost cannot resist the pull of what lies within. Natural curiosity overcomes him, and he peers through the dark, just able to make out the shine of the brass bed-knobs, the generous mass of the mattress made for two. He retreats, planning to leave them for the night, to conceal himself in some other part of the house until morning comes. He's heard enough of their conversation tonight, and certainly none of it makes his pain any easier to endure.

It's time for silence, he thinks, exhausted. *These thoughts are too much for any man to bear, alive or dead.* As he moves away, he presumes that they will return to their bedroom, to the blissful abyss of sleep. But Arthur's words, cutting through the quiet, bring him to a halt by the stairs.

"I didn't know what it would be like to take on a dead man's son."

What? The ghost turns. Each moment seems slower, time running in reverse, twisting the air around him, warping everything in its past. *What do you mean by that, Brother?*

Eleanor swallows hard, then closes her eyes. "*You* were the one who suggested marrying me so soon. It was *you* who offered to be a father to Georgie. I never asked you to be."

She closes the bedroom door behind her, leaving Arthur outside, staring dully at the polished surface, which is barely inches from his nose. The ghost can only watch in mute, anguished amazement, and try to grasp what has just been said. Slowly, he turns to Georgie's bedroom door, an innocuous, inoffensive slab of wood, the only thing standing between them both.

Georgie is mine?

The very idea swells in his head, blocking out all other thought. Arthur, even Eleanor, are both forgotten. Because *Georgie is his.*

I am a father, he thinks, with a sense of elation. It is something to cling to, a tiny bud of happiness amongst all this death and desperation.

Then, as he looks down at the misty, shapeless form of his existence, he realises the futility of his situation. He will *never* be a father, because being a parent requires the individual to be alive. He is merely a memory of one; no more, and no less. Georgie will never know him, *can* never know him. In time, he won't even be able to detect him as a ghostly presence, much less anything else. And all the while, he'll believe that Arthur is his father.

They will be happy, he thinks, looking miserably around him, at the sumptuous staircase, the elegant sash-windows, letting moonlight fall upon the floorboards below. Then, *it is time for me to leave this house. I cannot stay any longer.*

TWENTY-THREE

— 1878 —

I HELD MY breath for as long as I could, despite everything. It is human instinct to do so, and regardless of my knowledge that this river would be my coffin, I was unable to stop my body from resisting it with everything it had.

The surface was undetectable, the bottom of the Thames, invisible. I was floating in endless water, buoyed and bounced along by the current, and my limbs had become stone. Most painful of all; I had lost Eleanor. I'd *had* to lose Eleanor. I prayed, with the last remnants of oxygen available to me, that she would somehow survive this. But I suspected she too would be pulled down. The banks were too distant, the water too cold. She wasn't a strong swimmer at the best of times. There was very little chance that she could have made it.

I love you, my darling, I thought, as I involuntarily inhaled.

I'd heard rumours about death by drowning, tales of how it was a comforting, peaceful way to pass on; that the mind comprehended nothing of what was happening, only conjured pleasant hallucinations for the victim. It wasn't such for me. The water burned like hot coals through my throat, which was already constricting in protest, straight into my lungs.

Then the burning commenced in earnest.

I may have attempted to scream, down there in the dark. Certainly, my mouth was stretched in horror, incomprehension that such a thing could be happening to me, when only fifteen minutes earlier, I'd been enjoying a delightful evening with my wife. It was staggering that the world could turn so swiftly, that I could be flipped from contentment to desperation in so little time.

More water poured in. My lungs pulsed and spasmed in protest. All attempts at movement were pointless, for my arms and legs were no longer my own; only heavy, useless pillars by my sides. Was I sinking? Perhaps. Or perhaps bobbing upwards, tugged by the ceaseless current? Either way, it didn't much matter. Thought was becoming more difficult, but I was aware of the fact that I was dying, and that nothing could save me now.

Other forms passed me in the depths, bodies no doubt, of those who'd died before me. If they were corpses, then the Thames was filled with them. *And if that is so, what a terrible, terrible thing this is.*

My eyes were closing. My *mind* was closing. Yet still I clung to the image of her. *Please let her survive. And let her know how much I loved her.*

With that last thought, my heart ceased to beat.

And I ceased to be.

He is in the water, and he is not. This is the first thought he has, as he starts to *see* again, and become aware of his surroundings.

Where was I? he wonders, dimly aware of having just lost a sense of calm, of almost unbearable peace. *And why am I here? How long have I been like this?*

So many questions, none of them answerable. He turns, this way and that, confused by the world around him. It is undoubtedly water, though dark and filthy. He can see excrement bobbing past his eyes, and worse, the shapes of bodies, clothes blossoming around them like floating shrouds.

Why am I not wet? he wonders. None of this makes sense. Yet if this is a dream, it is the most peculiar dream he's ever had, because it feels so real. But it cannot be, his senses are not functioning as they should. He feels no wetness on his skin, and has no discomfort being down here, regardless of the lack of air.

Something dreadful has happened, he realises suddenly.

Fear prickles him, raw as an electric shock. Something is not right. A terrible event occurred, he is sure of it, but he cannot recollect what. His head snaps downwards, pulled by an urge he has no control over.

There's a man's body below him, though far too still to be alive. He focuses only on the man's billowing shirt, the lifeless stretch of the fingers, because he is too *frightened* to look any higher. He does not want to see the man's face, knows that if he does, he will see something that will change him forever. But of course, morbid curiosity overcomes him eventually; that all-too-human inability to ignore something, even when it's liable to cause terrible damage.

And so, he *looks.*

The dead man's face is only visible for a moment or so, before the body tumbles further into the darkness, losing itself in the clutching weeds. But the moment is all that is required.

He chokes. The *ghost* chokes. And all the while, thinks, *so now I know the truth.*

For a time, he simply floats, staring at the strange, incomprehensible world around him, willing his mind to remain empty. He waits, drifting along, unable to comprehend the truth of it all. For surely, if he is dead, there must be something more than this, somewhere for him to progress to?

Life did not prepare me for this, he thinks, and the first swell of despair washes through him. *And every word those vicars mumbled in their Sunday services was a lie.*

He sobs, for a few minutes, or an eternity. Time has warped and frayed, or maybe it's his sanity that's shattered, because of the devastation of knowing that he has *ceased to be.*

Thoughts clamour for attention, each more horrible than the last.

I am dead.

But I am not in Heaven.

I've lost everything.

I don't know what this means.

And lastly, most painfully, *where is Eleanor?*

If she was dead, wouldn't she be down here too, scrabbling in the depths like him? Come to mention it, why are there no other ghosts surrounding him? The water is mired with corpses, yet no other spirits lurk down here, or at least, not any that he can see.

I'm the only sentient creature here, he realises, bleakly scanning the murk. *I have died, and now I'm completely alone.*

Minutes, hours pass. The ghost becomes dimly aware of a hulking mass above him; a monstrous weight that blocks out the feeble light of the moon. He floats closer, marvelling, yet also repulsed by how easy it is to glide through the river. The water offers no resistance, nor can he feel it wetting his skin. It is even difficult to imagine how the coldness would feel, now he's without a body. *Surely I won't forget these things so soon,* he thinks, with something close to panic. *Or am I changing already? Is this what it means to be dead, to lose one's mind entirely?*

He knows he must calm himself, recover rational thought, and consider the most sensible course of action. The bulk above him widens as he closes in, confusing in its incongruousness. *That's a window,* he realises, edging closer, peering through the glass. *It's a row of windows.*

The force of the memory sends him spinning, propelled backwards by horror. *It's the saloon of the* Princess Alice. And far, far worse, it is overflowing with people; or things that were once people, before the Thames seeped into their screaming mouths. The bodies are wedged like potatoes in a sack, pressed inelegantly against the windows, all wrapped around one another. *So many lives.* It is hideous, all this needless, avoidable death.

He forces himself to look, just in case *she* should be amongst them, mouth twisted in horror, eyes whitening in death, but thankfully, there's no sign of her. *Eleanor wouldn't be inside,* he tells himself, remembering how her hand had slipped from his. *She was swimming for the riverbank. If her body is down here, she would be in amongst the weeds, or floating near the surface. I must keep searching.*

All the time he flits back and forth, he's aware of movement above. The occasional plank of wood slices cleanly through the water, which he soon realises is an oar. Nearer the surface, he can even detect the occasional shout, muffled by the river around him. *A rescue mission.* Not that there is any point. There's no one left alive anymore. The Thames has swallowed up hundreds of victims, and the men above stand no chance of finding anyone to rescue.

Sorrow hits him, as deftly as the paddling oars above. *I considered myself like those living creatures up there,* he thinks, reaching closer for the surface. *But I'm not any longer. Why did this have to happen? Why me? What sort of God would allow this to pass?*

Desperately, he breaks the surface, half-expecting water to fly from his rising body. The lack of physical impact disturbs him, reminding him again of his *nothingness.* It is a nightmare, and one that he prays will end soon. *For it cannot always be like this,* he thinks, raising his eyes to the moon. *No divine entity would let his creatures suffer so much in the afterlife, would it?*

There are several rowboats in the river, many men in uniform, hanging over the sides, peering through the water. The air ripples with the sound of shouting, whistles being blown, the occasional splash as something is thrown overboard. It is chaos, but a more muted, resigned form of chaos; a pale aftermath of the hell of the *Princess Alice's* collision.

Where are you, Eleanor? the ghost wonders, knowing that he *must* continue his search; that if he doesn't focus his efforts on finding her, he will surely lose his mind. If he doesn't set himself a task, what will be left for him? Nothing but a slow sink back down to the bottom, to spend the rest of his conscious moments mentally disintegrating next to his own decaying corpse?

I cannot give in, he tells himself with sudden resolution. Let the acceptance of death follow later, he will address the complexities of his new state of being later on. For now, he must find her, or at least find her body, just so he knows the truth of it. He wonders if she has passed on to the *other* place, like all the other dead people seem to have done.

But if she has, he thinks, fear burning inside him, *why have I not? Why would I be left behind?*

These are questions he cannot bear to think about at present. Instead, he glides seamlessly through the water, past the hoarse, freezing men and their rescue efforts, to the glossy mud of the riverbank.

It is a scene from the darkest nightmare. There, countless more bodies are piled on the grass, already pallid and distended with death. For a moment, he thinks he sees Eleanor, a glassy-eyed beauty laid carelessly beside a tree, arms twisted at unnatural angles. Then he realises this woman is younger, her hair a different colour. He sighs in relief, and renewed misery, for *where could she be?* He feels he has already seen so many.

There are other women who remind him of her, plus many more corpses from all walks of life. He spies one of the women he'd seen standing with Elizabeth Stride, the one with red hair and the impudent expression. One of her shoes is missing, and this disturbs him more than the sight of the rest of her; that drenched, naked foot, so vulnerable without its lace-up boot to cloak it. The light from the neighbouring oil lamp catches her toe, highlighting the bunion twisting it to one side. *That foot will never walk again,* he thinks sadly. *It will never dance, never run, never even twitch in bed. It is nothing now.*

Overcome, he simply stands and watches. The larger boat, the one that ploughed into the *Princess Alice,* is still sitting in the river. He notices, with bitterness, that it is almost completely undamaged. Some of her crew are even still aboard, helping those below to lift bodies from the water. They look like dead things themselves, glowing unnaturally in the waning moonlight.

The ghost looks up. It will be morning soon, and what then? Will he fly out of existence? Or will the sun drive him away to some dark corner of this city? Every ghost story he's ever heard is set at nighttime. *Have I become one of those creatures?* he wonders bleakly, thinking of the gory, blood-soaked phantoms that Fred used to conjure up in his stories, during those late nights as children. Even Arthur's pale, love-lorn apparitions seem unnerving now, those meandering tales of wandering spirits, howling out on the streets, looking for their lovers. *We mocked him so much at the time for his stories,* he remembers, closing his eyes. *But his version of the afterlife was more accurate than ours. Despair. Confusion. Relentless sadness. This is what it really is.*

Still the men work, tirelessly bobbing across the lightening water, heedless of the rising sun at their backs. The morning finally comes, weak and feeble as death itself, and the ghost looks upon his new, misted form, seeing it clearly for the first time. It is horrifying. His fingers, at times, seem like wispy echoes of their former selves, with lines and markings that echo what they once were. But when his emotion rises, they fade, mist over, sometimes disappearing completely.

What am I? he asks, knowing there is no answer. *An unnatural thing? A ghoul or monster? And what is to be done about it? How long must I endure it for?*

Without any answers to hand, he resumes his search. The light makes the landscape more nightmarish, not less; the faces of the dead shining pale, the vague bloat of their bellies and cheeks already evident. The officers check through jacket pockets, no doubt trying to discover the identities of the victims. Their distaste for the task is evident in every grimace, every wipe of the brow, and their reluctance to truly *look* at the corpses at their feet. The ghost does not blame them. He knows he would have been the same.

There are some survivors, he can see that now. A pitifully small huddle of people, some sitting by a neighbouring tree, others pacing restlessly like animals, blankets draped over their shoulders. Rather than congregate together, they have mostly chosen to disperse. Perhaps that way, it is easier to bear; by not talking about it, they can choose to pretend it has not happened.

A tall, mess-headed woman is talking to one of the officers. Although her back is turned, the ghost can tell it is Elizabeth Stride. Resentment flares within him, that such a person as she should survive, when he and Eleanor have died. *There is no God,* he thinks, hating her, and hating the world around him. *No God would allow this to happen.*

Despite himself, he drifts closer, keen to hear what she is saying. The officer's expression is unreadable from a distance, though his exhausted, hollow expression suggests he's losing patience with her.

The ghost stands between them, marvelling at their lack of awareness. He waves a tentative hand in Elizabeth Stride's face, but she doesn't flinch. Then he raises the other and punches her, with all his force, across the cheek. His hand flies through her skin, emerging cleanly the other side. He hadn't felt a thing, and neither had she. The ghost bites back a sob.

"I t-t-told you, you wouldn't b-b-be able to spell my name if I g-gave you it."

Why is she stuttering? he wonders, then notices her jaw; the swollen mass on the right-hand side, pulling her face into an uneven crescent. She was kicked when swimming for safety, he remembers that now.

The officer sighs and scratches his forehead. "Madam, surely you can see why we need to take names? Now, if you'd just—"

"—I d-don't wish to. You'll never find all the d-d-dead folks' names anyway, you're on a f-f-fool's mission."

"Well, do you see anyone you know down here?" He gestures to the piles of bodies, without looking at them. "Any names are of use to us, as I am sure you can understand."

Elizabeth Stride refuses to look, though the ghost notices the shine of her eyes, and softens. *This is harder for her than she's showing,* he realises. *She is only just keeping herself together.* "G-go and talk to someone else," she whispers, fingers clutched together at the front of her skirt. "I c-c-cannot help you."

With a grunt of exasperation, the officer moves along. Elizabeth Stride remains for a moment, staring at the river, as the rising sun gradually turns her skirts from grey to mud-brown. The tilt of her chin, though puffed out of proportion from the blow, is proud, unrelenting. *She looks like a warrior,* he realises, with grudging respect.

Finally, she turns, the sweep of her skirt brushing the grass-dew below. The ghost follows. There seems little else to do. He's confident that Eleanor is not here, that she's probably down in the depths with the hundreds of others, staring sightlessly upwards. The thought of it strangles him, and he pushes it down, turning his mind elsewhere.

Elizabeth's pace is surprisingly swift, considering the events of the night. Keeping her head down, she marches away, past the growing crowds of people, some survivors of the disaster, being comforted or tended to by others, and some gawping onlookers, avidly drinking in the details, storing them for a later retelling to family and friends.

Still, the ghost follows, keeping just behind her back. He does not want to be by her side, it expresses an intimacy that repulses him. *Better to float on after her and see where she goes,* he thinks, with a clinging desperation, for she is the only familiar thing here, the only anchor of his former life in all this chaos.

"Mrs Stride! Mrs Stride!"

That voice, the ghost thinks, with a sense of wonder. Plaintive, cracked, and damaged, but he'd know it anywhere. Relief pours through him like honey, warm, comforting, and *safe.* In amongst this hell, he's finally discovered the one thing to stop him falling off the edge. *Eleanor.*

She is alive, he thinks, and doesn't know whether to smile or weep.

Elizabeth stops, massages her jaw, and looks down.

There is Eleanor, slumped by the foot of a tree, hair tangled, dress sodden and stained. *My wife.* The ghost races towards her, seeing only her face, grimy and exhausted though it is; her familiar body, those delicate hands, now pressed cautiously to her stomach. He touches her, over and over, fingers tracing her nose, her cheekbone, her lip; but he can feel nothing.

"Oh, my love," he whispers, and knows that she cannot hear him.

"What are you doing here?" Elizabeth Stride's voice, though guarded, is curious. She crouches, ignoring the interested stares of the people nearby.

A tear gathers in Eleanor's eye, then rolls falteringly to her chin. "I was on that boat . . . so were you, I saw you on there. I—"

"Don't tell *anyone* you saw me on there." The brusqueness, the lack of social niceties, shocks the ghost. *Why does it matter if anyone knows she was on that boat?* he wonders, looking at her with renewed dislike.

A disjointed sob brings his attention back to his wife. He wishes he could envelop her in his arms, reassure her that she would be safe, that all would be well, and the impact of his physical state hits him like a hammer in the chest. *I can never touch her again,* he thinks, remembering the feel of her skin under his fingers, the soft bounce of her hair against his cheek. He cries too, and their sobbing combines; together in some distant way, if only for a minute or so.

"Where is your husband?" Elizabeth Stride asks eventually, in a gentler tone. "Did he not survive?"

Eleanor clutches her stomach more tightly and lets out a wail; child-like, plaintive. It tears the ghost open to hear it, that single raw note of grief.

Elizabeth Stride stands, still clutching at her face. Though the injury gives her pain, she goes to lengths to disguise the fact, only wincing slightly at sudden movement. "I am sorry for your loss," she says eventually, looking away. "This world is a damned cruel place, and it takes happiness from us as swiftly as breathing."

And then she is gone, a hunched, stalking figure, pushing her way through the crowds.

The ghost stays with Eleanor. What else is there for him to do? *This must be my purpose now,* he thinks, hovering his hand over hers, praying that she could feel it, at least on some subconscious level. *I must stay with her and protect her. And wait until she is ready to join me in death.*

At the thought, his spirits lift, just a little. They may be apart now, separated by the impenetrable gulf of life and death. But one day, Eleanor will surely die, as all humans must. And then, he will be waiting for her. He will make sure of it.

TWENTY-FOUR

— 2017 —

HERE THEY ARE again, walking by the River Thames. Strange how he always ends up here, one way or another. It calls to him, like a siren chorusing to its victim, and powerless, he answers its cry.

The Docks are so different now. A marina is choked with row after row of bobbing white yachts. Beige-bricked buildings overlook the waters, people's dwellings, he believes. It has become gentrified, freed of its grimy, arduous past. But then, everything has changed. It all races past him with increasing speed, and he fears where the future will take him next.

He fears existing another day, especially in this brutish, modern world.

The Fortune Teller paces beside him, quiet as ever, lost in her thoughts. A companion at least, in these dark, troubling days.

"Why did you do what you did?" she asks, finally. "Why did you try to destroy yourself?"

The ghost remembers the machine; diving through the screen, then the explosion. The blood on the boy's face. He hadn't meant to do that.

"I don't remember," he lies. "I don't recollect much, to be honest."

"Yet you said earlier that you remembered the Docks," she says pertly. "The memories are there, deep within you, don't you know that?"

He shakes his head. "That's not true. I need you to know what's *really* happening to me. I'm losing everything, every experience I ever had. It's all fading."

"I don't believe you."

"Why not?" Her tone aggravates him, belittles his pain.

"Because I think you do remember," the Fortune Teller says. "I think Eleanor, Arthur, Fred, Georgie; it's all buried within you, you just choose not to see it. I think you know what happened with your wife. You know how she survived, how she went on to find some sort of happiness. You know that you had a son, and you know what he grew into. You know all this. You've been travelling through time, thinking yourself a helpless onlooker, but that's not the case. That's not how it is at all, do you hear me? Do you hear me, S—"

"Shh." He holds out a hand, albeit a faded, foggy one. "Stop it, please." It is hard enough to hear her say the names of the people he loved, let alone his own.

"You won't let me remind you of what you're called?" She sighs, twitches in and out of view, showing her agitation. "Very well. How about mine? Do you remember me? I am sure that you do. It was you who led me here, after all. You cannot have such impact in a person's life, then forget that person's name."

The ghost stops, closes his eyes. It is a pleasant evening, though as ever, the sun casts no warmth upon him. "I don't know what you're called," he says heavily. "I remember nothing, and that is the problem."

"Do you remember what happened with Bo and Zoe? The boy we've been following? The beautiful girl he longs for?"

"Bits and pieces." He recollects letters on screens, anguished love, long-distance heartbreak. But that is different. That is recent history, and he is sure it will fade swiftly in a few days' time.

The Fortune Teller stares at him intently. "You remember further back than that, I am sure."

He shakes his head. "I do not."

"Try, then. Or at least let me tell you what I know."

The ghost winces. He wishes he could just walk away and leave this relentless onslaught. But where to walk to? This modern world is more intimidating than any other that he's inhabited, an alien planet with its polished metals and glass, its noisy machines, its impossible technology. Besides, he's never gone further than this small section of the city. It's all he knows. He dares not leave.

"You cannot continually tell me tales of the past." He starts to walk again, knowing that he is moving too swiftly, and that she will struggle to keep pace with him. But he wants to be alone. He craves solitude; he cannot take the pressure of her questioning.

"Why can't I keep reminding you of your memories?"

"It is impractical." He is aware that his voice sounds querulous, pompous, when what he actually means is *I cannot curse you to an existence like that.* Why can he not express what he wants to say? Why is he often so cold towards her, when it doesn't reflect the truth of the matter? *Because that is the only way I can navigate a path through this endless horror,* he realises. *Coldness prevents feeling too much. It numbs me.*

The Fortune Teller clutches him. The ice of her fingers breathes through his arm, then the sensation dies. "It's not impractical," she insists. "On the contrary. It is the only way we can carry on."

"Unless we choose not to carry on." He mutters the sentiment more loudly than he'd intended.

Stillness presides while she muses his words.

"That's the advice you gave me when I was living," she replies, without a trace of bitterness. "And look where it got me."

That's not how it happened, he thinks fiercely. He doesn't remember the exact details of that terrible night, but he knows he never meant for her to do what she did.

Perhaps she is right, he thinks, mulling it over. Maybe some memories are hidden within him, but the agonising truth is that he cannot access them when he needs to. They arise unbidden; these days less so than before.

"What do you propose, then?" he asks, ashamed of his harsh tone, even as the words tumble from him.

"That you let me be the keeper of your stories."

He laughs. "I have no tales that are worthy of storage. Perhaps it is best to simply let them disappear."

"No, that's not true. You *need* to know your past, so you can move on with your future."

The ghost's temper frays, then snaps, brittle as ancient twine tugged to its limits. "*What* future? We don't have a future, because we are *not alive*! All we have is a meaningless, impotent existence!"

Her form solidifies. *Those eyes,* he thinks, angered yet transfixed. Dark and full of earnestness. Despite himself, he is calmed, simply by meeting her steady, ceaseless gaze.

"Why not look at it another way?" she says simply, ignoring his outburst, much as a mother would at her offspring's childish tantrum.

"There is no other way."

"You are wrong. What about seeing this as an opportunity? Unlike every other soul, you and I will live forever. We don't know why, we don't know how it was that we were chosen and most others not, but why not see it as a positive thing?"

The ghost presses his hands to the ornate railing, wishing he could feel the cool, hard steel beneath his fingers. He needs the brutality of metal, something solid to tether himself to. *But I can only imagine what it feels like,* he realises, letting his hands slip helplessly through to the other side. *All we have left is pretence.* "It is not a positive thing," he says slowly, willing every word to come out correctly, so he can convince her once and for all. "Because all the other dead people have passed somewhere better, while we are stuck here."

"You don't know that," she presses. "They may have just vanished from existence. At least you still have a mind to think with, eyes to experience the world with."

"These are not eyes!" he hisses, astounded by her belligerence. "These are echoes of eyes! Mist and vapour, nothing more!"

"But they work, don't they? You see things with them, and more besides."

The ghost thinks of the darkness, swirling above certain humans, and shudders. "Nothing I'd want to see. Besides," he adds, "we cannot touch. We cannot *feel*."

"But we can hear. We can talk to one another."

It is exasperating to listen to, not least because her points make him feel petty, as though death were merely a minor condition to bear, rather than an entire way of being. He shakes his head, more to clear his thoughts than anything else. His feet move, quite without him realising it. He needs to keep going, or else stop and sink into further despair.

But the Fortune Teller will not give up so easily this time, that much is clear. He senses her presence, dogged and determined, lingering behind and waiting for him to turn.

I will not, he thinks childishly, and ploughs away from her, further down the towpath. Those machines have been here, he can tell, clipping away at the grass until it is lush, green, and shaven. It is unnatural, but then, what *is* natural about this modern world? Everything is artifice these days.

The smart residential buildings eventually give way to glass-fronted towers. People pass them, laughing, talking on their little plastic devices that they press to their ears, or simply out for a stroll. The sight of them embitters him further, but still, he walks. After a while, he wonders if the Fortune Teller has desisted, disappeared and returned to the boy's flat. A sneaky glance informs him that this is not the case. Although the waning afternoon light passes through her like rain through a muslin cloth, the shape of her is still visible; the firm shoulder, the line of her shawl.

I won't give in to her, he tells himself, and is surprised to feel the hint of a smile, tugging at his lips. For this has become a game, he knows that now; a darkly playful tug-of-war, to see who will falter first. A part of him respects her refusal to surrender, despite his irritation.

He turns, away from the river and into the narrow streets of the capital, past public houses that have stood there for centuries, and houses that survived fires and bombings. So much history, tumbled together with modernity; a crazed mishmash of old and new. Together, they dive into the city they know so well, one leading, the other following.

The sun sets, casting fire across the city skyline. The sky turns navy, then a gradual shade of grey. The north star glitters overhead. Still, he walks, and so does she.

Finally, when the moon is high and cold above the surrounding buildings, he stops.

"You win," he says, without turning.

The Fortune Teller smiles. He can *sense* her smiling. It is astonishing how well they know one another.

"Very well. First, will you start calling me by my name again?"

"I don't remember your name."

"Then I will remind you." She floats closer, extends a hand to his. "Every time you forget, I will remind you. It is *Agnes*."

The ghost nods, smiles, and takes her hand. "Yes. Of course it is." And she is right, because he does remember, the first time he ever heard her name, shouted across a field by a short, deep-voiced woman, far older than she. *Her mother?* he thinks, straining to recollect, then, *no, that's not it. Her aunt. She lived with her aunt.*

"Each time your memory runs dry," Agnes continues, as they walk together at a more leisurely pace, "I will be there to replenish it. Because I remember *all* the stories you told me. About Eleanor, your brothers, your little sister. Even about Elizabeth Stride."

Now there is a name I had forgotten, the ghost thinks incredulously. "She was killed," he mutters aloud, straining to remember the details. "My brother, he was—"

"—it wasn't your brother," she says gently. "Her death was in the newspapers, as were all the other poor women. They said it was a murderer called Jack the Ripper, do you remember?"

He shakes his head, unable to comprehend the jumbled images, vying for attention in his mind. A slit throat. Shadows on cobblestones. A man, shouting. None of it makes sense, and he cannot grasp sense from it, no matter how hard he tries. "But this is no life for you," he says instead, returning to the reassurance of the present. Crowds of baying young men herd out of the nearest public house, then walk straight through them. It doesn't matter, though. These things ceased to matter a long time ago. *We are a different species to them now,* he realises. *And their world is not ours.*

The Fortune Teller smiles gently. "It is the life I chose. Shall I tell you about Eleanor, and what happened after you died?"

He flinches. It is impossible not to, for even the mention of that time stirs something within him; a wretched agony that he's terrified to disturb. "I do not think I am ready," he whispers, frightened to meet her steadfast gaze.

"But you are," she corrects him. "And once it is done, it is done. Now, let's begin."

TWENTY-FIVE

— 1878 —

DEATH IS A complex state to adjust to.

Breathing, for example. The ghost *feels* that he breathes, is aware of the memory of his chest rising and falling; but when he considers the matter, he finds that he needs no air at all. He makes the effort to inhale, to draw in as much oxygen as he can into his lungs, only to find that there is no sensation to the process. Instead, air flows through him almost impudently, as oblivious to his presence as every other thing around him.

He needs no sleep, and so the days and nights blend seamlessly with one another; a drawn-out, endless swathe of time. He has tried closing his eyes and simply standing, which works to a certain extent, but never fully. He always seems to be *aware,* even when he's trying his hardest not to be.

And in those first dark days, he is *fully aware,* more than he'd want to be. Eleanor's parents are deceased, and naturally, the person she turns to is his mother, who looks alarmingly frailer, pinched to greyness, broken by the news. The shock of his death has devastated his family, and it is excruciating to watch their pain; Mother's wracking sobs at the kitchen table, Martha weeping by the fence in the garden, fretfully tugging handfuls of grass in her hands. And Arthur, maintaining stoic composure in front of the rest of them, only to shake with silent sobs behind a locked bathroom door.

The ghost's guilt is overwhelming; for it is not *right* that he should be the one to bring this much pain on the ones he loves. That was never his role in the family, he was always the peace-maker, the ever-reliable, the one everyone turned to for reassurance and stability. His world has flipped, his death has made him a destructive force, and he hates it.

Worst of all is the sight of Eleanor. At first, the ghost is relieved that she has chosen to move in with Mother, that she isn't on her own. But Mother's cottage at Battersea seems only to torment her; giving her a ceaseless succession of hours in which to brood, and none of the responsibility of her own household to distract her.

For weeks, she sits by the patio windows, which are covered, as is decorous for mourning. She stares at the heavy fabric without seeing, kneading her hands against her lap, and her curls hang unwashed over her face, dank as wet strips of rag. She has already become thinner, less substantial, and isn't even bothering to wear her corset, only the same dress, over and over each day. Normally, Mother would tend to her, gently bully her into taking more care over her appearance, but Mother's own grief is so encompassing, she can only mumble the occasional comment, then retreat from the room.

They tiptoe around one another; two tentative planets, orbiting at a safe distance. Martha avoids them both. It is hideous to see the three women who matter most to him, each locked in their own private misery, all of them diminished by their suffering. The house of his childhood, which he remembers as always being a place of noise and energy, is now still and silent as a tomb.

The ghost follows them, frequently reaching out to touch them, though he knows it will serve no purpose. He wishes he had appreciated the sense of touch more when he was alive; the glorious ability to simply reach out and make contact with someone, to feel the soft pliancy of their skin and the heat of the blood beneath it. Again and again, he reaches for Eleanor, particularly when she is sobbing in bed, her shoulders heaving with the force of her sadness.

I am here, he whispers in the darkness, over and over. And tries to wrap his arm around her, only to sink through to the mattress.

The day of the funeral is punctuated by a high wind, uncharacter-istically fierce for this time of year. He had listened to it building the night before, while standing in the guest room, gazing at his wife's sleeping body. The low howl had echoed down the chimney; a fitting sound of loss, he'd thought.

Now, Eleanor struggles to awaken. Her eyes are blacker than he's ever seen them, hollow, dead eyes that see the world but do not re-spond to it. His mother is the opposite, fussing over her dress, re-cently purchased for her by Arthur, from The London General Mourning Warehouse on Regent Street. It is usually improper for women to attend funerals, but Mother insists upon being there, as does Martha. The ghost does not think that Eleanor cares one way or another; she is too mired in her own silent world to notice the events around her.

The door knocker raps at eleven o'clock. Mother rushes to the door.

To the ghost's surprise, Arthur is accompanied by Fred, who is wearing what appears to be a new mourning suit. *Business must be good,* he notes, with a shade of a sneer. *Whatever suspicious sort of business it is, anyway.* He cannot help but notice that his older brother looks exhausted and fitful, standing awkwardly in the hallway. Even Mother's kindly words fail to put him at ease.

Arthur nods at Martha as she comes down the stairs. "You look very smart."

"Yes." Martha rests her hands on her dress, and casts her eyes to the floor. She accepts the warm hug of her youngest brother, and the stiff, uncomfortable embrace of the eldest, both with the same lack of emotion. *How will she get through this day?* the ghost wonders, wishing his little sister would change her mind and avoid the church service. It will not be a pleasant experience for one so young, even though she's more resilient than several adults he knows.

"I'm not sure it's proper to be there," Fred mutters, rubbing at his nose. "People will think you're a commoner, Mother. Ladies don't attend funerals, as you know."

"Oh, shush." Mother responds by shaking her head more earnestly than is necessary. "I'll mourn my boy how I wish, and the neighbours may prattle about it as much as they desire. But I'll say farewell to him, you mark my words." Then her voice breaks like a shattering dam, subsiding into fresh sobbing, muted swiftly by Arthur's reassuring shoulder.

"Where is Eleanor?" Arthur asks eventually, looking expectantly up the stairs. "Will she still be joining us?"

"Not if she's seen sense," Fred says darkly. "She'd do better here, at home."

"Perhaps she wants to say goodbye to him!" Martha snaps, taking an instinctive step backwards. "What would be the harm in that?"

"Women are too sensitive for such things."

"So say you *men*."

"Stop it, the pair of you!" The bite of Mother's anger silences them both. "Who knows? My boy's spirit may be waiting at the church, ready to bid us farewell too . . ."

He's not, the ghost thinks, with a wry smile. But the expression holds little weight, it is only a habitual attempt at levity, in the face of unrelenting anguish.

"He's not," Fred says flatly, unaware that he's echoed his deceased younger brother to the letter. "And all of this—" he gestures to the covered hallway mirror, the drawn curtains, just visible from the living room, "—won't bring him back. I am sorry to be brutish, Mother, but that's the way it is. Dead is *dead*."

With a wrenching gasp, Mother pulls away from Arthur and flees to the kitchen, Martha swiftly following, like a chick racing after a hen.

Arthur chews his lip. "That was a bit much," he murmurs eventually.

Fred sighs. "Perhaps it was. But I can't tolerate the falseness of it. Our brother's gone, that's all there is to it. No amount of covering mirrors or ordering fancy black stationary is going to bring him back."

"You received Mother's note then, I take it?" Arthur's mouth twitches into a grin, before resuming severity a moment later.

"Ridiculous item. I've no time for such things, this excessive mourning is a mere device to line the pockets of wealthy death-peddlers."

"But—" The air hangs heavy with Arthur's uncertainty.

"What?"

Watching Fred carefully, Arthur takes a deep breath, then speaks. "You do . . . you do *miss* him, don't you?"

Fred's expression softens. "Of *course* I do. He was my brother, despite what happened. And I wish to God he'd not died, I really do. Every night I find myself *remembering* things, like how he used to kick that damned ball against the shed, do you remember? And when the vicar tripped over in church, and none of us could stop laughing, until Mother had to take us out?"

"Gosh, I'd forgotten about that." Arthur chuckles softly. "That *was* funny."

It really was, the ghost thinks, and moves closer, until his shoulders are almost level with theirs. Together they stand for a moment, three brothers, two united by life and grief, the other excluded forever. The ghost wishes they would show some sign of awareness, anything that hints they sense his presence, but there is nothing. Only silence and stillness.

Finally, Fred coughs. "Of course, the memory of him stealing Eleanor from me isn't one I'm so fond of."

"It wasn't quite like that, was it?" Arthur says diplomatically.

Now he's deceased, the ghost isn't so sure. At the time, he'd believed that he'd done the right thing, that Eleanor deserved better than his brother, who'd treated her boorishly, with casual disinterest most of the time. *But I only saw what I wanted to see,* he wonders, remembering how overwhelmed he'd been in her presence, how he'd envied his brother for having her. *Maybe I did Fred wrong after all. Perhaps he's right to be angry, even after all this time.*

"It's funny," Fred continues, as they walk towards the kitchen, "the other night, I found myself thinking *now she's a widow, perhaps she'll look at me.*"

"Really?" Arthur stiffens, and the ghost is grateful for it, for someone to demonstrate his own personal feelings about the comment.

Fred nods. "But then, I realised I didn't have those feelings for her anymore. I haven't for a long time, you see."

The ghost relaxes. So too does Arthur. "Who has your heart now then, Brother?" he mutters, just as they enter the kitchen, to find Mother and Martha, huddled balefully around the table, each clutching cups of weak tea.

"I think you know very well," Fred retorts, then gives Arthur a meaningful nod, indicating a need to change the subject. He pats Mother on the shoulder, looming over her, almost bat-like in his black jacket and trousers. "My apologies, Mother, I spoke out of turn earlier. Will you forgive me?"

Goodness me, that's a first, the ghost thinks, unsure whether to be impressed or cynical.

Mother sobs in response, then seizes his hand in both of hers. The ghost can understand the desperation of the gesture, as it is so rare to hear Fred like this; emotional and open, as he was in childhood, before Father died.

The carriage clock chimes from the living room, and the others look up as one, knowing that it is *time,* that they need to make their way to the church. *I'm truly about to attend my own funeral,* the ghost thinks with disbelief. He's long given up on the hope that he might wake from this nightmare and return to his previous satisfying, mundane existence, but still finds it impossible to imagine himself taking a pew at the back, listening to the local vicar eulogise about his life. *It would be comedic,* he thinks, watching Arthur help Mother to her feet, *if it wasn't so awful.*

While they prepare themselves downstairs, the ghost races above to find Eleanor. He can *sense* her, far more strongly now than when he was alive; and sure enough, he locates her immediately, at the dressing table in the guest bedroom. The looking glass is still draped with black crinoline, but somehow, she has managed to pile her curls upon her head and reduce the puffiness of her eyes. *She looks better, yet worse,* he thinks, lingering at her shoulder, studying the graceful curve of her neck. *More presentable, but also less human. This is a mere mask that she is wearing to conceal her true emotions.*

He thinks upon what Fred has said. Perhaps he is right. She should not have to endure the horror of her husband's funeral, especially without a body to formally lay to rest. *How it must torture her to consider it, festering beneath the murky waters of the Thames,* he thinks with a shudder. *And how it torments me. It is not right.*

"Eleanor?" Mother's voice trails up the stairs like a creeping vine, edging its way into Eleanor's consciousness, nudging her out of her dazed reverie.

With a sigh, Eleanor stands, then freezes, eyes wide and alert. "Are you there?" she whispers, tentatively as a child. "Sometimes I feel that you are."

"I am!" the ghost says, tripping through her in his haste to reach out and make contact. He scans her face for signs of recognition, but her expression doesn't alter. "Can you hear me, my love? I'm here, I never left you."

She waits patiently, gaze flitting from one corner of the darkened room to the other. He tries again, whispering in her ear, speaking as clearly as possible, even shouting; but her expression doesn't change. He presses his lips to her cheek, desperately trying to feel the heat of her skin upon them.

It is futile, the ghost realises finally, twisted with misery, and watches as she leaves the room in a rustle of stiff material. It feels cavernous without her.

He wants to weep, had he tears to weep with. *I believed she felt my presence,* he thinks, staring bitterly at the curtained window. *But it was only wishful thinking on her part, and mine.* He travels down the stairs, just as Arthur pulls open the door.

"After you, my dear," he says gallantly, letting Eleanor pass out into the windy day.

She smiles at him, a watery, distracted gesture, then looks away.

For the next hour, the ghost feels strangely removed from proceedings; from the muted journey to the church, to the service itself. He is unsure where to place himself, momentarily concerned with the propriety of even being present at his own funeral, and eventually settles for the pew behind Eleanor, so he can rest the phantom of his hand upon her shoulder and imagine that she feels it.

The service is short and stilted. The vicar is a relatively young man, the replacement for Mr Giles, who'd held the position for many years before. He has no connection to the ghost, nor the ghost to him; and the lack of familiarity shows. Mother wails openly, and Martha squeezes her eyes shut, waiting for it all to end. Even Fred weeps for a minute or two, wiping the tears hastily with his sleeve.

Only Eleanor sits motionless, face unreadable, jaw clenched. The ghost notices that Arthur's eyes seldom leave her face, scrutinising her as a scientist might observe an intriguing experiment. The ghost supposes he should be grateful for his younger brother's concern for his widow's welfare, but there is something in Arthur's expression that unsettles him, something too avid, almost hungry.

He cannot tell what his brother is thinking, and it worries him.

Afterwards, the custom is to attend the burial, but without a corpse to bury, the family take a turn around the graveyard instead, gazing at the headstones without really seeing them. The ghost follows behind, a silent shadow, observing each minute movement they make; the slump of Mother's shoulders, the tension in Fred's cheeks as he takes too much interest in one grave inscription or another. And Arthur's hand, resting just once on the small of Eleanor's back. It is a supportive gesture, he supposes, a physical demonstration of his continued regard as her brother-in-law. But it disturbs him, perhaps more than it should do. It expresses intimacy, but also the sense of something restrained, an emotion rendered invisible by the misery of the day.

Eleanor pauses by a particular gravestone; a weeping cherub baby, sagging wings at his back. She clutches her stomach reflectively, no doubt sickened by the course of the day. Indeed, her face appears pinched and wan, and he wonders if she is unwell, whether she needs to return to the solitude of the cottage, to gather her thoughts.

Arthur hangs back, remaining with her while the others walk on into the windswept distance.

"How are you?" he asks in a low voice.

How do you think she is? the ghost thinks irritably, though he knows his brother only means well by it.

"Alone." She hangs her head, refuses to meet his eye. "Frightened. Much as you might expect."

Arthur nods curtly. The wind whips ceaselessly at them both, sending her curls flying free of her bonnet. It is cold, the ghost can tell by the tightness of their posture, the way Arthur continually pulls his jacket across his chest. He wishes he could feel it too.

"You know that I am here to help you," he mutters quietly, looking over his shoulder. "I meant what I said the other day, you know."

And what was that? The ghost was not privy to this conversation. It must have taken place when Arthur had last been round at the house, but when had he and Eleanor been alone? It makes no sense to him.

Eleanor shakes her head. A fat tear squeezes from her eye; the first she has cried all day. "I cannot think of that now," she says. "It is too soon."

"I understand." He nods down at her stomach, for reasons the ghost cannot discern. "But for propriety's sake, it might be better sooner, rather than later."

"Arthur, please, not now!" With a muted sob, she starts to walk after the others, a blind, scurrying gait, like a beggar trailing hopelessly towards the promise of food.

"Wait, Eleanor, do not take it like that. When we talked about it the other day, you—"

"—I am aware of that, but *not now*! Not here, of all places. Can't you see how inappropriate it is, Arthur?"

He nods, removing his hat and worrying the brim with his fingers. "Of course you're right. My poor brother, what would he—"

"—Your poor brother is lying at the bottom of the Thames, while we have this conversation. And I have to live with the guilt of that, Arthur. Don't you see?"

But I'm not in the Thames, the ghost yearns to protest. *I'm right here with you, if only you'd notice me.* But just what is this conversation about, exactly? He can only presume that Arthur has made some promise to protect Eleanor financially, and that she is reluctant to consider it. *Yes, that makes sense,* he tells himself, studying them both, looking for signs to confirm his guess.

Arthur flinches from her, as suddenly as if she'd struck him in the face. "Don't say that," he murmurs, biting his lip. "You don't know how it *tortures* me, to think of him like that."

She softens, draws out a handkerchief, and dabs her eyes. "I know," she says eventually. "It is unbearable, especially as it was I who persuaded him to get on that wretched boat in the first place. If I must be sentenced to bear that burden for the rest of my life, then you must learn to bear yours." She reaches across and squeezes his hand, briefly. "We will talk more of this at a later date. But for now, let me grieve for what I've lost, please."

"I will join you in the grieving," Arthur replies solemnly and replaces his hat. Together, they stroll along to the others. The ghost remains, staring after them both, and wonders why he feels *tighter* somehow, constricted painfully by the conversation he has just witnessed.

It was of no importance, he tells himself, trailing after them. *Put it from your mind. It did not mean anything at all.*

TWENTY-SIX

— 2017 —

"I REMEMBER THAT." The ghost looks at the Fortune Teller, at *Agnes,* and nods.

The pain returns, as sharp as he recollects. *This is why I forgot in the first place,* he thinks, as they pace slowly through the streets of Whitechapel. *Because the agony of the memories was overwhelming. I deliberately forced them from my mind, until I realised that I'd pushed them so far away, I couldn't retrieve them.*

The street lamps cast a stronger light over the pavement than they used to do. He knows the word for it, *electricity,* that strange force that powers everything in the modern world. The old oil lamps were preferable, he believes; softer, less showy. But then, what does it matter to them? The light causes their eyes no discomfort, nor do the surrounding shadows pose any threat. It may as well be just the two of them, secure in their own bubble.

"I am only telling you what you told me, all those years ago," Agnes reminds him. "These are your memories, not mine."

Already, the image of that windy day, the bleak grey clouds above the gravestones, is fading. He can still grasp elements though; his mother's shoulders shaking during the eulogy, the high, white walls of the church, the subtle press of Arthur's hand on Eleanor's back.

"And they married, didn't they." He declares it as a statement of fact, not a question; because he already knows the answer. The crushing sensation in his chest is evidence enough. The echo of his body is better at remembering the past than his mind.

"Eleanor and Arthur were wed, yes."

"And they had a child? I cannot remember his name, but I know he is important."

Agnes winces. "He is important because he was *your* son. Georgie was yours. You remember, we were with him regularly? We stayed with him when he was a teacher, at the school just down the road."

The ghost strains to recall it. Her words create pictures; a lazy young man taking a nap at the back of the classroom, with a female teacher sighing at him in frustration. *That teacher, we lived with her for a while,* he believes, but cannot remember her name, only her face; kindly, energetic, and passionate.

Though he cannot grasp these memories fully, the sensation of being able to see into his past is a relief. It reassures him that he is less lost than he thought.

"What happened to the child?" he asks.

Agnes nods solemnly. "I will tell you. We were with him for some time; when he shared rooms with Archibald, his lover. It was a heartbreaking end, but Georgie had already given up on life by then."

My son, the ghost thinks, remembering two images, side by side. One, a baby, gurgling happily in a cot, tugging at his toes and staring at the ghost with bright, inquisitive eyes. The other, a middle-aged man, bloated with alcohol and rich food, glassy-eyed in bed, while his lover sobbed over him. *His heart condition,* the ghost remembers, and casts his eyes to the street, overcome with sadness. *Georgie had a bad heart. My poor, poor son.*

"What of Eleanor?" he asks quietly. "What became of her?"

"You told me that you left her and Arthur, after learning that Georgie was yours." Agnes reaches for his hand again, eyes alight with compassion. She understands how hard this is for him, but also how *necessary,* like stitching a wound to allow it to heal. "I don't believe you could tolerate the sight of Arthur raising him as his own."

I think I returned from time to time, though, he muses, recollecting disconnected images of his family growing older without him. *I am sure of it, though the details escape me.* "Was Eleanor happy?" he presses, aware that his voice is cracking. "Did Arthur give her a happy life?"

"He gave her everything he could. But you told me that she often whispered out loud to you, when she believed she was on her own. She wasn't aware you could hear, of course, but I don't think she ever stopped loving you."

That is true, he realises. How painful her life must have been. Throughout, he'd always considered his own devastation, his misery at being removed from life. He'd taken little time to consider how hard it must have been to continue, day after day, with the press of grief upon her. *She had to continue, for Georgie's sake,* he realises. *And she and Arthur were good friends. I suppose, despite everything, it was for the best.*

The memories rise within him, sharp and bittersweet, only to fade almost immediately. But he cherishes them, nonetheless; the brief period that they flit through him, like leaves in the breeze.

"And when did she die?" he asks eventually, knowing that he must.

The street seems more silent than before. Time pauses, leaving them in stasis. He fears Agnes's answer, dreads and resists it with every part of his being, but *knows* she must tell him. For too long, he's purpose-fully driven it from his mind, until now, he has hardly any memories left.

Agnes composes herself. "I was there at the time," she says quietly. "So this part, I can tell you more fully. She was old, very old."

An image enters his mind; a thin, frail hand, blue with veins, resting on a pale pink bedspread. *Her hand,* he realises, and closes his eyes. *Yes, it was hers.*

"She outlived both of her husbands," Agnes continues, her voice as hushed and delicate as the tide. "And her son. The poor woman, to have lived through so much. She'd moved to a little terraced house in Fish Street Hill. Most of Arthur's money had run out by then."

"And I was there, with her, when she died?" Again, he already knows the answer, but needs to say the words aloud, to hear them hang on the air.

Agnes nods. "You were. I waited outside the room, out of respect. It was a peaceful night, just a few hours before sunrise. The war had only finished a few months earlier, the street was still a state, many of the houses just piles of rubble. But Eleanor lived quietly through it all, staying mostly in her bed.

"We were with another family at the time; Helen, her mother, and her two children, do you remember? On the occasions that you did remember who Eleanor was, you couldn't stand to see her like that; so ancient and vulnerable. So, we kept our distance, for the most part."

Helen. Yes, the ghost vaguely remembers her; a strong-jawed, resilient woman. She'd collapsed after the death of her husband, he remembers that. *A soldier,* he tells himself. *That's how it happened.*

"All the neighbours called Eleanor by her nickname, Ellie," Agnes continues softly. "That helped you to forget who they were talking about, I think."

"Did Eleanor . . . He pauses, unsure of the right words to say.

"Go on."

"Did she say anything, after she died?" *Did she see me?* he adds silently, desperate to hear the answer. He must know if Eleanor knew he was there, after all that time. But he cannot bear the possibility of the answer being no.

The glow from the streetlight shines through Agnes like the sun through glass. She nods, finally. "Eleanor *saw* you," she concludes. "You told me that she smiled, after she passed away."

"As though she remembered me, and was surprised to see me there," he finishes for her, because he *remembers* the moment himself now. How his Eleanor, so small and shrunken in her bed, had breathed her last breath, then stilled, and how her ghost had risen almost immediately; ready to venture into the life beyond.

He remembers how she'd changed, how the echoes of her had formed into her younger self; straight-backed, curly-haired, plump-cheeked. How she'd paused, studying her departed body with interest, then turned, sensing him.

And their eyes had met.

She sees me, he'd realised, unable to move or even speak. *Finally, she knows I am here.*

Then with a smile, a simple upturn of the lips, she had vanished. She had passed on, and left him behind.

The ghost had wept back then, and he weeps again now; for the final loss of his wife, for the years wasted, trying to find her. *I had her once,* he realises, feeling the core of himself crack and break, like a weary wall against a powerful tide. *But time went on, and she no longer needed me. That is the way it had to be.*

Agnes says nothing, only blends herself with him, their shimmering forms merging under the dark night sky. It is her way of holding him, reassuring him with every part of her presence, such that it is. He presses back into her, and weeps for everything he has lost.

So, that is how it happened, the ghost thinks finally. The memory is already fuzzing at the edges, retreating like a dying storm. *I know it. I understand now.* "What is left for us now?" he whispers, taking a step back, drinking in the sight of Agnes, the only constant through years of confusion and change.

"There's your family," she replies, with the hint of a smile. "Zoe is your great-great-great grand-niece. We used to stay with her, before she left London and left us behind."

"Zoe?" He remembers the photo on Bo's screen, the pretty young woman, displaying her flat stomach. *So that is why we remained with Bo,* he realises. *Because he was the link to my family.*

"Yes," Agnes continues. "We also stayed with her grandmother, Bernadette. Do you remember her flat, with the candles and all the music? And her horrible partner, Frank? The one that used to beat her?"

He strains to retrieve the memory, then shakes his head. There have been too many people over the years, person after person that they've attached themselves to, and it is impossible to differentiate between them.

"Whenever your family have been here in London, we've stayed as close to them as possible," Agnes says gently. She gestures down the street, back towards their home, or at least, the bleak dwelling they call home at the moment.

Back to Bo and his sad love letters, the ghost thinks, then wonders what the letters said, as the details have already vanished from his mind.

He nods, and they walk, keeping perfect pace with one another. The first weak grey of the forthcoming morning illuminates the tops of the surrounding buildings, then the road below. *It has been a long night,* the ghost thinks, and reaches over to touch Agnes's face. Although he feels no skin, he detects *something* there; a cold movement in the air where her cheek would have been, had she been alive. The gesture makes him warmer, for some reason. *At least I can feel something, and so can she,* he realises.

The crowds start to build around them; the usual Londoners, readying themselves for the day ahead; some jogging along pavements, others in suits, trotting rapidly to the underground train station. The ghost and Agnes continue as before; slowly, thoughtfully.

"Do you remember what I told you tonight?" she asks, as they arrive at the door to Bo's dingy flat. "Or has it faded already?"

The ghost ponders. He recalls elements of their conversation, but more important, he knows that he has *resolved* something within himself. *I remembered Eleanor,* he realises, knowing this to be significant. *And I must continue to do so. I cannot allow myself to fade to nothing.*

"I believe I recollect parts of it," he says.

Agnes beams. "That is good."

"Good enough for now," he adds, unwilling to admit that already the emotions are retreating, as inexorably as the tide from the shore. Soon, they will have gone altogether, and he will be as he was before. *I have become a leaking vessel,* he realises. *And no matter what memories flood in, they only seep out again, soon after.*

Agnes presses into him, tender, serious, and steadfast as she always is; a rock in the midst of this muddled, turbulent ocean. "Do not be afraid of the future," she whispers, voice soft as a night breeze. "I will continue to give you your memories back. Every night, we will walk, and every night, I will tell you what you want to know."

He studies her carefully. "But why would you offer? After all, this is of no benefit to you."

She smiles. The sun hits the street beneath them, making the surrounding walls glow with ember-like ferocity.

"You know why," she says simply.

I do, he thinks. Without saying anything, he reaches for her, and holds her as best as he can, knowing that if he must be cast adrift, she will anchor him to safety.

And that is enough, he realises.

For he remembers love.

ABOUT THE AUTHOR

GROWING UP IN a haunted house, Lucy Banks naturally developed a fascination with the strange, the curious, and the mysterious. She is the author of the Dr Ribero's Agency of the Supernatural series and co-host of review site The Book Scoop. She posts about writing craft and shares ghost stories from around Britain on her blog at lucy-banks.co.uk.

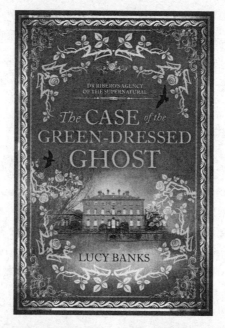

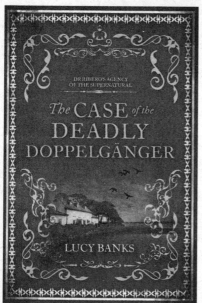

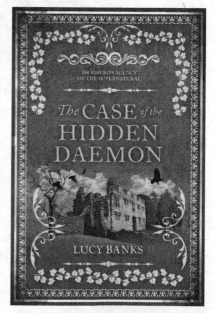